NEW YORK TIMES BESTSELLING AUTHOR

DIANA PALMER

TO TAME A TEXAN

Two Heartfelt Stories

Bentley* and *Boone

(Previously published as *Tough to Tame* and *Heart of Stone*)

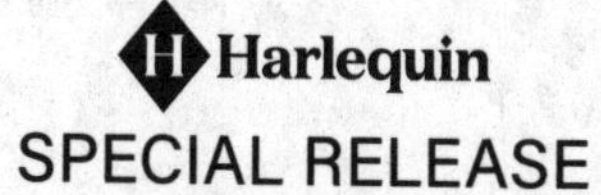

SPECIAL RELEASE

ISBN-13: 978-1-335-00213-6

To Tame a Texan

Bentley
First published as Tough to Tame in 2010. This edition published in 2026 with revised text.

Boone
First published as Heart of Stone in 2008. This edition published in 2026 with revised text.

For questions and comments about the quality of this book, please contact us at CustomerService@Harlequin.com.

Harlequin Enterprises ULC
22 Adelaide St. West, 41st Floor
Toronto, Ontario M5H 4E3, Canada
www.Harlequin.com

HarperCollins Publishers
Macken House, 39/40 Mayor Street Upper,
Dublin 1, D01 C9W8, Ireland
www.HarperCollins.com

26 27 28 29 30 LBC 5 4 3 2 1

Praise for *New York Times* bestselling author Diana Palmer

"Palmer's talent for character development and ability to fuse heartwarming romance with nail-biting suspense shines in *Outsider*."

—*Booklist*

"A gentle escape mixed with real-life menace for fans of Palmer's more than 100 novels."

—*Publishers Weekly* on *Night Fever*

"The ever-popular and prolific Palmer has penned another sure hit."

—*Booklist* on *Before Sunrise*

"Nobody does it better."

—Linda Howard, *New York Times* bestselling author

"Readers who enjoy stories by authors who know how to pack an emotional wallop will add Palmer to their list."

—*Booklist* on *Renegade*

"Nobody tops Diana Palmer when it comes to delivering pure, undiluted romance. I love her stories."

—Jayne Ann Krentz, *New York Times* bestselling author

Dear Reader,

I can't believe that it has been so many years since my first Long, Tall Texan book, *Calhoun*, debuted! The series was suggested by my former editor Tara Gavin, who asked if I might like to set stories in a fictional town of my own design. Would I! And the rest is history.

As the years went by, I found more and more sexy ranchers and cowboys to add to the collection. My readers (especially Amy!) found time to gift me with a notebook listing every single one of them, wives and kids and connections to other families in my own Texas town of Jacobsville. Eventually the town got a little too big for me, so I added another smaller town called Comanche Wells and began to fill it up, too.

You can't imagine how much pleasure this series has given me. I continue to add to the population of Jacobs County, Texas, and I have no plans to stop. Ever.

I hope all of you enjoy reading the Long, Tall Texans as much as I enjoy writing them. Thank you all for your kindness and loyalty and friendship. I am your biggest fan!

Love,

Diana Palmer

CONTENTS

A prolific author of more than one hundred books, **Diana Palmer** got her start as a newspaper reporter. A *New York Times* bestselling author and voted one of the top ten romance writers in America, she has a gift for telling the most sensual tales with charm and humor. Diana lives with her family in Cornelia, Georgia. Visit her website at dianapalmer.com.

Books by Diana Palmer

Long, Tall Texans

Lawbreaker
Fearless
Heartless
Dangerous
Merciless
Courageous
Protector
Invincible
Defender
Undaunted
Unbridled
Unleashed
Notorious
The Loner

Wyoming Men

Wyoming Tough
Wyoming Fierce
Wyoming Bold
Wyoming Strong
Wyoming Rugged
Wyoming Brave
Wyoming Winter
Wyoming Legend
Wyoming Heart
Wyoming True
Wyoming Homecoming

Visit the Author Profile page at Harlequin.com for more titles.

BENTLEY

I dedicate this book to all the fine veterinarians, technicians, groomers and office workers who do so much every day to keep our furry friends healthy. Thanks!

CHAPTER ONE

Cappie Drake peered around a corner inside the veterinary practice where she worked, her soft gray eyes wide with apprehension. She was looking for the boss, Dr. Bentley Rydel. Just lately, he'd been on the warpath, and she'd been the target for most of the sarcasm. She was the newest employee in the practice. Her predecessor, Antonia, had resigned and run for the hills last month.

"He's gone to lunch," came an amused whisper from behind her.

Cappie jumped. Her colleague, Keely Welsh Sinclair, was grinning at her. The younger woman, nineteen to Cappie's twenty-three, was only recently married to dishy Boone Sinclair, but she'd kept her job at the veterinary clinic despite her lavish new lifestyle. She loved animals.

So did Cappie. But she'd been wondering if love of animals was enough to put up with Bentley Rydel.

"I lost the packing slip for the heartworm medicine," Cappie said with a grimace. "I know it's here somewhere, but he was yelling and I got flustered and couldn't find it. He said terrible things to me."

"It's autumn," Keely said.

Cappie frowned. "Excuse me?"

"It's autumn," she repeated.

The older woman was staring blankly at her.

Keely shrugged. "Every autumn, Dr. Rydel gets even more short-tempered than usual and he goes missing for a week. He doesn't leave a telephone number in case of emergencies, he doesn't call here and nobody knows where he is. When he comes back, he never says where he's been."

"He's been like this since I was hired," Cappie pointed out. "And I'm the fifth new vet tech this year, Dr. King said so. Dr. Rydel ran the others off."

"You have to yell back, or just smile when he gets wound up," Keely said in a kindly tone.

Cappie grimaced. "I never yell at anybody."

"This is a good time to learn. In fact…"

"Where the hell is my damned raincoat?!"

Cappie's face was a study in horror. "You said he went to lunch!"

"Obviously he came back," Keely replied, wincing, as the boss stormed into the waiting room where two shocked old ladies were sitting beside cat carriers.

Dr. Bentley Rydel was tall, over six feet, with pale blue eyes that took on the gleam of steel when he was angry. He had jet-black hair, thick and usually untidy because he ran his fingers through it in times of frustration. His feet were large, like his hands. His nose had been broken at some point, which only gave his angular face more character. He wasn't conventionally handsome, but women found him very attractive. He didn't find them attractive. If there was a more notorious woman hater than Bentley Rydel in all of Jacobs County, Texas, it would be hard to find him.

"My raincoat?" he repeated, glaring at Cappie as if it were her fault that he'd left without it.

Cappie drew herself up to her full height—the top of her head barely came to Bentley's shoulder—and took a deep breath. "Sir," she said smartly, "your raincoat is in the closet where you left it."

His dark eyebrows rose half a foot.

Cappie cleared her throat and shook her head as if to clear it. The motion dislodged her precariously placed barrette. Her long, thick blond hair shook free of it, swirling around her shoulders like a curtain of silk.

While she was debating her next, and possibly job-ending, comment, Bentley was staring at her hair. She always wore it on top of her head in that stupid ponytail. He hadn't realized it was so long. His pale eyes narrowed as he studied it.

Keely, fascinated, managed not to stare. She turned to the old ladies watching, spellbound. "Mrs. Ross, if you'll bring—" she looked at her clipboard "—Luvvy the cat on back, we'll see about her shots."

Mrs. Ross, a tiny little woman, smiled and pulled her rolling cat carrier along with her, casting a wistful eye back at the tableau she was reluctantly foregoing.

"Dr. Rydel?" Cappie prompted, because he was really staring.

He scowled suddenly and blinked. "It's raining," he said shortly.

"Sir, that is not my fault," she returned. "I do not control the weather."

"A likely story," he huffed. He turned on his heel, went to the closet, jerked his coat out, displacing everybody else's, and stormed out the door into the pouring rain.

"And I hope you melt!" Cappie muttered under her breath.

"I heard that!" Bentley Rydel called without looking back.

Cappie flushed and moved back behind the counter, trying not to meet Gladys Hawkins's eyes, because the old lady was almost crying, she was laughing so hard.

"There, there," Dr. King, the long-married senior veterinarian, said with a gentle smile. She patted Cappie on the shoulder. "You've done well. By the time she'd been here a month, Antonia was crying in the bathroom at least twice a day, and she never talked back to Dr. Rydel."

"I've never worked in such a place," Cappie said blankly. "I mean, most veterinarians are like you—they're nice and professional, and they don't yell at the staff. And, of course, the staff doesn't yell…"

"Yes, they do," Keely piped in, chuckling. "My husband made the remark that I was a glorified groomer, and the next time he came in here, our groomer gave him an earful about just what a groomer does." She grinned. "Opened his eyes."

"They do a lot more than clip fur," Dr. King agreed. "They're our eyes and ears in between exams. Many times, our groomers have saved lives by noticing some small problem that could have turned fatal."

"Your husband is a dish," Cappie told Keely shyly.

Keely laughed. "Yes, he is, but he's opinionated, hardheaded and temperamental with it."

"He was a tough one to tame, I'll bet," Dr. King mused.

Keely leaned forward. "Not half as tough as Dr. Rydel is going to be."

"Amen. I pity the poor woman who takes him on."

"Trust me, she hasn't been born yet," Keely replied.

"He likes you," Cappie sighed.

"I don't challenge him," Keely said simply. "And I'm younger than most of the staff. He thinks of me as a child."

Cappie's eyes bulged.

Keely patted her on the shoulder. "Some people do." The smile faded. Keely was remembering her mother, who'd been killed by a friend of Keely's father. The whole town had been talking about it. Keely had landed well, though, in Boone Sinclair's strong arms.

"I'm sorry about your mother," Cappie said gently. "We all were."

"Thanks," Keely replied. "We were just getting to know one another when she was...killed. My father plea-bargained himself down to a short jail term, but I don't think he'll be back this way. He's too afraid of Sheriff Hayes."

"Now there's a real dish," Cappie said. "Handsome, brave..."

"...suicidal," Keely interjected.

"Excuse me?"

"He's been shot twice, walking into gun battles," Dr. King explained.

"No guts, no glory," Cappie said.

Her companions chuckled. The phone rang, another customer walked in and the conversation turned to business.

Cappie went home late. It was Friday and the place was packed with clients. Nobody escaped before six-thirty, not even the poor groomer who'd spent half a day on a Siberian husky. The animals had thick undercoats and it was a job to wash and brush them out. Dr. Rydel had been snippier than usual, too, glaring at Cappie as if she were responsible for the overflow of patients.

"Cappie, is that you?" her brother called from the bedroom.

"It's me, Kell," she called back. She put down her raincoat and purse and walked into the small, sparse bedroom where her older brother lay surrounded by magazines and books and a small laptop computer. He managed a smile for her.

"Bad day?" she asked gently, sitting down beside him on the bed, softly so that she didn't worsen the pain.

He only nodded. His face was taut, the only sign of the pain that ate him alive every hour of the day. A journalist, he'd been on overseas assignment for a magazine when he was caught in a firefight and wounded by shrapnel. It had lodged in his spine where it was too dangerous for even the most advanced surgery. The doctors said someday, the shrapnel might shift into a location where it would be operable. But until then, Kell was basically paralyzed from the waist down. Oddly, the magazine hadn't provided any sort of health care coverage for him, and equally oddly, he'd insisted that he wasn't going to court to force them to pay up. Cappie had wondered at her brother being in such a profession in the first place. He'd been in the army for several years. When he came out, he'd become a journalist. He made an extraordinary living from it. She'd mentioned that to a friend in the newspaper business who'd been astonished. Most magazines didn't pay that well, he'd noted, eyeing Kell's new Jaguar.

Well, at least they had Kell's savings to keep them going, even if it did so frugally now, after he paid the worst of the medical bills. Her meager salary, although good, barely kept the utilities turned on and food in the aging refrigerator.

"Taken your pain meds?" she added.

He nodded.

"Not helping?"

"Not a lot. Not today, anyway," he added with a forced grin. He was good-looking, with thick short hair even blonder than hers and those pale silvery-gray eyes. He was tall and muscular; or he had been, before he'd been wounded. He was in a wheelchair now.

"Someday they'll be able to operate," she said.

He sighed and managed a smile. "Before I die of old age, maybe."

"Stop that," she chided softly, and bent to kiss his forehead. "You have to have hope."

"I guess."

"Want something to eat?"

He shook his head. "Not hungry."

"I can make southwestern corn soup." It was his favorite.

He gave her a serious look. "I'm impacting your life. There are places for ex-military where I could stay..."

"No!" she exploded.

He winced. "Sis, it isn't right. You'll never find a man who'll take you on with all this baggage," he began.

"We've had this argument for several months already," she pointed out.

"Yes, since you gave up your job and moved back here with me, after I got...wounded. If our cousin hadn't died and left us this place, we wouldn't even have a roof over our heads, stark as it is. It's killing me, watching you try to cope."

"Don't be melodramatic," she chided. "Kell, all we have is each other," she added somberly. "Don't ask me to throw you out on the street so I can have a social life. I don't even like men much, don't you remember?"

His face hardened. "I remember why, mostly."

She flushed. "Now, Kell," she said. "We promised we wouldn't talk about that anymore."

"He could have killed you," he gritted. "I had to browbeat you just to make you press charges!"

She averted her eyes. Her one boyfriend in her adult life had turned out to be a homicidal maniac when he drank. The first time it happened, Frank Bartlett had grabbed Cappie's arm and left a black bruise. Kell advised her to get away from him, but she, infatuated and rationalizing, said that he hadn't meant it. Kell knew better, but he couldn't convince her. On their fourth date, the boy had taken her to a bar, had a few drinks, and when she gently tried to get him to stop, he'd dragged her outside and lit into her. The other patrons had come to her rescue and one of them had driven her home. The boy had come back, shamefaced and crying, begging for one more chance. Kell had put his foot down and said no, but Cappie was in love and wouldn't listen. They were watching a movie at the rented house, when she asked him about his drinking problem. He'd lost his temper and started hitting her, with hardly any provocation at all. Kell had managed to get into his wheelchair and into the living room. With nothing more than a lamp base as a weapon, he'd knocked the lunatic off Cappie and onto the floor. She was dazed and bleeding, but he'd told her how to tie the boy's thumbs together behind his back, which she'd done while Kell picked up his cell phone and called for law enforcement. Cappie had gone to the hospital and the boy had gone to jail for assault.

With her broken arm in a sling, Cappie had testified against him, with Kell beside her in court as moral support. The sentence, even so, hadn't been extreme. The boy drew six months' jail time and a year's probation. He also swore vengeance. Kell took the threat a great deal more seriously than Cappie had.

The brother and sister had a distant cousin who lived in Comanche Wells, Texas. He'd died a year ago, but the probation of the will had dragged on. Three months ago, Kell had a letter informing him that he and Cappie were inheriting a small house and a postage-stamp-size yard. But it was at least a place to live. Cappie had been uncertain about uprooting them from San Antonio, but Kell had been strangely insistent. He had a friend in nearby Jacobsville who was acquainted with a local veterinarian. Cappie could get a job there, working as a veterinary technician. So she'd given in.

She hadn't forgotten the boy. It had been a wrench, because he was her first real love. Fortunately for her, the relationship hadn't progressed past hot kisses and a little petting, although he'd wanted it to. That had been another sticking point: Cappie's impeccable morals. She was out of touch with the modern world, he'd accused, from living with her overprotective big brother for so long. She needed to loosen up. Easy to say, but Cappie didn't want a casual relationship and she said so. When he drank more than usual, he said it was her fault that he got drunk and hit her, because she kept him so frustrated.

Well, he was entitled to his opinion. Cappie didn't share it. He'd seemed like the nicest, gentlest sort of man when she'd first met him. His sister had brought her dog to the veterinary practice where Cappie worked. He'd been sitting in the truck, letting his sister wrangle a huge German shepherd dog back outside. When he'd seen Cappie, he'd jumped out and helped. His sister had seemed surprised. Cappie didn't notice.

After it was over, Cappie had found that at least two of her acquaintances had been subjected to the same sort of abuse by their own boyfriends. Some had been lucky, like Cappie, and disentangled themselves from the abusers. Others were trapped by fear into relationships they didn't even want. It was hard, she decided, telling by appearance what men would be like when they got you alone. At least Dr. Rydel was obviously violent and dangerous, she told herself. Not that she wanted anything to do with him socially.

"What was that?" Kell asked.

"Oh, I was thinking about one of my bosses," she confided. "Dr. Rydel is a holy terror. I'm scared to death of him."

He scowled. "Surely he isn't like Frank Bartlett?"

"No," she said quickly. "I don't think he'd ever hit a woman. He really isn't the sort. He just blusters and rages and curses. He loves animals. He called the police on a man who brought in a little dog with cuts and bruises all over him. The man had beaten the dog and pretended it had fallen down stairs. Dr. Rydel knew better. He testified against the man and he went to jail."

"Good for Dr. Rydel." He smiled. "If he's that nice to animals, he isn't likely the sort of person who'd hit women," he had to agree. "I was told by my friend that Rydel was a good sort to work for." He frowned. "Your boyfriend kicked your cat on your first date."

She grimaced. "And I made excuses for him." Not long after that, her cat had vanished. She'd often wondered what had happened to him, but he returned after her boyfriend left. "Frank was so handsome, so…eligible," she added quietly. "I guess I was flattered that a man like that would look twice at me. I'm no beauty."

"You are. Inside."

"You're a nice brother. How about that soup?"

He sighed. "I'll eat it if you'll fix it. I'm sorry. About the way I am."

"Like you can help it," she muttered, and smiled. "I'll get it started."

He watched her walk away, thoughtful.

She brought in a tray and had her soup with him. There were just the two of them, all alone in the world. Their parents had died long ago, when she was ten. Kell, who'd been amazingly athletic and healthy in those days, had simply taken over and been a substitute parent to her. He'd been in the military, and they'd traveled all over the world. A good deal of her education had been completed through correspondent courses, although she'd seen a lot of the world. Now, Kell thought he was a burden, but what had she been for all those long years when he'd sacrificed his own social life to raise a heartbroken kid? She owed him a lot. She only wished she could do more for him.

She remembered him in his uniform, an officer, so dignified and commanding. Now, he was largely confined to bed or that wheelchair. It wasn't even a motorized one, because they couldn't afford it. He did continue to work, in his own fashion, at crafting a novel. It was an adventure, based on some knowledge he'd acquired from his military background and a few friends who worked, he said, in covert ops.

"How's the book coming?" she asked.

He laughed. "Actually I think it's going very well. I spoke to a buddy of mine in Washington about some new political strategies and robotic warfare innovations."

"You know everybody."

He made a face at her. "I know almost everybody." He sighed. "I'm afraid the phone bill will be out of sight again this month. Plus I had to order some more books on Africa for the research."

She gave him a look of pride. "I don't care. You accomplish so much," she said softly. "More than a lot of people in much better shape physically."

"I don't sleep as much as most people do," he said wryly. "So I can work longer hours."

"You need to talk to Dr. Coltrain about something to make you sleep."

He sighed. "I did. He gave me a prescription."

"Which you didn't get filled," she accused. "Connie, at the pharmacy, told on you."

"We don't have the money right now," he said gently. "I'll manage."

"It's always money," she said miserably. "I wish I was talented and smart, like you. Maybe I could get a better-paying job."

"You're good at what you do," he replied firmly. "And you love your work. Believe me, that's a lot more important than making a big paycheck. I should know."

She sighed as she sipped her soup. "I guess." She gave him a quick glance. "But it would help with the bills."

"My book is going to make us millions," he told her with a grin. "It will hit the top of the *New York Times* bestseller list, I'll be in demand for talk shows and we'll be able to buy a new car."

"Optimist," she accused.

"Hey, without hope, what have we got?" He looked around with a grimace. "Unpainted walls, cracks in the paint, a car with two hundred thousand miles on it and a leaky roof."

"Oh, darn," she muttered, following his eyes to the yellow spot on the ceiling. "I'll bet another one of those stupid nails worked its way out of the tin. I wish we could have afforded a shingle roof."

"Well, tin is cheaper, and it looks nice."

She looked at him meaningfully.

"It's cheap, anyway," he persisted. "Don't you like the sound of rain on a tin roof? Just listen. It's like music."

It was like a tin drum, she pointed out, but he just laughed.

She smiled. "I guess you're right. It's better not to wish we had more than we do. We'll get by, Kell," she assured him. "We always do."

"At least we're in it together," he agreed. "But you should think about the military home."

"After I'm dead and buried, you can go into a home," she assured him. "For now, you just eat your soup and hush."

He smiled tenderly. "Okay."

She smiled back. He was the nicest big brother in the whole world, and she wasn't abandoning him while there was a breath in her body.

It had stopped raining when she got to work the next morning. She was glad. She hadn't wanted to get out of bed at all. There was something magical about lying in the bed with rain coming down, all safe and cozy and warm. But she wanted to keep her job. She couldn't do both.

She was putting her raincoat in the closet when a long arm presented itself over her shoulder and deposited a bigger raincoat there.

"Hang that up for me, please," Dr. Rydel said gruffly.

"Yes, sir."

She fumbled it onto a hanger. When she closed the door and turned, he was still standing there.

"Is something wrong, sir?" she asked formally.

He was frowning. "No."

But he looked as if he had the weight of the world on his shoulders. She knew how that felt, because she loved her brother and she couldn't help him. Her soft gray eyes looked up into his pale blue ones. "When life gives you lemons, make lemonade?" she ventured.

A laugh escaped his tight control. "What the hell would you know about lemons, at your age?" he asked.

"It isn't the age, Dr. Rydel," she said. "It's the mileage. If I were a car, they'd have to decorate me with solid gold accessories just to get me off the lot."

His eyes softened, just a little. "I suppose I'd be in a junkyard."

She laughed, quickly controlling it. "Sorry."

"Why?"

"You're sort of hard to talk to," she confessed.

He drew in a long breath. Just for a minute, he looked oddly vulnerable. "I'm not used to people. I deal with them in the practice, but I live alone. I have most of my life." He frowned. "Your brother lives with you, doesn't he? Why doesn't he work?"

She tightened up. "He was overseas covering a war and a bomb exploded nearby. He caught shrapnel in the spine and they can't operate. He's paralyzed from the waist down."

He grimaced. "That's a hell of a way to end up in a wheelchair."

"Tell me about it," she agreed quietly. "He was in the military for years, but he got tired of dragging me all over the world, so he mustered out and got a job working for this magazine. He said it would mean he wouldn't be gone so much." She sighed. "I guess he wasn't, but he's in a lot of pain and they can't do much for it." She looked up at him. "It's hard to watch."

For an instant, some fellow feeling flared in his eyes. "Yes. It's easier to hurt yourself than to watch someone you love battle pain." His face softened as he looked down at her. "You take care of him."

She smiled. "Yes. Well, as much as he'll let me, anyway. He took care of me from the age of ten, when our parents died in a wreck. He wants me to let him go into some sort of military home, but I'll never do that."

He looked very thoughtful. And sad. He looked as if he badly needed someone to talk to, but he had nobody. She knew the feeling.

"Life is hard," she said gently.

"Then you die," he added, and managed a smile. "Back to work, Miss Drake." He hesitated. "Your name, Cappie. What's it short for?"

She hesitated. She bit her lower lip.

"Come on," he coaxed.

She drew in a breath. "Capella," she said.

His eyebrows shot up. "The star?"

She laughed, delighted. Most people had no idea what it meant. "Yes."

"One of your parents was an astronomy buff," he guessed.

"No. My mother was an astronomer, and my father was an astrophysicist," she corrected, beaming. "He worked for NASA for a while."

He pursed his lips. "Brainy people."

"Don't worry, it didn't rub off on me. Kell got all that talent. In fact, he's writing a book, an adventure novel." She smiled. "I just know it's going to be a blockbuster. He'll rake in the money, and then we won't have to worry about money for medicine and health care."

"Health care." He harrumphed. "It's a joke. People going without food to buy pills, without clothes to afford gas, having to choose between essentials and no help anywhere to change things."

She was surprised at his attitude. Most people seemed to think that health care was available to everybody. Actually she could only afford basic coverage for herself. If she ever had a major medical emergency, she'd have to beg for help from the state. She hoped she could even get it. It still amazed her that Kell's employers hadn't offered him health care benefits. "We don't live in a perfect society," she agreed.

"No. Nowhere near it."

She wanted to ask him why he was so outspoken on the issue, which hit home for her, too. But before she could overcome her shyness, the phones were suddenly ringing off the hook and three new four-legged patients walked in the door with their owners. One of them, a big Boxer, made a beeline for a small poodle whose owner had let it come in without a lead.

"Grab him!" Cappie called, diving after the Boxer.

Dr. Rydel followed her, gripping the Boxer's lead firmly. He pulled up on it just enough to establish control, and held it so that the dog's head was erect. "Down, sir!" he said in a commanding tone. "Sit!"

The Boxer sat down at once. So did all the pet owners. Cappie burst out laughing. Dr. Rydel gave her a speaking glance, turned and led the Boxer back to the patient rooms without a single word.

CHAPTER TWO

When she got home, Cappie told her brother about the struggle with the Boxer, and its result. He roared with laughter. It had been a long time since she'd seen him laugh.

"Well, at least he can control animals and people," he told her.

"Indeed he can." She picked up the dirty dishes and stacked them from their light supper. "You know, he's very adamant about health care. For people, I mean. I wonder if he has somebody who can't afford medicines or doctors or hospitals? He never talks about his private life."

"Neither do you," he pointed out dryly.

She made a face. "I'm not interesting. Nobody would want to know what I do at home. I just cook and clean and wash dishes. What's exciting about that? When you were in the army, you knew movie stars and sports legends."

"They're just like you and me," he told her. "Fame isn't a character reference. Neither is wealth."

"Well, I wouldn't mind being rich," she sighed. "We could fix the roof."

"One day," he promised her, "we'll get out of the hole."

"You think?"

"Miracles happen every day."

She wasn't touching that line with a pole. Just lately, she'd have given blood for a miracle that would treat her just to a new raincoat. The one she had, purchased for a dollar at a thrift shop, was worn and faded and missing buttons. She'd sewed others on, but none of them matched. It would be so nice to have one that came from a store, brand-new, with that smell that clothes had when nobody had ever worn them before.

"What are you thinking about?" Kell asked.

"New raincoats," she sighed. Then she saw his expression and grimaced. "Sorry. Just a stray thought. Don't mind me."

"Santa Claus might bring you one," he said.

She glowered at him on her way out the door. "Listen, Santa Claus couldn't find this place if he had GPS on his sleigh. And if he did, his reindeer would slide off the tin roof and fall to their doom, and we'd get sued."

He was still laughing when she got to the kitchen.

It was getting close to Christmas. Cappie dug out the old, faded artificial Christmas tree and put it up in the living room where Kell could see it from his hospital bed. She had one new string of minilights, all she could afford, and she put the old ornaments on it. Finally she plugged in the tree. It became a work of art, a magical thing, when she turned out the other lights and looked at it.

"Wow," Kell said in a soft tone.

She moved to the doorway and smiled at him. "Yeah. Wow." She sighed. "Well, at least it's a tree. I wish we could have a real one."

"Me, too, but you spent every Christmas sick in bed until we realized you were allergic to fir trees."

"Bummer."

He burst out laughing. "Now, all we have to do is decide what we're going to put under it."

"Artificial presents, I guess," she said quietly.

"Stop that. We're not destitute."

"Yet."

"What am I going to do with you? There is a Santa Claus, 'Virginia,'" he chided. "You just don't know it yet."

She turned the lights back on and smiled at him. "Okay. Have it your way."

"And we'll put presents under it."

Only if they come prepaid and already wrapped, she thought cynically, but she didn't say it. Life was hard, when you lived on the fringes of society. Kell had a much better attitude than she did. Her optimism was losing ground by the day.

The beginning of the week started out badly. Dr. Rydel and Dr. King had a very loud and disturbing argument over possible treatments for a beautiful black Persian male cat with advanced kidney failure.

"We can do dialysis," Dr. King argued.

Dr. Rydel's pale blue eyes threw off sparks. "Do you intend to contribute to the 'let's prolong Harry's suffering' fund?"

"Excuse me?"

"His owner is retired. All she has is her social security, because her pension plan crashed and burned during the economic downturn," he said hotly. "How the hell do you think she's going to afford dialysis for a cat who's got, at the most, a couple of weeks of acute suffering to go before he faces an end to the pain?"

Dr. King was giving him very odd looks. She didn't say anything.

"I can irrigate him and pump drugs into him and keep him alive for another month," he said through his teeth. "And he'll be in agony all that time. I can do dialysis and prolong it even more. Or do you think that animals don't really feel pain at all?"

She still hadn't spoken. She just looked at him.

"Dialysis!" he scoffed. "I love animals, too, Dr. King, and I'd never give up on one that had a ghost of a chance of a normal life. But this cat isn't having a normal life— he's going through hell on a daily basis. Or haven't you ever seen a human being in the final stages of kidney failure?" he demanded.

"No, I haven't," Dr. King said, in an unusually gentle tone.

"You can take it from me that it's the closest thing to hell on earth. And I am not, repeat not, putting the cat on dialysis and that's the advice I'm giving his owner."

"Okay."

He frowned. "Okay?"

She didn't smile. "It must have been very hard to watch," she added quietly.

His face, for an instant, betrayed the anguish of a personal loss of some magnitude. He turned away and went back into his office. He didn't even slam the door.

Cappie and Keely flanked Dr. King, all big eyes and unspoken questions.

"You don't know, do you?" she asked. She motioned them off into the chart room and closed the door. "You didn't hear me say this," she instructed, and waited until they both nodded. "His mother was sixty when they diagnosed her with kidney failure three years ago. They put her on dialysis and gave her medications to help put off the inevitable, but she lost the battle just a year later when they discovered an inoperable tumor in her bladder. She was in agony. All that time, she had only her social security and Medicaid to help. Her husband, Dr. Rydel's stepfather, wouldn't let him help at all. In fact, Dr. Rydel had to fight just to see his mother. He and his stepfather have been enemies for years, and it just got worse when his mother was so ill. His mother died and he blames his stepfather, first for not letting her go to a doctor for tests in the first place, and then for not letting him help with the costs afterward. She lived in terrible poverty. Her husband was too proud to accept a dime from any other source, and he worked as a night watchman in a manufacturing company."

No wonder Dr. Rydel was so adamant about health care, Cappie thought. She saw him through different eyes. She also understood his frustration.

"He's right, too, about Harry's owner," Dr. King added. "Mrs. Trammel doesn't have much left after she pays her own medicine bills and utilities and groceries. Certainly she doesn't have enough to afford expensive treatments for an elderly cat who doesn't have long to live no matter what we do." She grimaced. "It's wonderful that we have all these new treatments for our pets. But it's not good that we sometimes make decisions that aren't realistic. The cat is elderly and in constant pain. Are we doing it a favor to order thousands of dollars of treatments that its owner can't afford, just to prolong the suffering?"

Keely shrugged. "Bailey, Boone's German shepherd, would have died if Dr. Rydel hadn't operated on him when he got bloat," she ventured.

"Yes, and he's old, too," Dr. King agreed. "But Boone could afford it."

"Good point," Keely agreed.

"We do have medical insurance for pets now," Cappie pointed out.

"It's the same moral question, though," Dr. King pointed out. "Should we do something just because we can do it?"

The phone rang, both lines at once, and a woman with a cat in a blanket and red, tear-filled eyes rushed in the door calling for help.

"It's going to be a long day," Dr. King sighed.

★ ★ ★

Cappie told her brother about Dr. Rydel's mother. "I guess we're not the only people who wish we had adequate health care," she said, smiling gently.

"I guess not. Poor guy." He frowned. "How do you make a decision like that for a pet?" he added.

"We didn't. We recommended what we thought best, but let Mrs. Trammel make the final decision. She was more philosophical than all of us put together. She said Harry had lived for nineteen good years, been spoiled rotten and shame on us for thinking death was a bitter end. She thinks cats go to a better place, too, and that they have green fields to run through and no cars to run over them." She smiled. "In the end, she decided that it was kinder to just let Dr. Rydel do what was necessary. Keely's barn cat has a new litter of kittens, solid white with blue eyes. She promised Mrs. Trammel one. Life goes on."

"Yes." He was somber. "It does."

She lifted her eyebrows. "Any day now, there's going to be a breakthrough in medical research and you're going to have an operation that will put you back on your feet and give you a new lease on life."

"After which I'll win the British Open, effect détente with the eastern communists and perfect a cure for cancer," he added dryly.

"One miracle at a time," she interrupted. "And just how would you win the British Open? You don't even play tennis!"

"Don't confuse me with a bunch of irrelevant facts." He sank back into his pillows and grimaced. "Besides, the pain is going to kill me long before they find any miraculous surgical techniques." He closed his eyes with a long sigh. "One day without pain," he said quietly. "Just one day. I'd do almost anything for it."

She knew, as many other people didn't, that chronic pain

brought on a kind of depression that was pervasive and dangerous. Even the drugs he took for pain only took the edge off. Nothing they'd ever given him had stopped it.

"What you need is a nice chocolate milkshake and some evil, fattening, over-salted French fries and a cholesterol-dripping hamburger," she said.

He made a tortured face. "Go ahead, torment me!"

She grinned. "I overpaid the hardware bill and got sent a ten-dollar refund," she said, reaching into her purse. "I'll go to the bank, cash it and we'll eat out tonight!"

"You beauty!" he exclaimed.

She curtsied. "I'll be back before you know it." She glanced at her watch. "Oops, better hurry or the bank will be closed!"

She grabbed her old denim jacket and her purse and ran out the door.

The ancient car was temperamental. It had over two hundred thousand miles on it, and it looked like a piece of junk. She coaxed it into life and grimaced as she read the gas gauge. She had a fourth of a tank left. Well, it was only a five-minute drive to Jacobsville from Comanche Wells. She'd have enough to get her to work and back for one more day. Then she'd worry about gas. The ten-dollar check would have come in handy for that, but Kell needed cheering up more. These spells of depression were very bad for him, and they were becoming more frequent. She'd have done anything to keep him optimistic. Even walking to work.

She cashed the check with two minutes to spare before the bank closed. Then she drove to the local fast-food joint and ordered burgers and fries and milkshakes. She paid for them—had five cents left over—and pulled out into the road. Then two things went wrong at once. The engine quit and a car flew out of a side road and right into the passenger side of her car.

She sat, shaking, amid the ruins of her car, with chocolate

milkshake all over her jeans and jacket, and pieces of hamburgers on the dirty floorboard. It was quite an impact. She couldn't move for a minute. She sat, staring at the dash, wondering how she'd manage without a car, because her insurance only covered liability. She had nothing that would even pay to repair the car, if it could be repaired.

She turned her head in slow motion and looked at the car that had hit her. The driver got out, staggering. He laughed. That explained why he'd shot through a stop sign without braking. He leaned against his ruined fender and laughed some more.

Cappie wondered if he had insurance. She also wondered if she didn't have a tire iron that she could get to, before the police came to save the man.

Her car door was jerked open. She looked up into a pair of steely ice-blue eyes.

"Are you all right?" he asked.

She blinked. Dr. Rydel. She wondered where he'd come from.

"Cappie, are you all right?" he repeated. His voice was very soft, nothing like the glitter in those pale eyes.

"I think so," she said. Time seemed to have slowed to a stop. She couldn't get her sluggish brain to work. "I was taking hamburgers and shakes home to Kell," she said. "He was so depressed. I thought it would cheer him up. I was worried about spending the money on treats instead of gas." She laughed dully. "I guess I won't need to worry about gas, now," she added, looking around at the damage.

"You're lucky you weren't in one of the newer little cars. You'd be dead."

She looked toward the other driver. "Dr. Rydel, do you have a tire tool I could borrow?" she asked conversationally.

He saw where she was looking. "You don't want to upset the police, Cappie."

"I won't tell if you won't."

Before he could reply, a Jacobsville police car roared up, lights flashing, and stopped. Obviously somebody in the fast-food place had called them.

Officer Kilraven climbed out of the police car and headed right for Cappie.

"Oh, good, it's him," Cappie said. "He'll scare the other driver to death."

Kilraven bent down on Cappie's side of the car. "You okay? Need an ambulance?"

"Heavens, no," she said quickly. As if she could afford to pay for that! "I'm fine. Just shaken up." She nodded toward the giggling driver who'd hit her. "Dr. Rydel won't loan me a tire iron, so could you shoot that man in the foot for me, please? I don't even have collision insurance and it wasn't my fault. I'll be walking to work on account of him."

"I can't shoot him," Kilraven said with a twinkle in his silver eyes. "But if he tries to hit me, I'll take him to detention in the trunk of my car. Okay?"

She brightened. "Okay!"

He straightened and said something to Dr. Rydel. A minute later, he marched over to the drunk man, smelled his breath, made a face and asked him to perform a sobriety test, which the subject refused. That would mean a blood test at the hospital, which Kilraven was fairly certain the man would fail. He told him he was under arrest and cuffed him. Cappie vaguely heard him calling for a wrecker and backup.

"A wrecker?" She groaned. "I can't afford a wrecker."

"Just don't worry about it right now. Come on. I'll drive you home."

Dr. Rydel helped her out of the car. She retrieved her purse, wincing. "I hope he has a Texas-size hangover when he wakes up tomorrow," she said coldly, watching Kilraven putting the prisoner in the back of his squad car. The man was still laughing.

"Oh, I hope he gets pregnant," Dr. Rydel mused, "and it's twins."

She laughed huskily. "Even better. Thanks."

He put her into his big Land Rover. "Wait here. I'll just be a minute."

She sat quietly, fascinated with the interior of the vehicle. It conjured up visions of the African veldt, of elephants and giraffes and wildebeest. She wished she could afford even a twenty-year-old version of this beast. She'd never have to worry about bad roads again.

He was back shortly with a bag and a cup carrier. He put them in her lap. "Two hamburgers and fries and two chocolate shakes."

"How…?"

"Well, it's easier to tell when you're wearing parts of them," he pointed out, indicating chocolate milk stains and mustard and catsup and pieces of food all over her clothes. "Fasten your seat belt."

She did. "I'll pay you back," she said firmly.

He grinned. "Whatever."

He started the engine and drove her out of town. "You'll have to direct me. I don't know where you live."

She named the road, and then the street. They didn't talk. He pulled up in the front yard of the dinky little house, with its peeling paint and rickety steps and sagging eaves.

He grimaced.

"Hey, don't knock it," she said. "It's got a pretty good roof and big rooms and it's paid for. A distant cousin willed it to us."

"Nice of him. Do you have any other cousins?"

"No. It's just me and Kell."

"No other siblings?"

She shook her head. "We don't have any family left."

He gave the house a speaking look.

"If we had the money to fix it up, it would look terrific," she said.

He helped her out of the car and onto the porch. He hesitated about handing her the bag with the food and the carrier of milkshakes.

"Would you like to come in and meet Kell?" she ventured. "Only if you want to," she added quickly.

"Yes, I would."

She unlocked the door and motioned him in. "Kell, I'm home!" she called. "I brought company."

"If it's wearing lipstick and has a good sense of humor, bring it in here quick!" he quipped.

Dr. Rydel burst out laughing. "Sorry, I don't wear lipstick," he called back.

"Oops."

Cappie laughed and walked toward the room a little unsteadily, motioning the vet to follow her.

Kell was propped up in bed with the old laptop. He paused, eyebrows arched, as they walked in. "We should have ordered more food," he said with a grin.

Cappie winced. "Well, see, the food is the problem. I was pulling out of the parking lot and the engine died. A drunk man ran into the car and pretty much killed it."

"Luckily he didn't kill you," Kell said, frowning. "Are you all right?"

"Just bruised a little. Dr. Rydel was kind enough to bring me home. Dr. Rydel, this is my brother, Kell," she began.

"You're the veterinarian?" Kell asked, and his silvery-gray eyes twinkled. "I thought you had fangs and a pointed tail…"

"Kell!" she burst out, horrified.

Dr. Rydel chuckled. "Only during office hours," he returned.

"I'll kill you!" she told her brother.

"Now, now," Dr. Rydel said complacently. "We all know I'm a horror to work for. He's just saying what you aren't comfortable telling me."

"And he does have a sense of humor," Kell said. "Thanks for bringing her home," he added, and the smile faded. "My driving days are apparently over."

"There are vehicles with hand controls now," Dr. Rydel pointed out.

"We're ordering one of those as soon as we get our new yacht paid off," Kell replied with a serious expression.

Cappie burst out laughing. "And our dandy indoor swimming pool."

Dr. Rydel smiled. "At least you still have a sense of humor."

"It's the only part of me that works," Kell replied. "I've offered to check myself into a military home, but she won't hear of it."

"Over my dead body," she reiterated, and glared at him.

He sighed. "It's nice to be loved, but you can take family feeling over the cliff with you, darlin'," he reminded her.

"Sink or swim, we're a matched set," she said stubbornly. "I'm not putting you out on the street."

"Military homes can be very nice," Kell began.

Cappie grimaced. "Your milkshake is getting warm," she interrupted. She took the carrier from Dr. Rydel and handed one to Kell, along with a straw. "There's your burger and fries," she said. "Working?"

"Taking a short break to play mah-jongg," he replied. "I'm actually winning, too."

"I play Sudoku," Dr. Rydel commented.

Kell groaned. "I can't do numbers. I tried that game and thought I'd go nuts. I couldn't even get one column to line up. How do you do it?"

"I'm left-brained," the other man said simply. "Numbers and science. I'd have loved to be a writer, but I'm spelling-challenged."

Kell laughed. "I'm left-brained, too, but I can't handle Sudoku. I can spell, however," he added, tongue in cheek.

"That's why we have a bookkeeper," Dr. Rydel said. "I think people would have issues if their names and animal conditions were constantly misspelled. I had a time in college."

"So did I," Kell confessed. "College trigonometry almost kept me from getting my degree in the first place. I also had a bad time with biology," he added pointedly.

Dr. Rydel grinned. "My best subject. All A's."

"I'll bet the biology-challenged loved you," Cappie said with a chuckle. "Blew the curve every time, didn't you?"

He nodded. "I bought pizzas for my classmates every Saturday night to make it up to them."

"Pizza," Cappie mused. "I remember what that tastes like. I think."

"I don't want to talk about pizza," Kell said and sipped his milkshake. "You and your mushrooms!"

"He hates mushrooms, and I hate Italian sausage," Cappie commented. "I love mushrooms."

"Yuuuuck," Kell commented.

She smiled. "We'll leave you to your supper. If you need anything, call me, okay?"

"Sure. What would you like to be called?"

She wrinkled her nose at him and went out the door.

"Nice to have met you," Kell told the vet.

"Same here," Dr. Rydel said.

He followed Cappie out into the living room. "You'd better eat your own burger and fries before they're cold," he said. "They don't reheat well."

She smiled shyly. "Thanks again for bringing me home, and

for the food." She wondered how she was going to get to work the following Monday, but she knew she'd come up with something. She could always beg one of the other vet techs for a ride.

"You're welcome." He stared down at her quietly, frowning. "You sure you're all right?"

She nodded. "I'm wobbly. That's because I was scared to death. I'll be fine. It's just a little bruising. Honest."

"Would you tell me if it was more?" he asked.

She grinned.

"Well, if you think you need to go to the doctor later, you call me. Call the office," he added. "They'll take a message and page me, wherever I am."

"That's very nice of you. Thanks."

He drew in a long breath. His blue eyes narrowed on her face. "You've got a lot on your shoulders for a woman your age," he said quietly.

"Some people have a lot more," she replied. "I love my brother."

He smiled. "I noticed that."

She studied him curiously. "Do you have family?"

His face tautened. "Not anymore."

"I'm sorry."

"People get old. They die." He became distant. "We'll talk another time. Good evening."

"Good evening. Thanks."

He shrugged. "No problem."

She watched him go with a strange sense of loss. He was in many ways the saddest person she'd ever known.

She finished her supper and went to collect her brother's food containers.

"Your boss is nice," he said. "Not what I expected."

"How could you tell him what I said about him, you horrible man?" she asked with mock anger.

"He's one of those rare souls who never lie," he said simply. "He comes at you head-on, not from ambush."

"How do you know that?"

"It's in his manner," he said simply. He smiled. "I'm that way myself. It does take one to know one. Now come here and sit down and tell me what happened."

She drew in a deep breath and sat down in the chair beside the bed. She hated having to tell him the whole truth. It wasn't going to be pretty.

CHAPTER THREE

Cappie hitched a ride to work with Keely, promising not to make a regular thing of it.

"I'll just have to get another car," she said, as if all that required was a trip to a car lot. In fact, she had no idea what she was going to do.

"My brother is best friends with Sheriff Hayes Carson," Keely reminded her, "and Hayes knows Kilraven. He told him the particulars, and Kilraven had a talk with the driver's insurance company." She chuckled. "I understand some interesting what-ifs were mentioned. The upshot is that the driver's insurance is going to pay to fix your car."

"What?"

"Well, he was drunk, Cappie. In fact, he's occupying a cell at the county detention center as we speak. You could sue his insurance company for enough to buy a new Jaguar like my brother's got."

She didn't mention that Kell had owned a Jaguar, and not too long ago. Those days seemed very far away now. "Wow. I've never sued anybody, you know."

Keely laughed. "Me, neither. But you could. Once the insurance people were reminded of that, they didn't seem to think fixing an old car was an extravagant use of funds."

"It's really nice of them," Cappie said, stunned. It was like a miracle. "I didn't know what I was going to do. My brother is an invalid, and the only money we've got is his savings and what I bring home. That's not a whole lot."

"Before I married Boone, I had to count pennies," the other girl said. "I know what it's like to have very little. I think you do very well."

"Thanks." She sighed. "You know, Kell was in the military for years and years. He went into all sorts of dangerous situations, but he never got hurt. Then he left the army and went to work for this magazine, went to Africa to cover a story and got hit with shrapnel from an exploding shell. Go figure."

Keely frowned. "Didn't he have insurance? Most magazines have it for their employees, I'm sure."

"Well, no, he didn't. Odd, isn't it?"

"They sent him to Africa to do a story," Keely added. "What sort of story? A news story?"

Cappie blinked. "You know, I never asked him. I only knew he was leaving the country. Then I got a call from him, saying he was in the hospital with some injuries and he'd be home when he could get here. He wouldn't even let me visit him. An ambulance brought him to our rented house in San Antonio."

Keely didn't say what she was thinking. But she almost had to bite her tongue.

Cappie stared at her. "That's a very strange story, even if I'm the one telling it," she said slowly.

"Maybe it's the truth," Keely said comfortingly. "After all, it's very often stranger than fiction."

"I guess so." She let it drop. But she did intend to talk it over with Kell that night.

★ ★ ★

When she got home, there was a big SUV parked in the driveway. She frowned at it as she went up the steps and into the house. The door was unlocked.

She heard laughter coming from Kell's room.

"I'm home!" she called.

"Come on in here," Kell called back. "I've got company."

She took off her coat and moved into the bedroom. Kell's visitor was very tall and lean, with faint silvering at the temples of his black hair. He had green eyes and a somber face, and one of his hands seemed to be burned. He moved it unobtrusively into his pocket when he saw her eyes drawn to it.

"This is an old friend of mine," Kell said. "My sister, Cappie. This is Cy Parks. He owns a ranch in Jacobsville."

Cappie held out her hand, smiling, and shook the one offered. "Nice to meet you."

"Same here. You'll have to bring Kell over to the ranch to see us," he added. "I have a terrific wife and two little boys. I'd love for you to meet them."

"You, with a wife and kids," Kell said, shaking his head. "I'd never have imagined it in my wildest dreams."

"Oh, it comes to all of us, sooner or later," Cy replied lazily. He pursed his lips. "So you work for Bentley Rydel, do you?"

She nodded.

"Does he really carry a pitchfork, or is that just malicious gossip?" Cy added, tongue in cheek.

She flushed. "Kell…!" she muttered at her brother.

He held up both hands and laughed. "I didn't tell him what you said. Honest."

"He didn't," Cy agreed. "Actually Bentley makes a lot of calls at my place during calving season. He's our vet. Good man."

"Yes, he is," Cappie said. "He brought me home after a drunk ran into my car."

Cy's expression darkened. "I heard about that. Tough break."

"Well, the man's insurance company is going to fix our car," Cappie added with a laugh. "It seems they were worried that we might sue."

"We would have," Kell said, and he wasn't smiling. "You could have been killed."

"I just got bruised a little," she said, smiling. "Nice of you to worry, though."

Kell grinned. "It's a hobby of mine."

"You need to get out more," Cy told the man in the bed. "I know you've got pain issues, but staying cooped up in here is just going to make things worse. Believe me, I know."

Kell's eyes darkened. "I guess you're right. But I do have something to do. I'm working on a novel. One about Africa."

Cy Parks's face grew hard. "That place has made its mark on several of us," he said enigmatically.

"It's still making marks on other men," Kell said.

"The Latin American drug cartels are moving in there, as well," Cy replied. "Hell of a thing, as if Africa didn't have enough internal problems as it is."

"As long as power-hungry tyrants can amass fortunes by oppressing other men, it won't lower the casualty rates for any combatants working there," Kell muttered.

"Combatants?" Cappie asked curiously.

"Two groups of people are fighting for supremacy," Kell told her.

"One good, one evil," she guessed.

"No. As far as African internal politics go, both sides have positive arguments. The outsiders are the ones causing the big problems. Their type of diplomacy is most often practiced with rapid-firing automatic weapons and various incendiary devices."

"And IEDs," Cy added.

Cappie blinked. "Excuse me?"

"Improvised explosive devices," Kell translated.

"Were you in the military, too, Mr. Parks?" Cappie asked.

Cy hesitated. "Sort of. Look at the time," he remarked, glancing at his watch. "Lisa wants me to go with her to pick out a new playpen for our youngest son," he added with a grin. "Our toddler more or less trashed the first one."

"Strong kid," Kell noted.

"Yes. Bullheaded, too."

"I wonder where he gets that from," Kell wondered aloud, with twinkling eyes.

"I am not bullheaded," Cy said complacently. "I simply have a resistance to stupid ideas."

"Same difference."

Cy made a face. "I'll come back and check on you later in the week. If you need anything…"

Kell smiled. "Thanks, Cy."

"I'd have come with Eb and Micah when they dropped by," Cy added, "but we were out of town with the kids. It's good to see you again."

"Same here," Kell said. "I owe you."

"For what?" Cy shrugged. "Friends help friends."

"They do."

Cappie stared at her brother with a blank expression. A whole conversation seemed to be going on under her nose that she didn't comprehend.

"I'll see you," Cy said. "Nice to have met you, Miss Drake," he added, smiling.

"You, too," she replied.

Cy left without a backward glance.

After he drove away, Cappie was still staring at her brother. "You didn't say you had friends here. Why haven't I seen them?"

"They came while you were at work," he said. "Several times."

"Oh."

He averted his eyes. "I met them when I was in the service," he said. "They're fine men. A little unorthodox, but good people."

"Oh!" She relaxed. "Mr. Parks has an injury."

"Yes. He was badly burned trying to save his wife and child from a fire. He was the only one who got out. It turned him mean. But now he's remarried and has two sons, and he seems to have put the past behind him."

"Poor guy." She grimaced. "No wonder he was mean. Who were the other men he mentioned?"

"Other friends. Eb Scott and Micah Steele. Micah's a doctor in Jacobsville. Eb Scott has a sort of training center for paramilitary units."

She blinked. "You do seem to attract the oddest friends."

"Men with guns." He nodded. He grinned.

She laughed. "Okay. I'm stonewalled. What do you want for supper?"

"Nothing heavy," he said. "I had a big lunch."

"You did?" She didn't recall leaving anything out for him except sandwiches in a Baggie.

"Cy brought a whole menu full of stuff from the local Chinese restaurant," he said. "The remains are in the fridge. I wouldn't mind having some of them for supper."

"Chinese food? Real Chinese food, from a real restaurant, that I don't have to cook?" She felt her forehead. "Maybe I'm delusional."

He chuckled. "It does sound like that, doesn't it? Go dig in. Bring me some of the pork and noodles, if you will. There's sticky rice and mangoes for dessert, too."

"I have died and am now in heaven," she said in a haunted tone.

"Me, too. Get cracking. I'm on the fourth chapter of this book already!"

"You are?" She laughed. He looked so much more cheerful. More than he'd been in weeks. "Okay, then."

He pulled the laptop back into place.

"Do I get to read it?"

He nodded. "When it's done."

"That's a deal." She went into the kitchen and got out the boxes of Chinese food. It was all she could do to keep back the tears. Cy Parks was a nice man. A very nice man. Except for their splurged hamburgers and milkshakes, for which she still owed Dr. Rydel, she reminded herself, there hadn't been any convenience food for a long time. This was a feast. She put some of it in the freezer for hard times and heated up the rest. Her day was already getting better.

It got even better than that. A tall man with sandy hair and blue eyes came driving up in Cappie's own car two days later. The big SUV was following close behind. Cappie gaped at the sight. Her old car had been refurbished, its dents beaten out and the whole thing repainted and repaired. There were even seat covers and floor mats. She stared at it helplessly surprised.

Cy Parks got out of the SUV and followed the sandy-haired man up onto the porch. "I hope you like blue," he told Cappie. "There was a paint sale."

She could barely manage words. "Mr. Parks, I don't even know what to say..." She burst into tears. "It's so kind!"

He patted her awkwardly on the shoulder. "There, there, it's just one of those random acts of kindness we're supposed to pass around. You can do the same thing for somebody else one day."

She dabbed at her eyes. "When I strike it rich, I swear I will!"

He chuckled. "Harley Fowler, here," he introduced his companion, "is as good a mechanic as he is a ranch foreman. I had him supervise the work on your car. The insurance company paid for it all," he added when she started to protest. He grinned. "We get things done here in Jacobsville. The insurance agent locally is the sister-in-law of my top wrangler."

"Well, thank you both," she said huskily. "Thank you so much. I was almost ashamed to ask Keely for rides. She's so nice, but it was an imposition. I live five miles out of her way."

"You're very welcome."

The front door opened and Kell wheeled himself out onto the porch. He whistled when he saw the car. "Good grief, that was quick work," he said.

Cy grinned. "You might remember that I always did know how to cut through the red tape."

"Thanks," Kell told him. "From both of us. If I can ever do anything for you…"

"You've done enough," Cy returned quietly. His green eyes twinkled. "But you could always put me in that novel you're writing. I'd like to be twenty-seven, drop-dead handsome and a linguist."

Kell rolled his eyes. "You can barely speak English," he pointed out.

Cy glared at him. "You take that back, or I'll have Harley shoot all the tires out on this car."

Kell held up both hands, his silver eyes twinkling. "Okay, you could get work as a translator at the UN any day. Honest."

Cy sighed. "Don't I wish." He frowned. "Do you still speak Farsi?"

Kell nodded, smiling.

"I've got a friend who's applying for a job with the company. Think you could tutor him? He's well-off, and he'd pay you for your time."

Kell frowned.

"It's not charity," Cy muttered, glowering at him. "This is a legitimate need. The guy wants to work overseas, but he'll never get the job unless he can perfect his accent."

Kell relaxed. "All right, then. I'll take him on. And thanks."

Cy smiled. "Thank you," he replied. "He's a nice guy. You'll like him." He glanced at Cappie, who was wondering what sort of company Cy's friend worked for. "You won't," he assured her. "I used to be a woman hater, but this guy makes me look civilized. He'll need to come over when you're at work."

Cappie was curious. "Why does he hate women?"

"I think he was married to one," Cy mused.

"Well, that certainly explains that," Kell chuckled.

"Thank you very much for fixing up my car," Cappie told Cy. "I won't forget it."

"No problem. We were glad to help. Oh, mustn't forget the keys, Harley!"

Harley handed the keys to her as Cy headed back and got into the other vehicle. "She purrs like a kitten now," Harley told her. "She drives good."

"The car is a girl?" she asked.

"Only when a guy is driving it," Kell told her with a wicked grin.

"Amen," Harley told him.

"Come on, Harley," Cy called from the SUV.

"Yes, sir." He grinned at the brother and sister and jumped into the passenger seat in Cy's SUV.

"What a nice man," Cappie said. "Just look, Kell!" She walked out to the car, opened the door and gasped. "They oiled the hinges! It doesn't squeak anymore. And look, they fixed the broken dash and replaced the radio that didn't work..." She started crying again.

"Don't do that," Kell said gently. "You'll have me wailing, too."

She made a face at him. "You have nice friends."

"I do, don't I?" He smiled. "Now you won't have to beg rides."

"It will be a relief, although Keely's been wonderful about it." She glanced at her brother. "I don't think the insurance paid for all this."

"Yes, it did," he said firmly. "Period."

She smiled at him. "Okay. You really do have nice friends."

"You don't know how nice," he told her. "But I may tell you one day. Now let's get back inside. It's cold out here today."

"It is a bit nippy." She turned and followed him inside.

The week went by fast. She got her paycheck on Friday and went shopping early Saturday morning in Jacobsville. Kell had said he'd love a new bathrobe for Christmas, so she went to the department store looking.

It was a surprise when she bumped into Dr. Rydel in the men's department. He gave her a curious look. She didn't realize why until she recalled that she'd left her hair long around her shoulders instead of putting it up. He seemed to find it fascinating.

"Shopping for anything particular?" he asked.

"Yes. Kell wants a bathrobe."

"Christmas shopping," he guessed, and smiled.

"Yes."

"I'm replacing a jacket," he sighed. "I made the mistake of going straight from church on a large animal call. A longhorn bull objected to being used as a pincushion and ripped out the sleeve."

She laughed softly. "Occupational hazard," she said.

He nodded. "Your car looks nice."

"Thanks," she said. She could imagine how her old wreck, even repainted, looked to a man who drove a new Land Rover, but she didn't say so. "Mr. Parks had his foreman supervise the work. The insurance company paid for it."

"Nice of him. He knows your brother?"

"They're friends." She frowned. "Mr. Parks doesn't look like a rancher," she blurted out.

"Excuse me?"

"There's something, I don't know, dangerous about him," she said, searching for the right word. "He's very nice, but I wouldn't want him mad at me."

He grinned. "A few drug dealers in prison could attest to the truth of that statement," he said.

"What?"

"You don't know?"

"Know what?"

"Cy Parks is a retired mercenary," he told her. "He was in some bloody firefights in Africa some years back. More recently, he and two other friends and Harley Fowler shut down a drug distribution center here. There was a gunfight."

"In Jacobsville, Texas?" she exclaimed.

"Yep. Parks is one of the most dangerous men I've ever met. Kind to people he likes. But there aren't many of those."

She felt odd. She wondered how it was that her brother had come to know such a man, because he and Cy seemed to be old friends.

"Where do you go from here?" Dr. Rydel asked suddenly.

She blinked. "I don't know," she blurted out, flushing. "I mean, I thought I might, well, stop by the game store in the strip mall."

He stared at her blankly. "Game store?"

She cleared her throat. "There's this new video game. *Halo*..."

"...*ODST*," he said, with evident surprise. "You're a gamer?"

She cleared her throat again. "Well...yes."

He said something unprintable.

She glared at him. "Dr. Rydel!" she exclaimed. "It's not a vice, you know, playing video games. They release tension and they're fun," she argued.

He chuckled. "I have all three Halo games from Bungie, plus the campaigns," he confessed, naming the famous company whose amazing staff had engineered one of the most exciting video game series of all time. "And the new one that just came out."

Now her jaw fell open. "You do?"

"Yes. I have *Halo: ODST,*" he said, pursing his lips. "Do you game online?"

She didn't want to confess that she couldn't afford the fees. "I like playing by myself," she said. "Or with Kell. He's crazy about the Halo series."

"So am I," Dr. Rydel told her. His blue eyes twinkled. "Maybe we could play split screen sometime, when we're both free."

She gave him a wicked look. "I can put down Hunters with a .45 automatic." Hunters were some of the most formidable of the alien Covenant bad guys, fearsome to engage in the Halo game because they were huge and it took a dead shot to hit them in their very few vulnerable places.

He whistled. "Not bad, Miss Drake!"

"Have you been a gamer for a long time?" she asked.

"Since college," he replied, smiling. "You?"

"Since high school. Kell was in the military and a bunch of guys in his unit would come over to the house when they were off duty and play war-game videos. We lived off base." She pursed her lips and her eyes twinkled. "I not only learned how to use tactics and weapons, I also learned a lot of very interesting and useful words to employ when I got killed in the games."

"Bad girl," he chided.

She laughed.

"I'll probably see you in the video store," he added.

She beamed. "You probably will."

He grinned and went back to the suits.

★ ★ ★

Fifteen minutes later, she parked in front of the video store and went inside. It was full of teenage boys mostly, but there were two men standing in front of a rack with the newest sword and sorcery and combat games. One of them was Dr. Rydel. The other, surprisingly, was Officer Kilraven.

Dr. Rydel looked up and smiled when he saw her coming. Kilraven's silver eyes cut around to follow his companion's gaze. His black eyebrows arched.

"She's Christmas shopping," Dr. Rydel announced.

"Buying video games for a relative?" Kilraven wondered aloud.

Dr. Rydel chuckled. "She's a gamer," he confided. "She can take down Hunters with a .45 auto."

Kilraven whistled through his teeth. "Impressive," he said. "I usually do that with a sniper rifle."

"I can use those, too," she said. "But the .45 works just as well, thanks to that magnified sight."

"Have you played all the Halo series?" Kilraven asked.

She nodded. "Now I'm shopping for *ODST*," she said. "Kell, my brother, likes it, too. He taught me how to play."

Kilraven frowned. "Kell Drake?"

"Yes…"

"I know him," Kilraven replied quietly. "Good man."

"Were you in the army?" she asked innocently.

Kilraven chuckled. "Once, a long time ago."

"Kell only got out a year ago," she said. "He was freelancing for a magazine in Africa and got hit by flying shrapnel. He's paralyzed from the waist down—at least until the shrapnel shifts enough so that they can operate."

Kilraven blinked. "He got hit by flying…he was working for a magazine?" He seemed incredulous. "Doing what?"

"Writing stories."

"Writing stories? Kell can write?"

"He has very good English skills," she began defensively.

"I never," Kilraven said in an odd tone. "Why did he get out of the army?" he wanted to know.

She blinked. "Well, I'm not really sure…" she began.

"Look at this one," Dr. Rydel interrupted helpfully, holding up a game. "Have you ever played this?"

Kilraven was diverted. He took the green case and stared at the description. He grinned. "Have I ever! *Elder Scrolls IV, Oblivion*," he murmured. "This is great! You don't have to do the main quest, if you don't want to. There are dozens of other quests. You can even design your own character's appearance, name him, choose from several races…ever played it?" he asked Cappie.

She chuckled. "Actually it's sort of my favorite. I love *Halo*, but I like using a two-handed sword, as well."

"Vicious girl," Kilraven mused, smiling at her.

Dr. Rydel unobtrusively moved closer to Cappie and cleared his throat. "You shopping or working today?" he asked Kilraven.

The other man looked from Cappie to Dr. Rydel and his silver eyes twinkled. "If you notice, I'm wearing a real uniform," he pointed out. "I even carry a real gun. Now would I be doing that if it was my day off?"

Dr. Rydel smiled back at him. "Would you be shopping for video games on city time?"

Kilraven glared at him. "For your information, I am here detecting crime."

"You are?"

"Absolutely. I have it on good authority that there might be an attempted shoplifting case going on here right now." He raised his voice as he said it and a young boy cleared his throat and eased a game out from under his jacket and back on the shelf. With flaming cheeks he gave Kilraven a hopeful smile and moved quickly to the door.

"If you'll excuse me," Kilraven murmured, "I'm going to have a few helpful words of advice for that young man."

"How did he know?" Cappie asked, stunned, as she watched the tall officer walk out the door and call to the departing teen.

"Beats me, but I've heard he does things like that." He smiled. "He's on his lunch hour, in case you wondered. I was just ribbing him. I like Kilraven."

She gave him a wry glance. "Sharks like other sharks, do they?" she asked wickedly.

CHAPTER FOUR

At first, Bentley wasn't sure he'd heard her right. Then he saw the demure grin and burst out laughing. She'd compared him to a shark. He was impressed.

"I wondered if you were ever going to learn how to talk to me without getting behind a door first," he mused.

"You're hard going," she confessed. "But so is Kell, to other people. He just walks right over people who don't talk back."

"Exactly," he returned. He shrugged his broad shoulders. "I don't know how to get along with people," he confessed. "My social skills are sparse."

"You're wonderful with animals," she replied.

His eyebrows arched and he smiled. "Thanks."

"Did you always like them?" she wondered.

His eyes had a faraway look. He averted them. "Yes. But my father didn't. It wasn't until after he died that I indulged my affection for them. It was just my mother and me until I was in high school. That's when she met my stepfather." His expression hardened.

"It must have been very difficult for you," she said quietly, "getting used to another man in your house."

He frowned as he looked down at her. "Yes."

"Oh, I'm remarkably perceptive," she said with amusement in her eyes. "I also suffer from extreme modesty about my other equally remarkable attributes." She grinned.

He laughed again.

Kilraven came back, looking smug.

"You look like a man with a mission," Bentley mused.

"Just finished one. That young man will never want to lift a video game again."

"Good for you. Didn't arrest him?"

Kilraven arched an eyebrow. "Actually he knows some cheat codes for *Call of Duty* that even I haven't worked out. So I called our police chief."

"Cheat codes are against the law?" Cappie asked, puzzled.

Kilraven chuckled. "No. Cash has a young brother-in-law, Rory, who's nuts about *Call of Duty*, so our potential shoplifter is going to go over to Cash's house later and teach them to him. Cash may have a few words to add to the ones I gave him."

"Neat strategy," Bentley said.

Kilraven shrugged. "The boy loves gaming but he lives with a widowed mother who works two jobs just to keep food on the table. He wanted *Call of Duty*, but he didn't have any money. If he and Rory hit it off, and I think they might, he'll get to play the game and learn model citizen habits on the side."

"Good psychology," Bentley told him.

Kilraven sighed. "It's tough on kids, having an economy like this. Gaming is a way of life for the younger generation, but those game consoles and games for them are expensive."

"That's why we have a whole table of used games that are more affordable," the owner of the store, overhearing them, commented with a grin. "Thanks, Kilraven."

The officer shrugged. "I spend so much time in here that I feel obliged to protect the merchandise," he commented.

The store owner patted him on the back. "Good man. I might give you a discount on your next sale."

Kilraven glared at him. "Attempting to bribe a police officer..."

The owner held up both hands. "I never!" he exclaimed. "I said 'might'!"

Kilraven grinned. "Thanks, though. It was a nice thought. You wouldn't have any games based on Scottish history?" he added.

The store owner, a tall, handsome young man, gave him a pitying look. "Listen, you're the only customer I've ever had who likes sixteenth-century Scottish history. And I'll tell you again that most historians think James Hepburn got what he deserved."

"He did not," Kilraven muttered. "Lord Bothwell was led astray by that French-thinking Queen. Her wiles did him in."

"Wiles?" Cappie asked, wide-eyed. "What are wiles?"

"If you have to ask, you don't have any," Bentley said helpfully.

She laughed. "Okay. Fair enough."

Kilraven shook his head. "Bothwell had admirable qualities," he insisted, staring at the shop owner. "He was utterly fearless, could read and write and speak French, and even his worst enemies said that he was incapable of being bribed."

"Which may be, but still doesn't provide grounds for a video game," the manager replied.

Kilraven pointed a finger at him. "Just because you're a partisan of Mary, Queen of Scots, is no reason to take issue with her Lord High Admiral. And I should point out that there's no video game about her, either!"

"Hooray," the manager murmured dryly. "Oh, look, a customer!" He took the opportunity to vanish toward the counter.

Kilraven's two companions were giving him odd looks.

"Entertainment should be educational," he defended himself.

"It is," Bentley pointed out. "In this game—" he held up a Star Trek one "—you can learn how to shoot down enemy ships. And in this one—" he held up a comical one about aliens "—you can learn to use a death ray and blow up buildings."

"You have no appreciation of true history," Kilraven sighed. "I should have taught it in grammar school."

"I can see you now, standing in front of the school board, explaining why the kids were having nightmares about sixteenth-century interrogation techniques," Bentley mused.

Kilraven pursed his lips. "I myself have been accused of using those," he said. "Can you believe it? I mean, I'm such a law-abiding citizen and all."

"I can think of at least one potential kidnapper who might disagree," Bentley commented.

"Lies. Vicious lies," he said defensively. "He got those bruises from trying to squeeze through a car window."

"While it was going sixty miles an hour, I believe?" the other man queried.

"Hey, it's not my fault he didn't want to wait for the arraignment."

"Good thing you noticed the window was cracked in time."

"Yes," Kilraven sighed. "Sad, though, that I didn't realize he had a blackjack. He gave it to me very politely, though."

Bentley glanced at Cappie. "Was it a sprained wrist or a fractured one?" he wondered.

Kilraven gave him a cold glare. "It was a figment."

"A what?"

"Of his imagination," Kilraven assured him. He chuckled. "Anyway, he's going to be in jail for a long time. The resisting-arrest charge, added to assault on a police officer, makes two felony charges in addition to the kidnapping ones."

"I hope you never get mad at me," Bentley said.

"I'd worry more about the chief," Kilraven replied. "He fed a guy a soapy sponge in front of the whole neighborhood."

"He was provoked, I hear," Bentley said.

"A felon verbally assaulted him in his own yard while he was washing his car. Of course, Cash has mellowed since his marriage."

"Not much," Bentley said. "And he's still pretty good with a sniper kit. Saved Colby Lane's little girl when she was kidnapped."

"He practices on Eb Scott's firing range," Kilraven said. "We all do. He lets us use it free. State-of-the-art stuff, computers and everything."

"Eb Scott?" Cappie asked.

"Eb was a merc," Kilraven told her. "He and Cy Parks and Micah Steele fought in some of the bloodiest wars in Africa a few years back. They're all married and somewhat settled. But like Cash Grier, they're not really tame."

Cappie only nodded. She was recalling what her brother had said about Cy Parks.

Kilraven cleared his throat. "Oops, lunchtime is over. I've got to go. See you."

"You didn't have lunch," Bentley observed.

"I had a big breakfast," Kilraven replied. "Can't waste my lunch hour eating," he added with a grin. "See you."

"Imagine him, a gamer," Cappie commented. "I'd never have thought it."

"A lot of military men keep their hand-eye coordination skills sharp playing them," he said.

"Were you in the military?" Cappie wanted to know.

He smiled and nodded. "I have it on good authority that it's all that saved me from a life of crime. I got picked up for hanging around with a couple of bad kids who knocked over a drugstore. I was just in the car with them, but I got charged with a felony." He sighed. "My mother went to the judge and promised him her next child if he'd let me join the army instead of standing trial. He agreed." He glanced down at her with a smile. "He's in his seventies now, but I still send him a Christmas present every year. I owe him."

"That was nice."

"I thought so, too."

"Kell got into some trouble in his senior year of high school. I don't remember it, I was so young, but he told me about it. He was hanging out with one of the inner-city gangs and there was a firefight. He didn't get shot, but one of the boys in the gang was killed. Kell got arrested right along with them. He drew a female judge who had grown up in gang territory and lost a brother to the violence. She gave him a choice of facing trial or going into the service and making something of his life. He took her at her word, and made her proud." She sighed. "It was tragic, about her. She was shot and killed in her own living room during a drug deal shootout next door."

"Life is dangerous," Bentley remarked.

She nodded. "Unpredictable and dangerous." She looked up at him. "I guess maybe that's why I like playing video games. They give me something that I can control. Life is never that way."

He smiled. "No. It isn't." He watched as she took a copy of *Halo: ODST* off the shelf. "Going to make him wait until Christmas to play it?"

"Yes."

His eyes twinkled. "I could bring my copy over. Let you get a taste of it before the fact."

She looked fascinated. "You could?"

"Ask Kell." He hesitated. "I could bring a pizza with me. And some beer."

She pursed her lips. "I'm already drooling." She grimaced. "I could cook something..."

"Not fair. You shouldn't have to provide for guests. Besides, I haven't had a decent pizza in weeks. I'll be on call tonight, but we might get lucky."

Her eyes brightened. "That would be nice. I'm sure Kell would enjoy it. We don't get much company."

"About six?"

Her heart jumped. "Yes. About six would be fine."

"It's a date."

"I'll see you then."

He nodded.

She walked, a little wobbly, to the counter and paid for her game. Her life had just changed in a heartbeat. She didn't know where it would lead, and she was a little nervous about getting involved with her boss. But he was very nice-looking and he had qualities that she admired. Besides, she thought, it was just a night of gaming. Nothing suspect about that.

She told Kell the minute she got home.

He laughed. "Don't look so guilty," he chided. "I like your boss. Besides, it's neat to see the game I might get for Christmas." He smiled angelically.

"You might get it," she said, "and you might not."

"You might get a new raincoat," he mused.

She grinned. "Wow."

He looked at her fondly. "It's hard, living like this, I know. We were better off in San Antonio. But I didn't want us to be around when Frank got out of jail." His face hardened.

Her heart jumped. She hadn't thought about Frank for several days in a row. But now the trial and his fury came back, full force. "It was almost six months ago that he was arrested, and three months until the trial. He got credit for time served.

We've been here just about three months." She bit her lower lip. "Oh, dear. They'll let him out pretty soon."

His pale eyes were cold. "It should have been a tougher sentence. But despite his past, it was the first time he was ever charged with battery, and they couldn't get more jail time for him on a first offense. The public defender in his case was pretty talented, as well."

She drew in a long breath. "I'm glad we're out of the city."

"So am I. He lived barely a block from us. We're not as easy to get to, here."

She stared at him closely. "You believe the threats he made," she murmured. "Don't you?"

"He's the sort of man who gets even," he told her. "I'm not the man I was, or we'd never have left town on the chance he might come after you. But here, I have friends. If he comes down here looking for trouble, he'll find some."

She felt a little better. "I didn't want to have him arrested again."

"It wouldn't have mattered," he told her. "The fact that you stood up to him was enough. He was used to women being afraid of him. His own sister sat in the back of the courtroom during the trial. She was afraid to get near him, because she hadn't lied for him when the police came."

"What makes a man like that?" she asked sadly. "What makes him so hard that he has to beat up a woman to make him feel strong?"

"I don't know, sis," Kell told her gently. "Honestly I don't think the man has feelings for anybody or anything. His sister told you that he threw her dog off a bridge when they were kids. He laughed about it."

Her face grew sad. "I thought he was such a gentleman. He was so sweet to me, bringing me flowers and candy at work, writing me love letters. Then he came over to our house and the first thing he did was kick my cat when it spit at him."

"The cat was a good judge of character," Kell remarked.

"When I protested, he said that animals didn't feel pain and I shouldn't get so worked up over a stupid cat. I should have realized then what sort of person he was."

"People in love are neither sane nor responsible," Kell replied flatly. "You were so crazy about him that I think you could have forgiven murder."

She nodded sadly. "I learned the hard way that looks and acts are no measure of a man. I should have run for my life the first time he phoned me at work just to talk."

"You didn't know. How could you? He was a stranger."

"You knew," she said.

He nodded. "I've known men like him in the service," he said. "They're good in combat, because they aren't bothered by the carnage. But that trait serves them poorly in civilian life."

She cocked her head at him. "Kilraven said that Eb Scott lets law enforcement use his gun range for free. Don't you know him, too?"

"Yes."

"And Micah Steele."

"Yes."

She hesitated. "They're all retired mercenaries, Kell."

"So they are."

"Were they involved with the military?" she persisted.

"The military uses contract personnel," he said evasively. "People with necessary skills for certain jobs."

"Like combat."

"Exactly," he replied. "We used certain firms to supplement our troops overseas in the Middle East. They're used in Africa for certain covert operations."

"So much secrecy," she complained.

"Well, you don't advertise something that might get you sued or cause a diplomatic upheaval," he pointed out. "Covert ops have always been a part of the military. Even what they call transparency in government is never going to threaten that. As long as we have renegade states that threaten our sovereignty, we'll have black ops." He glanced at the clock. "Shouldn't you warm up the game system?" he asked. "It's five-thirty."

"Already?" she exclaimed. "Goodness, I need to tidy up the living room! And the kitchen. He's bringing pizza and beer!"

"You don't drink," he said.

"Well, no, but you like a beer now and then. I expect somebody told him." She flushed.

"I do like a glass of beer." He smiled. "It's also nice to have friends who provide food."

"Like your friend Cy and the Chinese stuff. I'll get spoiled."

"Maybe that's the idea. Your boss likes you."

She'd gotten that idea, herself. "Don't mention horns, pitchforks or breathing fire while he's here," she said firmly.

He saluted her.

She made a face at him and went to do her chores.

"That's not fair!" Cappie burst out when she'd "died" for the tenth time trying to take out one of the Hunters in the Halo game.

"Don't throw the controller," Kell said firmly.

She had it by one lobe, gripped tightly. She grimaced and slowly lowered it. "Okay," she said. "But they do bounce, and they're almost shockproof."

"She ought to know," Kell told an amused Bentley Rydel. "She's bounced it off the walls several times in recent weeks."

"Well, they keep killing me!" she burst out. "It's not my fault! These Hunters aren't like the ones in *Halo 3*... They're almost invincible, and there are so many of them...!"

"I'd worry more about the alien grunts that keep taking you out with sticky grenades," Bentley pointed out. "While you're trying to snipe the Hunters, the little guys are blowing you up right and left."

"I want a flame thrower," she wailed. "Or a rocket launcher! Why can't I find a rocket launcher?"

"We wouldn't want to make it too easy, now would we?" Bentley chided. He smiled at her fury. "Patience. You have to go slow and take them on one at a time, so they don't flank you."

She gave her boss a speaking look, turned back to the screen and tried again.

It was late when he left. The three of them had taken turns on the controller. Bentley and Kell had wanted to try the split screen, but that would have put Cappie right out of the competition, because she was only comfortable playing by herself.

She walked Bentley outside. "Thanks for bringing the pizza and beer," she said. "Some other time, I'd like to have you over for supper, if you'd like. I can cook."

He smiled. "I'll take you up on that. I can cook, too, but I only know how to do a few things from scratch. It gets tiresome after a while."

"Thanks for bringing the game over, too," she added. "It's really good. Kell is going to love it."

"What did we all do for entertainment before video games?" he wondered aloud as they reached his car.

"I used to watch game shows," she said. "Kell liked police dramas and old movies."

"I like some of the forensic shows, but I almost never get to see a whole one," he sighed. "There's always an emergency. It's always a large animal call. And since I'm the only vet on staff who does large animal calls, it's always me."

"Yes, but you never complain, not even if it's sleeting out," she said gently.

He smiled. "I like my clients."

"They like you, too." She shook her head. "Amazing, isn't it?"

"Excuse me?"

She flushed. "Oh, no, not because of… I mean…" She grimaced. "I meant it's amazing that you never get tired of large animal calls when the weather's awful."

He chuckled. "You really have got to take an assertiveness course," he said, and not unkindly.

"It's hard to be assertive when you're shy," she argued.

"It's impossible not to be when you have a job like mine and people don't want to do what you tell them to," he returned. "Some animals would die if I couldn't outargue their owners."

"Point taken."

"If it's any consolation," he said, "when I was your age, I had the same problem."

"How did you overcome it?"

"My stepfather decided that my mother wasn't going to the doctor for a urinary tract infection. I was already in veterinary school, and I knew what happened when animals weren't treated for it. I told him. He told me he was the man of the house and he'd decide what my mother did." He smiled, remembering. "So I had a choice—either back down, or let my mother risk permanent damage to her health, even death. I told him she was going to the doctor, I put her in the car and drove her there myself."

"What did your stepfather do?" she asked, aghast.

"There wasn't much that he could do, since I paid the doctor." His face hardened. "And it wasn't the first disagreement we'd had. He was poor and proud with it. He'd have let her suffer rather than admit he couldn't afford a doctor visit or medicine." He looked down at her. "It's a hell of a world, when people have to choose between food and medicine and doctors. Or between heated houses and medicine."

"Tell me about it," she replied. She colored a little, and hoped he didn't notice. "Kell and I do all right," she said quickly. "But he'll go without medicine sometimes if I don't put my foot down. You'd think I'd be tough as nails, because I stand up to him."

"He's not a mean person."

"He could be, I think," she said. She hesitated. "There was a man I dated, briefly, in San Antonio." She hesitated again. Perhaps it was too soon for this.

He stepped closer. "A man."

His voice was very soft. Quiet. Comforting. She wrapped her arms around her chest. She had on a sweater, but it was chilly outside. The memories were just as chilling. She was recalling it, her face betraying her inner turmoil. He'd hit her. The first time, he said it was because he'd had a drink, and he cried, and she went back to him. But the second time, he'd have probably killed her if Kell hadn't heard her scream and come to save her. As it was, he'd fractured her arm when he threw her over the couch. Kell had knocked Frank out with a lamp, from his wheelchair, and made her call the police. He made her testify, too. She held her arms around herself, chilled by the memory.

"What happened?"

She looked up at him, wanting to tell him, but afraid to. Frank got a six-month sentence, but he'd already served three months and he was out. Would he come after her now? Would he be crazy enough to do that? And would Bentley believe her, if she told him? They barely knew each other. It was too soon, she thought. Much too soon, to drag out her past and show it to him. There was no reason to tell him anyway. Frank wouldn't come down here and risk being sent back to jail. Bentley might think less of her if she told him, might think it was her own fault. Besides, she didn't want to tell him yet.

"He was a mean sort of person, that's all," she hedged. "He kicked my cat. I thought it was terrible. He just laughed."

His blue eyes narrowed. "A man who'll kick a cat will kick a human being."

"You're probably right," she admitted, and then she smiled. "Well, I only dated him for a little while. He wasn't the sort of person I like to be around. Kell didn't like him, either."

"I like your brother."

She smiled. "I like him, too. He was just going downhill with depression in San Antonio. We were over our ears in debt, from all the hospital bills. It's lucky our cousin died and left us this place," she added.

Bentley's eyebrows lifted. "This place belonged to Harry Farley. He got killed overseas in the military about six months ago. He didn't have any relatives at all. The county buried him, out of respect for his military service."

"But Kell said…" she blurted out.

Her expression made Bentley hesitate. "Oh. Wait a minute," Bentley said at once. "That's right, I did hear that he had a distant cousin or two."

She laughed. "That's us."

"My mistake. I wasn't thinking." He studied her quietly. "Well, I guess I'd better go. This is the first Saturday night I can remember when I didn't get called out," he added with a smile. "Pure dumb luck, I guess."

"Law of averages," she countered. "You have to get lucky sooner or later."

"I guess. I'll see you Monday."

"Thanks again for the pizza."

He opened the door of the Land Rover. "I'll take you up

on the offer of supper," he said. "When we set a date, you can tell me what you want to fix and I'll bring the raw ingredients." He held up a hand when she started to protest. "It does no good to argue with me. You can't win. Just ask Keely. Better yet, ask Dr. King," he chuckled.

She laughed, too. "Okay, then."

"Good night."

"Good night."

He closed the door behind him. Cappie went back up on the porch and watched him throw up a hand as he drove away. She stood there for several seconds before she realized that the wind was chilling her. She went in, feeling happier than she had in a long time.

CHAPTER FIVE

Cappie felt awkward with Bentley the following Monday. She wasn't sure if she should mention that he'd been to her house over the weekend. Her coworkers were very nice, but she was nervous when she thought they might tease her about the doctor. That would never do. She didn't want to make him feel uncomfortable in his own office.

Having lived so long in San Antonio, she didn't know about life in small towns. It hadn't occurred to her that nothing that happened could be kept secret.

"How was the pizza?" Dr. King asked her.

Cappie stared at her in horror.

Dr. King grinned. "My cousin works at the pizza place. Dr. Rydel mentioned where he was taking it. And she's best friends with Art, who runs the software store, so she knew he was taking the game over to play with you and your brother."

"Oh, dear," Cappie said worriedly.

Dr. King patted her on the back. "There, there," she said in a comforting tone. "You'll get used to it. We're like a big family in Jacobs County, because most of us have lived here all our lives, and our families have lived here for generations, mostly.

We know everything that's going on. We only read the newspaper to find out who got caught doing it."

"Oh, dear," Cappie said again.

"Hi," Keely said, removing her coat as she joined them. "How was the game Saturday?" she added.

Cappie looked close to tears.

Dr. King gave Keely a speaking glance. "She's not used to small towns yet," she explained.

"Not to worry," Keely told her. "Dr. Rydel certainly is." She laughed at Cappie's tormented expression. "If he was worried about gossip, you'd better believe he'd never have put a foot inside your door."

"She thinks we'll tease her," Dr. King said.

"Not a chance," Keely added. "We were all dating somebody once." She flushed. "Especially me, and very recently." She meant her husband, Boone, of course.

"And nobody teased her," Dr. King added. "Well," she qualified it, "not where Boone could hear it, anyway," she added and chuckled.

"Thanks," she said.

Dr. King just smiled. "You know, Bentley hates most women. One of our younger clients made a play for him one day. She wore suggestive clothing and a lot of makeup and when he leaned over to examine her dog, she kissed him."

Cappie's eyes widened. "What did he do?"

"He left the room, dragged me in there and told the young lady that he was indisposed and Dr. King would be handling the case."

"What did the young lady do?" Cappie asked.

"Turned red as a beet, picked up her dog and left the building. It turns out," Dr. King added with a grin, "that the dog was in excellent health. She only used it as an excuse to get Dr. Rydel in there with her."

"Did she come back?"

"Oh, yes, she was an extremely persistent young woman. The third time she showed up here, she insisted on seeing Dr. Rydel. He called Cash Grier, our police chief, and had him come in and explain the legal ramifications of sexual harassment to the young lady. He didn't smile while he was speaking. And when he finished talking, the young lady took her animal, went home and subsequently moved back to Dallas."

"Well!" Cappie exclaimed.

"So you see, Dr. Rydel is quite capable of deterring unwanted interest." She leaned closer. "I understand that you like to play video games?"

Cappie laughed. "Yes, I do."

"My husband has a score of over 16,000 on Xbox LIVE," she said, and wiggled her eyebrows.

Keely was staring at her, uncomprehending.

"My scores are around 4,000," Cappie said helpfully. "And my brother's are about 15,000." She chuckled. "The higher the score, the better the player. Also, the more often the playing."

"I guess my score would be around 200," Dr. King sighed. "You see, I get called in a lot for emergencies when Dr. Rydel is out on large animal calls. So I start a lot of games that my husband gets to finish."

"Kell had buddies in the army who could outdo even those scores. Those guys were great!" Cappie said. "They'd hang out with us when they were off duty. Kell always had nice video gaming equipment. Some of them did, too, but we always had a full fridge. Boy, could those guys eat!"

"You lived overseas a lot, didn't you?" Keely asked.

"Yes. I've seen a lot of exotic places."

"What was your favorite?"

"Japan," Cappie replied at once, smiling. "We went there when Kell was stationed in Korea. Not that Korea isn't a beautiful country. But I really loved Japan. You should see the gaming equipment they've got. And the cell phone technology." She shook her head. "They're really a long way ahead of us in technology."

"Did you get to ride the bullet train?" Keely asked.

"Yes. It's as fast as they say it is. I loved the train station. I loved everything! Kyoto was like a living painting. So many gardens and trees and temples."

"I'd love to see any city in Japan, but especially Kyoto," Keely said. "Judd Dunn's wife, Christabel, went over there with him to buy beef. She said Kyoto was just unbelievable. So much history, and so beautiful."

"It is," Cappie replied. "We got to visit a temple. The Zen garden was so stark, and so lovely. It's just sand and rocks, you know. The sand is raked into patterns like water. The rocks are situated like land. All around were Japanese black pine trees and bamboo trees as tall as the pines, with huge trunks. There was a bamboo forest, all green, and a huge pond full of Japanese Koi fish." She shook her head. "You know, I could live there. Kell said it was his favorite, too, of all the places we lived."

"Are we going to work today, or travel around the world?" came a deep, curt voice from behind them.

Everybody jumped. "Sorry, Dr. Rydel," Keely said at once.

"Me, too," Cappie seconded.

"*Nihongo no daisuki desu,*" Dr. Rydel said, and made a polite bow.

Cappie burst out smiling. "*Nihon no tomodachi desu. Konichi wa, Rydel sama,*" she replied, and bowed back.

Keely and Dr. King stared at them, fascinated.

"I said that I liked the Japanese language," Dr. Rydel translated.

"And I said that I was a friend of Japan. I also told him

hello," Cappie seconded. "You speak Japanese!" she exclaimed to Bentley.

"Just enough to get me arrested in Tokyo," Bentley told her, smiling. "I was stationed in Okinawa when I was in the service. I spent my liberties in Tokyo."

"Well, isn't it a small world?" Dr. King wondered.

"Small, and very crowded," Bentley told her. He gave her a meaningful look. "If you don't believe me, you could look at the mob in the waiting room, glaring at the empty reception counter and pointedly staring at their watches."

"Oops!" Dr. King ran for it.

So did Keely and Cappie, laughing all the way.

There was a new rapport between Dr. Rydel and Cappie. He was no longer antagonistic toward her, and she wasn't afraid of him anymore. Their working relationship became cordial, almost friendly.

Then he came to supper the following Saturday, and she found herself dropping pots and pans and getting tongue-tied at the table while the three of them ate the meal she'd painstakingly prepared.

"You're a very good cook," Bentley told her, smiling.

"Thanks," she replied, flushing even more.

Kell, watching her, was amused and indulgent. "She could cook even when she was in her early teens," he told Bentley. "Of course, that was desperation," he added with a sigh.

She laughed. "He can burn water," she pointed out. "I had so much carbon in my diet that I felt like a fire drill. I borrowed a cookbook from the wife of one of his buddies and started practicing. She felt sorry for me and gave me lessons."

"They were delicious lessons," Kell recalled with a smile. "The woman was a *cordon bleu* cook and she could make French pastries. I gained ten pounds. Then her husband was reassigned and the lessons stopped."

"Hey, a new family moved in," she argued. "It was a company commander, and she could make these terrific vegan dishes."

Kell glared at her. "I hate vegetables."

"Different strokes for different folks," she shot back. "Besides, there's nothing wrong with a good squash casserole."

Kell and Bentley exchanged horrified looks.

"What is it with men and squash?" she exclaimed, throwing up her hands. "I have never met a man who would eat squash in any form. It's a perfectly respectable vegetable. You can make all sorts of things with it."

Bentley pursed his lips. "Door props, paperweights…"

"Food things!" she returned.

"Hey, I don't eat paperweights," Bentley pointed out.

She shook her head.

"Why don't you bring in that terrific dessert you made?" Kell prompted.

"I guess I could do that," she told him. She got up and started gathering plates. Bentley got up and helped, as naturally as if he'd done it all his life.

She gave him an odd look.

"I live alone." He shrugged. "I'm used to clearing the table." He frowned. "Well, throwing away plastic plates, anyway. I eat a lot of TV dinners."

She made a face.

"There is nothing wrong with a TV dinner," Kell added. "I've eaten my share of them."

"Only when I was working late and it was all you could get," Cappie laughed. "And mostly, I left you things that you could just microwave."

"Point conceded." Kell grinned.

"What sort of dessert did you make?" Bentley asked.

She laughed. "A pound cake."

He whistled. "I haven't tasted one of those in years. My mother used to make them." His pleasant expression drained away for a few seconds.

Cappie knew he was remembering his mother's death. "It's a chocolate pound cake," she said, smiling, as she tried to draw him out of the past.

"Even better," he said, smiling. "Those are rare. Barbara sells slices of one sometimes at her café, but not too often."

"A lot of people can't eat chocolate, on account of allergies," she said.

"I don't have allergies," Bentley assured her. "And I do hope it's a large pound cake. If you offered to send a slice home with me, I might let you come in an hour late one day next week."

"Why, Dr. Rydel, that sounds suspiciously like a bribe," she exclaimed.

He grinned. "It is."

"In that case, you can take home two slices," she said.

He chuckled.

Watching them head into the kitchen, Kell smiled to himself. Cappie had been afraid of men just after her bad experience with the date from hell. It was good to see her comfortable in a man's company. Bentley might be just the man to heal her emotional scars.

"Where do you want these?" Bentley asked when he'd scraped the plates.

"Just put them in the sink. I'll clean up in here later."

He looked around quietly. The kitchen was bare bones. There was an older microwave oven, an old stove and refrigerator, a table and chairs that looked as if they'd come from a yard sale. The coffeepot and Crock-Pot on the counter had seen better days.

She noticed his interest and smiled sadly. "We didn't bring a lot of stuff with us when we moved back to San Antonio. We sold a lot of things to other servicemen so we wouldn't have to pay the moving costs. Then, after Kell got wounded, we sold more stuff so we could afford to pay the rent."

"Didn't he have any medical insurance?"

She shook her head. "He said there was some sort of mix-up with the magazine's insurer, and he got left out in the cold." She removed the cover from the cake pan and got out cake plates to serve it on. Her mother's small china service had been one thing she'd managed to salvage. She loved the pretty rose pattern.

"That's too bad," Bentley murmured. But he was frowning behind her, his keen mind on some things he recalled about her mysterious brother. If Kell was friendly with the local mercs, it was unlikely he'd gotten to know them in the military. They were too old to have served anytime recently. But he did know that they'd been in Africa in recent years. So had Kell. That was more than a coincidence, he was almost sure.

His silence made her curious. She turned around, her soft eyes wide and searching.

His own pale blue eyes narrowed on her pretty face in its frame of long blond hair. She had a pert little figure, enhanced by the white sweater and blue jeans she was wearing. Her breasts were firm and small, just right for her build. He felt his whole body clench at the way she was looking at him.

He wasn't handsome, she was thinking, but he had a killer physique, from his powerful long legs in blue jeans to his broad chest outlined under the knit shirt. Beige suited his coloring, made his tan look bronzed, the turtleneck enhancing his strong throat.

"You're staring," he pointed out huskily.

She searched for the right words. Her mouth was dry. "Your ears have very nice lobes."

He blinked. "Excuse me?"

She flushed to her hairline. "Oh, good heavens!" She fumbled with the cake knife and it started to fall. He stepped forward and caught it halfway to the floor, just as she dived for it. They collided.

His arm slid around her to prevent her from going headlong into the counter and pulled her up short, right against him. Her intake of breath was audible as she clung to him to keep her footing.

She felt his chin against her temple, heard his breath coming out raggedly. His arm contracted.

"Th…thanks," she managed to say against his throat. "I'm just so clumsy sometimes!"

"Nobody's perfect."

She laughed nervously. "Certainly not me. Thanks for saving the cake knife."

"My pleasure."

His voice was almost a purr, deep and soft and slow. He lifted his head very slowly, so that his eyes were suddenly looking right into hers. She felt his chest rise and fall against her breasts in an intimacy that grew more smoldering by the second. She looked up, but her eyes stopped at his chiseled mouth. It was very sensuous. She'd never really paid it much attention, until now. And she couldn't quite stop looking at it.

She felt his fingers curling into her long hair, as if he loved the feel of it.

"I love long hair," he said softly. "Yours is beautiful."

"Thanks," she whispered.

"Soft hair. Pretty mouth." He bent and his nose slid against hers as his mouth poised over her parted lips. "Very pretty mouth."

She stood very still, waiting, hoping that he wasn't going to draw back. She loved the way his body felt, so close to hers. She loved his strength, his height, the spicy scent of his cologne. She hung there, at his lips, her eyes half closed, waiting, waiting…

"Where's that cake?" came a plaintive cry from the living room. "I'm starving!"

They jumped apart so quickly that Cappie almost fell. "Coming right up!" Heavens, was that her voice? It sounded almost artificial!

"I'll take the coffeepot into the living room for you," Bentley said. His own voice was oddly hoarse and deep, and he didn't look at her as he went out of the room.

Cappie cut the cake, forcing her mind to ignore what had almost happened. She had so many complications in her life right now that she didn't really need another one. But she did wonder if it was possible to put this particular genie back in its bottle.

And, in fact, it wasn't. When they finished the cake and a few more minutes of conversation, Bentley got a call from his answering service and hung up with a grimace.

"One of Cy Parks's purebred heifers is calving for the first time. I'll have to go. Sorry. I really enjoyed the meal, and the cake."

"So did we," Cappie said.

"We'll have to do this again," Kell added, grinning.

"Next time, I'll take the two of you out to a nice restaurant," Bentley said.

"Well…" Cappie hesitated.

"Walk me out," Bentley told her, and he didn't smile.

Cappie looked toward Kell to save her, but he only grinned. She turned and followed Bentley out the door.

He paused at the steps, looking down at her with a long, unblinking stare in the faint light that shone out from the windows.

She bit her lower lip and searched for something to say. Her mind wouldn't cooperate.

He couldn't seem to find anything to say, either. They just stared at each other.

"I hate women," he bit off.

She faltered. "I'm sorry," she said.

"Oh, what the hell. Come here."

He scooped her up against him, bent his head and kissed her with such immediate passion that she couldn't even think. Her arms went around his neck as she warmed to the hard, insistent pressure of his mouth as it parted her lips and invaded the soft, secret warmth of her mouth. It was too much, too soon, but she couldn't say that. He didn't leave her enough breath to say anything, and the pleasure throbbing through her body robbed her mind of the words, anyway.

Seconds later, he put her back on her feet and moved away. "Well!" he said huskily.

She stared up at him with her mouth open.

His eyebrows arched.

She tried to speak, but she couldn't manage a single word.

He let out a rough breath. "I really wish you wouldn't look at me in that tone of voice," he said.

"Wh...what?" she stammered.

He chuckled softly. "Well, I could say I'm flattered that I leave you speechless, but I won't embarrass you. See you Monday."

She nodded. "Monday."

"At the office."

She nodded again. "The office."

"Cappie?"

She was still staring at him. She nodded once more. "Cappie."

He burst out laughing. He bent and kissed her again. "And they say the way to a man's heart is through his stomach," he mused. "This is much quicker than food. See you."

He turned and went to his car. Cappie stood and watched

him until he was all the way to the main highway. It wasn't until Kell called to her that she realized it was cold and she didn't even have on a coat.

After that, it was hard to work in the same office with Bentley without staring at him, starstruck, when she saw him in between patients. He noticed. He couldn't seem to stop smiling. But when Cappie started running into door facings looking at him, everybody else in the office started grinning, and that did inhibit her.

She forced herself to keep her mind on the animal patients, and not the tall man who was treating them.

Just before quitting time, a little boy came careening into the practice just ahead of a man. He was carrying a big dog, wrapped in a blanket, shivering and bleeding.

"Please, it's my dog, you have to help him!" the boy sobbed.

A worried man joined him. "He was hit by a car," the man said. "The so-and-so didn't even stop! He just kept going!"

Dr. Rydel came out of the back and took a quick look at the dog. "Bring him right back," he told the boy. He managed a smile. "We'll do everything we can. I promise."

"His name's Ben," the boy sobbed. "I've had him since I was little. He's my best friend."

Dr. Bentley helped the boy lift Ben onto the metal operating table. He didn't ask the boy to leave while he did the examination. He had Keely help him clean the wound and help restrain the dog while he assessed the damage. "We're going to need an X-ray. Get Billy to help you carry him," he told her with a smile.

"Yes, sir."

"Is he going to die?" the boy wailed.

Dr. Rydel put a kindly hand on his shoulder. "I don't see any evidence of internal damage or concussion. It looks like a fracture, but before I can reduce it, I'm going to need to do X-rays to see the extent of the damage. Then we'll do blood work to make sure it's safe to anesthetize him. I will have to operate. He has some skin and muscle damage in addition to the fracture."

The man with the boy looked worried. "Is this going to be expensive?" he asked worriedly.

The boy wailed.

"I lost my job last week," the man said heavily. "We've got a new baby."

"Don't worry about it," Dr. Rydel said in a reassuring tone. "We do some pro bono work here, and I'm overdue. We'll take care of it."

The man bit his lower lip, hard, and averted his eyes. "Thanks," he gritted.

"We all have rough patches," Dr. Rydel told him. "We get through them. It will get better."

"Thanks, Doc!" the boy burst out, reaching over to rub a worried hand over the old dog's head. "Thanks!"

"I like dogs, myself," the doctor chuckled. "Now this is going to take a while. Why don't you leave your phone number at the desk and I'll call you as soon as your dog's through surgery?"

"You'd do that?" the man asked, surprised.

"Of course. We always do that."

"His name's Ben," the boy said, sniffing. "He's had all his shots and stuff. We take him every year to the clinic at the animal shelter."

Which meant money was always tight, but they took care of the animal. Dr. Rydel was impressed.

"We'll give her our phone number. You're a good man," the boy's father said quietly.

"I like dogs," Dr. Rydel said again with a smile. "Go on home. We'll call you."

"You be good, Ben," the boy told his dog, petting him one

last time. The dog wasn't even trying to bite anybody. He whined a little. "We'll come and get you just as soon as we can. Honest."

The man tugged the boy along with him, giving the vet one last grateful smile.

"I can take care of his bill," Keely volunteered.

Dr. Rydel shook his head. "I do it in extreme cases like this. It's no hardship."

"Yes, but…"

He leaned closer. "I drive a Land Rover. Want to price one?"

Keely burst out laughing. "Okay. I give up."

Billy, the vet tech, came to help Keely get Ben in to X-ray. Cappie came back after a minute. "I promised I'd make sure you knew that Ben likes peanut butter," she said. "Who's Ben?"

"Fractured leg, HBC," he abbreviated.

She smiled. "Hit by car," she translated. "The most frequent injury suffered by dogs. They know who hit him?"

"I wish," Dr. Rydel said fervently. "I'd call Cash Grier myself."

"They didn't stop?"

"No," he said shortly.

"I'd stop, if I hit somebody's pet," Cappie said gently. "I had a cat, when we lived in San Antonio, after Kell got out of the army. I had to give him away when we moved down here." She was remembering that Frank had kicked him, so hard that Cappie took him to work with her the next day, just to have him checked out. He had bruising, but, fortunately, no broken bones. Then the cat had run away, and returned after Frank was gone. She'd given the cat away before she and Kell left town, to make sure that Frank wouldn't send somebody to get even with her by hurting her cat. He was that sort of man.

"You're very pensive," he commented.

"I was missing my cat," she lied, smiling.

"We have lots of cats around here," he told her. "I think Keely has a whole family of them out in her barn and there are new kittens. She'd give you one, if you asked."

She hesitated. "I'm not sure if I could keep a cat," she replied. "Kell wouldn't be able to look out for him, you know. He has all he can do to take care of himself."

He didn't push. He just smiled. "One day, he'll meet some nice girl who'll want to take him home with her and spoil him rotten."

She blinked. "Kell?"

"Why not? He's only paralyzed, you know, not demented."

She laughed. "I guess not. He's pretty tough."

"And he's not a bad gamer, either," he pointed out.

"I noticed."

"Cappie, have you got the charges for Miss Dill's cat in here yet?" came a call from the front counter.

She grimaced. "No, sorry, Dr. King. I'll be right there."

She rushed back out, flustered. Dr. Rydel certainly had a way of looking at her that increased her heart rate. She liked it, too.

CHAPTER SIX

Cappie stayed late to help with the overflow of patients, held up by the emergency surgery on the dog. The practice generally did its scheduled surgeries on Thursdays, but emergencies were always accommodated. In fact, there was a twenty-four-hour-a-day emergency service up in San Antonio, but the veterinarians at Dr. Rydel's practice would always come in if they were needed. In certain instances, the long drive to the big city would have meant the death of a furry patient. They were considering the addition of a fourth veterinarian to the practice, so that they could more easily accommodate those emergencies.

The dog, Ben, came out of surgery with a mended foreleg and was placed in a recovery cage to wait until the anesthetic wore off. The next day, if he presented no complications, he would be sent home with antibiotics, painkillers and detailed instructions on post-surgical care. Cappie was glad, for the boy's sake. She felt sorriest for the children whose pets were injured. Not that grown-up people took those situations any easier. Pets were like part of the family. It was hard to see one hurt, or to lose one.

Kell was pensive when she got home. In fact, he looked

broody. She put down her coat and purse. "What's the matter with you?" she asked with a grin.

He put his laptop computer aside with deliberation. "I had a call from an assistant district attorney's office in San Antonio, from the victim support people," he said quietly. "Frank Bartlett got out of jail today."

It was the day she'd been dreading. Her heart sank. He'd vowed revenge. He would make her pay, he said, for having him tried and convicted.

"Don't worry," he added gently. "We're among friends here. Frank would have to be crazy to come down here and make trouble. In addition to the jail time, he drew a year's probation. They'll check on him. He wouldn't want to risk having to go back to jail to finish his sentence."

"You think so?" she wondered. She recalled what a hard-headed man Frank was. He got even with people. She'd heard things from one of her coworkers in San Antonio at the animal clinic, one who was friends with Frank's sister. She'd said that Frank had run a man off the road who'd reported him for making threats at one of his jobs. The man was badly injured, but he could never prove it had been Frank who'd caused the accident. Cappie was sure, now, that there had probably been other incidents, as well. Frank had admitted to her once that he'd spent time in juvenile hall as a youngster. He'd never said what for.

"He won't be able to get to you at home," Kell continued, "because I keep firearms and I know how to use them," he added grimly. "At work, I don't think he'd dare approach you. Dr. Rydel would likely propel him headfirst out the front door," he chuckled.

Cappie was reminded that Dr. Rydel had actually done that. Dr. King told her about it. A man had come in with a badly injured dog, one with multiple fractures, claiming that the animal had fallen down some steps. After examining the dog, Dr. Rydel knew better. He'd accused the man of abusing the dog, and the man had thrown a punch at him. Dr. Rydel had picked him up and literally thrown him out onto the front porch, while fascinated pet owners watched. Then he'd called the police and had the man arrested. There had been a conviction, too.

Cappie, remembering that, smiled. "Dr. Rydel gets very upset when people abuse animals," she told her brother.

"Obviously." He pursed his lips. "I wonder why he decided to become a veterinarian?"

"I'll have to ask him that."

"Yes, you will. I made macaroni and cheese for supper," he said, "when you called to say you'd be late."

She made a face before she could stop herself.

Kell just grinned. "It's frozen," he said. "I heated it up in the oven."

She sighed with relief. "Sorry. It's just that I've had my carbon for today."

He laughed. "I know I can't cook. One day, though, I'll learn how. Then watch out."

"Some men are born to be chefs. You aren't one of them. I'll make a salad to go with the macaroni."

"I did that already. It's in the fridge."

She went to kiss his cheek, bending over him in the wheelchair. "You're the nicest brother in the whole world."

"I could return the compliment." He ruffled her hair. "Listen, kid, if the surly vet proposes, you take him up on it. I can take care of myself."

"You can't cook," she wailed.

"I can buy nice frozen things to heat up," he returned.

She sighed. "As if Dr. Rydel would ever propose," she laughed. "He likes me, but that doesn't mean he'll want to marry me one day."

"You need to invite him over again and make that shrimp and pasta dish you do so well. I have it from a spy that Dr. Rydel is partial to shrimp."

"Really? Who knows that?"

"Cy Parks told me."

She gave him a suspicious look. "Did you try to pump Cy Parks for inside information?"

Kell gave her his best angelic look. "I would never do such a sneaky thing."

"Sure you would," she retorted.

"Well, Dr. Rydel knew why Cy was asking him, anyway. He just laughed and asked if there was any other inside information that Cy would like to have for us."

She flushed. "Oh, my."

"Cy said the good doctor talked more about you than he did about the heifer he was helping to deliver," Kell added. "It's well-known that Dr. Rydel can't abide women. People get curious when a notorious woman hater suddenly starts seeing a local woman."

"I wonder why he hates women?" she wondered aloud.

"Ask him. But for now, let's eat. I'm fairly empty."

"Goodness, yes, it's two hours past our usual suppertime," she agreed, moving into the kitchen. "I'm sorry I was late."

"How's the dog?" he asked, joining her at the table.

"He'll be fine, Dr. Rydel said. The poor boy was just devastated. I felt sorry for his dad. He'd just lost his job. You could see he was torn between getting the dog treated and taking care of his family. There's a new baby. Dr. Rydel didn't charge him a penny."

"Heart of gold," Kell said gently.

"We were going to take up a collection, when Dr. Rydel reminded us that he drove a Land Rover," she laughed. "He inherited money from his grandmother, Dr. King said, and he makes a good living as a vet."

"That means he'll be able to take care of you when you get married."

She made a face. "Horses before carts, not carts before horses."

"You wait and see," he replied. "That's a man who's totally hooked. He just doesn't know it yet."

She smiled from ear to ear as she started putting food on the table. She'd already pushed her fears about Frank to the back of her mind. Kell was right. He surely wouldn't risk his freedom by making trouble for Cappie again.

Dr. Rydel took her to a carnival Friday night. She was shocked not only at the invitation, but at the choice of outings.

"You like carnivals?" she'd exclaimed.

"Sure! I love the rides and cotton candy." He'd smiled with reminiscence. "My grandmother used to save her egg money to take me to any carnival that came through Jacobsville when I was a kid. She'd even go on the rides with me. I get tickled even now when I hear somebody talk about grandmothers who bake cookies and knit and sit in rocking chairs. My grandmother was a newspaper reporter. She was a real firecracker."

She was remembering the conversation as they walked down the sawdust-covered aisles between booths where carnies were enticing customers to pitch pennies or throw baseballs to win prizes.

"What are you brooding about?" he teased.

She looked up, laughing. "Sorry. I was remembering what you said about your grandmother. Did you spend a lot of time with her?"

His face closed up.

"Sorry," she said again, flushing. "I shouldn't have asked something so personal."

He stopped in the aisle and looked down at her, enjoying the glow of her skin against the pale yellow sweater she was wearing with jeans, her blond hair long and soft around her shoulders.

His big, lean hand went to her hair and toyed with it, sending sweet chills down her spine when he moved a step closer. "She raised me," he said quietly. "My mother and father never got along. They separated two or three times a year, and then fought about who got to keep me. My mother loved me, but my father only wanted me to spite her." His face hardened. "When I made him mad, he took it out on my pets. He shot one of my dogs when I talked back to him. He wouldn't let me take the dog to a veterinarian, and I couldn't save it. That's why I decided to become a vet."

"I did wonder," she confessed. "You talk about your mother, but never about your father. Or your stepfather." Her hands went to his shirtfront. She could feel the warm muscle and hair under the soft cotton.

He sighed. His hand covered one of hers, smoothing over her fingernails. "My stepfather thought that being a vet was a sissy profession, and he said so, frequently. He didn't like animals, either."

"Some sissy profession," she scoffed. "I guess he never had to wrestle down a sick steer that weighed several hundred pounds."

He chuckled. "No, he never did. We got along somewhat. But I don't miss seeing him. I had hard feelings against him for a long time, for letting my mother get so sick that medical science couldn't save her. But sometimes we blame people when it's just fate that bad things happen. Remember the old saying, 'Man proposes and God disposes'? It's pretty much true."

"Ah, you advocate being a leaf on the river, grasshopper," she said in a heavily accented tone.

"You lunatic," he laughed, but he bent and kissed her nose. "Yes. I do advocate being a leaf on the river. Sometimes you have to trust that things will work out the way they're meant to, not the way you want them to."

"Why do you hate women?"

His eyebrows arched.

"Everybody knows that you do. You even told me so." She flushed a little as she remembered when he'd told her so; the first time he'd kissed her.

"Remember that, do you?" he teased softly. "You don't know a lot about kissing," he added.

She moved restlessly. "I don't get in much practice."

"Oh, I think I can help you with that," he said in a deep, husky tone. "And for the record, I don't hate you."

"Thank you very much," she said demurely, and peered up at him through her lashes.

He bent slowly to her mouth. "You're very welcome," he whispered. His lips teased just above hers, coaxing her to lift her chin, so that he had better access to her mouth.

Before he could kiss her, a deep voice mused from behind him, "Lewd behavior in public will get you arrested."

"Kilraven," Bentley groaned, turning to face the man. "What are you doing here?"

Kilraven, in full uniform, grinned at the discomfort in their faces as he moved closer and lowered his voice. "I'm investigating possible cotton candy fraud."

"Excuse me?" Cappie said.

"I'm going to taste the cotton candy, and the candy apples, and make sure they're not using illegal counterfeit sugar."

They both stared at him as if he'd gone mad.

He shrugged. "I'm really off duty, I just haven't gone home to change. I like carnivals," he added, laughing. "Jon, my brother, and I used to go to them when we were kids. It brings back happy memories."

"They have a sharpshooting target," Bentley told him.

"I don't waste my unbelievable talent on games," Kilraven scoffed.

"I am in awe of your modesty," Bentley said.

"Why, thank you," Kilraven replied. "I consider it one of my best traits, and I do have quite a few of them." He peered past them. Winnie Sinclair, in jeans and a pretty pink sweater and matching denim jacket, was walking around the penny-pitching booth with her brother, Boone Sinclair, and his wife, Cappie's coworker, Keely. Kilraven looked decidedly uneasy. "I'll see you around," he added.

But instead of going to the cotton candy booth, he turned on his heel and walked right out of the carnival.

"How odd," Cappie murmured, watching him leave.

"Not so odd," Bentley replied. His eyes were on Winnie Sinclair, who'd just seen Kilraven glare in her direction and then walk away. She looked devastated. "Winnie Sinclair is sweet on him," he explained, "and he's even a worse woman hater than I am."

Cappie followed his glance. Keely smiled and waved. She waved back. Winnie Sinclair smiled wanly, and turned back to the booth. "Poor thing," she murmured. "She's so rich, and so unhappy."

"Money doesn't make you happy," Bentley pointed out.

"Well, the lack of it can make you pretty miserable," she said absently.

His hand reached down and locked into hers, bringing her surprised eyes back up to meet his.

She was hesitant, because Keely was grinning in their direction.

"I don't care about public opinion," Bentley pointed out,

"and she wouldn't dare tease me in my own practice," he added with a grin.

Cappie laughed. "Okay. I won't care, either."

His strong fingers linked with hers, while he held her gaze. "I can't remember the last time I smiled so much," he said. "I like being with you, Cappie."

She smiled. "I like being with you, too."

They were still smiling at each other when two running children bumped into them and broke the spell.

Bentley drove her home, but he didn't move to open the door after he cut off the lights and the engine. He unfastened her seat belt, and his own, and pulled her across the seat and into his lap. Before she could speak, his mouth was hard on hers, grinding into it, and his fingers were lazily searching under the soft hem of her sweater.

He found the hooks on her bra and loosened them with one quick motion of his hand. Then he found soft flesh and teased around it with such expertise that she squirmed backward to give him access.

"Too quick?" he whispered against her mouth.

"No," she bit off, and arched her back.

He smiled as his mouth covered hers once more, and his hand settled directly over the hard little nub that raised against his palm.

After a few minutes, kissing was no longer enough. His hand moved in at the base of her spine and half lifted her against him, so that her belly ground against his in the rapt silence of the vehicle, broken only by the force of their audible breaths, and her soft moan. She could feel him wanting her. It had been exciting with Frank, but not like this. She wanted what Bentley wanted. She was on fire for him.

He unfastened the buttons on his shirt and pulled her against him, so that her soft breasts ground against the hair-roughened muscles of his chest. His hand moved her hips against his in a slow, anguished rotation that made her moan louder.

"Oh, God," he bit off, shivering. "Cappie!"

Her nails were scoring his back as she held on for dear life and began to shudder. "Don't stop," she whimpered. "Don't stop!"

"I've…got to!"

He moved abruptly, pushing her back into her seat. He opened the door and got out of the Land Rover, standing with his back to her as he sucked in deep breaths and tried to regain the control he'd almost lost.

Embarrassed, Cappie fumbled her bra closures into place and pulled her sweater down. She was still shaky. It had been a near thing. Thank goodness they were parked in her driveway instead of on some lonely road where there might not have been as much incentive to stop. Despite her passionate response to him, Cappie didn't move with the times. Did he know that? Was he hoping for some brief fling? She couldn't. She just couldn't. Now, she reasoned with something like panic, he wouldn't want to see her again, not if she said no. And either way, how was it going to affect her job? There was only one veterinary clinic in Jacobs County, and she worked for it. If she lost her job, she couldn't get another, not in her field.

While she was torturing herself with such thoughts, the door suddenly opened.

"I know," Bentley said in a strangely calm and amused tone, "you're kicking yourself mentally for taking advantage of me in a weak moment. But it's okay. I'm used to women trying to ravish me."

She stared up at him wide-eyed and speechless. Of all the things she expected he might say, that was the last.

"Come on, come on, you're not going to get a second shot

at me in the same night," he teased. "I have my reputation to think of!"

Her mind started working again, and she laughed with relief. She picked up her purse and scrambled out the door, her discarded coat over one arm.

"Listen," he said gently, "don't start brooding. We got a little too involved, too quickly, but we'll deal with it."

She hesitated. "I'm not, well, modern," she blurted out.

"Neither am I, honey," he said softly.

She could have melted into the ground at the husky endearment. She blushed.

He bent and kissed her with tender respect. "I know what sort of woman you are," he said gently. "I'm not going to push you into something you don't want."

"Thanks."

"On the other hand, you have to make me a similar promise," he pointed out. "I'm not going to keep dating you if I have to worry about being ravished every time I bring you home. I'm not that sort of man," he added haughtily.

She grinned from ear to ear. "Okay."

He walked her to the door, smiling complacently. "I'll see you at work Monday," he said. He framed her face in his hands and looked at her for a long time. "Just when you think you're safe," he mused, "you jump headfirst into the tiger trap."

"You know, I was just thinking the same thing," she said facetiously.

He chuckled as he bent to kiss her again. "We'll take it at a nice, easy pace," he whispered. "But I know already how it's going to end up. We're good together. And I'm tired of living alone."

Her heart almost burst with joy. "I… I don't think I could just live with someone," she blurted out, still a little worried.

He kissed her eyes shut. "Neither could I, Cappie," he whispered. "We can talk about licenses and rings." He lifted his head. His eyes were soft with feeling. "But not tonight. We have all the time in the world."

"Yes," she whispered. Her eyes were bright with the force of her emotions. "It's happening so fast."

He nodded. "Like lightning striking."

She felt her heart racing. But in the back of her mind, there was a sudden fear, a foreboding. She bit her lower lip. "You don't really know much about me," she began. "You see, when I lived in San Antonio, there was this man I dated..."

Before she could tell him about Frank, his phone rang. He jerked it out and answered it. "Rydel," he said. He listened, grimaced. "I'll be in the office in ten minutes. Bring the cat right in, I'll see it. Yes. Yes. You're welcome." He hung up. "I have to go."

"Be careful," she said.

He smiled. "I will. Good night."

"Good night, Dr. Rydel."

"Bentley."

She laughed. "Bentley."

He ran back to the Land Rover, started it and drove away with a wave of his hand. Cappie watched him go, then walked into her house, feeling as if she could have floated all the way.

Monday morning, Cappie still felt light-headed and ecstatic. She'd half expected Bentley to phone her Saturday or Sunday, considering how involved they'd gotten when he brought her home from the carnival on Friday night. But maybe he'd had emergencies. She hoped he hadn't had second thoughts. She was so crazy about him that she couldn't bear to even think about having him reconsider what he'd said. But she knew that wasn't going to happen. They were already so close that she knew it was going to be forever.

So it came as a shock when she walked in the office and Dr. Rydel met her beaming smile with a cold glare that sent chills down her spine.

"You're late, Miss Drake," he said curtly. "Please try to be on time in the future."

She looked as if she'd been hit in the head by a brick. Keely, at the counter, gave her a sympathetic look.

"I'm… I'm sorry, sir," she stammered.

"I need you to help Keely with an X-ray," he said, and turned away abruptly.

"Right away." She put up her coat and purse and rushed to join Keely, who was going in the room where they kept the medical cages. She took a hair band out of her pocket and scrunched her thick hair into a ponytail with it. Inside, she felt numb.

"It's Mrs. Johnson's cat," Keely explained, wary of being overheard by the vet, who was just going into a treatment room. "She stepped on his paw. It's swollen, and Dr. Rydel is afraid it may be broken. Mrs. Johnson is no lightweight," she added with a grin.

"Yes, I know."

"She had to leave him with us while she went to see her heart doctor. She was very upset. She's just getting over a heart attack, and she's worried about her cat!" she said, smiling. Keely opened the cage and Cappie lifted the old cat. It just purred. It didn't even offer to bite her, although it was obvious that it was in pain.

"What a sweet old fellow," Cappie murmured as they went toward the X-ray room. "I thought he might want to bite us."

"He's a sweetheart all right. Here." Keely motioned to the X-ray table and closed the door behind them. "What in the world is wrong with Dr. Rydel?" she whispered. "He came in looking like a thundercloud."

"I don't know," Cappie said. "We went to the carnival Friday night and he was happy and laughing..."

"You didn't have a fight?" Keely persisted.

"No!" She wanted to add that they'd talked about rings, but this wasn't a good time. The tall man who met her at the door didn't look as if he'd ever said any such thing to her.

"I wonder what happened."

"So do I," Cappie said miserably.

They got the X-ray and Cappie took the old cat back to his cage while Keely developed it. Dr. King gave her a worried look, but she was too busy to say much. Cappie felt sick. She couldn't imagine what had turned Dr. Rydel into an enemy.

She waited and worried all day through two dozen patients and one long emergency. Mrs. Johnson came to pick up her cat, his paw in a neat cast, crying buckets because she'd been so worried about him. Cappie helped her out the door, smiling even though she didn't feel like it. Earlier, she'd thought maybe Dr. Rydel would say something to her, explain, anything. But he didn't. He treated her just as he had when she first joined the practice, courteous but cold.

At the end of the day, she wanted to wait around and see if she could get him to talk to her, but a large animal call took him out the door just minutes before the staff went home. She drove to her house with her heart in her shoes.

"You look like the end of the world," Kell remarked when she walked in. "What happened?"

"I don't know," she said sadly. "Dr. Rydel looked at me as if I had some contagious disease and he didn't say one kind word all day. It was business as usual. He was just like he was when I first went to work for him."

"He seemed pleasant enough when he picked you up Friday night," he remarked.

"And when he brought me home," she added. "Maybe he got cold feet."

Kell studied her sad face. "Maybe he did. Everybody says he was the biggest woman hater around town. But if that's the case, he might warm up again when he's had time to think about it. If he's really interested, Cappie, he's not going away."

"You think so?" she asked, hopeful.

"I know so. Men who act like he did when he came to supper don't suddenly turn ice-cold for no reason. Maybe he just had a rough weekend."

Which was no reason for him to take it out on Cappie. On the other hand, she didn't really know him that well.

"Maybe I can get him to talk to me tomorrow," she said.

He smiled. "Maybe you can."

She nodded. "I'll go make supper."

"Try not to worry."

"Of course."

But she did worry, and she didn't sleep. She went in to work the next morning with a feeling of foreboding.

Dr. Rydel was at the counter when she came in.

"I'm five minutes early," she said abruptly when he glared at her.

"Come into my office, please," he said.

She brightened. At last, he was going to explain. Surely it was something that didn't have anything to do with her.

He let her in and closed the door behind her. He didn't offer her a seat. He perched on the edge of his desk and stared at her coldly. "I had a visitor Saturday morning."

"You did?" An ex-girlfriend, she was thinking, and he wanted her back, was that it?

"Yes," he replied curtly. "Your boyfriend."

"My what?"

"Your boyfriend, Frank Bartlett," he said coldly.

She felt sick all the way to her toes. Frank had come down here! He'd come to Jacobsville! She held on to a chair. She should have told Bentley about him. She shouldn't have waited. "He's my ex-boyfriend," she began.

He laughed coldly. "Is he, really? Now that's not what he said."

CHAPTER SEVEN

Cappie could almost imagine what sort of story Frank had told Bentley. But now she understood his anger.

"I can explain," she began.

"You told me Friday night that you had an ex-boyfriend," he said icily. "I didn't get to hear the rest of the story, but Bartlett was kind enough to fill me in. You accused him of assaulting you and had him arrested. He actually spent time in jail and now he has a felony record because of you."

Her eyes widened. "Yes, but that isn't what happened…!"

"I know all about women who like to play with men," he interrupted. "When I was in my early twenties, I worked for a veterinarian while I was in college. It supplemented my grants and scholarships. He had a vet tech who was very pretty, but never got dates. I felt sorry for her. She could only work for him part-time, because I had the full-time position. She stayed late one weekend and teased me into kissing her. Then she very calmly tore her shirt, messed up her hair and phoned the police."

Cappie felt her face go pale.

"She wanted my job," Bentley continued cynically. "I dipped into my savings to hire a private detective, who discovered that it wasn't the first time she'd pulled that stunt. She was arrested and my record was cleared. The vet hired me back in a heartbeat and spent years trying to make it up to me."

"I had no idea," she whispered.

"Of course not, or you wouldn't have tried the same stunt on me."

She blinked in disbelief. "What?"

"You were always talking about what you'd do if you had money. You knew I was well-to-do. When were you going to accuse me of assaulting you? Have you got a lawyer waiting in the wings to sue me?"

She couldn't believe her ears. He actually thought she was playing him for cash. Frank had lied to him, and with his background, Bentley had fallen for the tall tale.

"I've never accused anyone falsely," she defended herself.

"Only Frank Bartlett?"

She swallowed, hard. "He broke my arm," she said with quiet dignity. "It wasn't the first time he hit me, either."

"He told me you'd say that," he replied. "Poor guy. You ruined his life. Well, you aren't going to get the chance to ruin mine. You can work your two weeks' notice." He got to his feet.

"You're firing me?" she asked weakly.

"No, you're quitting," he returned coldly. "That way, you won't be able to let the state support you with unemployment insurance, or sue me for unlawful termination of employment."

"I see."

"Women," he muttered coldly. "You'd think I'd already learned my lesson. You all look so innocent. And you all lie."

He opened the door. "Back to work, Miss Drake," he said in a formal tone. "It's going to be a long day."

She worked mechanically, even managed to smile at old Mr. Smith's jokes and Dr. King's bland comments. Keely was looking at her oddly, but nobody else seemed to find her behavior out of the ordinary.

At the end of the day, she went to her car almost gratefully. She still couldn't believe that Dr. Rydel had fallen for Frank's lies. But she was going to do something about it. She just didn't know what. Yet.

She pulled up in the front yard, puzzled at the colorful cloth piled at the foot of the steps. Was Kell cleaning house…?

She slammed on the brakes, cut off the engine and ran as fast as she could to the front door. That wasn't a bundle of cloth, it was Kell. Kell! He was unconscious, lying beside the wreck of his wheelchair and he was bleeding from half a dozen cuts. She felt for a pulse and, thank God, found one! At least he was still alive.

She saw the front door standing open and didn't dare go inside, for fear someone might be waiting there. She ran back to her car, jerked out her cell phone and punched in 911. Then she ran back to Kell and waited.

The next hour was a blur of ambulance sirens, police sirens, blue uniforms, tan uniforms and abject terror.

She waited for Dr. Micah Steele to come out and tell her what Kell's condition was. She was sick and chilled to the bone. If Kell died, she'd have nobody.

He came back out to the waiting room a few minutes after Kell was brought in, tall and blond and somber.

"How is he?" she asked frantically.

"Badly beaten," he told her, "which you already know. His back is one long bruise. We're still doing tests, but he has some feeling in his legs, which indicates that the shrapnel in his back may have shifted. If the tests verify that, I'm having him transported to the medical center in San Antonio. I have a friend who's an orthopedic surgeon there. He'll operate."

"You mean, Kell could walk again?" she asked, excited.

He smiled. "Yes." The smile faded. "But that's not my immediate concern. He said there were three men. One of them was a man you've had dealings with, I understand. Frank Bartlett."

"Beating up a paralyzed man, with a mob," she gritted. "What a brave little worm he is!"

"Sheriff's got an all-points bulletin out for him and his friends," Micah told her. "But you're in danger until they're found. You can't stay out there at the house by yourself."

"If you send Kell to San Antonio," she said, "I'll call a friend who works for the same veterinary practice that employed me until I moved here. She'll let me stay with her."

"You'll have to be in protective custody," Micah said firmly.

She smiled. "Her brother is a Texas Ranger. He lives with her."

"Well!"

"I'll call her as soon as I see Kell."

"That will be another twenty minutes," he said. "We have to finish the tests first. But he's going to be fine."

"Okay. Thanks, Dr. Steele."

He smiled. "Glad I can help. I like Kell."

"I do, too."

She phoned Brenda Banks in San Antonio. Brenda's brother, Colter, was a Texas Ranger. He'd been based out of Houston until his best friend, a Houston police officer named Mike Johns, was killed trying to stop a bank robbery. Colter had asked for reassignment to Company D of the Texas Rangers, based in Bexar County, and moved in with his sister. Since Company D now had an official Cold Case sergeant, Colter applied for and obtained the job. Brenda said he loved solving old cases.

She tried the apartment, first, and sure enough, Brenda was

at home and not at work. "How do you like your new job?" Brenda asked when she heard Cappie's voice.

"I like it a lot. Do you still have a spare bedroom, and is there a job opening there at the vet clinic?"

"Oh, dear."

"Yes, well, things didn't work out as well as I hoped," Cappie said quietly. "Frank and a couple of friends came down and almost beat Kell to death. He's on his way up to San Antonio for back surgery and I need a place to stay, just until after the surgery. They wanted me in protective custody, but I told them Colter lived with you..."

"You poor kid! You can come and stay as long as you like," Brenda said at once. "But Colter's out of the country on a case. He has an apartment of his own now. What's that about Kell?" she asked worriedly. "Is he going to be all right?"

"He's just banged up, mostly," Cappie said, "but the shrapnel in his back has shifted and he has feeling in his legs. They may be able to operate."

"What a blessing in disguise," the other woman said quietly. "But what about you? Don't tell me Frank went to your house just to beat up your brother."

"He was probably looking for me," she confessed. "But he'd already done enough damage to my working relationship with my new boss. I don't have a job anymore, either."

"I'll ask Dr. Lammers about something part-time," she said immediately. "I know they'd love to have you back. The new tech doesn't have the dedication to the job that you had, and doesn't show up for work half the time, either. I'll phone her right now. Meanwhile, you come on up here. You know where the spare key's kept."

"Thanks a million, Brenda." Her voice was breaking, despite her efforts to control it.

"Honey, I'm so sorry," Brenda said gently. "If there's anything I can do, anything at all, you just tell me."

Cappie swallowed. "I've missed you."

"I've missed you, too. You just hang on. Get Kell up here and then come on yourself. We'll handle it. Okay?"

"Okay."

"I'll phone Dr. Lammers right now." She hung up.

Cappie went back to the waiting room and sat, sad and somber, while she waited for the test results and a chance to talk to Kell.

Dr. Steele was smiling when he came back. "I think it's operable," he said. "I'm going to send Kell to San Antonio by chopper. It's quicker and it will be easier on his back. We don't want that shrapnel to shift again. You can see him, just for a minute. Want to fly up with him?"

"Yes, if I can," she said.

He nodded toward Kell's room. "Cash Grier is in there with him. He wants a word with you, too."

"Okay. Thanks, Dr. Steele."

She opened the door and walked in. Cash Grier was leaning against the windowsill, very somber. Kell looked terrible, but he smiled when she bent over to kiss him.

"Dr. Steele thinks they may be able to operate," she told him.

"So I heard." He smiled. "I don't know how I'll afford it, but maybe they take IOUs."

"You get better before you worry about money," she said firmly. "We can always sell the car."

"Sure, that will pay for my aspirin," Kell chuckled.

"Stop that. It's going to work out," she said firmly. "Hi, Chief," she greeted Cash.

"Hi, yourself. Your ex-boyfriend was after you," he said without preamble. "He won't quit. He knows he'll go back to jail for what he did to Kell. He'll get you, if he can, before we catch him."

"I'm going to fly up to San Antonio with Kell," she said slowly, "and I'll be staying with my best friend. Her brother's a Texas Ranger." She didn't add that he was out of town. After all, Cash wouldn't know. But would she be putting Brenda in danger, just by being there?

"Colter's out of the country, and Brenda doesn't own a weapon," Cash said, stone-faced. He nodded when she gasped. "I know Colter. I used to be a Texas Ranger, too. We've kept in touch. You don't want to put Brenda in the line of fire."

"I was just worrying about that." She bit her lower lip. "Then what do we do?"

"You stay in a hotel near the hospital," he said. "We're sending security up to watch you."

"Police officers from here?" she wondered.

"Not really," Cash said slowly. "Actually Eb Scott is detailing two of his men to stay with you. One is just back from the Middle East, and the other is waiting for an assignment."

"Mercenaries," she said softly.

"Exactly."

She looked worried.

"They're not the sort you see in movies," Kell assured her. "These guys have morals and they only work for good causes, not just for money."

"Do you know the men?" she asked him.

He hesitated.

"I know them," Cash said at once. "And you can trust them. They'll take care of you. Just go with Kell to the hospital and they'll meet you there."

She frowned. "I'll have to phone somebody at my office, to tell them what's happened."

"Everybody at your office already knows what happened,"

Cash told her. "Well, except your boss," he added, just when her heart had skipped two beats. "He had to fly to Denver on some sort of personal business. Something to do with his stepfather."

"Oh." It was just as well, she thought. Now she wouldn't have to see him again. Kell didn't know Dr. Rydel had fired her, but this wasn't really the time to tell him. It could wait. "What about our house?"

"Kell gave me the key," he said. "I'll get it to Keely. She'll make sure the lights are off and everything's locked up and the fridge is cleaned out."

"I don't want to live there anymore," she told Kell in a subdued tone.

"We don't have to make decisions right now," he replied, wincing as he moved. "Hell, I think it was better when I couldn't feel my legs!"

"You'll enjoy walking again," Cappie said gently. "Kell, it would be like a miracle. At least some good would have come out of all this."

"Just what I was thinking." He smiled at her. "Now don't worry. It's going to work out."

"Yes, it is," Cash agreed. "Rick Marquez is going to make sure every cop in San Antonio has a personal description of Frank Bartlett, and he's talked to a reporter he knows at one of the news stations. Your nemesis Frank is going to be so famous that if he walks into a convenience store, ten people are going to tackle him and yell for the police."

"Really? But why?"

"Did I mention that there's a reward for his capture?" Cash added. "We took up a little collection."

"How kind!"

"You should stay here," Cash said seriously. "It's a good town. Good people."

Her face closed up. "I'm not living in any town that also houses Dr. Rydel."

Cash and Kell exchanged a long look.

"But Kell might like to stay," she added.

Kell wondered what was going on. Cappie had been crazy about her boss until today. "I think we need to have a talk about why you're down on your boss," he told her.

"Tomorrow," she said. "First thing."

"I'll probably be in surgery tomorrow, first thing," Kell replied.

She smiled wanly. "Then I'll tell you while you're unconscious. When do we leave?" she added.

Kell wanted to argue, but they'd given him something for pain, and he was already drooping. "As soon as the helicopter gets here. Need anything from the house? I'm sure Cash would run you over there."

She shook her head. "I've got my purse and my phone. Oh, here's the house key," she added, pulling it off her key ring and handing it to Cash. "I know you gave Kell's to Keely, but you may need mine. Thanks a lot."

"If you need anything, you can call Keely. She'll run it up to you, or her husband or her sister-in-law will."

"I'll do that."

"And try not to worry," Cash added, moving away from the window. "Things always seem darkest before the dawn. Believe me, I should know," he added with a smile. "I've seen my share of darkness."

"You're a wonderful police chief," she told him.

"Another good reason to stay in Jacobs County," he advised.

"We can agree to disagree on that point," she replied. "I might reconsider if you'd lock Dr. Rydel up and throw away the key."

"Can't do that. He's the best veterinarian around."

"I guess he is, at that."

Cash wisely didn't add to his former statement.

The trip in the helicopter was fascinating to Cappie, who'd never flown in one, despite Kell's years in the military. She'd had the opportunity, but she was afraid of the machines. Now, knowing that it was helping to save Kell's legs, she changed her opinion of them.

She sat quietly in her seat, smiling at the med techs, but not talking to them. She'd had just about all she could stand of men, she decided, for at least the next twenty years. She only hoped and prayed that Kell would be able to walk again. And that somebody would find Frank Bartlett before he came back to finish what he'd started.

Bentley Rydel walked into his office three days later, out of sorts and even more irritable than he'd been when he left. His stepfather had suffered a stroke. It hadn't killed him, but he was temporarily paralyzed on one side and in a nursing home for the foreseeable future. Bentley had tracked down the man's younger brother and made arrangements to fly him to Denver to look after his sibling. All that had taken time. He didn't begrudge giving help, but he was still upset about Cappie. Why had he been stupid enough to get involved with her? Hadn't he learned his lesson about women by now?

The office hadn't officially opened for business; it was ten minutes until it did. He found every employee in the place standing behind the counter glaring at him as if he'd invented disease.

His eyebrows arched. "What's going on?" His face tautened. "Cappie's suing me for asking her to quit, is she?" he asked with cold sarcasm.

Dr. King glared back. "Cappie's in San Antonio with her

brother," she said. "Her ex-boyfriend and two of his friends beat Kell within an inch of his life."

He felt the blood drain out of his face. "What?"

"They've got Cappie surrounded by police and volunteers, trying to keep the same thing from happening to her," Keely added curtly. "Sheriff Carson checked into Frank Bartlett's background and found several priors for battery against women, but nobody was willing to press charges until Cappie did. She wasn't exactly willing at that—her brother forced her to, when she got out of the hospital. Bartlett beat her bloody and broke her arm. She said that she'd probably be dead if Kell hadn't managed to knock out Bartlett in time."

He felt as if his throat had been cut. He'd believed the man. How could he have done that to Cappie? How could he have suspected her of such deceit? She'd been the victim. Bentley had believed the lying ex-boyfriend and fired Cappie. Now she was in danger and it was his fault.

"Where is she?" he asked heavily.

"She told us not to tell you," Dr. King said quietly. "She doesn't want to see you again. In fact, she's got her old job back in San Antonio and she's going to live there."

He felt sick all over. No, she wouldn't want to stay in Jacobs County now. Not after the job Bentley had done on her self-esteem. It had probably been hard for her to trust a man again, having been physically assaulted. She'd trusted Bentley. She'd been kind and sweet and trusting. And he'd kicked her in the teeth.

He didn't answer Dr. King. He looked at his watch. "Get to work, people," he said in a subdued tone.

Nobody answered him. They went to work. He went into his office, closed the door and picked up the telephone.

"Yes?" Cy Parks answered.

"Where's Cappie?" he asked quietly.

"If I tell you, I'll have to change my name and move to a foreign country," Cy replied dryly.

"Tell me anyway. I'll buy you a fake mustache."

Cy chuckled. "Okay. But you can't tell her I sold her out."

"Fair enough."

Cappie was worn-out. She'd been in the waiting room around the clock until Kell was through surgery, and it had taken a long time. The chairs must have been selected for their comfort level, she decided, to make sure nobody wanted to stay in them longer than a few minutes. It was impossible to sleep in one, or even to doze. Her back was killing her. She needed sleep, but she couldn't leave the hospital until she knew Kell was out of the recovery room.

Beside her, two tall, somber men sat waiting also. One of them was dark-eyed and dark-headed, and he never seemed to smile. The other one had long blond hair in a ponytail and one pale brown eye and an eye-patch on the other. He was good-natured about his disability and referred to himself as Dead-Eye. He chuckled as he said it. She didn't know their names.

Detective Sergeant Rick Marquez had dropped by earlier in the day to talk to her about Frank Bartlett's family and friends. She did know about Frank's sister, but she hadn't met any of his friends. Detective Marquez was, she thought, really good-looking. She wondered why he didn't have a steady girlfriend.

Marquez had assured her that he was doing everything possible to track down Frank Bartlett, and that a friend of his who was a news anchor was going to broadcast a description of Bartlett and ask for help from the public to apprehend him. There was a two-thousand-dollar reward being offered for information leading to his arrest and conviction.

Brenda came with her to the hospital and stayed until she was called into her own office for an emergency surgery on a dog patient. She'd promised to return as soon as she could. She was upset that Cappie wasn't going to stay with her. She could borrow a gun, she muttered, and shoot that two-legged snake if he came near the apartment. But Cappie smiled and said she hadn't been thinking straight when she'd called and asked for a place to stay. She wasn't risking Brenda. Besides, she had security. Brenda gave the two men a long, curious glance. She did mention that she wouldn't want to mess with them, if she was a bad man. The one with the ponytail grinned at her.

After Brenda left, Cappie sat with her two somber male attachments while people came and went in the waiting room. She drank endless cups of black coffee and tried not to dwell on her fears. If Kell could just walk again, she told herself, the misery of the past few days would be worth it. If only!

Finally the surgeon on Kell's case came out to speak with her, smiling in his surgical greens.

"We removed the shrapnel," he told her. "I'm confident that we got it all. Now we wait for results, once your brother has time to heal. But I'm cautiously optimistic that he'll walk again."

"Oh, thank God," she breathed, giving way to tears. "Thank God!"

"Now, will you please go and get some sleep?" he asked. "You look like death walking."

"I'll do that. Thank you, Dr. Sims. Thank you so much!"

"You're very welcome. Leave your cell phone number at the nurses' desk and they'll phone you if they need you."

"I'll do that right now."

She went to the nurses' desk with her two companions flanking her and looking all around them covertly.

"I'm Kell Drake's sister," she told a nurse. "I want to give you my cell phone number in case you need to get in touch with me."

"Certainly," a little brunette replied, smiling. She pulled a pad over to her and held a pen poised over it. "Go ahead."

Cappie gave the number to her. "I'll always have it with me, and I won't turn it off."

The brunette looked from one man to the other curiously.

"They're with me," Cappie told her. She leaned over the counter. "You see, they're in terrible danger and I have to protect them."

The two men gave her a simultaneous glare that could have stopped traffic. The brunette managed to smother a giggle.

"Okay, guys, I'm ready whenever you are," she told them.

The one with the eye-patch pursed his lips. "Want a head start?" he asked pointedly.

She grinned up at him. "You want one?" she countered.

He chuckled, and indicated that she could go first. He turned and winked at the little brunette, who flushed with pleasure. He was whistling as he followed Cappie out through the waiting room.

"You, protect us," the other man scoffed. "From what… bug bites?"

"Keep that up," Cappie told him, "and I'll show you a bite."

"Now, now, let's try to get along," Dead-Eye murmured as they waited for the elevator to come back up.

"I'm getting along. She's the one with the attitude problem," the other man muttered.

"Says you," Cappie told him.

He stared at Dead-Eye and pointed at Cappie.

"I never take sides in family squabbles," Dead-Eye told him.

"She is not a member of my family!" the other man said.

"A likely story," Dead-Eye said. "Anyway, how can you be sure? Have you had your DNA compared to hers?"

"I know I'm not related to you," the man told Dead-Eye.

"How do you know that?" came the dry retort.

"Because you're too ugly to be any kin to me."

"Well, I never," Dead-Eye harrumphed. "Look who's calling who *ugly*."

"Your mother dresses you funny, too."

Cappie was already light-headed with relief. These two were setting off her quirky sense of humor. "I can't take the two of you anywhere," she complained. "You embarrass me to tears."

"Can I help it if he's ugly?" the second man said. "I was only stating a fact."

"He's not ugly," Cappie defended Dead-Eye. "He's just unique."

Dead-Eye grinned at her. "We can get married first thing in the morning," he said. "I've been keeping a wedding ring in my chest of drawers for just such an emergency."

Cappie shook her head. "Sorry. I can't marry you tomorrow."

"Why not?"

"My brother won't let me date ugly men."

"You just said I wasn't ugly!" he protested.

"I lied."

"I can have my nose fixed."

She frowned. It was a very nice nose.

"I can alter it for you with my fist," the other man volunteered.

"I can alter you first," Dead-Eye informed him.

"No fighting," Cappie protested. "We'll all end up in jail."

"Some of us have probably escaped from one recently," the other man said with a pointed look at Dead-Eye.

"I didn't have to escape. They let me out on account of my extreme good looks," Dead-Eye scoffed.

"Your looks are extreme," came the reply. "Just not good."

"If you two don't stop arguing, I'm going to have my best friend come over to spend the night with us, and you two will be sharing the sofa," she assured them.

"Just shoot me now," Dead-Eye muttered, "and be done with it. I'm not sharing anything with him. Not unless he's got proof he isn't rabid."

The elevator door had opened while they were arguing. Dr. Bentley Rydel stepped off it and stared at the younger man while Cappie gaped at his sudden appearance.

"He isn't rabid," Bentley assured Dead-Eye.

"And how would you know?" Dead-Eye asked.

"I'm a veterinarian," Bentley replied curtly.

"We should go," Cappie said, avoiding Bentley's eyes.

"We?" he asked, scowling.

"These are my two new boyfriends," Cappie told him with a cold scowl. "We're sharing a room."

He knew she wasn't involved with two strangers. He had a pretty good idea of who they were and why she was with them. She probably expected him to believe the bald statement, with his track record.

"I heard about Kell," he said quietly. "How is he?"

"Out of surgery and resting comfortably, thank you," she said formally. "We have to go."

"Can we talk?" Bentley asked somberly.

"If you can get them," she indicated her companions, "to tie me up and gag me, sure. Let's go, guys."

She walked into the elevator and stood with her back to the door until she heard it close.

CHAPTER EIGHT

Cappie didn't sleep, of course. She was replaying the last forty-eight hours in her mind all night, sick with worry about Kell. It was her fault that Frank Bartlett had ever gotten near them. If only she hadn't been so flattered by his attention, so crazy about him that she ignored Kell's warnings. If only she hadn't gone out with him at all.

Pity, she thought, that people couldn't set the clock backward and erase all the stupid things they did. Like getting involved with Dr. Bentley Rydel, for example, she told herself. It had surprised her to find him at the hospital. Somebody in Jacobsville must have told him what had happened, and he felt sorry for her. Maybe he was willing to overlook her smarmy past long enough to check on her brother's condition. That didn't mean he believed her innocence or wanted to get involved with her again. Which was just as well, she told herself, because she certainly wanted nothing more to do with him!

She got up and dressed…in the same clothes she'd worn the day before. She hadn't packed anything. She'd have to call Keely and ask her to go to the house and pack a few items of clothing for her and Kell. But she'd make sure Keely got an armed person to go with her, in case Frank was waiting around to see if Cappie turned back up.

When she opened her bedroom door, the two men were arguing over the coffee in the tiny little coffeepot that came, with coffee, as a perk for staying in the hotel.

"There's not enough for three people," Dead-Eye was muttering, refusing to let go of the pot.

"Then you can get yours at a café, because I'm having mine here," the other man said coldly.

"We're all having ours at the hospital, because I'm leaving right now," Cappie informed them, starting for the door.

"See what you get for starting a fight? Now neither of us is having coffee," Dead-Eye scoffed as he turned off the coffeepot and put the little carafe back in it.

"You started it first," the other man said coolly.

Cappie ignored the banter and opened the door.

"Hold it right there."

Dead-Eye was in front of her in a heartbeat, his hand under his jacket as a tall man walked into view in the hall. He stood immobile, waiting.

But it wasn't Frank. It was another man, and a woman and child suddenly appeared behind him and started talking to him.

"Nice day," Dead-Eye told them with a smile.

"Huh? Oh. Yeah." The man smiled back and herded his family ahead of him down the hall.

Dead-Eye stood aside to let Cappie out. "Wait until one of us makes sure it's safe," he told her in a kind tone. "Men who commit battery without fear of arrest are usually not planning to go back in prison, if you get my drift. He might decide a bullet is better than a fist."

"Sorry," she said. "I didn't think."

"That's what we're here for," the other man said, following her out the door and closing it. "We'll think for you."

"Were you thinking, just then?" Dead-Eye grinned.

The other man indicated his sleeve. The hilt of a large knife was in his palm. He flexed his hand and snapped it back in place. "Learned that from Cy Parks," he said. "He taught me everything I know."

"Then what are you doing with Eb?"

"Learning…diplomacy." He said it through gritted teeth. "They say my attitude needs work."

Dead-Eye opened his mouth to speak.

Cappie beat him to it. "And you think I need an attitude adjustment?" she exclaimed.

The other man shifted restlessly. "We should get to the hospital."

Cappie just smiled. So did Dead-Eye.

When they got to the hospital cafeteria, it was already full. One of the tables was occupied by a somber Dr. Rydel, moving eggs around on a plate as if he couldn't decide between eating them or throwing them.

Cappie's traitorous heart jumped at the sight of him, but she didn't let her pleasure show. She was still fuming about his assumption of her guilt, without any proof except the word of a man who was a stranger.

He looked up and saw her and grimaced.

"Want me to frisk him for you?" Dead-Eye asked pleasantly. "I can do it discreetly."

"Yeah, like you discreetly frisked that guy at the airport," the dark-eyed man muttered. "Isn't he suing?"

"I apologized," Dead-Eye retorted.

"Before or after airport security showed up?"

"Well, after, but he said he understood how I might have mistaken him for an international terrorist."

"He was wearing a Hawaiian shirt and flip-flops!"

"The best disguise on earth for a spy, and I ought to know. I used to live in Fiji."

"Did you, really?" Cappie asked, fascinated. "I've always wanted to go there."

"Have you?" Dead-Eye looked past her to Bentley, who had gotten up from the table and was moving toward them. "Now might not be a bad time," he advised.

Bentley had dark circles under his eyes from lack of sleep. But he was just as arrogant as ever. He stopped in front of Cappie.

"I'd like to talk to you for a minute."

She didn't want to talk to him, and almost repeated her words of the night before. But she was tired and worried and a little afraid of Frank. It didn't matter now, anyway. Her life in Jacobsville was already over. She and Kell would start over again, here in San Antonio, once the threat was over.

"All right," she said wearily. "I'll only be a minute, guys," she told Dead-Eye and his partner. "You can get coffee."

"Finally," Dead-Eye groaned. "I'm having caffeine withdrawal."

"Is that why you look so ugly?" the other man taunted.

They moved off, still fencing verbally.

"Who are they?" Bentley asked as he seated her at his table.

"Bodyguards," she said. "Eb Scott loaned them to me."

"Want coffee?"

"Please."

He went to the counter, got coffee and a sweet roll and put them in front of her. "You have to eat," he said when she started to argue. "I know you like those. You bring them to work in the morning sometimes when you have to eat on the run."

She shrugged. "Thanks."

He pushed sugar and cream to her side of the table.

"I phoned the nurses' desk on the way here, on my cell phone," she said wearily. "They said Kell's having his bath and then breakfast, so I'd have time to eat before I went up to see him."

"I talked to him briefly last night," he said.

She lifted her eyebrows. "It's family only. They posted it on the door!"

"Oh, that. I told them I was his brother-in-law."

She glared at him over her coffee as she added cream.

"Well, they let me in," he said.

She lifted the cup and sipped the hot coffee, with an expression of absolute delight on her face.

"He was about as friendly as you are," he sighed. "I screwed up."

She nodded. "With a vengeance," she added, still glaring.

He pushed his plate of cold scrambled eggs to one side. His pale blue eyes were intent on her gray ones. "After what happened to me, I was down on women for a long time. When I finally got to the stage where I thought I might be able to trust one again, I found out that she was a lot more interested in what I could give her than what I was." His face tautened. "You get gun-shy, after a while. And I didn't know you, Cappie. We had supper a few times, and I took you to a carnival, but that didn't mean we were close."

She stared at the roll and took a bite of it. It was delicious. She chewed and swallowed and sipped coffee, all without answering. She'd thought they were getting to be close. How dumb could she be?

He drew in a long breath and sipped his own coffee. "Maybe we were getting close," he admitted. "But trust comes hard to me."

She put down the cup and met his eyes evenly. "How hard do you think it comes to me?" she asked baldly. "Frank beat me up. He broke my arm. I spent three days in the hospital. Then at the trial, his defense attorney tried his best to make it look as if I deliberately provoked poor Frank by refusing to go to bed with him! Apparently that was enough to justify the assault, in his mind."

He scowled. "You didn't sleep with him?"

The glare took on sparks. "No. I think people should get married first."

He looked stunned.

She flushed and averted her eyes. "So I live in the past," she muttered. "Kell and I had deeply religious parents. I don't think he took any of it to heart, but I did."

"You don't have to justify yourself to me," he said quietly. "My mother was like you."

"I'm not trying to justify myself. I'm saying that I have an idealistic attitude toward marriage. Frank thought I owed him sex for a nice meal and got furious when I wouldn't cooperate. And for the record, I didn't even really provoke him. He beat me up because I suggested that he needed to drink a little less beer. That was all it took. Kell barely got to me in time."

He let out a long breath. "My stepfather hit my mother once, for burning the bacon, when they were first married. I was fifteen."

"What did she do?" she asked.

"She told me. I took him out back and knocked him around the yard for five minutes, and told him if he did it again, I'd load my shotgun and we'd have another, shorter, conversation. He never touched her again. He also stopped drinking."

"I don't think that would have worked with Frank."

"I rather doubt it." He studied her wan, drawn face. "You've been through hell, and I haven't helped. For what it's worth, I'm sorry. I know that won't erase what I said. But maybe it will help a little."

"Thanks." She finished her roll and coffee. But when she

got through, she put two dollar bills on the table and pushed them toward him.

"No!" he exclaimed, his high cheekbones flushing as he recalled with painful clarity his opinion of her as a gold digger.

"I pay my own way, despite what you think of me," she said with quiet pride. She stood up. "Money doesn't mean so much to me. I'm happy if I can pay bills. I'm sorry I gave you the impression that I'd do anything for it. I won't."

She turned and left him sitting there, with his own harsh words echoing in his mind.

Kell was lying on his stomach in bed. His bruises were much more obvious now, and he was pale and weak from the surgery. She sat down beside him in a chair and smiled.

"How's it going?" she asked gently.

"Badly," he said with a long sigh. "Hurts like hell. But they think I might be able to walk again. They have to wait until I start healing and the bruising abates before they'll know for sure. But I can wiggle my toes." He smiled. "I'm not going to prove it, because it hurts. You can take my word for it."

"Deal." She brushed back his unkempt hair.

"Your old boss came by last night," he said coldly. "He explained what happened. I gave him an earful."

"So did I. He's back."

"I'm not surprised. He was pretty contrite."

"It won't do any good," she said sadly. "I won't forget what he said to me. He didn't believe me."

"Apparently he's had some hard knocks of his own."

"Yes, that explains it, but it doesn't excuse it."

"Point taken." He glanced past her toward the door. "You've got bodyguards."

"Yes. Some of Eb Scott's guys. They don't like each other."

"Chet has a chip on his shoulder, and Rourke likes to take potshots at it."

"Which is which?" she asked.

"Rourke lost an eye overseas."

"Oh. Dead-Eye."

He chuckled and then winced. "That's what he calls himself. He's got quite a history. He worked for the CIA over in the South Pacific for several years. Now he's trying to get back in. His language skills are rusty, and he's not up on the latest communications protocols, so he's studying with Eb. Chet, on the other hand, is trying to land a job doing private security for overseas embassies. He has anger issues."

"Anger issues?"

"He tends to slug people who make him angry. Doesn't go over well in embassies."

"I can understand that." She frowned. "How do you know them?"

He sighed. "That's a long story. We'll have to talk about it when I get out of here."

She was adding up things and getting uncomfortable totals. "Kell, you weren't working for a magazine when you went to Africa, were you?" she asked.

He hesitated. "That's one of the things we'll talk about. But not now. Okay?"

She relented. He did look very rocky. "Okay." She laid a gentle hand on his muscular arm. "You're my brother and I love you. That won't change, even if you tell me blatant lies and think I'll never know about them."

"You're too sharp for your own good."

"I've been told that."

"Don't stray from your bodyguards," he cautioned. "I have to agree with them. I think Frank's not planning to go back to jail. He'll do whatever it takes to get even with you, and then he'll try suicide-by-cop."

"Jail would be better than dead, certainly?"

"Frank has anger issues, too."

She flexed the arm he'd broken. "I noticed."

"Don't take chances. Promise me."

"I promise. Please get well. Being an orphan is bad enough. I can't lose you, too."

He smiled. "I'm not going anywhere. After all, I've got a book to finish. I have to get well in order to do that."

She hesitated. "Kell, he wouldn't come here, and try to finish the job he did on you?" she asked worriedly.

"I have company."

"You do?"

"Move it, you military rejects," came a deep voice from the door. A tall, familiar-looking man with silver eyes and jet-black hair moved into the room, dressed in boots and jeans and a chambray shirt, carrying a foam cup of coffee.

"Kilraven?" she asked, surprised. "Aren't you working?"

He shook his head. "Not tonight," he said. "I had a couple of vacation days I was owed, so I'm babysitting your brother."

"Thanks," she said with a broad grin.

"I'm getting something out of it," he chuckled. "I'm stuck on the middle level of a video game, and Kell knows how to crack it."

"Is it *Halo: ODST*?" Dead-Eye asked. "I beat it."

"Yeah, on the 'easy' level, I'll bet," Chet chided.

"I did it on 'normal,' for your information," he huffed.

"Well, I did it on *Legendary*," Kell murmured, "so shut up and take care of my sister, or I'll wipe the floor with you when I get back on my feet."

Dead-Eye gave him a neat salute. Chet shrugged.

"See you later," Cappie said, kissing her brother's cheek again.

"Where are you going?" he asked.

"On a job interview," she said gently. "Brenda's boss might have something part-time."

"Are you sure you want to move back here?" Kell asked.

"Yes," she lied.

"Good luck, then."

"Thanks. See you, Kilraven. Thank you, too."

He grinned. "Keep your gunpowder dry."

"Tell them." She pointed to her two companions. "I hate guns."

"Bite your tongue!" Kilraven said in mock horror.

She made a face and went out the door, her two companions right behind her.

Bentley met them at the elevator. "Where are you going now?" he asked her.

She hesitated.

"Job interview," Rourke said for her.

"You can't leave the clinic," Bentley said curtly. "I don't have anybody to replace you yet!"

"That's your problem," she shot back. "I don't want to work for you anymore!"

He looked hunted.

"Besides, Kell and I are moving back to San Antonio as soon as he heals," she said stubbornly. "It's too far to commute."

Bentley looked even more worried. He didn't say anything.

"Aren't you supposed to be at work?" she added.

"Dr. King's filling in for me," he said.

"Until when?"

His pale eyes glittered. "Until I can convince you to come home where you belong."

"Please. Hold your breath." She walked around him and into the next open elevator. She didn't even look to see which direction it was going.

It was going up. She was stuck between two oversize men and two perfume-soaked women. She started to cough before the women got off. The men left two floors later and the elevator slowly started down.

"Wasn't that heaven?" Rourke said with a dreamy smile, inhaling the air. "I love perfume."

"It makes me sick," Chet muttered, sniffing.

"It makes me cough," Cappie agreed.

"Well, obviously, you two don't like women as much as I do," Rourke scoffed.

They both glared at him.

He raised both hands, palms-out in defense, and grinned.

The elevator stopped at the cafeteria again and Bentley was still there, smoldering.

Cappie glared at him. It didn't help. He got on the elevator and pressed the down button.

"Where do you think you're going?" Cappie asked him.

"On a job interview," he said gruffly. "Maybe they need an extra veterinarian where you're applying."

"Does this mean that you're not marrying me?" Rourke wailed in mock misery.

Bentley gaped. "You're marrying him?" he exclaimed.

"I am not marrying anybody!" Cappie muttered.

Bentley shifted restlessly. "You could marry me," he said without looking at her. "I'm established in a profession and I don't carry a gun," he added, looking pointedly at the butt of Rourke's big .45 auto nestled under his armpit.

"So am I, established in a profession," Rourke argued. "And knowing how to use a gun isn't a bad thing."

"Diplomats don't think so," Chet muttered.

"That's only until other people start shooting at them, and you save their butts," Rourke told him.

Chet brightened. "I hadn't thought of it like that."

"Come on," Cappie groaned when the elevator stopped. "I swear, I feel like I'm leading a parade!"

"Anybody got a trombone?" Rourke asked the people waiting around the elevator.

Cappie caught his arm and dragged him along with her.

They took a cab to the veterinarian's office. The car was full. The men were having a conversation about video games, but they left Cappie behind when they mentioned innovations they'd found on the Internet, about how to do impossible things with the equipment in the Halo series.

"Using grenades to blow a Scorpion up onto a mountain?" she exclaimed.

"Hey, whatever works," Rourke argued.

"Yeah, but you have to shoot your buddies to get enough grenades," Chet said. "That's not ethical."

"This, from a guy who lifted a policeman's riot gun right out of the trunk of his car!" Rourke said.

"I never lifted it, I borrowed it! Anyway, everybody was shooting rifles or shotguns and I only had a .45," he scoffed.

"Everybody else's was bigger than his," Rourke translated with an angelic pose.

Chet hit his arm. "Stop that!"

"See why he can't get a job with diplomats?" Rourke quipped, holding his arm in mock pain.

"I'm amazed that either of you can get a job," Cappie commented. "You really need to work on your social skills."

"I'm trying to, but you won't marry me," Rourke grumbled.

"Of course she won't, she's marrying me," Bentley said smugly.

"I am not!" Cappie exclaimed.

"No woman is going to marry a veterinarian when she can have a dashing spy," Rourke commented.

"Do you know one?" Bentley asked calmly.

Rourke glared at him. "I can be dashing when I want to, and I used to work for the CIA."

"Yes, but does sweeping floors count as a real job?" Chet wanted to know.

"You ought to know," Rourke told the other man. "Isn't that what you did in Manila?"

"I was the president's bodyguard!"

"And didn't he end up in the hospital?"

"We're here!" Cappie said loudly, indicating where the cab was stopping. "And the ride is Dutch treat," she added. "I'm not paying cab fare for bodyguards and stubborn hangers-on."

"Who's a hanger-on?" Rourke asked.

But Cappie was already out of the cab. The three men followed her when they settled their part of the fare.

She walked into the veterinarian's front office, where Kate Snow was still holding down the job of receptionist. She was twenty-four, tall, brunette and had soft green eyes and a pleasant rather than pretty face. She smiled.

"Hi, Cappie," she greeted. "Come to visit your old stomping grounds?"

"Actually I'm here to apply for something part-time," she replied.

"Brenda said that, but I didn't believe her," Kate replied, stunned. "You just moved to Jacobsville."

"Well, I'm moving back."

"I'll buzz Dr. Lammers," she said, and pressed a button on the phone. She spoke into the receiver, nodded, spoke again and hung up. "He's with a patient, but he'll be out in a minute." She looked past Cappie. "Can I help you?" she asked the three men.

"I'm with her," Rourke said.

"Me, too," Chet seconded.

"I'm applying for a job, too," Bentley said. "I thought you might need an extra vet." He smiled.

"Who are you?" Kate asked, surprised.

"He's my ex-boss," Cappie muttered.

"You're Dr. Rydel?" Kate exclaimed. "But you have your own practice in Jacobsville!"

"I do, but if Cappie moves here, I move here," he said stubbornly.

"We might move here, too," Rourke interrupted. "I can interview for a job here, too. I can type."

"Liar," Chet said. "He can't type."

"I can learn!"

"All you know how to do is shoot people," Chet scoffed.

"Sir, it's illegal to carry a concealed weapon," Kate began nervously.

Rourke gave her his most charming smile. "I'm a professional bodyguard, and I have a permit. If you'd like to see it, I'll take you to this lovely little French bistro downtown and you can look at it while we eat."

Kate stared at him as if he'd grown horns.

"There's a guy stalking her," Chet told her. "We're going to catch him if he tries anything and turn him over to local law enforcement."

"Stalking you?" Kate stammered.

Cappie glared at the two men. "Thank you so much for making me an employment liability!"

Rourke made her a bow. Chet just glowered. Bentley beamed.

"I don't mind employing you. Not one bit," Bentley said. "These two can work for the groomer and we'll protect you."

"I'm not grooming anything," Chet told him bluntly.

"Okay. Then you can deal with surly clients," Bentley compromised.

Chet gave him an appreciative look.

"Actually I know how to groom things," Rourke said. "I once shaved a monkey."

Cappie hit him.

"There you are!" Brenda exclaimed, coming out of the back in a green-and-blue polka-dotted lab coat. "I talked to Dr. Lammers, but he said we've already got more part-timers than we can spare. I'm so sorry," she added miserably.

"What's your address?" Bentley asked. "I'll send you flowers."

"I thought you wanted to marry her," Chet pointed at Cappie.

Brenda's eyes widened. "Who are you?" she asked the dark-eyed man.

"I'm a hired…"

"…assassin," Rourke finished for him.

"I don't kill people, I just shoot them!" Chet growled.

"I only wound them," Rourke added. "Are we going back to Jacobsville, then?"

"Who are these men?" Brenda asked again.

"Well, these two are my bodyguards—" she indicated them "—and that's my ex-boss."

"Why is your ex-boss here?" she asked, all at sea.

"He was going to get a job here, too, but there are no openings for part-timers or vets, so I guess we're all going back to Jacobsville," Cappie said miserably. "That is, if Frank doesn't shoot me first."

"Nobody's shooting you," Rourke assured her.

"You can bet on that," Chet said.

Brenda smiled at them. "Thanks. She's my best friend."

Cappie hugged her. "Thanks anyway, for trying. I'll call you. See you, Kate!"

Kate waved as she picked up the ringing telephone. Her eyes were still on Rourke, who grinned at her.

"Come on, let's go," Cappie told the men.

"How's Kell?" Brenda asked, walking them out.

"He's going to make it. We won't know if he can walk for several days, though."

"If you have to go home, I'll visit him for you."

"I can't leave just yet," Cappie said. "Not until we find Frank."

Brenda stared at Bentley, who was all smiles. "Aren't you going back to your practice?"

"When we find Frank," he commented pleasantly.

"You're not part of this bodyguard unit," Chet reminded him.

"I am now," Bentley assured him. His eyes smoothed over Cappie. "I'm in it until the end."

Cappie hated the rush of pleasure that comment gave her. So she disguised it by hugging Brenda and promising to keep in touch.

CHAPTER NINE

Bentley went with them back to the hotel where Cappie was staying. He left them at the desk to get a room for himself. He managed one on the same floor, two doors down, and then went back to the other hotel where he'd been staying to pack his bags and check out.

"Great," Cappie muttered when they were back in her suite. "Now we're really going to be a parade."

"He likes you," Rourke pointed out. "And at this point, the more eyes, the better. He might see something we'd miss. After all, he knows what Frank looks like. We only have a mug shot. And you said it didn't really look much like him," he added, because he'd shown it to her earlier.

"All right," she sighed. She moved to the window and looked down at the busy street. "At least Kell's in good hands. I wouldn't want to walk in on Kilraven, even if he was in a good mood, with evil intent."

"There's an odd bird," Rourke commented. "We can't even find out which branch of the government he really works for, and we've tried. His brother works for the FBI, but Kilraven's true affiliations are less obvious."

She turned to him. "Is he CIA?"

"If he was, he wouldn't say so. And just for the record," he added with a grin, "no CIA office address is ever listed, in any city where we have offices. We don't even mention which cities those are."

"What a shadowy bunch you are," she commented.

He just grinned. "That's why we're so good at what we do."

"What we *do?*" she asked, hitting on the obvious assumption.

"I didn't say I was still with them," he pointed out.

"You didn't say you weren't, either," she replied.

He made a face at her.

"At least my job is up-front and everybody knows what it is," Chet said.

They both looked at him with wide eyes.

He glared at them. "I'm a bodyguard!"

"Well, so am I, right now," Rourke said. "But it's not what I do full-time." He gave the other man a narrow-eyed appraisal. "And it isn't what you do full-time, either."

Chet looked uncomfortable.

"What does he do full-time?" Cappie asked, curious.

"It involves long-range rifles and black ops."

"It does not," Chet muttered.

"It used to."

"Well, after I broke my leg, I was less enthusiastic about jumping out of Blackhawks," he muttered.

"You broke both legs, I heard."

Chet sighed. "And an arm. Breaks never heal properly, even with good medical care." He sighed again. "You try getting good medical care in..." He caught himself and closed his mouth.

"I wasn't going to say a word," Rourke told him.

"Well, don't. I'm out of cigarettes. I'm going down the street and see if I can find anybody in the mob to sell me a pack under the table, if the police aren't looking."

"Smoking's not illegal, is it?" Cappie asked.

"Any day now, it probably will be," Chet said despondently. "Can't spit without a federal permit these days," he said, and kept muttering all the way out the door.

"Quick, tell me," Cappie said to Rourke, "was he a sniper?"

"I've never been sure," he told her with a grin. "But he and Cash Grier are pretty chummy."

"Should that mean something?"

"Grier was a high-level government assassin in his younger days, but I didn't tell you that," he said firmly. "Some secrets have to be kept to save one's skin."

"Well!" she exclaimed. "I'd never have guessed."

"Neither would most other people. I'm going down the hall to loiter and see if I see anybody I recognize. Keep the door locked and don't answer it unless you recognize my voice, or Chet's. Got that?"

She nodded. "Thanks."

"When I do a job, I do a job," he told her. He closed the door behind him when he left.

She was jumpy. With her protection, she shouldn't have been, but she kept remembering her last sight of Frank Bartlett, cursing her for all he was worth when the judge announced his sentence. He'd been yelling vengeance at the top of his lungs, and he'd almost managed to get away from the sheriff's deputy who had him in handcuffs. It had been a scary moment. Almost as scary as the memory of the night he'd beaten her.

She wrapped her arms around her rib cage and closed her eyes. She did hope they'd catch him before he got to her. Surely the job he'd done on Kell would guarantee him some quality prison time. But what if he got out again, after that? Would she have to live her entire life being afraid of Frank? After all, he could get out on good behavior, no matter how long his sentence was. Or he could hang a jury at his next trial. Or he could break out of prison. There were plenty of horrible possibilities, all of which would leave Cappie hiding behind locked doors as long as she lived. It wasn't a possibility she looked forward to.

The sudden knock on the door brought a cry of panic to her lips. She moved toward the door, but she didn't touch the knob. "Who…is it?" she called.

"Room service. We're checking to see if your veterinarian has been delivered yet."

She burst out laughing. She knew that curt voice, as well as she knew her own. "Bentley!" She moved closer to the door. "I don't recall ordering a veterinarian."

"Well, we're delivering one to you anyway, just in case you regret not ordering him later," he drawled.

She unlocked the door and gave him a droll look. "Nice tactics."

He shrugged. "I'm desperate. You wouldn't let me in if I just asked." He looked behind her and the smile faded. "Where are your bodyguards?"

"Chet went looking for cigarettes and Rourke is down the hall checking for intruders."

"And you're in here alone."

"Well, the door was locked until you asked to come in," she pointed out.

"Fair enough. Want to come downstairs and have coffee and pie with me? Then we can go to see Kell."

"I guess that would be okay. But I have to tell Rourke where I'm going…"

"He already knows," came an amused voice from the general direction of her purse.

"How did you get in here?" she asked, lifting the purse.

"I hid a microphone in there earlier, in case you escaped."

"I'm going downstairs to have coffee and pie, then Bentley and I are going to see Kell."

"Okay. I'll be around. Have fun. And don't hit him with the pie. You will be going to a hospital."

"On your way to a hospital is the best time to hit people with things," she retorted. "There are doctors there."

"Yes, I know," Bentley spoke into her purse. "I am one."

"You're a veterinarian," Rourke shot back.

"I can treat injuries if I want to."

"Try not to let her give you any."

"You stop that," Cappie told her purse. Nobody answered. "Hello?" she said, looking inside it.

"Don't do that in public, okay?" Bentley asked as they walked to the door. "There are probably psychiatrists around the hospital, too."

She rolled her eyes and went out into the hall just ahead of him.

The hospital cafeteria was crowded. They found a table, but they had to share it with an elderly couple who'd come all the way from the Mexican border to visit their daughter, who'd just had a baby. They had photographs, and showed every single one to Bentley and Cappie, who made the correct responses between sips of coffee and bites of apple pie.

Finally the elderly couple finished their soft drinks and went off toward the elevator.

"Alone at last," Bentley teased.

"One more photograph would have done me in," she confessed. "I swear, if I ever have a grandchild…"

"…you'll have even more photos than they did, and show them to total strangers, too," he chuckled.

She shrugged and smiled. "Yes. I guess I would."

"Babies are nice. I used to think I'd like one or two, myself."

"You don't anymore?" she asked.

He moved his coffee mug around on the table. "I sort of gave up hope. Until you came along." He didn't look at her as he said it.

She felt her toes tingle. She hated the rush of pleasure she felt. "Really?"

He looked up. His pale blue eyes made sparks as they met hers. "Really."

She hesitated.

"I never should have believed a man I just met, who sat in my office and told lies about you with perfect innocence. But, then, I was afraid you were too good to be true."

"Nobody's perfect."

"I realize that. You don't have to be perfect. I just don't want to get in over my head and get kicked in the teeth again."

"I'm not that sort of person," she told him.

His eyes narrowed on her face. "He really hurt you, didn't he?"

"I thought I loved him," she said quietly. "He seemed to be kind and considerate…but the first date we had, he kicked my cat. I should have known then. Kind people aren't cruel to animals, ever. I found out later that he'd been abusive to at least two other women he dated, but they were too afraid of him to press charges." She smiled wanly. "Well, so was I. But Kell insisted. He said that Frank might end up killing someone if I didn't have him prosecuted. Then I'd have it on my conscience. I just didn't realize that it might be me that Frank killed." She put her face in her hands. "It won't ever end. Even if he goes back to trial, he could get off, or they could release him for good behavior, or he could break out… I'll never be free of him as long as I live."

"Don't talk like that," he said softly. "I won't let him hurt you."

She took her hands away. She looked older. "What if he hurt you? What if he killed you? Anybody around me will be a target. I almost put Brenda in danger without even realizing it."

"I'm not afraid of the little weasel," he told her. "And you're not going to be afraid of him, either. That's how he controls women. With fear. Don't give him a foothold in your mind."

She bit her lip. "I'm just scared, Bentley."

"Yes, but you did the right thing. And you'll do it again, anytime you have to. You aren't the type of person who runs from trouble, any more than I am."

"You think so?"

"I know so."

She searched his eyes. "I was scared to death of you, at first. Then I was in a wreck and you drove me home." She smiled. "You aren't as horrible as you seem."

"Thanks. I think." He smiled back.

"Okay. I'll stick it out. If Frank escapes another jail sentence, maybe I can get Rourke to hide him in a jungle overseas, so deep that he'd never find his way out."

"Ahem," her purse replied, "I do not kidnap American citizens and carry them out of the country for nefarious purposes. Not even for pretty women."

"Spoilsport," she told him.

"However, I know people who would," he added, with a smile in his voice.

"Good man," Bentley said.

"Why don't you marry him?" Rourke asked. "At least he'd make sure you were never in harm's way."

"If you'll give me your boss's telephone number," Bentley told the purse, "I'll call him and give you a glowing recommendation."

"What a pal!"

"I always..."

Bentley stopped talking because three people were standing at their table with open mouths, watching him speak into Cappie's purse. He cleared his throat. "There, the radio's turned off now," he said in a deep, deliberate tone. He handed her back the purse.

The three people looked sheepish, smiled and left the cafeteria in a bit of a rush.

Cappie burst out laughing. Bentley's cheeks were the color of bubble gum.

"Quick thinking, there, Dr. Rydel," Rourke called over the radio. "Want to come work for us?"

"Go away," Cappie told him. "I am not going to consider marrying anybody in your line of work."

"Spoilsport," Rourke said. "Shutting up now."

Cappie met Bentley's eyes, and they both laughed.

Kell was groggy and quiet. The pain must have been pretty bad, Cappie thought, once the anesthetic wore off. He was much less talkative than he'd been when he was just out of the recovery room. He was pale and he looked as if it was an effort to say anything at all. They only stayed a couple of minutes. Kell was asleep before they got out the door.

"Do you think it would be safe to step outside just for a minute and get a breath of air?" Cappie asked. "There are people everywhere."

"I don't know," Bentley said, his eyes roving.

"Rourke, what do you think?" she asked her purse.

But there was no reply. She looked around. She didn't see Rourke or Chet. That was odd. They'd been visible every minute since she came to San Antonio.

"Maybe it would be all right," she said. "I just want to stretch my legs for a minute."

"All right," Bentley said. "But you stay close to me." He

slid his big hand into her small one and closed it warmly. "I'll take care of you."

She smiled wearily and laid her head against his shoulder for a minute. "Okay."

They walked out into the cold night air. The sidewalk was crowded. Traffic passed by. There was a policeman on the corner, leaning back against a storefront, talking into a cell phone. Nearby, two men in suits were talking, oblivious to passersby.

All around them, neon signs and holiday lights brightened the darkness. "It's almost Christmas," she exclaimed. "With all that's happened, I forgot." She grimaced. "We won't get to open presents under the tree this year. Kell will never be able to go home by Christmas Eve."

"Then we'll put up a small tree in his room and transfer the presents up here from Jacobsville," he promised her. "We'll have Christmas here."

She looked up at him with soft, quiet eyes. "We?"

His jaw tautened. "I'm not leaving you again. Not even for a day," he said huskily.

The words made tears brim in her eyes. The way he said it was so poignant, so passionate. He didn't even need to say what he was feeling. She read it in his face.

He pulled her into his arms and held her close, hugged her tight, buried his face in her long, soft hair. "Marry me."

She closed her eyes. "Yes. Yes!" she whispered.

His chest rose and fell heavily. "Of all the places to get engaged," he groaned. "With a thousand eyes watching."

"It doesn't matter," she whispered.

No, he thought. It didn't.

"Hold him! I'll get her!"

The voices came suddenly into what was the sweetest dream of Cappie's life. She was so relaxed, so happy, that it took precious seconds for her to realize what was about to happen. She felt Bentley torn from her arms. Two men were pulling his arms behind him. A violent jerk brought her around as two bruising hands caught her shoulders and twisted them. Above her, Frank Bartlett's angry, contorted features came into view, his narrow dark eyes promising retribution.

"Got you at last, didn't I?" he growled. "Now, you're going to pay for what you did to me!"

She cried out and tried to pull away from him, but his hands were too strong. He drew one back and slapped her as hard as he could, so hard that she staggered and would have fallen if he hadn't jerked her back up brutally with the other hand.

Her face stung like fire. There would be a bruise. But it only made her mad. She drew back her high-heeled foot and kicked him in the calf muscle as hard as she could. He yelled in pain and slapped her again. But before he could draw back another time, he suddenly went down under a vicious tackle.

"That's the way, brother!" came a cheering cry from the sidelines.

"Go get him!" came another hearty voice.

Bentley was knocking the stuffing out of Frank Bartlett, his big fists making the other man, a match for him pound for pound, cry out in pain.

"Now isn't he talented?" Rourke murmured as he drew a shaky Cappie back from the crowd. He looked at her bruised face and winced. "Sorry we didn't rush right in, but we wanted to make sure we had plenty of witnesses and an excellent case for the prosecution." He jerked his head toward Chet and the two men in suits. They had the two men with Frank subdued and handcuffed. The uniformed officer who'd been on the corner was standing with them.

"We had you staked out," Rourke told her. "I wouldn't have done it this way, if there had been any other choice."

She reached up and patted his cheek. "You did good, Dead-

Eye," she said with a smile, and winced when it hurt. "I'm going to look like an accident victim for a few days, I'm afraid."

"No doubt about that. Your poor face!"

She glanced back toward Frank. Bentley was still pounding him. "Shouldn't you save Bentley?"

"Bentley?" he exclaimed.

"From a homicide charge, I mean," she clarified.

"Oh. Right. Probably should."

He moved forward and pulled Bentley off the other man. It took some doing. The veterinarian was obviously reluctant to give up his pastime.

"Now, now," Rourke calmed him, "we have to have enough left to prosecute. Besides, Cappie needs some TLC. She's pretty bruised."

Bentley was catching his breath as he walked quickly back to Cappie. He winced at the sight of her face. "My poor baby," he exclaimed, bending to kiss her bruised cheek with exquisite tenderness. "Let me just go back over there and hit him one more time…!"

"No," she protested, grabbing his suit coat. "Rourke's right, we have to have enough of him left to prosecute. Bentley, you were magnificent!"

"So were you, kicking him in the leg," he chuckled.

"I guess we make a pretty good team," she mused.

"You can say that again."

She put a hand to her cheek. "Boy, that stings."

"It looks like hell. You'll have to see a doctor."

"Fortunately there are plenty of those right inside," Rourke came back in time to reply. "See the letters? They spell out *hospital*."

She drew back a fist.

Rourke held up both hands. "Now, now, I'm on your side."

He nodded toward one of the men in suits who had a long black ponytail. "Recognize him?"

She frowned. "No…"

"That's Detective Sergeant Rick Marquez," he told her. "He was just on his way to the opera when we phoned and said an assault with intent was going down in front of the hospital. He broke speed records getting here."

"How kind of him," Cappie said.

"Not really. He always goes to the opera alone. He can't get women."

"But, why not?" she wondered. "He's a dish."

"He carries a gun," Rourke pointed out.

"You carry a gun."

"I can't get women, either."

"What a shame."

He moved closer. "I'm available."

She laughed as Bentley stepped in front of her, glowering.

"Wait, scratch that, I just remembered, I'm not available," Rourke said quickly.

"Even if you were, she's not," Bentley said.

"There you are, again, starting trouble," Rick Marquez chuckled, joining them. He looked at Cappie's face and grimaced. "Damn, I'm sorry we didn't get here sooner," he apologized. "I couldn't get a cab and I had to run all the way."

"Fortunately you're in great shape," Rourke said.

"Fortunately I am," Marquez agreed. "What are you and Billings doing here?"

"Trading favors with Eb Scott." Rourke grinned. "We're bodyguards. Well, not anymore. Not now that you have those three jackals in custody."

Marquez moved a step closer to him. "How about telling Chet that he's not allowed to smoke here?"

"Why don't you tell him?" Rourke asked, surprised.

"Too many windows overlook my apartment," came the amused reply. "He might not be able to resist the temptation to get even."

"Good point. I'll just pass that along. About the smoking!" Rourke added quickly. "Anyway, he wouldn't shoot you. He's not sanctioned."

"Yet," Marquez enunciated.

Rourke shrugged, grinned and went to find his partner.

"They really were great," Cappie told the detective. "I've never felt safer. Well, until tonight."

"We let you walk into the trap," Marquez replied quietly. "It was the only way we could guarantee a case against Bartlett that he couldn't escape. His sort doesn't give up."

"Yes, but he could get out again..."

"He won't," Marquez said curtly. "I promise you that. See that guy I was standing with? He's the assistant D.A. who put Frank away in the first place."

"I thought he looked familiar," Cappie returned.

"He cursed a blue streak because the judge gave him such an easy sentence. He's been working behind the scenes to get depositions in case Frank slipped." He grinned. "And did Frank ever slip! In front of all these witnesses, too." He indicated the uniformed officer, and two others who'd joined him, who were questioning bystanders. "Frank is going back in jail for a long time."

"What about his friends?" Cappie asked.

"I know what they helped him do to your brother. We couldn't have proved it, before, but I'm betting one of them will be happy to turn state's evidence in return for a reduced sentence."

"Meanwhile," Bentley said, sliding an affectionate arm around Cappie, "we're going to have a nice Christmas celebration with Kell in the hospital and then plan a wedding."

"A wedding?" Marquez sighed. "I used to think I'd find a nice woman someday who liked cops and opera, who'd love to marry me. But, I'm really happy to be single. I mean, I have all sorts of free time, and I get to watch whatever television programs I like, and TV dinners are just wonderful. In fact, I think I might like to do commercials for them." He smiled.

"They have psychiatrists in there, don't they?" Bentley asked, nodding toward the hospital.

Marquez glared at him. "I'm happy, I said! I love living alone! I never want my private life messed up by some sweet, loving woman who can cook!"

"Anybody got a straitjacket?" Bentley asked.

Marquez threw up his hands and walked away.

Cappie felt her face begin to throb. Tears stung her eyes. "Could we go back inside and find the emergency room, you think?" she asked Bentley.

"Right this minute," he said with obvious concern.

Marquez followed them inside. "I've got my digital camera with me," he said, suddenly all business. "We want to get photos, to make sure a jury sees what Frank did to you."

"Be my guest," Cappie replied. "But then I want aspirin and an ice pack!"

"You can come down to my office in the morning to give me a statement. For now, we'll get the photos and have a doctor look at your face. After that, you can even have a beer if you like, and I'll buy," Marquez promised.

She made a face. "Sorry, but I'd rather have the ice pack."

Bentley's arm contracted. "Then we have to find some way to keep Kell from seeing your poor face, until he's through the worst of his own ordeal."

"Yes, we do," she said. "That isn't going to be easy."

Marquez, seeing the bruising increase by the second, had to agree. And she didn't know yet how it was going to look a day later. But he did.

* * *

They did take X-rays of Cappie's face. Marquez got his photos and left. The doctor treating her came back into the cubicle where she and Bentley were waiting in the busy emergency room.

"There are two small broken bones," he said. "I want you to take these X-rays to your primary physician and let him refer you to a good plastic surgeon. Meanwhile, I'm going to write you something for pain. Keep ice on the swelling. Nothing is going to disguise the bruises, I'm afraid." He glanced curiously at Bentley.

"I didn't do it," Bentley said easily. "The man who did was taken away in a squad car, with his accomplices, and he's going to be prosecuted to the full extent of the law. Those X-rays we asked for a copy of are going to help put him away."

The young resident nodded somberly. "I see far too many injuries like this. A boyfriend?" he queried.

"No," Cappie said heavily. "An ex-boyfriend who spent six months in jail for breaking my arm," she added. "He got out and came looking for me. This time, I hope he'll stay as a guest of the state for much longer."

"I'll be happy to testify," the resident said. He pulled a card out of his wallet and handed it to her. "That happens too often, you know, a brutal man seeking revenge. We had a young woman killed a few weeks ago for the same thing."

Cappie felt sick to her stomach.

Bentley put his arm around her. "Nobody's killing you," he said.

She leaned her head against him. "Thanks."

They took the extra X-ray in its envelope, paid the bill and left the emergency room, hand-in-hand.

"Do you want to go and see Kell tonight?" Bentley asked.

She shook her head, wincing, because it hurt. "I'm too sick.

I just want to lie down." She looked up. "Will you go with me to Marquez's office in the morning?"

"You'd better believe I will."

"Thanks."

His arm contracted around her. "Not necessary. Let's get you back to your room. It's been a long day."

"Tell me about it," she mused. At least, she thought, her ordeal was over for the moment. Tomorrow she could worry about the details, including telling poor Kell what had happened.

CHAPTER TEN

Cappie groaned at her own reflection in the hotel mirror when she climbed out of bed the next morning. One whole side of her face was a brilliant purple, and swollen to boot.

"You okay in there?"

She smiled. Bentley had insisted on sleeping on the sofa in the suite, just in case. Rourke and Chet were already up and packing their things for the trip back to Jacobsville. Cappie and Bentley were staying for another day or two, while she gave statements to the police and looked after Kell.

"I think so," she said. "I just can't bear to look at myself."

"I'll bet Chet knows exactly how that feels!" Rourke called from the doorway of the room he and Chet had shared.

"Will you shut up?" Chet muttered.

"Now, that's a good example of how much work your diplomatic skills need," Rourke admonished.

"I'm through trying to be diplomatic," Chet said curtly. "I'm going back to the company and let them send me off on lone assignments, all by myself. Anywhere I don't have to try to be nice to people!"

"Yes, and you can take those smokes with you," Rourke

added. "Having to share a room with you is punishment enough for any lawbreaker! Man, you reek!"

"Cigarette smoke is beneficial," Chet told him.

"It is not!"

"If your quarry smokes, you can smell him from five hundred meters," Chet returned, and he actually smiled.

Rourke's jaw dropped. He'd never seen the other man smile.

Chet gave him a haughty, arrogant stare, picked up his bag and walked out. "Hope things go well for you, Miss Drake," he said as she came out of her room wrapped in a thick robe. He winced. "It will look much better in a week or so," he assured her.

She tried to smile, but it hurt too much. "Thanks for helping keep me alive, Chet."

"My pleasure. See you back at Scott's place, Rourke."

"You wait for me—I'm not paying cab fare back to Jacobsville all alone," Rourke said. He picked up his own bag, shook hands with Bentley and bent to kiss Cappie's undamaged cheek. "If he ever walks out on you, just get word to me, and I'll bring him back to you in a net," he said in a stage whisper.

"Thanks, Rourke. But I don't think that will ever happen."

Bentley smiled. "I can guarantee it won't."

"Cheers, then. See you."

They waved the two men off. Bentley studied her poor, damaged face warily. "I wish there had been some way to prevent that."

"Me, too. But it's insurance. Let's get breakfast. Then we can go down to Detective Marquez's office and start giving statements. Later," she added reluctantly, "we can go see Kell and try not to upset him too much when we tell him what happened."

"Suits me."

Detective Marquez had a small office in a big department. It was noisy and people seemed to come and go constantly. The phones rang off the hook.

"This looks like those crime shows on television," Cappie remarked.

Marquez chuckled. "It's much worse. You can't get five minutes' peace to type up a report." He got up to retrieve the report he'd typed at the computer as he questioned her. He took it out of the printer tray and handed it to her. "Check over that, if you will, and see if I've got it right." He pulled out another one. "This one's for you, Dr. Rydel." He handed the vet another sheet of paper.

They went over their statements, made a couple of corrections. Marquez inserted the corrections and printed the statements out again. They signed them.

"I'll bet Frank's foaming at the mouth," Cappie mused.

"He really is, but this time he's not going to fool any jury into thinking he's the injured party," Marquez assured her.

"I'll bet that judge is feeling bad about now," Bentley muttered.

"The judge did feel bad," Marquez agreed. "So did the district attorney, especially after Frank and his cohorts beat up your brother. The whole justice system here in San Antonio went into overdrive to catch the perp."

"Really?" Cappie asked, surprised.

"Really. The assistant district attorney who prosecuted your case was in the vanguard."

"Somebody needs to take him out for a big steak dinner," Cappie commented.

"I'm taking him out for one, at my mother's café in Jacobsville," he chuckled. "Of course, he's eligible and so is my mother."

"I see wheels turning in your head," Cappie said.

He grinned. "Always," Marquez said easily. "He and I have worked several cases together. I like him."

"Me, too," Cappie said. She hesitated. "Frank won't get out until the trial, will he?"

Marquez shook his head. "The assistant D.A. is having the bond set in the six-figure range. I don't think Frank knows a bail bondsman who'll take a chance on him for that amount of money."

"Let's hope not," Bentley said.

Marquez gave him a keen glance. "He'll probably stay in jail voluntarily, to keep from having you come at him again. That was some tackle."

Bentley shrugged. "I used to play football in college."

"I played soccer. Don't get to do much tackling, but I can knock a ball half a block with my head."

"Is that why it looks that way?" a familiar voice drawled from the cubicle doorway.

"Kilraven," Marquez grumbled, "will you stop stalking me?"

"I'm not stalking you," the tall man said easily. "I'm just waiting for you to answer my ten phone calls, six voice mails and twenty e-mails." He glowered at the younger man.

Marquez held up his hands. "Okay. Just let me finish up with Miss Drake and Dr. Rydel and I'll be right with you. Honest."

"No hurry," Kilraven said, smiling. "I'll be standing right out here, intimidating lawbreakers."

"Thanks for looking out for Kell," Cappie told him.

"What are friends for?" he asked.

"How would you know, Kilraven, you don't have any friends," a passing detective drawled.

"I have lots of friends!"

"Oh, yeah? Name one."

"Marquez!"

"He's your friend?" the detective asked Marquez, sticking his head into the cubicle.

"He is not," Marquez said without looking up as he glanced over the statements one last time.

"I am so," Kilraven said in a surly tone.

Marquez gave him a speaking glance.

Kilraven moved back out of the cubicle, muttering to himself in some foreign language.

"I know what that means in Arabic," Marquez called after him. "Your brother speaks Farsi fluently and he taught me what those words mean!"

A rolling barrage in yet another language came lilting into the cubicle.

"What's that?" Marquez asked.

Kilraven poked his head in and grinned. "Lakota. And Jon can't teach you that—he doesn't speak it. Ha!"

He left.

Marquez grimaced.

"He's really very nice," Cappie said.

Marquez leaned toward her. "He is, but I'm not saying it out loud." His expression became somber. "I'm working on a cold case with him and another detective," he said quietly. "It involves him. He's impatient, because we got a new lead."

Bentley nodded quietly. "I know about that one. One of my vet techs is married to the best friend of our local sheriff. I hear most of what's going on."

"Tragic case," Marquez agreed. "But hopefully we're going to crack it."

Bentley got to his feet, tugging Cappie up with him. He winced as she turned toward him.

"I appreciate the copies of those X-rays," Marquez added, walking out with them. "Everything we can throw against Bartlett will help put him away."

"He'd better hope he never gets out," Cappie said. "My brother will be waiting for him if he does."

Marquez chuckled. "If it hadn't been three to one against, and your brother hadn't been in a wheelchair, I'd probably be helping defend him on homicide charges."

"No doubt," Bentley replied somberly.

Cappie frowned. "Is there a conversation going on that I don't know anything about?" she asked.

Bentley and Marquez exchanged covert glances. "Just commenting on your brother's justifiable anger," Bentley told her easily. He caught her fingers in his. "Let's go see your brother and tell him he's about to have a new brother-in-law."

Kell was a little better, until he saw Cappie's face. He swore brilliantly.

"I know how you feel," Bentley said. "But for what it's worth, Bartlett probably looks much worse. It took two detectives to pull me off him."

Kell brightened. "Good man." He winced at his sister's face, though. "I'm so sorry."

"I'll heal." She didn't mention the potential surgery she might have to undergo. There was no need to worry him even more. "Detective Marquez said that Frank won't get out for a long time. He expects one of Frank's accomplices to turn state's evidence. If they charge him with battery on both of us, he'll do some serious time."

"I expected Hayes Carson to show up here and ask me for a statement for what Frank did to me in Comanche Wells," he murmured.

"I imagine he's giving you time to get over the surgery," Cappie said.

"Probably so."

"Have you spoken to the surgeon yet?" Cappie asked.

He smiled. "Yes. He's optimistic, especially since I have feeling in my legs now."

"At least something good may come out of all this misery," she said gently.

Kell was looking at Bentley. "Just before we came up here to the hospital, she said she didn't want to live in a town that also contained you. You told me part of the story, but not any more than you had to. She was going to explain, then they knocked me out with a shot. Care to comment?"

"I made a stupid decision," Bentley said with a sigh. "I expect to be apologizing for it for the rest of my life. But she's going to marry me anyway." He gave her a tender smile, which she returned. "I can eat crow at every meal, for however long it takes."

"I stopped being mad at you while you were beating the stuffing out of Frank Bartlett," she pointed out.

He glanced at his bruised, swollen knuckles. "I'll have permanent mementoes of the occasion, I expect."

"You're getting married?" Kell asked.

"Yes," Cappie said. She touched her face gingerly. "Not until the swelling goes down, though."

"And not until I'm able to walk down the aisle and give you away," Kell interjected.

Bentley pursed his lips. "I could get Chet and Rourke to carry you down the aisle to give her away," he offered.

"The last wedding Chet went to, he spent the night in jail for inciting a riot," Kell pointed out.

Cappie frowned. "Exactly how well do you know Chet and Rourke?" she asked pointedly.

He groaned. "Oh. The pain. I need to rest. I really can't talk anymore right now."

Cappie's eyes narrowed on the drip catheter. "Doesn't that thing automatically inject painkiller into the drip while you're post-surgical?" she asked.

Kell kept his eyes closed. "I don't know. I feel terrible. You have to leave now." He opened one eye. "You can come back later, when I'll be much better as long as you don't ask potentially embarrassing questions. If you do, I may have a relapse."

"All right," Cappie sighed.

He brightened. "Be good and I'll tell you how to get past the Hunters in *ODST*."

"Cash told you?" she asked.

He chuckled and winced, because moving hurt. "Not without a bribe."

"What sort of bribe?"

"Remember that old Bette Davis movie, where she murders her lover and then has to blackmail the man's widow over a letter that could convict her?" he asked.

"Yes. It's called *The Letter*...it's one of my favorite..." She stopped. "You didn't!"

"Hey, it's not as if you watch it that much," Kell protested.

"Kell!"

"Do you want to get past the Hunters, or don't you?" he asked.

She sighed. "I guess I can always find another copy of it somewhere."

"That's a nice sister," Kell said.

"If I buy you another one," Bentley interrupted, "will you tell *me* how to get past the Hunters?" he asked her.

They all laughed.

Two weeks later, Kell was walking down the hall, wobbling a little, in his pajamas and robe while Cappie held him up. The swelling in her cheek had gone down, but it still had a yellowish tinge to it. Kell was much better. He was learning how to walk all over again, courtesy of the rehab department in the Jacobsville hospital.

"This is slow," he muttered.

"It is not," Bentley retorted, and the sound of gunfire came from the television in the living room. "Ha! That's one Hunter down!"

"Rub it in," she called. "It wasn't even your favorite movie you had to sacrifice to learn how to do that!"

"I bought you a new one. It's in the DVD player," he called back.

"Fat lot of good it's doing me, since that game console hasn't been off for five minutes all day," she muttered.

"Stop picking on my future brother-in-law," Kell chided. "It isn't every man who can make tortillas from scratch."

"He only did it to butter you up," she told him.

"It worked. When's the wedding, again?"

"Three weeks from now. Micah Steele says you'll be able to manage the church aisle with just a cane by then. And we can hope there won't be a large animal emergency anywhere in the county during the ceremony!" she raised her voice.

"I'm borrowing a vet from San Antonio to cover the practice for me until we're back from our honeymoon in Cancún," he said. They'd picked the exotic spot because it had been the dream of Cappie's life to see Chichen Itza, the Mayan ruin.

"I hope the vet knows he's covering for you," she said.

He chuckled. "He does."

"The guest list just keeps growing," Cappie sighed. "I've already sent out fifty invitations."

"Did you put Marquez and the assistant D.A. on the list?"

"Yes," she said. "And Rourke and Chet, too."

Kell groaned.

"Chet won't start any riots. I'll have a talk with him," she promised. "They took good care of me in San Antonio," she added.

"Yes, but I was the one who took down Frank," Bentley

called. "Can you believe that little weasel tried to sue me for assault?" he added huffily.

"He didn't get as far as first base," Kell assured him. "Blake Kemp had a long talk with his attorney."

"Why would our D.A. be talking to a defense attorney in San Antonio?" Cappie wanted to know.

"Because the defense attorney wasn't aware of the familial connections of the defendant's assailant," Bentley murmured. "Ha! There went another Hunter!" he exclaimed.

Cappie blinked. "Familial connections…?"

Kell leaned down to her ear. "Don't ask. The upshot is that the lawsuit is going nowhere. Fast."

Cappie was still staring at Bentley. "What familial connections?" she persisted.

"The governor is my first cousin. Ha! Another one!"

"Our governor?" she exclaimed.

"We only have one. This game is great!"

Cappie sighed. She looked up at her handsome big brother. "The game is not going with us on our honeymoon," she said firmly.

Bentley gave her a roguish glance. "Not even if I tell you how to get past the Hunters?"

"Well, in that case, maybe I could reconsider," she chuckled.

Kell did make it down the aisle with a cane. The little country church in Comanche Wells was filled to capacity. Only people they knew got an invitation, but there was still standing room only. A good many of the guests were in uniform, either military or law enforcement, on one side of the church, while a number of Eb Scott's guys were seated across the aisle from them. Covert glares were exchanged. Down the center aisle marched Cappie in her lovely white gown with what seemed acres of lace and a pretty fingertip veil. She was carrying a bouquet of yellow roses and wearing a smile that went from ear to ear.

She held on to Kell's arm tightly, so proud of his progress that she beamed with happiness. He was already talking about a new job working for Eb Scott at his anti-terrorism school. She was really curious about how well her brother seemed to know any number of Eb's employees, but she hadn't made any comments. She was still indebted to Eb for lending her Chet and Rourke, who were seated together in the front of the church. Around them were her former and present coworkers, including Keely and Boone Sinclair. Boone's sister, Winnie, was being watched with real intensity by Kilraven, dressed in an expensive suit in the row behind her.

She and Kell stopped at the altar, where he gave her hand to Bentley. He was beaming, too, so handsome that Cappie just sighed, looking up at him with gray eyes that adored him.

The wedding service was brief, but poignant. Bentley lifted the veil and bent to kiss her with such tenderness that she had to fight tears.

Then he led her down the aisle to the back of the church. The people who hadn't been able to squeeze into the church were waiting outside with what seemed like buckets of rice and confetti. They were totally drenched in both as they ran to the white limousine that was to take them to the town civic center, for the reception.

They fed each other cake, posed for wedding pictures and generally had a wonderful time. There was a live band and they danced together to a slow, romantic tune, which lasted for all of two minutes before Cash Grier, with his beautiful wife, Tippy, signaled to the band leader.

There were grins, a fanfare and then a furious and delicious rendition of the classic tune "Brazil." But Cash didn't start dancing, as everyone expected him to. He glanced toward Bentley with a chuckle and a flourish.

Bentley gave Cappie a wicked look. "Shall we?"

"But, Bentley, you can't dance…can you?" she exclaimed.

"I couldn't," he confessed, taking her onto the dance floor. "But Cash gave me lessons. Okay. One, two…three!"

He twirled her around in the most professional sort of way, in a mixture of samba, cha-cha and mambo that she followed with consummate ease while people on the sidelines began to clap.

"You're terrific!" Cappie panted.

"So are you, gorgeous," he chuckled. "Are we good, or what?"

About a day and a half later, they repeated the same exact dialog to each other, but for a totally different reason.

Lying exhausted and bathed in sweat in a huge double bed in a beachfront hotel in Cancún, they could barely move.

"And I thought you danced well!" she laughed. "You're just amazing!"

"Why, thank you," he drawled, grinning. "May I return the compliment?"

"Yes, well, I think I'm a quick study," she sighed.

"Not so nervous anymore, I notice," he murmured.

She laughed. She was almost a basket case of nerves when they checked into the hotel that afternoon. She loved Bentley, but she had no real idea of what it was going to be like when they were alone together. But he was understanding, patient and gentle as he cradled her in his arms in a big easy chair and fed her shrimp from a big platter of seafood that room service had brought up. Of course, he'd also fed her champagne in increasing amounts, until she was so relaxed that nothing he suggested seemed to disturb her.

Slow, tender kisses grew slower and more insistent. He

coaxed her out of her clothing with such ease that she barely noticed until she felt the cool air on her skin. Even then, the way he was touching her was so electrifying that her only conscious thought was to see how much closer to him she could get. There was one little flash of pain, easily forgotten as he kissed her with delicate sensuality and lifted her back into the fiery hunger the hesitation had briefly interrupted. Her mind had gone into eclipse while her body demanded and pleaded for an end to the tension which he built in her so effortlessly. Finally, finally, she fell over the edge of it into a blazing heat of fulfillment that exceeded her wildest expectations.

"And I used to think you were reserved!" she laughed.

"Only when I'm wearing a white lab coat," he murmured drowsily. He opened his eyes, rolled over and studied her pretty pink nudity with lazy appreciation. "Would you like me to get up and put on a lab coat, and be reserved?"

"I would not," she retorted, pulling him back down. She kissed him intensely. "I'd like you to be unreserved all over again, starting right now."

He slid over her, his hair-roughened chest grazing the hard tips of her pretty breasts. "I can't think of anything I'd enjoy more, Mrs. Rydel."

She would have answered him back, but she was much too involved for speech.

They wandered through the ruins at Chichen Itza hand in hand, fascinated as they strolled around the wide plain that contained the pyramidal Castillo and the other buildings that made up the Mayan complex.

"It must have looked much different when it was occupied, all those hundreds of years ago," Cappie mused, her eyes everywhere.

"There were probably even more people," he chuckled,

glancing at the crowds of tourists that abounded, even this time of year. He handed her his huge water bottle and waited for her to take a sip before he followed suit. The bus trip here was hours long, and it would be after dark before they got back to their hotel. It was something they'd both wanted to see.

"It's a lot different, being here, than seeing it on television," she remarked.

"Most things are," he replied. "Until they can discover a way to let you touch and smell distant ruins, it won't be as much fun to watch it on a small screen."

She stopped and looked up at him with her heart in her gray eyes. "I never thought being married would be so much fun."

He hugged her close. "And we're only at the beginning of our marriage," he agreed, his blue eyes soft as they scanned her face. "I hope we have a hundred years ahead of us."

"Me, too." She pressed into his arms and closed her eyes. "Me, too, Bentley."

She went back to work for him in the practice. She'd argued that if Keely, who was happily married and well-off, could keep working, she could, too. He hadn't protested too much. It delighted him to be able to see her all day long.

"Don't you want a cat?" Keely coaxed the week after they came back from their honeymoon. "I've got six little white kittens that Grace Grier asked me to find homes for, and I've only placed four of them."

Cappie laughed. "I'd love one."

"Me, too," Bentley agreed, poking his head around the corner. "Did Cy Parks call back about that new bull of his that got cut on the barbed wire?"

"He did. He said if you'd drop by on your way home, he and Lisa would feed you both," Keely chuckled. "They're having homemade chili and corn bread."

"My favorite," Bentley said.

"Mine, too," Cappie replied almost at the same time as Bentley.

"He said you could bring Kell along," the other girl added.

"Kell's gone off somewhere with Rourke and Chet," Cappie sighed. "No telling where. They vanish for days at a time, and nobody knows where. He's my own brother. You'd think he could trust me."

"And me," Bentley added.

"I'm sure he has his reasons," Cappie said. "Whatever they are."

"It's bound to be something covert and dangerous and exciting," Keely said out loud.

"More than likely, they're helping Detective Marquez stake out a nightclub or something," Bentley chuckled. "He did mention that he needed a couple of willing volunteers for a special project he and that assistant district attorney are working on."

"We owe that district attorney," Cappie agreed. "He talked Frank's accomplices into testifying against him for reduced sentences. He says Frank won't get out until his hair turns gray. Made my day," she added.

"Mine, too," Bentley assured her. "Okay, people, back to work."

"Yes, sir, Dr. Rydel, sir," Cappie said, saluting him.

He made a face at her. Then he grinned.

She grinned back, turning back to her coworker behind the counter. "Who's next, Keely?"

"Mrs. Anderson and her Chihuahua. Got the chart right here."

Cappie took it from her and went out into the waiting room, which was full. Her eyes were bright with happiness as she exchanged a glance with her handsome husband, just before he went into the back to examine a surgical patient. She felt as if she could walk on air.

"Okay, Mrs. Anderson," she told an elderly little woman with a smile. "If you'll bring Tweedle on back, we'll get Dr. Rydel to take a look at his bruised paw."

"He's a very nice doctor," the little woman told Cappie. "You're a lucky young woman!"

"Yes, you are!" Bentley called from the back. "Not every woman gets a husband who's as accomplished and modest as I am! You should be proud of yourself!"

"I am, dear, and how do you like your potatoes…burned or charbroiled?"

There was a pause. "Not every husband gets a wife as accomplished and modest as you are, dear!" he called back.

She chuckled. "Now that will get you a nice scalloped potato dish and a beautifully cooked pot roast!"

An amused Mrs. Anderson wiggled her eyebrows at Cappie as she followed her to a treatment room. Cappie just grinned.

* * * * *

BOONE

To my sister, Dannis Spaeth Cole, and my niece Maggie
in Cuthbert, Georgia, and to my other niece Amanda Hofstetter,
in Portland, Oregon. Love you all.

CHAPTER ONE

Keely Welsh felt his presence before she looked up and saw him. It had been that way from the day she met Boone Sinclair, her best friend's eldest brother. The man wasn't movie-star handsome or gregarious. He was a recluse, a loner who hardly ever smiled, who intimidated people simply by walking into a room. For some unknown reason, Keely always knew when he was around, even if she didn't see him.

He was tall and slender, but he had powerful legs and big hands and feet. There were rumors about him that grew more exaggerated with the telling. He'd been in Special Forces overseas five years earlier. He'd saved his unit from certain destruction. He'd won medals. He'd had lunch with the president at the White House. He'd taken a cruise with a world-famous author. He'd almost married a European princess. And on and on and on.

Nobody knew the truth. Well, maybe Winona and Clark Sinclair did. Winnie and Clark and Boone were closer than brothers and sisters usually were. But Winnie didn't talk about her brother's private life, not even to Keely.

There hadn't been a day since she was thirteen when Keely hadn't loved Boone Sinclair. She watched him from a distance, her green eyes soft and covetous. Her hands would shake when she happened on him unexpectedly. They were shaking now. He was standing at the counter, signing in. He had an appointment for his dog's routine shots. He made one every year. He loved the old tan-and-black German shepherd, whose name was Bailey. People said it was the only thing on earth that he did love. Maybe he was fond of his siblings, but it didn't show. His affection for Bailey did.

One of the other vet techs came out with a pad and called in Bailey, with a grin at Boone. It wasn't returned. He led the old dog into one of the examination rooms. He walked right past Keely. He never looked at her. He didn't speak to her. As far as he was concerned, she was invisible.

She sighed as the door closed behind him and his dog. It was that way anyplace in town that he saw her. In fact, it was like that at his huge ranch near Comanche Wells, west of Jacobsville, Texas. He never told Winnie that she couldn't have Keely over for lunch or an occasional horseback ride. But he ignored her, just the same.

"It's funny, you know," Winnie had remarked one day when they were out riding. "I mean, Boone never makes any comment about you, but he does make a point of pretending he doesn't see you. I wonder why." She looked at Keely then, with her dark eyes mischievous in their frame of blond hair. "You wouldn't know, I guess?"

Keely only smiled. "I haven't got a clue," she said. It was the truth.

"It's only you, too," her friend continued thoughtfully. "He's very polite to our brother Clark's occasional date—even to that waitress that Clark brought home one night for dinner, and you know what a snob Boone can be. But he pretends you don't exist."

"I may remind him of somebody he doesn't like," Keely replied.

"There was that girl he was engaged to," Winnie said out of the blue.

Keely's heart jumped. "Yes, I remember when he was engaged," she replied. It had been when she was fourteen, almost fifteen years old, just before he came back from overseas. Keely's young heart had been broken.

"It was just before you came back here to live with your mom," Winnie continued as if she'd read Keely's mind. "In fact, it was just about the time she started drinking so much more..." She hesitated. Keely's mother was an alcoholic and it was a sensitive subject to her friend. "Anyway, Boone was mustering out of the Army at the time. His fiancée rushed to Germany where he'd been taken when he was airlifted out of combat, wounded, and then...poof. She was gone, Boone came home, and he never mentioned her name again. None of us could find out what happened."

"Somebody said she was European royalty," Keely ventured shyly.

"She was distantly related to some man who was knighted in England," came the sarcastic reply. "Anyway, she ran out on Boone and he was bitter for a long time. So three weeks ago the phone rings and he gets a call from her. She's been living with her father, who owns a private detective agency in San Antonio. She told Boone she'd made a terrible mistake and wanted to make up."

Keely's heart fell. A rival who had a history with Boone. It made her miserable just to think about it, despite the fact that she would never get close enough to Boone to give the other woman any competition. "Boone doesn't forgive people," she said, thinking aloud.

"That's right," Winnie replied, smiling. "But he's mellowed a bit. He takes her out on dates occasionally now. In fact, they're going to a Desperado concert next week."

Keely frowned. "He likes hard rock?" she asked, surprised. He looked so staid and dignified that she couldn't picture him at a rock concert. She said so.

Winnie laughed. "I can," she said. "He's not the conservative, quiet man he seems to be. Especially when he loses his temper or gets in an argument."

"Boone doesn't argue," Keely mused aloud.

He didn't. If he was angry enough, he punched. Never women, of course, but his men knew not to push him, especially if he was broody. One horse handler had found out the hard way that nobody made jokes at the boss's expense. Boone had been kicked by a horse, which the handler thought was hilarious. Boone roped the man, tied him to a post and anointed him with a bucket of recycled hay. All without saying a word.

Keely laughed out loud.

"What?" Winnie asked.

"I was remembering that horse wrangler…."

Winnie laughed, too. "He couldn't believe it, he said, even when it was happening. Boone really does look so straitlaced, as if he'd never stoop to dirty his hands. His cowboys used to underestimate him. Not anymore."

"The rattlesnake episode is noteworthy, as well," came the amused reply.

"That cook was so shocked!" Winnie blurted out. "He was a really rotten cook, but he threatened to sue Boone if he fired him, so it looked as if we were stuck with him. He'd threatened to cook Boone a rattler if he made any more remarks about the food. He added a few spicy comments about why Boone's fiancée took a powder. Then one morning he looks in his Dutch oven to see if it's clean enough to cook in, and a rattlesnake jumps up right into his face!"

"Lucky for the cook it didn't have any fangs."

"The cook didn't know that!" Winnie laughed. "He didn't know who did it, either. He resigned on the spot. The men actually cheered as he drove off. The next cook was talented, and the soul of politeness to my brother."

"I am not surprised."

She shook her head. "Boone does have these little quirks," his sister murmured. "Like never turning on the heat in his bedroom, even in icy weather, and always going around with his shirts buttoned to the neck."

"I've never seen him with his shirt off," Keely remarked. It was unusual, because most of the cowboys worked topless in summer heat when they were branding or doctoring cattle. But Boone never did.

"He used to be less prudish," Winnie said.

"Boone, prudish?" Keely sounded shocked.

Winnie glanced at her and chuckled. "Well, I guess that really doesn't fit at all."

"No, it doesn't."

Winnie pursed her lips. "Come to think of it, he's not the only prude around here. I've never even seen you in a T-shirt, Keely. You always wear long sleeves and high necklines."

Keely had a good reason for that, one she'd never shared with anyone. It was the reason she didn't date. It was a terrible secret. She would have died rather than tell Winnie, who might tell Boone....

"I was raised very strictly," Keely said quietly. And she had been; for all their odd tendencies, both her parents had insisted that Keely go to Sunday School and church every single Sunday. "My father didn't approve of clothing that was too flashy or revealing."

Probably because Keely's mother propositioned any man she fancied when she drank. She'd even tried to seduce Boone.

Keely didn't know that, and Winnie didn't know how to tell her. It was one reason for Boone's antagonism toward Keely.

Things would have been better if Keely knew where her father was. She'd told people she thought he was dead, because it was easier than admitting that he was an alcoholic, just like her mother, and linked up with a bunch of dangerous men. She'd missed her father at first. But she'd have been in more danger if she'd stayed with him.

She still loved him, in her way, despite what had happened to her.

"Come to think of it, Keely, you don't even date."

Keely shrugged. "I'm a vet tech. I have a busy life. I work on call, you know. If there's an emergency at midnight on a weekend, I still go to the office."

"That's a lot of hogwash," Winnie said gently as they paused to let the horses drink from one of the crystal-clear streams on the wooded property where they were riding. "I've even tried to set you up with nice men I know from work. You freeze when a man comes near you."

"That's because you work with the police, Winnie, and you bring cops home as prospective dates for me," Keely said mischievously. It was true. Winnie worked as a clerk in the Jacobsville Police Department's office during the day, and now she was doing a stint two nights a week as a dispatcher for the 911 center. In fact, she was hoping that job would work into something permanent, because being around Officer Kilraven all day when he was on the day shift was killing her.

"Policemen make me nervous," Keely was saying. "For all you know, I might have a criminal past."

Winnie wasn't smiling. She shook her head. "You're hiding something."

"Nothing major. Honest." What she suspected about her father, if true, would have shamed her. If Boone ever found out, she'd really die of shame. But she hadn't heard from her father since she was thirteen, so it wasn't likely that he'd just turn up someday with his new outlaw friends. She prayed that he wouldn't. Her mother's behavior was hard enough to live down as it was.

"There's this really handsome policeman who's been working with us for a few weeks. He's just your type."

"Kilraven," Keely guessed.

"Yes! How did you know?"

"Because you talk about him all the time," Keely returned. She pursed her lips. "Are you sure you aren't interested in him? I mean, you're single and eligible yourself."

Winnie flushed. "He's not my type."

"Why not?"

Winnie shifted in the saddle uneasily. "He told me he wasn't my type. He said I was too young to be mooning over a used-up lobo wolf like him and not to do it anymore."

Keely gasped out loud. "He didn't!"

The older girl nodded sadly. "He did. I didn't realize that I was so obvious with it. I mean, he's drop-dead gorgeous, most women look at him. He just noticed more when I did it. Because I'm who I am, I guess," she added darkly. "Boone might have said something to him. He's very protective of me. He thinks I'm too naive to be let loose on the world."

"In his defense, you have led a sheltered life," Keely said gently. "Kilraven is street smart. And he's dangerous."

"I know," Winnie muttered. "There have been times that he's been in situations where I sweat blood until he walks back into the station. He's noticed that, too. He didn't like it and he said so." She took a long, sad breath and looked at Keely. "So you can know all about my private agony, but you won't share yours? It's no use, Keely. I know."

Keely laughed nervously. "Know what? I don't keep secrets."

"Your whole life is a secret. But your biggest one is that you're in love with my brother."

Keely looked as if she'd been slapped.

"I would never tell him," Winnie said quietly. "That's the truth. I'm sorry for the way he treats you. I know how much it hurts."

Keely shifted her eyes, embarrassed.

"Don't be like that," Winnie said, her voice gentle. "I won't tell. Ever. Honest."

Keely relaxed. She drew in a breath, watching the creek bubble over rocks. "It doesn't hurt anything, what I feel. He'll never know. And it helps me to understand what it might be like to love a man—even if that love is never returned. It's a taste of something I can never have, that's all."

Winnie frowned. "What do you mean? Of course you'll be loved one day! Keely, you're only nineteen. Your whole life is ahead of you!"

Keely looked at her friend, and her dark eyes were soft and sad. "Not that way, it isn't. I won't ever marry."

"But one day…"

She shook her head. "No."

Winnie bit her lower lip. "When you're a little older, it might be different," she began. "Keely, you're nineteen. Boone is thirty. That's a big age difference, and he thinks about things like that. His fiancée was only a year younger than he was. He said that people should never marry unless they're the same age."

"Why?"

Winnie sighed. "I've never talked about it much, but our mother was twelve years younger than dad. He died a broken man because she ran away with his younger brother. He always said he made a major mistake by marrying someone from another generation. It was just too many years between them. They had nothing in common."

Keely felt heartsick for the family. "Is your mother still alive?"

She bit her lip. "We...don't know," she said. "We've never tried to find her or our uncle. They married, after the divorce, and moved to Montana. Neither one of them ever tried to contact us again."

"That's so sad."

"It made Boone bitter. Well, that and then his fiancée cutting out on him. He doesn't have a high opinion of women."

"You can't blame him, really," Keely had to admit. She patted her horse's neck. "It's sad, isn't it, that we're both too young for the men we care about?"

"Only in their minds," Winnie returned. "But we can always change their opinions. We just have to find an angle. One that works."

Keely laughed. "Doesn't that sound easy?"

Winnie grimaced. "Not really." She tugged on the reins, backing her horse out of the creek. Keely followed suit. "Let's talk about something more cheerful," Winnie said on the way back to the ranch. "Are you coming to the big charity dance?"

Keely shook her head. "I'd like to, even without a date, but both my junior bosses are going, and so is our senior tech. I have to be on call."

"That's awful!"

"It's fair, though. I was off last year."

"I remember. Last year you stayed home."

Keely studied the pommel as the leather squeaked under the steady motion of the horse's body. "Nobody asked me to go with them."

"You don't encourage men," Winnie pointed out.

Keely smiled sadly. "What for?" she asked. "Any man who asked me would have been second best. I don't want to get involved with anyone."

Winnie had always been curious about Keely's odd private

life. She wondered what had happened to the other woman to leave her so alone. "It's just a dance," she pointed out. "You don't have to agree to marry the man when he takes you home."

Keely burst out laughing. "You're terrible!" she choked.

"Just pointing out an obvious fact," came the amused reply.

"Anyway, I'll be working. You go and have enough fun for both of us."

"Any man who took me would be second choice, too," she reminded her friend. "The difference is, I want to go so I can rub my date in Kilraven's face."

"He won't go," Keely murmured.

"What makes you think so?"

"Just a guess. He keeps to himself. He reminds me of Cash Grier, the way he was before he married Tippy Moore. Grier was a bona fide woman hater. I think Kilraven is, too."

Winnie hesitated. "I wonder."

Keely didn't follow up on the remark. She felt sorry for Winnie. She felt sorry for herself, too. Men were such a headache….

She came back to the present in time to see Boone coming out of the examination room with Bailey on a leash. He walked right past Keely without looking at her or saying a word to her. She stared after him with her heart breaking right inside her chest. Then she turned and went back to work, putting on a happy face for the benefit of her coworkers.

Keely hated Boone's ex-fiancée on sight. Misty Harris's father ran a private detective agency in San Antonio, and she was wealthy. She was pretty, she was very intelligent and she looked down on other women. Boone, Winnie had told Keely, liked a woman with a good mind and an independent spirit. She also thought that the woman probably was good in bed, which made Keely uncomfortable.

The woman had a poisonous tongue, and she didn't like

Keely. It was obvious when she arrived for a date with Boone the next Friday night and found Keely sitting in the living room with Winnie.

"No dates?" she chided the other women, looking sleek in a black cocktail dress with her long black hair flowing over her shoulders. Her deep blue eyes were twinkling with malicious amusement. "Too bad. Boone's taking me to the Desperado concert. He's going to introduce me to the lead singer. We've had tickets for two months. It's going to be a great evening!"

"I love Desperado," Winnie had to agree.

"I wouldn't miss this concert for anything," the brunette purred.

There was a noise at the side door, scratching and howling.

"Oh, it's that dog," the brunette muttered. "He's filthy. For God's sake, Winnie, you aren't going to let him in? The Persian rugs are priceless! He'll get mud all over them!"

"Bailey is a member of the family," Winnie said icily as she opened the door and pulled a towel from a shelf nearby. "Hello, old fellow!" she greeted the old German shepherd. "Did you get wet?"

She started toweling him dry and wiping his paws. He was panting and whining. His tongue was purple. He shuddered. His stomach was swollen.

With a practiced eye, Keely observed him. Something was wrong. She got up and joined Winnie at the sliding glass door, going down on one knee. Her hands touched the dog's distended belly.

She clenched her teeth. "He's got bloat," she told Winnie.

"What was that?" Boone asked, taking the steps two at a time.

Keely looked up at him, trying not to betray her pleasure at just the sight of him. "Bailey's got bloat. He needs to be seen by a vet right now."

"Don't be absurd," Boone shot back. "Dogs don't get bloat."

"Big dogs do," Keely said urgently. "You must have seen the condition in cattle at one time or another. Here. Feel!"

She grabbed his hand and carried it to the dog's belly.

He felt it and scowled.

"Look at the color of his tongue," Keely persisted. "He isn't getting enough oxygen. If you don't get him to the vet soon, he'll be dead."

"Oh, that's ridiculous," the brunette spat. "He's just eaten too much. Put him in his kennel. He'll be fine by morning."

"He'll be dead," Keely repeated flatly.

"Listen, you, I'm not missing that concert for a stupid old dog with an upset stomach!" the brunette raged. "You're just trying to get Boone to notice you by telling him something's wrong with that dog! He knows what a crush you have on him. This is a pathetic act!"

Boone looked at Keely, who was pale and sick at heart to have her innermost secret spoken aloud for Boone to hear.

He ran his hand over Bailey's stomach one last time. "It's not bloat," he pronounced. "He's just had too much to eat and he's got gas." He got to his feet, patting the old dog on the head, smiling. "You'll be fine, won't you, old man?"

Keely glared at him. The dog was still panting and now he was whimpering loudly.

"He's not your dog," Boone shot at her. "Misty's right. This is a bid for attention, just like old Bailey whining so that I'll pet him. But it won't work. I'm taking Misty to the concert."

Keely was so infuriated that she wouldn't even look at him. Bailey was dying.

"Let's go," Boone told Misty.

He didn't speak to Keely again, or to Winnie. He and his date walked back to the garage. Minutes later, his car roared out down the driveway.

"What are we going to do?" Winnie asked, because she believed her best friend.

"We can let him die or take him to the vet," Keely said curtly.

"Who's driving?" was all the other woman asked.

The oldest of the three vets, Bentley Rydel, and the owner of the clinic, was on call. He was the best surgeon of the group. At thirty-two, he was the only unmarried one. People said it was because he was so antagonistic that no woman could get near him. It was probably the truth.

He helped Keely get Bailey into the X-ray room and onto the table. She held him while the X-rays were taken, petting him and talking soothingly to him. For a man who resembled nothing more than a human pit viper with other members of his own species, he was the soul of compassion with animals.

He and Winnie were back in ten minutes with the X-rays. He looked somber as he showed them the proof that Bailey's stomach had turned over. "It's a complicated and expensive procedure, and I can't promise you that it will succeed. If I don't operate, the necrosis will spread and he'll die. He may die anyway. You have to make a decision."

"He's my brother's dog," Winnie said uneasily, petting the whimpering old animal.

"Your brother will have to give consent."

"He won't," Keely said miserably. "He doesn't think it's bloat."

Bentley's eyebrows arched. "And what veterinary school did he graduate from?"

Winnie's phone playing the theme from *Star Wars* interrupted the conversation. She answered it nervously. She'd recognized Boone's number on the caller ID screen.

"It's Boone!" she whispered with her hand over the phone. She grimaced. "Hello?" she said hesitantly.

"Where the hell is my dog?" he demanded.

Winnie took a deep breath. "Boone, we brought Bailey here to the vet..."

"*We?* Keely's mixed up in this, isn't she?" he demanded, outraged.

The vet, seeing Winnie's pained expression, held out his hand for the phone. Winnie gave it to him gladly.

"This animal," the vet began firmly, "has a severe case of bloat. I can show you on the X-rays where necrosis of tissue has already begun. If I don't operate, he will be dead in an hour. The decision is yours, but I urge you to make it quickly."

Boone hesitated. "Will he live?"

"I can't promise you that," Bentley said curtly. "He should have been brought in when the symptoms first presented. The delay has complicated the procedure. This conversation," he added acidly, "is another delay."

The curse was audible two feet from the cell phone. "Do it," Boone said. "I'll give you permission. My sister can be your witness. Do what you can. Please."

"Certainly I will." He handed the phone to Winnie. "Keely, we need to prep him for surgery."

"Yes, sir." Keely was smiling. Her boss was a great negotiator. Now, at least Bailey had a chance, no thanks to the heartless woman who'd have sacrificed his life for a concert ticket.

The operation took two hours. Keely stood gowned beside the vet, administering anesthetic to the dog and checking his vital signs constantly. There was only a small amount of dead tissue, luckily, and she watched Bentley's skillful hands cut it away efficiently.

"What was the delay?" he asked her.

She clenched her teeth. "Concert tickets for Desperado. Boone's date didn't want to miss it."

"So she decided that Bailey should die."

She grimaced. "I'm not sure she was being deliberately cold-hearted."

"You'd be surprised at how many people consider animals inanimate objects with no feelings. Old-timers come in sometimes and tell me in all seriousness that no animal feels pain."

"Baloney," she muttered.

He laughed shortly. "My opinion exactly."

"How's he doing?" she asked.

He nodded as he worked. "All right. There are no complications to worry about. I operated on Tom Walker's Shiloh shepherd for this about two months ago, remember, and he had a tumor the size of my fist. We lost him despite the timely intervention."

"We aren't going to lose Bailey?" she asked worriedly.

"Not a chance. He's old, but he's a fighter."

She smiled. Even if Boone gave her hell, it would be worth it. She was fond of the old dog, too, even if Boone felt she was using his pet. It made her furious that Boone believed that heartless brunette. Keely wasn't stupid enough to think that such a play would work on a man with a head like a steel block. Boone wouldn't care if she was Helen of Troy, he'd walk right by her without looking. She knew better than to try to chase him. She was amazed that he didn't realize that.

"Done," Bentley announced finally when the last suture was in place. Keely took away the anesthetic and waited while the vet examined the old dog. "I think he'll do, but don't quote me. We'll know in the morning."

"Yes, sir."

"I'll carry him in for you," he volunteered, because the dog was very heavy and Keely had problems carrying weight.

"You don't have to," she began self-consciously.

His pale blue eyes were kind as they met hers. "You've had some sort of injury to your left shoulder. I don't have to see it to know it's there. It won't let you bear weight."

She grimaced. "I didn't realize it was so obvious."

"I won't give you away," he said with a smile. "But I won't make you carry loads too heavy, either."

"Thanks, boss," she said, smiling back.

He shrugged. "You're the hardest worker I've got." He seemed self-conscious after he said that, and he made a big production of lifting Bailey, very carefully, to one of the recovery cages where he'd be kept and monitored until he came out from under the anesthetic.

"I can stay and watch him," she began.

He shook his head. "I had a call on my cell phone while we were prepping Bailey," he reminded her. "There's a heifer calving over at Cy Parks's place. She's having a hard time. It's one of his purebred herd and he wants me there to make sure the calf is born alive."

"So you have to go out there."

He nodded. "I'll check on Bailey when I get back. It's Friday night," he added with a faint smile. "Usually we get emergency cases all night, you know."

"Want me to stay and answer the phone?" she asked.

He studied her quizzically. "It's Friday night," he repeated. "Why don't you have a date?"

She shrugged. "Men hate me. If you don't believe that, just ask Boone Sinclair."

He looked over her shoulder and his eyebrows lifted as a door opened. "Speak of the devil," he said in a voice that didn't carry over Winnie's greeting to her brother.

CHAPTER TWO

Boone stalked into the room where Keely and Bentley were standing together beside the recovery cage, which contained Bailey. He didn't look very belligerent now, and his concern for the old dog was evident as he knelt beside the cage and touched the head of the sleeping animal gently with his fingertips.

"Will he live?" he asked without looking up.

"We'll know that in the morning," Bentley said curtly. "He came through the surgery very well, and I didn't find anything that would complicate his recovery. For an animal his age, he's in excellent shape."

Boone stood up, facing the vet. "Thank you."

"Thank Keely," came the short reply. "She ignored your suggestion to leave the animal alone until morning. At which time," the vet added with a glitter in his eyes, "you'd have found him dead."

Boone's own eyes flashed. "I thought he was trying to get attention. Like Keely," he added with icy sarcasm.

Bentley's eyebrows lifted. "Do you really think Keely needs to beg any man for attention?" he asked, as if the remark was incredible to him.

Boone stiffened. "Her social life is not my concern. I'm grateful to you for saving Bailey."

"We'll know how successful I was in the morning," Bentley replied. "Keely, can you get my medical bag for me, please?"

"Yes, sir." She left the room, glad for something that would take her out of Boone's immediate presence.

Boone glanced again at the cage. "He and I have been through some hard times together," he told the vet. "If I'd realized how dangerous his condition was, I'd never have left him." He looked at Bentley. "I didn't know that dogs got bloat."

"Now you do," the vet replied. "Most large dogs are at risk for it."

"What causes it?"

Bentley shook his head. "We don't know. There are half a dozen theories, but no definite answers."

"What did you do?"

"I excised the dead tissue and tacked his stomach to his backbone," Bentley replied quietly. "I'll prescribe a special diet for him. For the next couple of days, of course, he'll get fluids."

"You'll let me know?" Boone added slowly.

Bentley recognized the worry in those dark eyes. "Of course."

Boone turned to Winnie. His eyes were accusing.

She grimaced. "Now, listen, Keely knows what she's doing, whatever you think," she began defensively. "I agreed with her and I'll take full responsibility for bringing Bailey over here."

"I'm not complaining," he said. His stern expression lightened. He bent and brushed an affectionate kiss onto Winnie's forehead. "Thanks."

She smiled, relieved that he wasn't angry. "I love old Bailey, too."

Keely came back with the medical bag and handed it to Bentley. She was holding his old raincoat, as well.

"I hate raincoats," he began angrily.

She just held it up. He grimaced, but he slid his long arms into it and pulled it up. "Worrywart," he muttered.

"You got pneumonia the last time you went out into a cold rain," she reminded him.

He turned and smiled down at her; actually, it was more of a faint turning up of one side of his mouth. Bentley Rydel never smiled. "Go home," he said.

She shook her head. "I won't leave Bailey until I'm sure he's out from under the anesthesia," she said, and she didn't look at Boone. "Besides, you're sure to have at least one emergency call waiting for you when you get back."

"I don't pay you enough for all this overtime," he pointed out.

She shrugged. "So I'll never get rich." She grinned.

He sighed. "Okay. I'm on my cell phone, if you need me."

"Drive carefully."

He made a face at her. But his expression was staid and impassive as he nodded to the Sinclairs on his way out.

Boone was glaring at Keely. She averted her eyes and went back to Bailey's cage to check on him.

"We should go," Winnie told her brother. "See you later, Keely."

Keely nodded. She didn't look at them.

Boone hesitated uncharacteristically, but he didn't speak. He took Winnie's arm and led her out the door.

"You couldn't even say thanks to Keely for saving Bailey's life?" she chided as they paused beside their respective vehicles.

He looked down at her coldly in the misty rain. "I could sue her for bringing Bailey here without permission."

Winnie was shocked. "She saved his life!"

He avoided her gaze. "That's beside the point. Let's go. We're getting wet."

"What about your concert?" Winnie asked, and there was a faint bite in her tone.

"It's not over. I'm going back."

She wanted to say that his ex-fiancée wasn't going to be pleased that he'd deserted her, even for a few minutes. But she didn't say it. He was obviously out of humor, and it was never wise to push him.

Keely stayed with Bailey until he came to and Bentley returned from his call. There was a new emergency, a woman whose champion English springer spaniel was whelping and one of the puppies wouldn't emerge. Once again, they had to do an emergency surgery to save mother and child.

It was two in the morning before they finished and Keely cleaned up. "Now go home," Bentley said gently.

"I'll have to." She laughed. "I can't keep my eyes open."

"No matter what Boone Sinclair says," he told her, "you did the right thing." He glanced at Bailey, who was now sleeping peacefully thanks to a painkiller. "I think he'll do."

She smiled. Even though Boone had been a pain in the neck, he did love the old dog. She was glad that he wouldn't have to give up his companion just yet.

She went home, tiptoeing past her mother's room, and went to bed.

The next day, she worked until noon and then went home to do all the housework that her mother never bothered with. She finished just in time to start supper. By then, her mother was finishing the second whiskey highball and her best friend, Carly, had shown up for supper. Keely, who'd prepared enough just for her mother and herself, had to add potatoes and carrots to her stew to stretch it out. The grocery budget was meager. It took second place to the liquor budget.

It was the same every Saturday night that she was home, Keely thought miserably, hiding her discomfort while she served up a light supper in the dining room. Her mother, Ella, already drunk, was making fun of Keely's conservative clothing while her best friend, Carly, added her own sarcastic comments to the mix. Both women were in their forties, and highly unconventional. Carly was no beauty, but Ella was. Ella had a lovely face and a good figure, and she used both to good advantage. A list of her past lovers, despite her substance abuse problem, would fill a small notebook. The mischief she caused was one of her favorite sources of amusement. Next to ridiculing Keely, that was. She and Carly considered virtue obsolete. No man, they emphasized, wanted an innocent woman these days. Virginity was a liability to a single woman.

"All you need is a man, Keely." Carly Blair giggled, hoisting a potent Turkish cigarette to her too-red lips. "A few nights in the sack with an experienced man would take that prudish pout out of your lips."

"You need to wear makeup," her mother added, in between sips of her third whiskey highball. "And buy some clothes that don't look like they came out of a mission thrift shop."

Keely would have reminded them that she worked with animals in a veterinary clinic, not in an exclusive boutique, and that men were thin on the ground. But it only amused them more if she fought back. She'd learned to keep her head down when she was under fire.

The beef stew she'd had cooking all day in her Crock-Pot was fragrant and thick. She'd made yeast rolls to go with it, and a simple pound cake for dessert. Her efforts were unappreciated. The women hardly noticed what they were eating as they gossiped about a woman they knew in town who was having an affair. Their comments were earthy and embarrassing to Keely.

They knew that, of course; it was why they did it. What the

two women didn't know was that Keely couldn't sustain a relationship with a boyfriend, much less a lover. She had a secret that she'd never shared with anyone except the doctor who had treated her. It would keep her alone for the rest of her life. She'd made sure that her mother didn't know what she was hiding. The older woman was bitter and miserable and she loved making a victim of her daughter. Keely's secret would have been more fodder for her attacks. So Keely kept a good distance between herself and her coldhearted parent.

She wondered often what had become of her father. She'd loved him very much, and she'd thought that he loved her. But he hadn't been the same since he'd lost his game park. He'd turned to alcohol and then drugs to numb the pain and disappointment. He'd had no way to support himself, much less an adolescent daughter. He'd had to leave her with her mother. She'd done her best to make him let her stay, offering to get a job after school, anything! But he'd said that she needed security while she was growing up, and he could no longer provide it. Her mother wasn't such a bad person, he'd said. Keely knew better, but she couldn't change her father's mind, so she rationalized that he'd probably forgotten what a cruel woman Ella could be. Besides that, she was terrified of his new friends; especially one of them, who'd slapped her around.

Ella owned land that she'd inherited, along with a sizable amount of money from her late parents. She'd loaned her husband the money for his game park to get him out of her life, Ella said. She'd quickly gone through the money she'd inherited, spending it on luxurious vacations, fancy cars and a mansion while Keely was living in meager circumstances with her father. But her mother's wealth or lack of it was no concern to Keely. As soon as she was settled comfortably in her job, she was going to get another part-time job so that she could afford to move into a boardinghouse. She'd had all she could take of living here.

Her father had just left her on Ella's front porch, crying and still pleading to go with him. Ella hadn't been happy to find the adolescent back in her life, but she took her in, at least. At the age of thirteen, Keely had settled down slowly with the mother she barely remembered from childhood, who proceeded to make her life a misery.

"Boone Sinclair is dating that ex-fiancée of his who threw him over when he got out of the Army," Carly Blair drawled, with a quick glance at Keely.

"Is he?" Ella looked at Keely, too. "Have you seen her?" she asked, because she knew that her daughter was friendly with Clark and Winnie Sinclair. "What does the woman look like?"

"She's very pretty," Keely replied calmly between bites of stew. "Long black hair and dark blue eyes."

"Very pretty." Ella laughed. "Nothing like you, Keely, right? You look like your father. I wanted a beautiful little girl who looked like me." She wrinkled her nose. "What a disappointment you turned out to be."

"We can't all be beautiful, Mother," Keely replied. "I'd rather be smart."

"If you were smart, you'd go to college and get a better job," Ella retorted. "Working as a technician for a veterinarian," she added haughtily. "What a vulgar sort of job."

"The senior veterinarian where Keely works is very good-looking," Carly interrupted, shifting in her chair. She chuckled. "I tried to get him to take me out, but he gave me an icy glare and went back into his office." She shrugged. "I guess he's got a girlfriend somewhere."

Keely was surprised at the remark. Carly was in her mid-forties and Bentley Rydel was only thirty-two years old. Bentley had mentioned, only once, that he couldn't stand Carly. He probably didn't like Keely's mother, either, but he was too polite to say so. Not that they had pets that would need his services. Ella hated animals.

"Keely's boss is a cold fish, like Boone Sinclair," Ella said. She leaned back in her chair and studied her daughter with a cold expression. "You'll never get anywhere with that man, you know," she added in a slow drawl. "He may take his ex-fiancée around with him, but he's no passionate lover."

"How would you know?" Keely returned, stung by the comment and the way her mother aimed it at her.

Ella smiled mockingly. "Because I tried to seduce him myself, on more than one occasion," she said, enjoying the look of horror on her daughter's face. "He's ice-cold. He doesn't respond normally to women, not even when they come on to him physically. No matter what people say about his hot relationship with his ex-fiancée, I can assure you that he isn't all that responsive to women."

"Maybe he just doesn't like older women," Keely muttered icily, her eyes sparkling with temper as she pictured her mother using her wiles on Boone.

A cruel look passed over Ella's face. "Well, he certainly doesn't like you," she retorted with deliberate sarcasm. "I told him you're hot for your veterinarian boss and sleeping with him on the side."

Keely was horrified. "What!" she burst out. "But, why?"

Ella laughed at her expression. "I wanted to see what he'd say," she mused. "It was a disappointment. He didn't react at all. So I asked him if he hadn't noticed what a nice figure you've got, even if you aren't pretty, and he said he didn't feel attracted to children."

Children. Keely was nineteen. That wasn't childish. She didn't think of herself as a child. But Boone did…

"Then I said that you might look like a child, but you knew

what to do with a man, and he just walked away," Ella continued. She saw Keely's stricken expression. "So I suppose your little fantasy of love isn't going to be fulfilled." Her face took on a wicked cast. "I did mention in the course of conversation, before he left so rudely, that you had a crush on him and he could probably cut you out with your boss if he tried. He said that you were the last woman on earth he'd want."

Keely wanted to sink through the floor. Some of Boone's antagonistic behavior began to make sense. Her mother was feeding him lies about Keely, and he was swallowing them whole. She wondered how long Ella had been doing it, and if it was revenge because Boone wouldn't touch her. Maybe she saw Keely as a rival and wanted to make sure there was no chance that Boone would weaken toward her daughter. Either way, it was devastating to the younger woman. She left the rest of her food untouched. She couldn't choke down another bite.

"You might get somewhere with him if you stopped dressing out of thrift shops and wore a little makeup," Ella chided.

"On my salary, all I can afford are clothes from thrift shops," Keely said.

There was a hot silence. "Is that a dig at me?" Ella demanded, eyes flashing. "Because I give you a roof over your head and food to eat," she added curtly. "You only have to do a little cooking and housework from time to time to earn your keep. That's more than fair. I'm not obligated to dress you, as well!"

"I never said you were, Mother," Keely replied.

"Don't call me 'Mother'!" Ella shot back, weaving a little in her chair. "I never wanted you in the first place. Your father was hot to have a son. He was disappointed when you turned out to be a girl, and I refused to get pregnant again. It ruined my waistline! It took me years to get my figure back!

"I wanted to give you up for adoption when you were eleven and your father divorced me, but he said he'd take you if I'd loan him enough money to open that game park. So I loaned him the money—which he never repaid, by the way—and he took you off my hands. He didn't want you, either, Keely," she added with a drunken smile. "Nobody wanted you. And nobody wants you now."

"Ella," Carly interrupted uneasily, "that's harsh." Keely's face was as white as flour.

Ella blinked, as if she wasn't quite aware of what she was saying. She stared blankly at Carly. "What's harsh?"

Carly winced as Keely got to her feet and began clearing the table without saying a word.

She carried empty plates into the kitchen, trying desperately not to let the women see her cry. Behind her, she heard murmuring, which grew louder, and then her mother's voice arguing. She went out into the cold night air in her shirtsleeves, tears pouring down her cheeks. She wrapped her arms around herself and walked to the front yard, stopping at the railing that looked out over Comanche Wells, at the rolling pastureland and little oasis of deciduous trees that shaded the fenced land where purebred cattle grazed. It was a beautiful sight, with the air crisp and the moon shining on the leaves on the big oak tree that stood in the front yard, making it look as if the leaves had been painted silver. But Keely was blind to the beauty of it. She was sick to her stomach.

She heard the phone ring in the house, but she ignored it. First Boone's fierce antagonism and the argument over Bailey and the ex-fiancée's taunts the night before, and then her mother's horrible assertions tonight. It was the worst two days of Keely's recent life. She didn't want to go back in. She wanted to stay out in the cold until she froze to death and the pain stopped.

"Keely?" Carly called from the back door. "It's Clark Sinclair. He wants to speak to you."

Keely hesitated for a moment. She turned and went back inside without meeting Carly's eyes or looking toward the dining room where her mother sat finishing her drink.

She picked up the phone and said "Hello?" in a subdued tone.

"The old girl's giving you hell, is she?" Clark mused. "How about going out? I know it's late notice, but I just got in from Jacksonville and I want to talk to somebody. Winnie's working late at dispatch, and God knows where Boone's off to. How about it?"

"Oh, I'd really like that," Keely said fervently.

"Need an escape plan, do we? I'll be there in ten minutes."

"I'll be ready. I'll wait for you on the front porch."

"God, it must be bad over there tonight!" he exclaimed. "I'll hurry, so you don't catch cold." He hung up. So did Keely.

"Got a date?" Ella drawled, coming to the doorway in a zigzag with her highball glass still in her hands. It was empty now. "Who's taking you someplace?"

Keely didn't answer her. She went down the hall to her room and closed and locked the door behind her.

"I told you it was a mistake to tell her that," Carly said plaintively. "You'll be sorry tomorrow when you sober up."

"Mistake to tell her what?" Ella muttered. "I need another drink."

"No. You need to go to bed and sleep it off. Come on." Carly led her down the hall to her own bedroom, pushed her inside and closed the door behind them. "How could you tell her that, Ella?" she asked softly as she helped her friend down onto the big double bed with its expensive pink comforter.

"I don't care," Ella said defiantly. "She's in my way. I don't want her here. I never did."

"She does all the housework and all the cooking," Carly said in one of her rare moments of compassion. "She works all day and sometimes half the night for her boss, and then she comes home and works like a housekeeper. You don't appreciate how much she does for you."

"I could hire somebody to do all that." Ella waved the idea away.

"Could you afford to pay them?" Carly retorted.

Ella frowned. She was hard put just to pay utilities and buy groceries. But she didn't reply.

Carly eyed her quietly. "If you push her, she'll leave. Then what will you do?"

"I'll do my own housework and cooking," Ella said grandly.

Carly shook her head. "Okay. It's your life. But you're missing out."

"On what?" Ella muttered.

"On the only family you have," Carly replied in a subdued tone. "I don't have anybody," she added. "My parents are dead. I had no siblings. I was married, but I was never able to have a child. My husband is dead, too. You have a child, and you don't want her. I'd have given anything to have a child of my own."

"You can have Keely," Ella said, laughing. "I'll give her to you."

Carly moved toward the door. "You can't give people away, Ella." She looked back. "You don't really have anybody, either."

"I have men." Ella laughed coldly. "I can have any man I want."

"For a night," her friend agreed. "Old age is coming up fast, for both of us. Do you really want to drive your only child away? She'll marry someday and have children of her own. You won't even be allowed to see your grandchildren."

"I'm not having grandchildren," Ella shot back. "I'm not going to be old. I'm only in my late thirties!"

Carly laughed. "You're heading toward fifty, Ella," she reminded her friend. "All the beauty treatments in the world aren't going to change that."

"I'll have a face-lift," the other woman returned. "I'll sell more land to pay for it."

That was unwise. Ella had already sold most of the land her family had left her. If she sold the rest, she was going to be hard-pressed just to pay bills. But Carly could see that it did no good to argue with her.

"Good night," she told Ella.

Ella made a face at her, collapsed on the pillow and was asleep in seconds. Carly didn't say anything else. She just closed the door.

Keely put on a pair of brown corduroy slacks and a beige turtleneck sweater and ran a brush through her thick, straight blond hair. She hoped Clark didn't have an expensive date in mind. She couldn't dress for it. She threw an old beige Berber coat over her clothes and grabbed her purse.

True to his word, Clark pulled up in the yard in exactly ten minutes, driving his sports car.

Carly came out of Ella's bedroom just as Keely was leaving.

"Is she asleep?" Keely asked dully.

"Yes." Carly was worried, and it showed. "She should never have said that to you," she added. "She loved you when you were a baby. You wouldn't remember, you were too little, but I do. She was so happy..."

"So happy that she now treats me this way?" Keely asked, hurt.

Carly sighed. "She was different after your father left. She started drinking then, and it's just gotten worse year after year." She saw that she wasn't getting through to the younger woman. "There are things you don't know about your parents, Keely," she said gently.

"Such as?"

Carly shook her head. "That's not my place to tell you." She turned away. "I'm going home. She'll sleep until morning."

"Lock the door when you leave, please," Keely said.

"I'm leaving now. You can lock it." Carly got her purse and stopped just as the door closed behind the two women.

"I'm as bad as she is, sometimes," the older woman confessed quietly. "I shouldn't make fun of the way you are, and neither should she. But you don't fight back, Keely. You must learn to do that. You're nineteen. Don't spend the rest of your life knuckling under, just to keep peace."

Keely frowned. "I don't."

"You do, baby," Carly said softly. She sighed. "Ella and I are a bad influence on you. What you need to do is get an apartment of your own and live your own life."

Keely searched the other woman's eyes. "I've thought about that...."

"Do it," Carly advised. "Get out while you can."

Keely frowned. "What do you mean?"

Carly hesitated. "I've said too much already. Enjoy your date. Good night."

Carly walked off to her small import car. Keely watched her for a minute before she went down the steps to where Clark was waiting in his sleek Lincoln. He leaned across and opened the door for her.

He grinned. "I'd come around and open it, but I'm too lazy," he teased.

She smiled back. He was like a kinder version of Boone. Clark had the same black hair and dark eyes, but he was a little shorter than his brother, and his hair was wavy—unlike Boone's, which was straight.

"Neither one of you resemble your sister," she remarked.

He shrugged. "Winnie got our mother's coloring. She doesn't like that. We hated our mother."

"So Winnie said."

He glanced at her as they pulled out of her mother's yard. "We share the feeling, don't we, Keely?" he probed. "Your mother is a walking headache."

She nodded. "She was in high form tonight," she said wearily. "Drunk and vicious."

"What was Carly saying to you?"

"That I have to learn to stand up to her," she said. "Surprising, isn't it, coming from Mother's best friend? The two of them make fun of me all the time."

Clark glanced at her, and he didn't smile. "She's right about that. You need to stand up to my brother, too. Boone walks all over people who won't fight back."

She shivered. "I'm not taking on your brother," she said. "He's scary."

"Scary? Boone?"

She averted her gaze to the window. "Can't we talk about something else?"

He was disconcerted by her remark, but he pulled himself together quickly. "Sure! I just heard that the Chinese are launching another probe toward the moon."

She gave him a wry look.

"You don't like astronautics," he murmured. "Okay. Politics?"

She groaned out loud. "I'm so sick of presidential candidates that I'm thinking of moving to someplace where nobody runs for public office."

"The Amazon jungle comes to mind."

Her eyes narrowed. "If I went far enough in, I might escape television and the internet."

"I can see the headlines now," he said with mock horror.

"Local vet technician eaten by jaguar in darkest jungles of South America!"

"No self-respecting jaguar would want to eat a human being," she retorted. "Especially one who eats anchovies on pizza."

"I didn't know you liked anchovies."

She sighed. "I don't. But when I was little, I discovered that if I ordered them, my dad would let me have more than two slices of pizza."

He laughed. "Your father must have been a card."

"He was." She smiled reminiscently. "Animals loved him. I've seen him feed tigers right out of his hand without ever being bitten. Even snakes liked him."

"That animal park must have been something else."

"It was wonderful," she replied. "We all loved it. But there was a tragic accident, and Dad lost everything."

"Somebody got eaten?"

"Almost," she replied, unwilling to say more. "There was a lawsuit."

"And he lost," he guessed.

She didn't correct him. "It destroyed him."

He frowned. "Did he commit suicide?"

She hesitated. This was Clark. He was her friend. She knew that he'd never tell Boone or even Winnie without asking her first. "He's not dead," she said quietly. "I don't know where he is or what he's doing. He developed a…a drinking problem." She couldn't tell him the whole truth. She glanced at him worriedly. "You won't tell anybody?"

"Of course not."

She studied her purse in her lap, turning it restlessly in her hands. "He left me with Mother and took off. That was six years ago, and I haven't heard a word from him. For all I know, he could be dead."

"You loved him."

She nodded. "Very much." She moved restlessly.

"What is it?"

She felt the pain of her mother's words go right through her. "My mother said that she never wanted me. I ruined her figure," she added with a hollow laugh.

"Good God! And I thought our mother was bad!" He stopped at a traffic light heading into Jacobsville and looked toward her. "Isn't it a hell of a shame that we can't choose our parents?"

"Yes, it is," she agreed. "I was just sick when she said it. I should have guessed. She didn't like me when I left, and she liked me even less when Dad dumped me on her, and now I think she hates me. I've tried to please her, keeping house and cooking and cleaning, but she doesn't appreciate it. She grudges me the very food I eat." She turned toward him. "I've got to get out of that house," she said desperately. "I can't take it anymore."

"Mrs. Brown runs a very respectable boardinghouse," he began.

She grimaced. "Yes, and charges a respectable price for rooms. I can't afford it on my salary."

"Hit Bentley up for a raise," he suggested.

"Oh, right, I'll do that first thing tomorrow," she drawled.

"You're scared of Bentley. You're scared of Boone." He pulled out into traffic. "You're even scared of your mother. You have to step up and claim your own life, Keely."

"What do you mean?"

"You can't go through life being afraid of people. Especially people like my brother and Bentley Rydel. Do you know why they're scary?" he persisted. "It's because it's hard work to talk to them. They're both basically introverts who find it difficult to relate to other people. Consequently they're quiet and somber and they don't go out of their way to join in activities. They're loners."

She sighed. "I'm a loner, too, in my own way. But I don't stand on the sidelines and glare at people all the time—or, worse, pretend they're not there."

"Is that Boone's latest tactic?" he mused, chuckling. "He ignores you, does he?"

"He did until I argued about Bailey's condition."

"Thank God you did," he said fervently. "Bailey belongs to Boone, but we all love the old fellow. I'll never understand why Boone didn't realize what had happened to him. He's a cattleman—he's seen bloat before."

"His girlfriend convinced him that I was trying to get attention, using Bailey to lure Boone to my place of work."

"Oh, for heaven's sake!" he burst out. "Boone's not that stupid!"

"Well, apparently my mother's been telling him that I have a crush on him, and now he thinks everything I do or say is an attempt to worm my way into his life," she said bitterly.

"Ella told him that?" he exclaimed.

"Yes. And she told him that I'm sleeping with Bentley."

"Does Bentley know that you're sleeping with him?" he asked innocently.

She laughed. "I don't know. I'll ask him."

He burst out laughing, too. "That's more like it, kid," he said. "You have to learn to roll with the punches and not take life so seriously."

"It feels pretty serious to me lately," she replied. "I feel like I've hit a wall tonight."

"You should push your mother into one," he told her. "Or better yet, tell her what a lousy mother she's been."

"She doesn't listen when she's drunk, and she's mostly away from home when she's sober." She pursed her lips. "I work for veterinarians. I've been professionally taught to let sleeping dogs lie."

He smiled. "Have you, now?"

"Where are you taking me?" she asked when he took a state highway instead of the Jacobsville road. "I thought we were going to a movie."

"I'm not in the mood for a movie. I thought we might go to San Antonio for shrimp," he replied. "I'm in the mood for some. What do you think?"

"We'll be very late getting back," she reminded him worriedly.

"What the hell," he scoffed. "You can tell your mother you're sleeping with me now instead of Bentley and she can mind her own business about when you come home."

Her eyes almost popped.

He saw that and grinned. "Which brings to mind a matter I need a little help with. I think," he added, "that you and I can be the solution for each other's problems. If you're game."

All the way to San Antonio, she wondered what he meant, and how she would fit into his "solution."

CHAPTER THREE

The restaurant Clark took Keely to was one of the most exclusive in town, famous for its seafood. Keely was worried that she was dressed too casually for such a grand place, but she saw people dressed up and dressed down for the evening out. She relaxed and followed Clark and the hostess to a corner table. They were seated and provided with menus. Keely had to bite her tongue at the prices. Any one of these dishes would have equaled a day's salary. But Clark just gave her a grin and told her to order what she wanted. They were celebrating. She wondered what they were celebrating, but he wouldn't say.

Keely had eaten earlier, so she just had a very light meal. After she'd finished, she wondered if it was really the food that drew him here. He couldn't take his eyes off the waitress who took their orders. And the waitress blushed prettily when he stared at her.

"Do you know her?" Keely asked softly when the waitress went to turn in their orders.

"Yes," he said, grimacing. "I'm in love with her."

Immediately Keely recalled Boone's attitude toward his siblings becoming involved with someone from a lower economic class. He'd been vocal about it in the past. The look on Clark's face was painful to see. She knew without asking that he was seeing the hopelessness of his own situation vividly.

"Is she the one you took to supper at the ranch?" she asked, remembering something she'd heard from Winnie.

He nodded. "Boone was polite to her, but later he asked me if I was out of my mind. He sees all working women as gold diggers who can't wait to marry me and then divorce me for a big settlement."

"Not all women want money," she pointed out.

"Tell Boone. He doesn't know."

"That woman he goes out with seems to be obsessed with it," Keely muttered.

"She doesn't count, because she's rich in her own right."

"Yes. She's beautiful, too," she added with more bitterness than she realized.

He studied her across the white tablecloth with its fresh flowers, candles and silverware. "Think about it—would a man like Boone stick his head into the same noose he escaped once? That woman walked away from him when he was lying in a hospital with shrapnel wounds that could have killed him. She didn't like hospitals. She thought he might be crippled, so she gave him back his ring. Now she's in San Antonio and wants to go back to where they started. How do you think Boone feels about that?"

For the first time, she felt a glimmer of hope. "Your brother doesn't forgive people," she said softly. It was what she'd said once to Winnie.

"Exactly. Much less people who stick pins in his pride."

"Then why is he taking her around with him?" Keely wanted to know.

He shrugged. "She's beautiful and she has polished manners. Maybe he's just lonely and he wants a showpiece on his arm. Or," he added slowly, "maybe he has something in mind that she isn't expecting. She wants to marry him again. But I don't think he wants to marry her. And I think he's got a good reason for going out with her at all."

"God knows what it is," Keely murmured.

"God does know. He probably doesn't like it, either."

"You think Boone is working on revenge?"

"Could be. He doesn't often share his innermost thoughts with Winnie or me. Boone plays his hand close to his chest. He doesn't give away anything."

"What was he like before he came home wounded?" she wanted to know.

"He was less somber," he told her. "He played practical jokes. He laughed. He enjoyed parties, and he loved to dance. Now, he's the total opposite of the man he used to be. He's bitter and edgy, and he won't say why. He's never talked to any of us about what happened to him over there."

"You think whatever it was is what changed him so much?"

He nodded. "I miss the brother I had. I can't get close to the man he's become. He avoids me like the plague. More so, since I brought Nellie home with me for supper. He gave me a long lecture on the dangers of encouraging hired help. He was eloquent."

"So you're uneasy about taking her out on a date."

"I'm uneasy about Boone finding out that I'm dating her," he confessed. "Which brings me," he added with a glance, "to the solution I need your help with."

She gave him a wary look. "Why do I get the feeling that I shouldn't have agreed to come here with you?"

"I can't imagine." He leaned toward her, smiling. "But if you'll just cooperate in my little project, I'll return the favor one day."

She noticed that Nellie, waiting on another table, was sending pained looks toward Clark, who was oblivious to her interest. "This is upsetting Nellie," she pointed out.

"Not for long. I'll speak with her before we leave. Listen, you're my best friend. I need you to be a friend and help me divert Boone from guessing how involved I am with Nellie. We're going to pretend to get involved, if you're game."

"Involved?" Keely squeaked. "Listen here, Boone already thinks I'm sleeping with Bentley, thanks to my mother. He won't believe I'm turning my attention to you. He hates me!" she exclaimed. "He'll go out of his mind if he thinks you're serious about me, and he'll stop it any way he can. I'll lose my job and have to stay at home, my mother will drive me crazy—"

"Your mother will be thrilled if you go out with me, because I'm rich," Clark said sardonically. "She won't cause trouble. And Boone will spend his time trying to think up ways to get you out of my life, unaware of what's really going on."

"Boone isn't stupid," she worried. "He's going to wonder what you see in me. I'm poor, I work at a menial job..."

"I'll take care of all that," he said, smoothing it over. "All you have to do is pretend to find me fascinating." He grinned. "Actually I *am* fascinating," he added. "Not to mention highly eligible and charming."

She made a face at him.

"But my brother can't know it's not for real," Clark added seriously. "He's got control of all my money until I turn twenty-seven. Then I can get to my trust. That's next year. I can't afford to tick him off just yet. But I'm not giving up Nellie." He glanced toward the young waitress, who blushed again at his interest and almost overturned a tray looking at him. "You have to help us," he told her. "You helped Bailey and he's just a dog. I'm a kind, thoughtful man who treats you like a little sister."

"That's it, play on my heartstrings," Keely muttered.

He grinned. "Come on. It will drive Boone nuts, you know it will. You'll love it!"

Thinking of the way Boone had treated her, she had to admit that the deception would pay dividends in the form of revenge. But Boone was a formidable enemy and Keely was uncertain about making one of him. That was funny, considering his hostile and condescending attitude toward her. He was her enemy already.

"I'll save you if it gets too rough," he promised.

She knew it was a bad idea. She was going to regret giving in. "If I agree to do it, I have to tell Winnie the truth," she began.

"No," he said immediately. "Winnie can't keep a secret, and she's afraid of Boone, too. If he puts on the pressure, she'll tell him everything she knows."

Keely grimaced. "I just know this is going to end badly."

"But you'll do it, won't you?" he asked with a cajoling smile.

She sighed. She grimaced. Clark had been her friend as long as Winnie had. He'd helped her out of half a dozen scrapes involving her mother. "Okay," she said at last.

He grinned from ear to ear. "Okay! Now. How about dessert?"

Before they left the restaurant, he introduced her to Nellie and explained to the waitress who Keely was and what her place was in his life. Nellie brightened at once. She was glowing when Clark added that Keely was going to be the red herring so that he and Nellie could go on dates without Boone knowing.

Keely noticed that the other woman was very demure and meek, and Clark seemed to love that attitude. But Keely noticed something that he didn't; there was a faint glint in Nellie's eyes that didn't go with a meek demeanor. She couldn't help but be apprehensive. Maybe Nellie's allure for him was Boone's disapproval; in many ways, he'd only just started to try the boundaries of his big brother's control. And Nellie had to know that the family was rich. She was a working girl, like Keely. If she turned out to be a gold digger, Keely stood to be burned at the stake by Clark's older brother for her part in this. She wished she'd refused. She really did.

They were very late getting home. It was one o'clock in the morning when Clark drove up at Keely's front door.

Until that moment, she hadn't remembered her mother's vicious words. They came back with cruel force when she saw the living-room light still on. She didn't want to go inside. If she'd had anywhere else to go, she wouldn't set foot in the place.

But her choices, like her salary, were limited. She had to live with her mother until she could make better arrangements.

Clark was watching her with open sympathy. "She probably doesn't even remember saying it," he murmured. "Drunks aren't big on memory."

She glanced at him, curious. "How would you know that?"

He hesitated, but only for a minute. "After Boone's fiancée threw him over, he went on a two-week bender. He didn't remember a lot of the things he said to me, but I've never forgotten any of them. The crowning jewel," he added with taut features, "was that I'd never measure up to him and that I wasn't fit to run a ranch."

"Oh, Clark," she sympathized. She could only imagine being a man and having Boone as a big brother to try to live up to. Those were very big shoes to have to fill.

"He sobered up and didn't remember anything he'd said to me. But words hurt."

"Tell me about it," Keely sympathized.

He turned to her. "We're both in the same boat, aren't we? We're people who don't measure up to the expectations of the people we live with."

"Winnie and I think you're great just the way you are," she replied doggedly.

He laughed, surprised. "Really?"

"Really. You've got a wonderful sense of humor, you're never moody or sarcastic and you've got a big heart." Her eyes narrowed. "If I'd told you that Bailey needed emergency care immediately, you'd have packed him into the car and taken him right to the vet."

He sighed. "Yes, I guess I would have."

"Boone thought it was a pitiful plea for attention on my part," she added sadly. "I guess my mother's said a lot of things to him about me."

"Apparently. She doesn't like you, does she?"

"The feeling is mutual. We're sort of stuck together until I can get a raise or a second job."

"How would you manage a second job?" he asked.

"Getting away from my mother's constant abuse would make me manage. I can't imagine living in a place where nobody makes fun of me."

"You could work for me," he suggested.

She shook her head. "Thanks, but no thanks. I want to be completely independent."

"I figured that, but it didn't hurt to ask."

She smiled. "You really are a nice man."

"I'll pick you up next Saturday morning. We can go riding at the ranch. We might as well make a start at getting on Boone's nerves," he added with a dry chuckle.

"Take all his bullets away before I get there," she pleaded.

"He's not so bad," he told her.

She shivered. "Sure he isn't."

The front door opened and Keely's mother came out onto the porch. "Who's that out there?" she drawled, hanging on to one of the supporting posts. She was wearing floral silk slacks with a fluffy pink robe. Her hair was disheveled and she looked sleepy.

"Don't pay her any attention," Keely advised Clark with a sad little sigh. "She doesn't even know what she's saying. I'll see you next Saturday."

"Thanks, Keely," he told her with sincere affection.

She shrugged. "You'd do it for me," she said, and smiled. "Good night."

"Good night."

She got out of the car and walked up to the porch, shaking inside, dreading another confrontation with her parent. She tried to walk past Ella, but the older woman stopped her.

"Where have you been?" she demanded.

Keely looked at her. For the first time she didn't back down, even though her knees were shaking. "Out," she replied tersely.

The older woman's face tautened. "Don't talk to me like that. You live in my house, in case you've forgotten!"

"Not for much longer," Keely gritted. "I'm moving out as soon as I can get a night job to go with my day job. I don't care if I have to live in my car, it will be worth it! I'm not staying here any longer."

She brushed past her mother and went into the house, down the hall, into her room. She locked the door behind her. She was shaking. It was the first time in memory that she'd stood up to her abusive parent.

Ella came to her door and knocked. Keely ignored her.

She knocked again, with the same result.

Ella was sobering up quickly. It had just dawned on her that if Keely left, she'd have nobody to do the chores. She couldn't even cook. She'd been able to afford help until the past two or three years. But she was facing a drastic reduction in her capital, due to her bad business decisions. And there was something else, something more worrying, that she didn't dare think about right now.

"I didn't mean what I said!" she called through the door. "I'm sorry!"

"You're always sorry," Keely replied tightly.

"No. This time I'm really sorry!"

There was a hesitation. Keely started to weaken. Then she remembered her mother's track record and kept quiet.

"I can't cook!" Ella yelled through the door a minute later. "I'll starve to death if you leave!"

"Buy a restaurant," was Keely's dry retort.

With what, Ella was thinking, but Keely's light went off. She stood there, weaving, her mind dimmed, her heart racing. A long, long time ago, she'd cuddled Keely in her arms and sung lullabies to her. She'd loved her. What had happened to that soft, warm feeling? Had it died, all those years ago, when she learned the truth about her husband? So many secrets, she thought. So much pain. And it was still here. Nothing stopped it.

She needed another drink. She turned back down the hall toward her own room. She could plead her case with Keely tomorrow. There was plenty of time. The girl couldn't leave. She had no place to go, and no money. As for getting a second job, how would Keely manage that when she worked all hours for that vet? She relaxed. Keely would stay. Ella was sure of it.

Saturday morning, Clark came to pick her up to go riding with him at the ranch.

She'd done that several times with Winnie. But she'd never done it with Clark. Winnie and Boone were usually both home on the weekend, but Winnie's red VW Beetle was nowhere in sight when Clark drove up in front of the stables with Keely beside him.

He got out and opened the door for her with a flourish.

Boone, who was saddling a horse of his own in the barn, stopped with the saddle in midair to glare at them.

"Oh, dear," Keely muttered under her breath.

"He's just a man," Clark reminded her. "He can kill you, but he can't eat you."

"Are you sure?"

Boone had put the saddle back on the ground at the gate that kept his favorite gelding from leaving his stall. He stalked down the brick aisle toward Clark and Keely, who actually moved back a step as he approached with that measured, quick, dangerous tread.

He loomed over them, taller even than Clark, and looked intimidating. "I thought you were flying to Dallas today," he told Clark.

Clark was intimidated by his older sibling and couldn't hide it. He tried to look defiant, but he only looked guilty. "I'm going Monday," he said, and it sounded like an apology. "I brought Keely. She's going riding with me."

Boone looked down at Keely, who was staring at her feet and mentally kicking herself for ever agreeing to Clark's hare-brained scheme.

"Is she, now?" Boone mused coldly. He glanced at Clark. "Fetch me a blanket for Tank from the tack room, will you? You can ask Billy to saddle two horses for you on the way."

Clark brightened. His brother sounded almost friendly. "Sure!"

He grinned at Keely and moved quickly down the aisle of the barn toward the tack room, leaving Keely stranded with Boone, who looked oddly like a lion confronted by a thick, juicy steak.

"Tell Clark you don't want to go riding, Keely," he said slowly. "And ask him to take you home. Right now."

First her mother, now Boone. She was so tired of people telling her what to do. She looked up at him with wide, dark green eyes. "Why do you care if I go riding with Clark?" she asked quietly. "I go riding with Winnie all the time."

"There's a difference."

She felt threatened. Then she felt insulted. She met his dark, piercing stare with resignation. "It's because my people aren't rich or socially important, isn't it?" she asked. "It's because I'm poor."

"And uneducated," he added tauntingly.

Her face colored. "I have a diploma for the work I do," she stammered.

"You're a glorified groomer, Keely," he said flatly. "You hold dogs and cats while the vet treats them."

Her whole body tautened. "That isn't true. I give anesthesia and shots..."

He held up a hand. "Spare me the minute details," he said, sounding bored.

"We can't all go to Harvard, you know," she muttered.

"And some of us can't even face community college," he shot back. "You had a scholarship and you threw it away."

She felt sick. "A scholarship that paid just for textbooks," she corrected. "And only half of that. How in the world do you think I could afford to pay tuition and go to classes and hold down a full-time job, all at once?"

"You could give up the job."

She laughed hollowly. "My mother would love that. Then she wouldn't even have groceries."

His dark eyes narrowed. "Do you pay rent?"

Her big, soft green eyes met his. "I do all the housework and all the cooking and cleaning and shopping. That's my rent."

"Who buys her liquor?" he asked with a cold smile. "And her see-through negligees?"

Keely's face went scarlet. He was insinuating something. Her stare asked the question without words.

He stuck his hands in the pockets of his jeans, pulling the thick fabric taut over the hard, powerful muscles of his legs. "I dropped by your house to thank you, belatedly, for getting Bailey to the vet in time to save him," he said curtly. "You weren't home, but she was. She answered the door in a see-through negligee and invited me inside."

The shame was overpowering. She averted her face.

"Embarrassed?" he scoffed. "Why? Like mother, like daughter. I'm sure you wear similar things for Bentley," he added with honey-dripping sarcasm.

She couldn't manage a reply. His opinion of her was painful. She'd loved him secretly for years, and he could treat her like this. He wouldn't even give her the benefit of the doubt.

Her lack of response made him angry. Why it should also make him feel guilty was a question he couldn't answer. "You keep away from Clark," he said shortly. "I don't want you going out with him. Do you hear me, Keely?"

"It's just for a ride…."

"I don't give a damn what it's for!" he snapped, watching her body tense, her eyes grow frightened. That made him even angrier. He stepped toward her and was infuriated when she backed up. "Get out of Clark's life. Today!" he told her in a goaded undertone.

She felt her knees go weak. He was intimidating. She couldn't even force her eyes back up to his. She was so tired of being afraid of everybody; especially of Boone.

Before he could say anything else, Clark came up with a blanket. He was grinning. "Billy's got the horses saddled. He's bringing them right up!"

Boone glared down at Keely. "I think Keely wants to go home," he said.

"You do?" Clark exclaimed, surprised.

Keely drew in a quick breath and stepped close to Clark. "I'd like to go riding," she replied.

Clark glanced at Boone, whose eyes were black as jet. "What's going on?" he asked his brother. He frowned. "Do you really mind if I just take Keely riding?"

Boone glared at Keely as if he'd like to roast her on a spit. He glared at his brother, too. His lips made a thin line. "Oh, hell!" Boone bit off. "Do what you damned well please!"

He turned and strode out of the barn, apparently oblivious to the blanket Clark was holding out and the saddle he'd left sitting at the stall gate. His long, quick strides were audible on the paved floor, echoing down the aisle.

Clark ground his teeth together as he watched Boone's departure. "I hope he doesn't run into any of his men on the way to wherever he's going," he said with visible misgivings.

"Why?" Keely asked, relieved that Boone hadn't said anything more.

Suddenly there was a distant voice, a sharp curse and the sound of water being splashed.

"Oh, boy," Clark said heavily.

Keely stared down the aisle. A tall, dripping wet cowboy came into the barn, sloshing water as he walked. He was wringing out his felt hat, muttering. He looked up and saw Keely and Clark and grimaced.

"What happened to you, Riley?" Clark exclaimed.

The cowboy glowered at him. "I just made a comment about how good you and Miss Keely looked together," he said defensively. "Boone picked me up and tossed me into the watering trough!"

Clark exchanged a glance with Keely. She had to bite her lip to keep from laughing as the cowboy passed on down the aisle, muttering about his freshly laundered clothing having to go right back into the washing machine. He headed out the back door of the barn toward the bunkhouse beyond.

"Poor guy," Keely said. She looked up. "Your brother has a very nasty temper."

"Yes." He drew in a breath. "Well, it wasn't as bad as I expected it to be," he added, smiling. "Let's go for a nice ride and pretend that my brother likes you and can't wait to welcome you into our family!"

"Optimist," Keely said and grinned.

Boone was gone when they came back from the lazy ride around the ranch, but Winnie was just putting her car into the garage. She drove a cute little red Volkswagen Beetle, her pride and joy because she was paying for it herself.

She came out of the garage frowning. She didn't even notice Clark and Keely at first, not until she'd passed right by the barn.

"What's wrong with you?" Clark called to her.

She stopped, glanced at them and looked blank. "What?"

"I said, what's wrong with you?" Clark repeated as he and Keely joined his sister near the corral.

"Bad day at work?" Keely asked sympathetically.

Winnie was tight-mouthed. "I had a little upset with Kilraven," she muttered.

Keely's eyebrows arched. "What sort of upset?"

Winnie grimaced. "I didn't mention the ten-thirty-two involved in a ten-sixteen physical," she said, describing a possible weapon involved in a domestic dispute. "The caller said her husband was drunk, had beaten her up in front of the kids and was holding a pistol to her head. The phone went dead and I dispatched Kilraven. I'd just managed to get the caller back on the phone and I was listening to her while I gave him the information, and the caller was hysterical, so I got rattled and didn't tell him about the gun. When he got to the address I gave him, he had a .45 caliber Colt automatic shoved into his face."

Keely gasped. "Was he shot?"

"No thanks to me, he wasn't," Winnie said miserably. "I was also supposed to put out a ten-three, ten-thirty-three, calling for radio silence while he went into the house. I messed up everything. It was my first shift working all alone without my instructor, and I just blew it! My supervisor said I could have gotten someone killed, and she was right." She burst into tears. "Kilraven called for backup and talked the man out of the gun, God knows how. After the man was in custody on the way to the detention center, Kilraven called me on his cell phone and said that if I ever sent him on a call again and left out vital details of the disturbance, he'd have me fired."

Keely hugged her, muttering sympathetic things, while Clark patted her on the shoulder and said that it would all blow over.

Winnie blew her nose and wiped her eyes. "I'm going to put in my resignation at the police station and at 911 dispatch and come home," she sobbed. "I'm a menace! Kilraven said I was taking up jobs that some other woman needed desperately, anyway. He said rich women who got bored should find some other way to entertain themselves!"

"That's harsh," Clark muttered. "I'll have a talk with him."

Winnie looked up at her sweet brother through tear-filled eyes. "Are you kidding? Kilraven makes Boone look civilized!"

"Well, we could ask Boone to speak to him," Clark compromised.

Just as Winnie was starting to answer him, a Jacobsville police car came flying up the long driveway and skidded to a halt in front of the barn. A tall, black-haired, powerful-looking policeman got out and stalked toward them.

"Uh-oh," Winnie whispered, going pale.

"Who is that?" Clark asked.

Winnie took a breath. "Kilraven," she said heavily.

CHAPTER FOUR

Winnie looked like a professional mourner. Her long, wavy blond hair was ruffled by the wind and her dark eyes were red from crying.

"It's all right," she said, trying to deflect trouble as Kilraven came to a stop, towering over her. "You didn't need to come all the way out here to tell me I'm fired. I'm going to put in my resignation first thing tomorrow morning."

He propped his hand on his holstered gun and stared down at her with glittering silver eyes. "Who asked you to quit?"

"You said I should," she accused, and dabbed at new tears. "You said I needed to leave law enforcement to people who were qualified to work in it."

The tall man grimaced. The tears were real. He'd been browbeaten into coming out here by his boss, Jacobsville Police Chief Cash Grier, protesting all the way because he thought Winnie was putting on an act for sympathy. But this was no act. His rage dissolved like tears on hot pavement.

"I could have gotten you killed," Winnie told him, red-eyed, and started crying all over again. "That man held a pistol to your head!"

Kilraven's perfect teeth clenched. "It wasn't loaded."

Winnie stared at him through a mist. "What?"

"It wasn't loaded," Kilraven repeated. "He was too drunk to realize the clip was missing."

"Wouldn't there still be one bullet chambered?" Winnie asked.

Kilraven shrugged. "Didn't matter."

Winnie frowned. "It didn't matter? Why?"

He drew in a long breath. "He couldn't remember how to get the safety off."

Winnie was just looking at him now, not saying anything.

"But it could have ended in tragedy," Kilraven continued quietly. "I mean, if he'd managed to actually fire the damned thing…" He left the rest unsaid.

Winnie blew her nose and wiped her eyes again. "I know."

"They stuck you in that dispatch job with no real training," he muttered. "Any big city 911 staff goes through a training program. Well, Jacobs County has one, too," he conceded. "But the director thought you were just playing around, that you weren't really serious about working in the 911 center since you worked full-time for us in the police department. So he just stuck you in as an assistant to one of the regulars and let you get on with it. He thought you'd fold after a few days, that you only took the job because you were bored with being at home, and that you thought working for the police and emergency dispatch was entertainment. I had a long talk with the director before I came here."

"You did?" Winnie was fascinated. She hesitated. "You didn't…hit him or anything?"

"I do not hit people," the tall officer replied haughtily.

"That's not what Harley Fowler says," Keely murmured under her breath.

Kilraven glared at her. "That guy pulled a knife on me and

threatened to cut off my…well, never mind what he threatened, he was lunging at me with it. It was hit him or shoot him."

"How many pins did they have to put in his jaw?" Keely wondered aloud.

"It was better than having to have a bullet dug out," Kilraven protested. "And I should know. I've had three bullets dug out, over the years, along with various bits of shrapnel, and I'm wearing two steel pins, as well. The pins hurt less."

Winnie was studying him curiously.

"I'm not telling you where they are," Kilraven said. "And shame on you for what you're thinking!"

Winnie flushed. "You don't know!"

"The hell I don't," he huffed. "My great-grandfather was a full fledged shaman who could read minds."

"That's not what Harley Fowler says he was," Keely interrupted.

He gave her an exasperated glance. "What does Harley Fowler know about me? I've never even met the man!"

"He doesn't know you, but he plays poker with Garon Grier, who works with Jon Blackhawk, who's your half brother," Keely explained.

"Damn the FBI!" Kilraven cursed.

"Harley doesn't belong to the FBI," Winnie pointed out.

"Garon and my brother do," Kilraven said. "And they can stop telling people lies about me and my family."

"Jon *is* your family," Winnie replied. "And Harley didn't tell lies, he said your great-grandfather got mad at a local sheriff and smeared him with fresh meat and shoved him headfirst into a wolf den."

"Well, the wolf den was empty at the time," Kilraven defended his ancestor.

"Yes, but your great-grandfather didn't know that." Keely laughed.

Kilraven made a face at her. "You didn't get that from Harley Fowler, you got it from Bentley Rydel."

Keely blushed.

Kilraven threw up his hands. "You take your dog to a vet and expect him to stick to medicine, instead of which he pumps you for personal information and then tells the whole community!"

"You don't get to join the family unless we know everything about you," Clark pointed out.

Kilraven scowled. "What family?" he asked suspiciously, and glanced at Winnie, who blushed as warmly as Keely had.

"The Jacobsville family," Clark returned. "We're not a town. We're a big extended family."

"You don't live in Jacobsville, you live in Comanche Wells," Kilraven retorted.

"It's an extension of Jacobsville, and you're avoiding the issue," Clark said with a grin.

Kilraven's wide, sexy mouth pulled up into a faint snarl. "I'm leaving. I don't want to be part of a family."

"With that attitude, I wouldn't worry about it," Winnie said under her breath.

He paused to look down at her. "Your director will talk to you in the morning about some more training. He's going to do it personally. I don't want you fired. Neither do any of the other law enforcement and rescue personnel. You've got a real knack for the job."

Kilraven turned on his heel and stalked off back to his patrol car. He got in under the wheel, coaxed the engine into a roar and shot out of the driveway without a glance, a wave or anything else.

"Well, he's sort of nice," Clark had to admit.

"He's sort of scary, too," Keely said, watching Winnie.

Winnie was smiling through her tears. "Maybe I'm not a lost cause, after all."

Keely hugged her. "Definitely not a lost cause," she laughed.

"Well, I guess I'll go inside and find something to eat..." She stopped, her gaze moving from Clark to Keely. "What are you two doing together?"

"Driving Boone mad," Clark said, and he grinned.

"Would you like to explain how?" his sister asked.

"I invited Keely over to ride horses with me, and Boone was in the barn when we drove up together."

"So that's why," Winnie began thoughtfully.

"Why, what?" Keely wanted to know.

"Why my brother was sitting on the shoulder of the road in his car with a Texas Department of Public Safety car flashing its lights behind him, with a trooper sitting inside running wants and warrants."

"How do you know what he was doing?" Keely asked.

"Because I run tags all the time at work for the troopers and the local police," she replied.

"What was Boone doing?" Clark asked hesitantly.

Winnie chuckled. "Teaching the trooper new words, from the look of it. I didn't dare stop to ask."

"Oh, dear," Keely said, glancing at Clark.

"Stop that," Clark said firmly. "It's none of Boone's business if I want to ask you over here to go riding with me."

"It shouldn't be," Winnie told her brother. "But he'll make it his business. He thinks Keely's too young to go out with men. Any men."

Clark's eyes popped. "She's almost twenty years old!"

"Well, of course she is," Winnie said gently. "But not to Boone. To him, she's still in pigtails trying to teach her dog how to fetch newspapers."

"Don't dig that up," Keely moaned.

"That was when your folks rented that place down the road while your house was being remodeled. You'd have been about eleven. That dog was very good at fetching newspapers," Winnie replied. "It was just that it was easier for him to bring you Boone's paper from our front porch than it was to fetch yours out of the paper box at the end of your driveway."

"Boone yelled at me," Keely recalled with a shudder.

"Boone yells at everybody," Winnie reminded her.

"Almost everybody," Clark qualified.

Keely's eyebrows arched. "Almost?"

"It didn't work when he yelled at Bentley Rydel, did it?" He chuckled. "Winnie told me," he added when Keely looked puzzled.

"Bentley isn't afraid of anybody," Keely agreed, smiling. "He's been good to me."

"I'd think he had a crush on you, except for his age," Clark said. "He's even older than Boone."

"I guess he is, at that," Keely said.

"Want some lunch?" Winnie asked them after a moment of silence. "We'll have to get it ourselves, because our Mrs. Johnston is off today, but I can make a salad and Keely can make real bread."

"I'd love homemade bread," Clark sighed. "The lunchroom ladies used to make it at school when I was a kid."

"Would you mind?" Winnie asked her best friend.

Keely smiled. "Not at all. I love to cook."

It would also give her an excuse not to have to go home for a while. Her mother would be getting up pretty soon, hungover as usual and driving Keely nuts. With a little luck, maybe Carly would come over and take Ella out partying, since it was Saturday. It would give Keely a lovely quiet night at home alone if she didn't get called out; something she rarely experienced.

The three of them worked in a companionable silence while they whipped together a light lunch. Keely took a little of the dough she was using for rolls and added real butter, pecans, cinnamon and sugar and made cinnamon buns for dessert.

Winnie's pasta salad had time to chill while the dough sat rising. Within an hour, Keely had fresh bread on the table and cinnamon buns cooking in the oven while they ate their way through pasta and fresh fruit.

In the middle of the impromptu feast, Boone walked in. He stopped in the doorway, his nostrils flaring.

"I smell fresh bread," he remarked, scowling. "Where the hell did you get fresh bread? Is there a bakery in town that I don't know about?"

"Keely made it," Clark mumbled, working his way through a third yeast roll liberally spread with butter. "Mmmm!" he added, closing his eyes and groaning at the delicious taste.

"Did you get a ticket?" Winnie asked, trying to divert him from the penetrating glance he was aiming at Keely, who squirmed in her chair.

"Ticket for what?" Boone asked, digging in the china cabinet for a plate.

"Speeding," she replied.

He put his plate on the table and fetched silverware and a napkin. He poured himself a cup of coffee from the pot and sat down with the other three. Keely's heart was already doing overtime, and she had to work at acting normal while Boone was so close.

"I got a warning," he said tautly.

"My friend Nora is the county deputy clerk of court," she reminded him. "If you get a speeding ticket, it will go through her office and she'll tell me."

His mouth twitched. "I got a small ticket."

"There's only one size," she said.

He ignored her. He reached for a roll, buttered it and took a bite. He wore the same expression that was dominating

Clark's face. Fresh rolls were a treat. Their cook, Mrs. Johnston, couldn't make bread, although she was a great cook otherwise.

"There's some salad left," Winnie commented, pushing the bowl toward him.

"Where did you learn to make rolls?" he asked Keely, and seemed really interested in her answer.

"When I lived with my father, he ran a big game park. One of his temporary workers had been in the military and traveled all over the world," she recalled. "He was a gourmet chef. He taught me to make bread and French pastries when I was twelve years old."

"What sort of animals did your father have?" Boone persisted.

"The usual ones," she said, without meeting his eyes. "Giraffe, lions, monkeys and one elephant."

"African lions?"

She nodded. "And one mountain lion," she added. No one noticed that her fingers, holding her fork, went white.

"They have mean tempers," Boone said. "One of my ranch hands had to track one down and kill it when he worked over in Arizona some years ago. It was bringing down cattle. He said it killed one of his tracking dogs before he could get a clear shot at it."

"They tend to be vicious, like most wild animals," she agreed. "They're not malicious, you know. They're just wild animals. They do what they do."

"What was your job at a wild game park?" Boone murmured.

"I fed the animals and watered them and made sure the gates were locked at night so they couldn't get out," she said.

He finished his roll and followed it with sips of black coffee. "Not a smart job for a twelve-year-old kid," he remarked.

"It was just Dad and me," she said, "except for old Barney, and he was crippled. He'd hunted a lion who became a man-killer in Africa and it fought back. He lost an arm and a foot to it."

"Did he keep the pelt when he killed it?" Boone asked.

She smiled faintly. "He made a rug out of it and slept on it every night. When he left us, he was still carrying it around."

"The rolls were good," Boone said unexpectedly.

"Thanks," Keely replied shyly.

"You could get a job cooking," he pointed out.

She frowned. "Why would I want to give up working for Bentley?"

His pleasant expression went into eclipse. "God knows."

Winnie gave her brother a piercing look. He ignored it. He studied her face and frowned. "You've been crying," he said abruptly. "Why?"

She paled. She didn't want to talk about it.

"Why?" he persisted.

She knew it was useless to try to hide it from him. Someone would tell him, anyway.

"I almost got Kilraven killed," she confessed, putting down her fork.

"How?"

"I got rattled and forgot to warn him that the man involved in a domestic dispute was armed," she said quietly. "Luckily for Kilraven, the clip was missing and the man couldn't figure out how to get the safety off."

"Luckily for the man," Clark elaborated dryly. "If he'd shot Kilraven, he'd be awaiting trial in the hospital."

"That would depend on where he shot him," Winnie replied.

"Kilraven's steel right through," Keely teased. "No bullet could get through that hard shell."

"She's right." Clark chuckled. "They'd have to hit him with a bomb to make a dent in him."

None of them noticed that Boone was sitting rigidly, with

his eyes staring blindly into space. There was a look in them that any combat veteran would have recognized immediately. But nobody in his family had ever been in the military, except for himself.

Keely did notice. She knew that Boone had been in the war, that he'd been a front line, Special Forces soldier. She knew that he was reliving some terrible memory. Keely knew about those, because she had her own. Without saying a word, her eyes communicated that knowledge to the taciturn man across from her. He frowned and averted his eyes.

He finished his coffee and got to his feet. "I've got to make a few phone calls," he murmured.

"Keely made cinnamon buns," Winnie said. "Don't you want one?"

He hesitated uncharacteristically. "Bring me one in the office, with a second cup of coffee, will you?" he asked.

"Sure," Winnie said.

"No." His dark eyes slid to Keely. "You bring it," he said.

Before she could answer him, he strode out of the room.

"Well!" Clark said, surprised.

"He's in a mood to bite somebody," Winnie said solemnly. "Boone's a horror when there's no audience to slow him down. If he disapproves of you dating Clark, he'll make your life hell. I'll take his dessert to him."

"No," Clark said. He looked at Keely. "You have to stop being afraid of him and stand up to him," he told her. "This is a good time to start."

Keely became pale. She hesitated and looked to Winnie to save her.

But Winnie hesitated, too. She frowned. "Maybe Clark's right," she said after a minute. "You're afraid of Boone. He knows it, and uses it against you."

Keely bit her lower lip. "I suppose you're right. I'm a wimp."

"You're not," her best friend replied, smiling. "Here's your chance to prove it."

"With your shield or on it," Clark intoned dramatically.

Keely glowered at him. "I am not a Spartan."

"An Amazon, then," Clark compromised, and grinned. "Go get him!"

"We'll be right here," Winnie promised. "You can yell for help and we'll come running."

Keely had her doubts about that. Winnie and Clark loved Boone, but neither of them had ever been a match for his temper. If she yelled for help, they'd assume that Boone was bristling and ready for a fight, and they'd be under heavy pieces of furniture trying not to get noticed. Still, they had a point. She was almost twenty years old. It was time she learned to fight back.

She poured a cup of black coffee from the pot and took the cinnamon buns out of the oven. She put two of them on a saucer and added a napkin to her burdens. She glanced at her audience.

Clark flapped his hand at her.

Winnie mouthed, "Go on!"

She would have made a smart remark, but her heart was in her throat. It bothered her that Boone had asked her to bring dessert to him. Considering his reaction to her friendship with Clark, he had to be up to something.

She tapped nervously on the door.

"Come in," he called curtly.

She balanced the saucer holding the cinnamon buns on the cup of coffee and gingerly opened his office door, closing it with her back once she was inside.

It was a small, intimate room, with ceiling-to-floor bookcases on two walls, French windows opening onto a small patio, and a fireplace with gas logs. The carpet was deep beige, the curtains echoing the earth tones. But the furniture was red leather, as if the very sedateness of the room commanded a touch of color. Boone looked right at home in a big red leather-upholstered chair behind his enormous solid oak desk. Over the mantel was a painting of Boone's father. It was a prophecy of what Boone would look like in old age—with silver hair and a distinguished, commanding expression.

"You look like him," Keely mused as she put the coffee and its accompanying dessert gently in a bare spot on the paper-littered desktop. Her hands were cold and shaking and the cup rattled in the saucer. She hoped he hadn't noticed.

"Do I?" He glanced at the portrait. "He was a head shorter than I am."

"You can't see height in a painting," she pointed out.

She didn't want to argue. She started toward the door.

"Come back here," he said curtly. It wasn't a request.

It was now or never. She took a steadying breath and turned. "Winnie's waiting for me."

"Winnie?" he asked with a cynical smile. "Or Clark?"

She swallowed. Her hands began to shake again. She clasped them at her waist to still them. "Both of them," she compromised.

He leaned back in the chair, ignoring the buns and the coffee. "You and Clark have been like siblings for years. Why the sudden passion?"

"Passion?" she parroted.

"He's dating you. Didn't you notice?" he asked sarcastically.

"We went horseback riding," she pointed out. "There are a lot of things you can't do on a horse!"

His eyebrows made arches. "Really? What sort of things?"

He was baiting her. She glared at him. "You said you wanted cinnamon buns and coffee. There it is."

She started toward the door again.

Incredible, how fast he could move, she thought dazedly

when he was already at the door before she reached it. She had to stop suddenly to keep from running right into his tall, powerful body.

He turned so that her back was against the door. His dark eyes narrowed as he looked down at her. She felt like a small, delicious and decidedly alarmed bunny.

He knew it. He smiled slowly and his eyes began to glitter. "You're afraid of me," he said in a slow, deep tone.

Her hands spread behind her against the door and she tried to melt into it. He was very close. She could feel the heat from his tall, powerful body, smell the clean, spicy scent of him as he leaned closer.

Now he had an advantage, and he knew it. She'd done a stupid thing, trying to run.

"You aren't afraid of Clark or Bentley, though, are you?" he persisted.

"They're nice people."

He made a short, rough sound deep in his throat. "And I'm not?"

She dragged in a ragged breath. Her eyes would only go as high as his top shirt button, which was unfastened. Thick, black curling hair peeked out from under it. She wondered if there was more across his broad, muscular chest under the fabric. He never took his shirt off, or even opened it past that top button. She was curious. Her thoughts surprised her. She hadn't thought that way about a man in a long time.

He recognized her fear for what it was. One lean hand came up to her cheek and brushed back strands of soft blond hair, the gesture sensuous enough to make her shiver. She couldn't hide her reaction to him. She didn't have the experience.

Pressing his advantage, he bent and brushed his nose lazily against hers in an odd, intimate little caress that made her breath stop in her throat.

"You smell of lilacs," he whispered. "It's a scent I never connect with any other woman."

"It's only shampoo," she blurted out. She was shy and nervous. She didn't understand what he was doing. Was this a pass? She couldn't remember a man ever treating her like this.

"Is it?" He shifted, just a little, but enough to bring his long legs in contact with hers, in an intimacy she'd never shared with a man.

Instinctively her small hands went to his chest and pushed once, jerkily.

He pulled back from her with a rough word. His eyes were blazing when he looked down at her. "Did you think I was making a pass at you?" he challenged tightly. "You'd be lucky! I don't waste my time on children."

She was shivering. His whole posture was threatening, and he looked murderous.

"Hell!" he burst out, furious at his own weakness and her cold reaction to it. She was just a little icicle.

Her lower lip trembled. He was scary like that. She still connected anger with physical violence, thanks to a friend of her father's. She cringed involuntarily when he lifted his hand.

Her blatant fear put a quick cap on his temper. He stopped for a moment, puzzled. What he was learning about her, without a word being spoken, fascinated him. She really *was* afraid of him. Not only of his ardor, but his temper, as well. She thought he was raising his hand to strike her. Which posed a worrying question. Had some man hit her in the past?

"I was going to open the door, Keely," he said in a totally different tone, the one he used with children. "I don't hit women. That's a coward's way."

She forced her eyes up to his. She couldn't tell him. She kept so many secrets. There were nightmares in her past.

He frowned. His fingers went to her cheek and drew down

it with an odd tenderness. They moved to her soft mouth and traced it, and then lifted to smooth back her hair.

"What happened to you?" he asked in the softest tone he'd ever used with her.

She met his eyes evenly. "What happened to *you*?" she countered in a voice that was barely louder than a whisper to divert him.

"Me?"

She nodded. "When Clark was talking about bombs, you got all quiet and your eyes were terrible."

The expression on his face went from tender to indifferent, in seconds. He was shutting her out. "You'd better go back to the others," he said. He opened the door for her and stood aside, waiting for her to leave.

She went through it hesitantly, as though there was something unfinished between them.

"Thanks for the coffee and dessert," he said tautly, and closed the door before she could say another word.

CHAPTER FIVE

Boone came out of the office an hour later and left without saying a word. Keely and Winnie and Clark watched a new movie on pay-per-view and then shared a pizza before Clark drove Keely home. Boone still hadn't come back.

Keely didn't often get premonitions, but she had one now. It was getting dark and when they drove up at the Welsh house, two things registered at once. There were no lights on in the house and a Jacobs County Deputy Sheriff's car was sitting in the driveway.

"Oh, dear," Keely murmured fearfully, grabbing at the door handle.

Clark, concerned, got out of his car and walked with her to the deputy, who got out of his car when Keely approached.

"Sorry, ma'am," he told her with a quiet demeanor, "but we couldn't contact you by phone and there's, well, there's sort of an emergency."

"Something's happened to my mother?" Keely asked nervously.

"Not exactly." The deputy, a kind man, grimaced. "She's over at Shea's Roadhouse," he added, naming a sometimes notorious bar on the Victoria road. "She's very drunk, she's breaking bottles and she refuses to leave. We'd like you to come with us and see if you can get her to go home before we're forced to arrest her." He, like most of Jacobs County, knew that Ella's fortunes had dwindled, even if Keely didn't. Keely likely wouldn't have enough money to bail Ella out of jail.

"I'll come right now," Keely agreed.

"I'll drive you and help you get her home," Clark said at once without being asked.

She smiled at the deputy. "Thanks."

He shrugged. "I used to have to drag my old man out of bars," he said. "It's why I went into law enforcement when I grew up. I'll follow you out there, in case there's any more trouble."

"Thanks."

"It goes with the job, but you're welcome."

When they got to Shea's, Ella was screaming bloody murder and holding an empty whiskey bottle over her head while the bartender crouched in a corner.

"For goodness' sake!" Keely exclaimed, walking up to her mother with Clark and the deputy close behind. "What are you doing?"

Ella recognized her daughter and slowly put the bottle on the bar. She shivered. "Keely." In a rare show of emotion, she caught her daughter around the neck, hugged her and held on for dear life. "What will we do?" she sobbed. "Oh, Keely, what will we do?"

"About what?" Keely asked, shocked at the older woman's behavior. She was never affectionate.

"All my fault," Ella mumbled. "All my fault. If I'd told what I knew..."

Before she could elaborate on that cryptic remark, she began to collapse.

"Help!" Keely called.

The deputy and Clark got on both sides of the older woman and held her up.

"Do you want to press charges?" the deputy asked the bartender.

The man looked torn. But Keely's face decided him. "Not if she'll agree to pay for the damages."

"Of course we will," Keely replied, unaware of her mother's financial status.

"Where in the world is Tiny?" the deputy asked the bartender, because their bouncer usually prevented trouble like this.

"He's having knee replacement surgery," he confided. "One of our more volatile customers kicked him in the leg and put him out of commission. We usually have a relief bouncer, but we can't find one. Nobody except Tiny wants the job."

"If you get in trouble, all you have to do is call us," the deputy told him.

"I know that. Thanks." The bartender hesitated, frowning, as if he wanted to say more, but he glanced worriedly at Keely.

The deputy was a veteran of law enforcement. He knew the man wanted to tell him something. "I'll help them get Mrs. Welsh to the car, then I'll come back and get a list of the damages," he promised, and saw the bartender relax a little.

"Okay," he said.

Keely followed the deputy and Clark, with her mother, out to Clark's car.

"Do you have a blanket or something, in case she gets sick?" Keely asked worriedly. It would be terrible if her mother threw up in that luxurious backseat.

Clark popped the trunk lid and pulled out a big comforter, throwing it over the backseat. "I keep it in case I have to carry

Bailey somewhere," he confessed. "He doesn't like to ride in the car."

They got Ella down on the seat and closed the door. After a couple of words with the deputy, they went back to the Welsh place and bundled Ella into the house and onto her bed. Keely was careful to use her right arm in the process. The left one was too weak and fragile for lifting.

"It's like deadweight," Clark commented when they'd placed her.

"She usually is," Keely replied, breathless. She frowned at the prone sight of her mother, who was still wearing slacks and a blouse and sweater and shoes. She'd take those off later, when Clark left. "I just wonder what set her off? She doesn't ever go to bars except with Carly, and she doesn't usually get this drunk even then."

"No telling," Clark said. "Well, I'll get home," he added, smiling. "Thanks for everything, Keely."

She smiled. "Thank you."

"I'll call you."

She waved as he drove away. It was already dark. She went back inside, still puzzled about Ella's condition.

But there were more puzzles to come. She'd tugged off her mother's shoes and thrown a coverlet over her. Undressing an unconscious person was heavy work and Keely's shoulder was already aching.

She was watching the news on their small color TV while doing a load of clothes when there was a knock at the door.

Most Saturday nights, there was an emergency at work and she was called in to assist. But the phone hadn't rung. There weren't even any messages, except for an odd call with nothing but static and then a click. She wondered if Bentley had driven over to collect her for an emergency.

When she opened the door, it was another surprise. Sheriff Hayes Carson was standing on her front porch. He wasn't smiling.

"Hi, Keely," he said. "Mind if I come in?"

"Of course not." She held the door wide so that he could enter. He was a head taller than Keely, with brown-streaked blond hair that had a stubborn wave right over his left eyebrow. He had dark eyes that seemed to see right through people. In his midthirties, he was still a confirmed bachelor, and considered quite a catch. But Keely knew he hadn't come calling in the middle of the night because he found her irresistible.

She went to turn the television down, and motioned him into a chair. She perched on the edge of the sofa.

"If it's about the bar tonight," she began worriedly.

"No," he said gently. "Not quite. Keely, have you heard from your father lately?"

She was stunned. It wasn't the question she'd anticipated. "No," she stammered. "I haven't heard a word from him since he dropped me off here when I was about thirteen," she added. "Why?"

He seemed to be considering his options. He leaned forward. "You knew he'd fallen into some bad company before you left?"

"Yes," she said, and shuddered. "One of his new friends slapped me around and left bruises," she recalled. She'd never told that to anyone else. "I think it was the main reason he brought me back to my mother."

Hayes's sensuous mouth made a thin line. "Pity he wasn't living in Jacobs County at the time," he muttered.

Keely knew what he meant. She'd heard that Hayes was hell on woman-beaters. "It is, isn't it?" she agreed. "Is my father in some sort of trouble?"

"We think he needs money. He may get in touch with you or your mother. This is important, Keely. If he does, you need to call me right away." He was solemn as he spoke. "You could both be in terrible danger."

"From my own father?" she asked, agape.

He was hesitant. "He's not the father you remember. Not anymore."

He never had been the father she'd wanted, she recalled, even if she'd tried to give him the love a father was due from his daughter. She could remember times when she was sick and her father left her alone, going out at odd hours and staying gone, sometimes for two days at a time, while Keely and the hired help kept the game park going. At the last, his drinking and his violent friends worried Keely more than she'd ever admitted.

"Is he mixed up in something illegal, Sheriff Carson?" she asked worriedly.

His face was a closed book, revealing nothing. "He's got friends who are," he said, sharing with a little of the truth. "They're pushing him for money that he doesn't have, and they want it very badly. We think he may have tried to contact your mother."

"Why would you think that?" she asked slowly.

He sighed. "The bartender at Shea's said she was yelling that her husband was going to kill her if she didn't buy him off, and she was broke."

Her heart skipped. "Broke? She said she was broke?" she exclaimed. "But she owns property, she gets rent—"

He hated being the one who had to tell her this. He ground his teeth. "She's sold all the property, Keely, probably to pay her bar bills," he said heavily. "One of the Realtors who was at the bar at the time mentioned it to me. There's nothing left. She's probably drained her savings, as well."

Keely felt sick. She sank down into the sofa and felt wounded all over again. No wonder Ella didn't want her to leave. Her mother couldn't afford to hire someone to replace her for domestic work.

"I'm sorry," Hayes said genuinely.

"No, it's all right," she replied, forcing a smile. "I did wonder. She let things slip from time to time." Her green eyes were troubled. Her own small salary barely allowed her to own an ancient used car and buy gas to get to work, much less pay for utilities and upkeep. What Hayes had told her was terrifying. "What do you want me to do?" she asked, surmising why he'd come.

"I want you to tell me if you hear anything from or about your father," he said gently. "There's a lot at stake here. I wish I could tell you what I know, but I can't."

Keely recalled that her father's friend had a police record. He'd bragged when he slapped her that he'd killed a woman for less than Keely had done, talking back to him.

She frowned. "Just before I came to Jacobsville," she recalled, "Dad's friend, Jock, said he'd killed a woman."

"Jock?" He drew out a PDA and pulled up a screen. "Jock Hardin?"

Her heart flipped. "Yes. He was the one who hit me."

He frowned. "Why did he hit you?"

She drew in a long breath. "I burned the rolls."

Hayes cursed roundly and then apologized. He leaned forward and stared right into her eyes. "Did he do anything more than hit you?" he asked.

"He wanted to." She couldn't say more. Jock had gotten her shirt halfway off and then pushed her away, revolted. Her pride wouldn't let her admit that to Hayes.

"He was prevented?"

She nodded. Her green eyes looked into his. "Do you know where he is? I mean, he isn't going to come here and make trouble for Mama and me, is he?"

"I don't know, Keely. He's on the run from a new charge, one he shares with your father. Don't ask. I can't tell you," he added when she started to speak. "Suffice it to say that we can put him away for life if we can catch him."

"And my father?" she prodded gently.

He bit his full lower lip. "He'll probably get the same sentence. I'm sorry. He's done some bad things since he left you here. Some very bad things. People have died."

Her heart sank right into her shoes. She remembered her father laughing, buying her a puppy and taking her around with him in the game park, teasing her about her affection for the big mountain lion, Hilton. He hadn't been a bad man in those days, and he'd been affectionate with her, and always kind. The man she remembered at the last had been very different, with violent mood swings. Jock had taken over his life. And Keely's. She'd realized, belatedly, that her father had probably saved her life by bringing her back to Jacobsville.

"He wasn't a bad man when we had the game park," she told Hayes. "He had a nice girlfriend who took me to church and he never teased me about it. She was also our bookkeeper. In those days, he was religious, in his own way. He loved the animals. They loved him, too. He could walk right in with the tiger and the mountain lion and pet them." She laughed, remembering. "They purred..." Her face fell. "What if Jock comes here?" she asked, and she was really afraid. The man had terrified her for weeks. Her father had been so far out of reality that he hadn't even intervened.

Hayes's face hardened. "I'll lock him up so tight he'll never get out," he promised.

She relaxed a little. "He was vicious to me."

"You were lucky he didn't kill you."

She nodded.

"We'll all keep a watch on you," he promised, rising to his

feet. "I've worked it out with my deputies, and the Jacobsville police will increase patrols by your office at night when you work late. Call dispatch when you start home and let them know you're on the road. We'll watch your back."

"I will. Thanks, Sheriff Hayes," she added when they were at the front door.

"I'm sorry about the way things worked out for your father," he told her abruptly. "I know how it is. My only brother was an addict. He died of an overdose."

She did know. Everybody did. "I'm sorry, for you, too."

"Keep your doors locked."

"I will."

"Good night."

"Good night."

She watched him drive away. Then she locked the door and sat down, heavily, giving way to tears.

Her mother sobered up the next day and became very quiet. Keely cooked and cleaned, equally silent. Neither of them mentioned the financial situation. Her mother was very watchful and she locked doors. But when Keely asked why, she would not reply.

Carly came over the next Friday night to take Ella out bar crawling, but Ella was sober and didn't want to go.

They were in the next room, talking softly, but Keely was listening and could hear them above the soft noise of the dishwasher.

"Are you going to tell Keely?" Carly was asking.

"I suppose I'll have to," Ella said tautly. "I hoped it would never come to this," she added brokenly. "I thought it was all over. I prayed he'd die, that he'd stay away forever."

"I know how you feel," Carly said. "But it's too late for that. You talked to the sheriff, didn't you?"

"Yes. I told him everything I know. He said he'd told Keely that she and I might be in danger and that she had to tell him if she heard from her father." She hesitated. "She loved her father. I know she still does, in spite of everything. She might not tell anybody if he called."

"He isn't the man she loved," Carly said tightly. "He'd kill her in a heartbeat if she got in his way. And that Jock man, he'd kill anybody without a reason. He's heartless."

"Yes," Ella said, and shuddered. "He came with Brent to bring Keely here. He wouldn't let Brent out of his sight for a second, and they didn't stay long."

"I remember," Carly replied. "He was the scariest man I ever met. He made my skin crawl when he looked at me."

"They can't come back here," Ella said forcefully. "I don't care how much trouble they're in. I can't give them money I don't have!" She coughed. "He wanted me to sell the house!"

"It's all you've got left, you can't do that!"

"I'm not going to," Ella said. "But he threatened—"

"You told Sheriff Carson. They'll all watch out for Keely."

Keely felt her heart stop. Had one of the men threatened her? Surely not her father!

"Jock was in the military," Ella said dully. "Brent said he'd been in some top-secret pacification program. He knows how to torture people and he likes it. Brent said he still had a yen for Keely, despite what happened to her."

"What did he mean, what happened to her?" Carly wondered aloud.

"I don't know. He wouldn't tell me." There was a long pause. "So many secrets. I've kept them from Keely and Brent's kept them from me. Apparently Keely's keeping some of her own. So many secrets. Oh God, I need a drink!"

"We can't go out," Carly said at once. "Not now."

"I had a little whiskey left," Ella said wistfully. "I don't know where it is."

"You're better off without it," Carly said. "You have to think of the consequences. Now, of all times, you need to think clearly!"

There was another pause. "Yes. I suppose I do."

Keely, her head full of what they were saying, felt numb. She didn't say a word. She only smiled at Carly when she left, and avoided being alone with her mother, who was as quiet as a church. It was so uncharacteristic that Keely felt chilled, as if she'd stepped over her own grave.

She did try, once, to get her mother to open up about her father. Ella changed the subject and went to watch the news on television. She'd started doing that every day, as if she were waiting for some story to break. It made Keely nervous.

Clark came the next night, Saturday, to get her for one of their dates, and he was glum when they drove away from her mother's house.

"What's wrong with you?" Keely asked.

He glanced at her. "I wanted to drive us over to San Antonio for dinner and to take in a play. Boone said we couldn't go." He frowned, glancing at her. "He says you're in some sort of trouble, and you aren't supposed to go out of the county."

Her breath stopped in her throat. How had Boone known? What did he know? Then she remembered. Hayes Carson was his best friend. They went out together every week to play poker with Garon Grier and Jon Blackhawk, Officer Kilraven's half brother.

"What's going on, Keely?" Clark asked. "What does Boone know that I don't?"

She ground her teeth together. She didn't want to talk about it, but it would be nice to get some of her worries off her chest.

"My father is in some sort of trouble and Sheriff Carson thinks Mama and I might be in danger. He wants money. Apparently he called my mother and threatened her. She won't tell me what he said."

"Good Lord!" Clark exclaimed. He glanced in the rearview mirror. "Would that have anything to do with why we're being followed?"

"Followed?"

"Yes. By a sheriff's car when I picked you up, and by a Jacobsville police car now that we're here in town."

Keely remembered what Hayes had told her. She clutched her purse in her lap. "Sheriff Carson said they'd look out for me," she confessed. "They think I might be in danger if I go out at night."

"With me?"

"You could be in the line of fire, too, Clark," she said, just realizing it. "Maybe we should stop seeing each other…."

"No." His voice was firm. "I'm not giving up Nellie. This is a good plan. We'll work around your father. After all, a threat is just a threat. How is he going to hurt you when we're surrounded by uniforms?" he asked, grinning.

"I don't know."

"We'll be perfectly safe," he said. "When Boone said I couldn't take you to San Antonio, I called Nellie and had her drive down here. I'll leave you at the local library. It stays open until nine o'clock. That will give me a little time with her, if you're game. You'll be safe at the library," he added.

She knew that. The police would be able to watch her through the many glass windows if she sat at a table. "Okay," she agreed.

He grinned at her. "You're the nicest girl I know."

"Thanks, Clark."

"I mean it." He hesitated. "You don't think your own father would really hurt you?" he added, worried.

"Of course not," she lied.

"That makes me feel better."

"Will Nellie be safe, driving down here from San Antonio and back, alone at night?" she added, and she was concerned.

"She drives one of those huge SUVs," he said. "A tank couldn't dent it. And she has a cell phone that I pay for. She can call for help if she has to."

"She seems very nice," she replied.

"She's the best thing that's ever happened to me," he murmured, smiling wistfully. "She's just dynamite in bed, and when I give her presents, she embarrasses me with the gratitude. The diamond earrings made her cry."

She wondered if Clark realized what he was admitting. The woman was trading sex for expensive gifts, and he thought it was love. She didn't. She'd seen the greed in Nellie's eyes when Clark had talked to her at the restaurant. Men were so dim, she thought sadly. Even Boone, going out with that traitorous woman who'd left him in the lurch when he was wounded overseas. He'd taken her back in a heartbeat.

"You're very quiet," Clark remarked. "Sorry. I shouldn't have made that remark about Nellie being hot. I guess you think of sex outside marriage as a sin."

"I do," she confessed.

"Our dad never thought of it like that," he returned. "He enjoyed women. He never remarried, but he sure played the field. Winnie, though, didn't approve of his lifestyle. She's a lot like you." He glanced at her. "She didn't like Nellie at all." He grimaced. "I guess Nellie doesn't appeal to women," he added. "She has a lot of trouble at work. Her coworkers think she gets too many tips. They say she plays on men's vanity just so they'll leave her big tips. Ridiculous!"

It wasn't, but Keely wasn't going to say so. With any luck, when Clark spent enough time with his pretty girlfriend, he'd learn the truth for himself. If Winnie didn't like the girl, it meant something. Winnie loved people, and she wasn't possessive about her brothers.

"You don't mind staying here alone?" he asked when he pulled up in front of the library. He'd called Nellie on the way there.

She smiled. "Of course not. Go have fun."

He bent and kissed her on the cheek. "You're sweet. I'll make it up to you. How about some emerald earrings? I know you love emeralds…"

She frowned. "I don't want anything from you, Clark," she said, puzzled. "You're my friend!"

He looked as if she'd knocked him in the head. "But you love emeralds," he persisted.

She reached up and kissed his cheek. "If I want any, I'll buy them. One day," she added, laughing. "Isn't that Nellie?" she asked, indicating a big green SUV that had just pulled up next to them in the parking lot. The woman inside was openly glaring at them.

"Uh-oh." Clark laughed. "She saw you kiss me. She's terribly jealous. I'll have to sweeten her up." He pulled a jeweler's box out of his pocket, opened it and showed it to Keely. It was a diamond necklace. A real, glittery, very expensive diamond necklace. "I asked her what she'd really like, and she said one of these. Think she'll like it?"

Keely had to bite her tongue. "Sure!"

He closed the box. "It will put her in a good mood." He chuckled. "I'll be back in a little while."

"Okay."

She got out of the car. Nellie came around the SUV, locking it with her remote. She gave Keely, who was wearing corduroy slacks with a cotton blouse and Berber coat, a superior sort of look. Nellie was wearing a designer dress and expensive shoes with a coat that would cost Keely a year's salary—probably another gift from Clark. She looked expensive and greedy and very jealous.

"Why did you kiss him?" she asked Keely, keeping her back to Clark. "I don't want you touching him, do you hear? He's all mine."

"I noticed," Keely said, indicating the coat and dress. "Bought and paid for?"

"How dare you!" Nellie snapped.

Keely smiled sweetly. "One day he'll get a look at this side of you," she whispered. "And you'll be out on your ear."

"Think I care?" Nellie drawled. "There's always another one, a richer one. Besides, men are stupid."

She bypassed Keely and went rushing into Clark's outstretched arms. "Oh, darling, I missed you so!" she exclaimed, and kissed him hungrily. Clark was eating it up.

Keely shook her head. She walked into the library, thinking that P. T. Barnum was right. A sucker actually was born every minute. She wished she could tell Clark the truth. A man that much in love wouldn't hear her, or believe her, and it would ruin their friendship. But worse was to come, she knew. She wished she and Boone weren't enemies, so she could tell him what was going on. She knew that she was going to end up, inevitably, right in the middle of all the trouble.

CHAPTER SIX

The library was one of Keely's favorite places. She didn't get much time to spend there, because she was usually on call on the weekends. But this weekend, the senior vet tech had unexpectedly offered to take Keely's place. Her husband was in the military, and his unit had been called up for overseas deployment. She was blue about it and didn't want to spend so much time alone. Keely sympathized with her, but was glad to have the time off. Or she had been, until her life suddenly became complicated.

She was reading a thick biology text on canine anatomy when a shadow fell over her. She looked up, straight into Boone Sinclair's dark eyes. Her heart raced. She fumbled with the book and it fell onto the floor.

He picked it up and, glancing at the title with an odd smile, put it back on the table. He pulled up a chair and sat down next to her. Here, in the reading area, she was alone. The librarian was in the back cataloging, so they had the room to themselves.

"I thought you and Clark had a date," he murmured suspiciously.

She couldn't think. He was leaning toward her, and she

could smell the minty scent of his breath on her face. She bit her lower lip nervously.

"I wanted to look up something," she stammered inventively. She flushed. She wasn't good at lying. "He went to get gas. He's coming back for me." She forced a glare. "We were going up to San Antonio to the theater when you told him we couldn't go."

"San Antonio is too big and we don't know many police officers there," he said, unexpectedly somber. "You don't need to be out of sight of the police. It's easier to watch you here."

"You've been talking to Sheriff Hayes," she accused.

He nodded. "Hayes is pretty laid-back most of the time. When he worries, there's good reason." His eyes narrowed on hers. "Your mother hasn't been seen out at Shea's for a week?" It was a question.

She needed so desperately to talk to someone. Her face was drawn with worry. Clark was sweet, but he was too concerned with Nellie to pay more than a little attention to Keely's problems. Not that he didn't care about her. He just cared more about Nellie.

Incredibly Boone's big hand smoothed over hers where it lay on the book cover. He linked his warm, strong fingers into hers. "Talk to me," he said quietly.

She actually shivered. It had been years since a man had touched her. Not even a man, really, just a boy she dated. She hadn't been held, kissed, caressed. She was a woman with a woman's feelings, and she couldn't, didn't dare, indulge them.

Boone knew more about women than she realized. He understood her reaction to him, and was puzzled by it. "For a woman who's getting regular sex, you sure don't act as if your needs are being met," he commented.

She went as red as the book cover and her hand jerked under his.

He smiled, but not in a mean way. His fingers contracted more. "Tell me what's really going on, Keely."

His hand was comforting. She didn't fight the firm, caressing clasp. It felt so good. She wanted to climb into his lap and put her head on his shoulder and cry her eyes out. She wanted comfort, just a little comfort. But this wasn't the man, or the place or the time.

She took a deep breath. "Something's going on about my father," she confessed in a hushed tone. "I don't know what. Nobody will tell me anything. He's mixed up in something bad, and he has this friend..." Her soft features contracted and her eyes were full of pain at the memory.

"This friend," he prompted, squeezing her hand. He was very intent.

"Jock." The name tasted like poison in her mouth. "My mother thinks he has something to do with whatever's going on. I overheard her talking to Carly. She won't tell me anything."

"This man, Jock," he persisted. "You look frightened when you say his name."

"He...hit me," she confessed, fascinated by the expression on his face. "I was just barely thirteen. He'd been watching me while I was cooking. He made me nervous. He'd been in prison. He said he'd killed a woman. I let the biscuits burn." She bit her lip again. "He hit me so hard he knocked me down. My father heard him yelling and came into the kitchen and managed to get Jock out of the room." She wrapped her arms around her chest, cold with the memory. "It was just after that when Dad brought me back here to live with Mama."

"Good God." Boone's eyes were soft and quiet with sympathy. "No wonder you're uncomfortable around men." He was remembering. His jaw tautened. "That's why you were afraid of me in my office."

"I don't really know you," she confessed apologetically. "And you don't like me," she added uneasily. "You don't like me being friends with Winnie and you don't like me going around with Clark."

"No, I don't," he replied honestly. But he looked troubled.

"I understand," she said unexpectedly. "You know that I'm poor and you think I use Winnie and Clark..."

"The hell I do!" He lowered his voice quickly, looking around to make sure he hadn't drawn the attention of the librarian. He looked back at Keely, scowling. "You don't use people," he bit off. "You work like a soldier for your paycheck. Unpaid overtime, trips out to old Mrs. McKinnon's place to give her dog its diabetic injections because she can't do it, walking dogs at the shelter on weekends so the staff can handle adoptions..." He stopped, as if he hadn't wanted her to know that he was aware of her activities.

"Mrs. McKinnon loves her dog," she replied. "Maggie handles the shelter on Saturdays and feeds and waters the animals on Sunday. There's this tiny little budget. She already spends twice the hours she gets paid for to do all that. I just help a little."

His dark, quiet eyes studied her soft, oval face in its frame of thick blond hair, down to her pretty bow mouth. She wasn't a beauty, but she radiated a sort of loveliness that most women didn't.

"It's a pity," he said, almost to himself, "that you aren't older."

"I'll be twenty in December," she said, misunderstanding.

"Twenty whole years old." He looked down at her hand. It was a useful hand, not an elegant one. Short nails, immaculately kept, no polish. No jewelry on those fingers, either. He frowned. "No rings?" he asked. He looked up at her ears where her hair was pushed back. "No earrings?"

She flushed. "I have little silver studs, but I forgot to put them on...."

"Clark hasn't given you anything?" he persisted. "He walked out tonight with a huge jewelry case."

"Oh, that was for—" She stopped at once, horrified.

His eyebrows arched and the corner of his mouth tugged up. "Not for you?"

She swallowed hard. "I don't like jewelry."

"Liar."

She flushed. "I don't have to be paid to give a man attention," she said curtly, and then realized how that sounded, and flushed even more. "I mean, I don't want expensive things from Clark."

He cocked his head to one side and watched her like a hawk. "In the past few weeks, he's gone through half the inventory of a jewelry store. I see the receipts, Keely, even if I don't pay the bills. I have an accountant to do that."

She was in a quandary now. She couldn't admit that Clark hadn't given that expensive jewelry to her, and if she denied it, she'd only get him in trouble.

"Your car is a piece of junk," he persisted. His practiced eye swept over the blouse and slacks she was wearing, the coat hung over the back of the chair beside her. "You've worn that same outfit to the house half a dozen times. You don't drive unless you have to, so you can save on gas money. And you won't let Clark give you a pair of earrings?"

Her teeth clamped down. She wasn't telling him anything else. She tugged at her hand.

He wouldn't let it go. "That waitress he brought to the house," he said softly, "was looking around between every bite, cataloging paintings and silver and furniture and putting mental price tags on the rugs and the chandelier."

She was horrified that she might react to that statement. Her eyes were almost bulging.

He pursed his lips and his dark eyes twinkled. "Clark thinks he's putting one over on me," he said in a hushed, soft tone. "He doesn't realize that Misty's father has a private detective agency that I can hire when I need to. Apparently, Nellie doesn't realize it, either, or she'd be more careful about going with Clark to motels."

She made a soft exclamation and her horror showed.

"You don't use people," he continued. "But Clark does. He's using you. And you're letting him."

"You don't know that," she protested weakly.

"I'm only surprised that your boss is so forgiving about it," he added, and his expression hardened. "Isn't he the jealous type?"

She sank down into her chair. She felt limp. She'd failed Clark. He'd never forgive her. "Dr. Rydel is thirty-two, Boone," she said gently, and didn't notice the reaction when she spoke his name. His eyes had flashed.

"Thirty-two." He parroted the words. He'd gone blank for an instant.

"Thirty-two," she repeated, looking up. "I'm nineteen. Even if I were a femme fatale, I'd have my work cut out. Dr. Rydel hates women. He only likes me because he thinks of me as a child. Like you do," she added in a different tone.

His eyes were unreadable. "There are times," he said softly, "when you seem older than you are." He frowned slightly. "Why don't you date, Keely?" he asked suddenly.

She was shocked by the question. "I…my job takes up so much time…" She'd walked right into the trap. She glared at him. "I date Clark," she said doggedly.

"Clark loves you," he replied unexpectedly. "Like a sister," he added almost at once. "He never touches you. He doesn't light up when you walk into a room. His hands don't shake when you're close to him. That doesn't add up to a romance."

What he was describing was exactly what happened with Keely when she saw Boone. She didn't dare admit it, of course. What had he been saying about Clark?

"When he brought the waitress home with him," he continued, "he spilled coffee all over the linen tablecloth trying to pour her a second cup. He actually fell out of his chair when he touched her hands as she passed him the salad bowl."

She grimaced.

"And I don't need a declaration to tell me who got that diamond necklace. It sure as hell wasn't you."

"You won't tell him?" she asked worriedly. "He's my friend, he and Winnie. I don't have many. I gave my word..."

His eyes glittered. "It bothers me that you didn't mind helping him get around me."

Her eyes were apologetic. "He said she was the most important thing in the world to him and that he'd die if he had to give her up. He thought it would make you so angry, seeing me with him, that you wouldn't think about Nellie."

He looked down at her hand. He caressed the back of it absently with his fingers. He didn't want to admit how angry it *had* made him. Uncharacteristically angry. Keely was a child. He couldn't afford to become involved with her. Just the same, he didn't want Clark taking advantage of her. Odd, how relieved he felt that she wasn't sleeping with Bentley Rydel. Her mother had been lying to him, trying to hurt him because he rejected her.

"Your mother is a piece of work," he muttered angrily.

She was puzzled, not having been privy to his complicated thoughts. "Why do you say that?"

He looked up. "What do you think of Nellie?" he asked, changing the subject.

She hesitated.

"Tell me," he prodded.

She sighed and met his eyes. "I think she's the worst sort of opportunist," she confessed. "She adds up presents and gives sex in return. Clark thinks that's love," she added cynically.

"You don't."

Her eyes were old. "Living with my father taught me some things. He was almost broke when he lost the game park because this woman played up to him and pretended to be awed at the way he handled the animals. She stroked his vanity and he bought her expensive things. Then there was a lawsuit, and we had absolutely nothing. Meanwhile," she added, "there was this sweet woman who kept the books for us, who took me to church and dated my father. She was shy and not beautiful, but he dropped her as soon as the other woman came along."

"What happened?"

"When he went bankrupt, his flashy girlfriend was suddenly interested in a local Realtor who'd just inherited a lot of property from his late father."

"I see."

"Clark is a sweet man," she said quietly. "He deserves better."

He leaned back, finally letting go of her hand. His eyes narrowed on her face. "She works for a living. So do you. I expected you to take her side."

"She's a snake," she returned. "And she doesn't exactly work that hard for a normal living. Her coworkers say she plays up to her male customers to get big tips. Clark told me. He thinks they're jealous because she's pretty."

He had a faraway look. "Beauty is subjective," he said oddly. "It isn't always manifested in surface details."

She smiled. Then she laughed. "Maybe I'm subjectively beautiful and nobody noticed," she said.

He realized, belatedly, that she'd made a joke. He laughed softly.

She looked around. The librarian was starting to close doors and turn out lights. She bit her lip. Clark was nowhere in sight.

"I don't think they'll let you stay the night," he pointed out.

She got up, grimacing. She picked up her coat and her purse.

"At least there's a bench out front. I told Clark they closed at nine."

He got up, too, towering over her. "You haven't learned yet that intimacy makes people lose track of time."

She couldn't meet his eyes. He sounded very worldly. She put her purse down and gingerly eased her left arm into the coat. He was behind her at once, easing the rest of the garment over her other arm and onto her shoulder.

"What happened to your arm?" he asked.

She felt his warm hands on her shoulders, the warm strength of his body behind her. She wanted to lean back and have him hold her. Insane thoughts.

"An accident," she said after a minute. "Nothing terrible," she lied. "But it left a weakness in that arm. I can't lift much."

There was a pause. His usually impassive face had a ragged look. "I have a similar problem with one of my legs," he said hesitantly. "If I overdo, I limp."

She turned and looked up at him. She'd noticed that. She'd never expected him to admit it to his enemy. "You were hurt overseas worse than you told Winnie and Clark," she said with keen insight. "Worse than you've told anyone. Except maybe Sheriff Carson."

His jaw firmed. "You see too much."

"In my own way, I've been through the wars, too," she replied quietly. "Scars don't go away, even if wounds heal. And they destroy people."

She wasn't looking at him as she said it. Her eyes had the same expression as his did. It was a moment of shared tragedy, shared pain. He moved a step closer to her. She looked up at him expectantly. It was as if the wall between them had lowered just a little, letting in new light. But even as he started to speak, a car drove up outside.

Boone tugged Keely back into the shadows of a row of books.

Outside the tinted glass windows, they saw Clark glance furtively at Boone's big Jaguar sitting next to Nellie's SUV. He bundled her out of his car and into the SUV and waved her out of the parking lot. He looked hunted. He stood at the front bumper of his car, looking toward the library and hesitating.

"The jig's up," Keely told Boone with twinkling eyes.

"No, it isn't. Come here." He took her hand and tugged her farther down the row of books, out of sight of the glass windows. "I hope you're a good actress."

"Excuse me?"

They heard the door open. Clark whispered something to the librarian. There was a returned whisper and muffled footsteps on carpet coming closer.

Boone let go of Keely's hand. "You won't tell me a damned thing," he said in a low voice, but one that carried at least to the end of the aisle. "I want to know where Clark is, why he isn't here with you." He nodded at her meaningfully.

She caught on at once. "I told you, he just went to get gas—"

Clark turned into the aisle where they were. His look of fear eclipsed when he overheard what Keely said. He seemed to relax.

"I'm back," he told her. "In the nick of time." He joined them and grinned at his brother. "What are you doing here?"

"I came in to get a book and found Keely," Boone muttered. "Why didn't you take her with you to get gas?" he asked suspiciously.

"I told him that I wanted to check out that canine anatomy book I was telling you about," she said to Clark.

"Oh. Right," he agreed quickly.

Boone gave them both a glare as the light overhead went out. "Now I won't have time to check on mine, no thanks to both of you." He turned on his heel and stalked out, pausing only long enough to speak to the librarian.

Keely rushed back to grab her own book and take it to the desk, telling the harassed librarian that she'd be back on Monday to check it out and apologizing for keeping her late.

The librarian smiled and said it was all right, but she followed them right out the door, locking up behind her.

"That was close!" Clark exclaimed when they were in the car heading back toward Keely's house. "How long had he been there?"

"Just a couple of minutes," she lied. "I thought we were in big trouble!"

"We would have been if he'd seen Nellie get out of my car and into hers," he said. "What a break that he was talking to you down an aisle instead of in front of the window!"

"Yes, wasn't it?" she agreed.

"I'll have to plan better next time," he said, almost to himself.

"Did she like the necklace?"

He chuckled. "She loved it! I ordered her a Gucci suit to go with it and had it sent to her apartment," he added. "She was very grateful."

She could imagine the form that gratitude took, but she wasn't saying anything. She was still wondering what Boone expected her to do now. She couldn't bear to tell Clark she'd sold him out. Not that she had, really. Boone wasn't stupid. Clark underestimated him, as usual. It was par for the course that Boone was always three steps ahead of everybody else.

"Nellie really is beautiful," she commented, for something to say.

"Absolutely." He grinned at Keely. "You didn't have any trouble before Boone showed up?"

"None at all. I was fine."

"I'll have to plan better next time," he repeated. "Boone's smart. I have to work hard to keep him in the dark."

"I'm sure you'll come up with something," she replied.

"We will," he replied. "We're in this together, remember."

This was likely to end in despair for Clark, either way, and she hated having agreed to being a party to it. Especially now that Boone was clued in. She wondered if she should tell Clark the truth. Probably she should, but she was wary of Boone's temper if he found out. She felt stifled.

"Don't look so worried," he said gently. "Everything will work out. Really it will."

"Did you know that Misty's father had a private detective agency in San Antonio?" she asked abruptly, and then could have bitten her tongue for the slip.

"Some agency," Clark muttered. "I had them check out a cowboy for us when we were hiring on a new horse wrangler. He had a rap sheet and their brilliant staff didn't find a thing."

She stared at him. "How did you find that out if they didn't tell you?"

"Boone found it out," he said. "He was suspicious of something the man did, so he asked Hayes to look into the man's background. He had a prior for burglary. A conviction, no less, and he'd served time. Boone fired him the same day."

"I thought even a bad detective could find out something like that," she replied.

He frowned. "That's what I thought. I mentioned it to Boone, too. He said that they hired a man with false credentials, but found it out only after they assigned him our background check. They thanked us for flushing him out."

She was curious about that. It seemed a little easily explained. But they were already pulling up in front of her house, and there was no more time for questions.

When Clark pulled up at the porch, Ella was standing just outside the screen door in just her slip with a full glass of whiskey.

"So there you are!" she raged as Keely opened her door. "Where have you been?"

"Why don't you come back home with me?" Clark suggested quickly, leaning over the passenger seat to look out at her.

Even her mother in that shape was preferable to being in the same house with Boone after their awkward conversation. She needed time to think over what he'd said. Not to mention her disquiet at having to listen to another long recital of Nellie's assets, which had lasted all the way home. She forced a smile. "I can handle her," she told him gently. "It's okay."

"If you say so." He sounded dubious. "You never did say what happened in Boone's office the last time you were at the house. We heard him close the door."

"He was just warning me off you," she prevaricated, and smiled again. "It didn't work."

He laughed, relieved. "Thank God. I couldn't handle having all my plans go south before we even get started good, and this is just the beginning for me and Nellie! You're positive you want to stay?" He gestured toward her mother.

She nodded. "Thanks for the ride. I'll see you soon."

"Sure. Take care." Keely closed the passenger door. He waved to her mother, who ignored him, almost dancing in her impatience to talk to her daughter. He drove away with a wave.

"What's wrong?" Keely asked when she got onto the porch, because this wasn't a simple case of a few drinks too many. Her mother's face was stark-white and she was visibly frightened.

Ella bit her lip. "Your father called again."

"Again? Where is he?" she asked. "Is he coming here?"

"I don't know." She took a big sip of her drink.

"What did he want?" Keely persisted.

She turned and looked at her daughter with wide, frightened eyes. The hand holding the drink was shaking. "He… he didn't say."

"Why did he call, then?"

Ella looked around nervously. "Let's go inside."

They did, and Ella locked the door. She was rattled, all right. She couldn't even find the right light switch to turn off the porch light.

"I'll get it," Keely volunteered.

Ella stood watching her, biting her lower lip. She was so pale that her skin looked like milk.

Keely stood quietly, waiting for the older woman to speak.

CHAPTER SEVEN

"I don't know where to start," Ella said hesitantly. "I know your father didn't tell you anything about what happened here before he left with you."

"Nobody ever tells me anything," Keely replied bitterly. "I know that Dad's mixed up in something, that the police are interested in him for whatever it is and that Jock is involved somehow." She straightened. "And I know that you're broke and Dad is threatening you for money."

Ella bit her lower lip hard enough to draw blood. "You couldn't know that. Who told you that?" she demanded.

"Is it true?" Keely prevaricated.

Ella looked around wildly and brushed her untidy hair back from her thin face.

Keely moved forward a step. "Is it true?" she repeated softly.

Ella took a deep breath. For once, she really looked her age. "Yes," she said. "I thought the money would never run out. There was so much of it. Your grandparents invested in land when it was cheap. As the town grew, more people needed land, so they started renting it out for businesses. When they died, I continued the practice, raising the rents as the land prices increased."

"What happened?" Keely prodded.

Ella laughed hollowly. "I got greedy. My parents would never buy me designer clothes or even a good car. They made me pay my own way, from the day I started working. They wanted me to go to college, but I thought I was smart enough. Your father thought I'd get all that money the minute I married, so he married me. But it didn't work out that way." She drew in a long breath, her eyes with a faraway look. "All I had was an allowance. Brent and I bought expensive cars and diamonds and ate in the best restaurants and took long trips overseas. We ran up a fortune in bills. My parents paid it, then they stopped my checks." She laughed again as she glanced at her daughter. "Brent got used to living high. He couldn't go back to wages. He found a way to make a lot of money quick." Her face tautened. "You were far too young to understand what was going on. My parents died in a plane crash and we inherited the estate, but there wasn't much left. Mostly just the land—we'd spent the rest. I wanted him out of my life. He wanted that game park, so I made a deal with him. I sold land and gave him the proceeds. I was free, still relatively young, and I wanted to celebrate. So I did. Then your father dumped you here and the luxury lifestyle was a thing of the past. I resented you for that. But it probably saved us from being tossed out into the street with the clothes we were wearing. I'd gone hog wild and didn't even realize it. By the time I did, it was too late."

She moved into the living room and sat down, heavily, in a chair. Keely sat down on the arm of the sofa across from her. It was unusual for her parent to speak to her like this, as an equal, without even sarcasm.

Ella brushed back her hair. "I managed to salvage a couple of the properties before they were foreclosed on for unpaid bills. But my renters found cheaper rents and moved out. I was left with empty buildings that I couldn't repair, and nobody wanted to use them. Within the past six months, it was suddenly all gone, except for the house and the land it sits on." She looked up at Keely. "Your father and Jock are broke and they need a grubstake. They want me to sell the house and property to fund it."

"But it's all you have left," Keely argued. "Tell them you won't do it. Sheriff Carson will look out for you."

Ella bit her lower lip. "It's more complicated than that, Keely," she replied quietly. "You see, your father and I did something…illegal, when you were very small. If he tells what he knows, I can go to prison."

Keely's mouth thinned. "If he uses it, he'll be incriminated, as well, and he can go there, too."

The older woman smiled sadly. "They'd have to catch him first, wouldn't they?" she asked. "He's been one jump ahead of the law all his life."

"What did you do?" Keely asked, reasoning that her mother would probably close up and say nothing else.

Ella took a sip of her drink. "I've lived with the guilt for years," she said, almost to herself. "I thought it wasn't going to bother me, what we did. I thought…" She took another sip of the drink. "A local boy saw Brent bringing in a shipment of cocaine and hiding it in our basement. He was going to tell the sheriff." She grimaced. "My father was dying and he'd already threatened to disinherit me because of Brent. If there had been a scandal, and Brent and I had been prosecuted, I'd have lost everything. They could have proved that I…paid for the shipment that Brent was going to cut and resell on the streets."

"What did you do?" Keely asked apprehensively.

"The boy liked to get high," Ella continued miserably. "He did it all the time, anyway. He had a supplier, one of Brent's dealers—she died and her sister married a local cattleman a few months ago. We promised him that we'd send the boy a kilo of coke, all for himself, if he wouldn't tell on us."

Keely was feeling sick. She already had an idea of who her mother was talking about. "And?"

"Oh, he agreed. In fact, we promised him a dime bag on the spot. That's a hundred dollars of cocaine in street talk. What we didn't tell him was that it was one-hundred-percent pure—it wasn't cut with anything to lessen the effect. We gave it to his supplier, and he had her inject him. And he died. Of course, she didn't know, either. But we had her in our pocket then, too, because she couldn't prove that she didn't know she was killing him."

Keely's eyes closed. "It was Sheriff Hayes Carson's younger brother, Bobby, wasn't it?" she asked huskily.

Ella sighed. "Yes. I've lived with the guilt and the fear all these years, terrified that Sheriff Hayes would find out. He wouldn't rest until he put me in prison. He's blamed others, and that took the heat off me. It was the only hope I had…"

"No wonder you paid for the game park for Dad," she said, seeing clearly the pattern of the past. "It's why you let him take me along."

Her mother nodded slowly. "After Bobby died, I couldn't bear to look at Brent anymore. He made me feel like a murderess. I was afraid, too, that he might get high one night and tell someone what we'd done. So he promised to leave town if I'd let him have the money for the game park. He even said he'd straighten up, give up drugs, try to get his life back together. He said he'd never wanted anything more than he wanted that game park."

Keely's eyes became tormented as she remembered what her mother had said; she'd had to pay her husband to take Keely with her.

"No," Ella said quickly, reading Keely's expression. "I wanted to hurt you that night. It wasn't true. Brent wanted you with him. He said that if I fought him, he'd go to the police with the truth. He had nothing to lose by then. He'd already been arrested for possession twice and gotten off with the help of a lawyer. But he'd never get away with murder, and neither would I. So I let him take you." She looked up. "I never even asked if Jock was the reason. You see, Jock had noticed you when he came by to see Brent and told him about the old game park that he was running. The owner wanted out. Brent said that Jock liked young girls. I didn't even connect it, at the time." She shivered. "I should be shot."

Keely felt sick all over. Perhaps that accident, as terrible as it was, had saved her from something much more terrible. Now she realized what had probably happened. Soon after her father had purchased the rickety old game park where Jock worked and started renovating it, Jock had been arrested. Apparently he'd served time in prison, too, because it was only two years later that he showed up at the park. That was when things started to go downhill, and only about a week before Keely's accident. After that, Jock couldn't bear to touch her. Probably it was his idea for Brent to dump Keely, so the two of them could pursue other illegal enterprises. Keely might have been part of the plan for those jobs, she thought with muted terror. She'd been saved from more than she knew at the time, even though she'd resented being deserted.

She hadn't known her father at all. She'd thought he loved her. In those two years when it was just the two of them, and Dina keeping books, her young life had been happy and secure. Her father had, twice, even given up drinking; although Keely hadn't known he was using drugs. But just before Jock had turned back up, Brent Welsh had involved himself with the flashy woman who took him for everything he'd saved;

and there had been a good bit. Jock had been livid when he'd discovered that.

"What are you thinking?" Ella asked.

She looked up. "How happy we were for a couple of years. I guess it was while Jock was in prison, because he left when Dad and I settled into the game park and only came back a few days before Dad brought me here."

Ella looked relieved. "At least Jock didn't have much access to you, did he?"

"No," Keely replied. "I was afraid of him."

"I still am," Ella confessed. "Your father could be dangerous when he was drunk. But he said Jock was dangerous cold sober."

Keely smoothed her hands over her knees. "Thank you for telling me the truth."

Ella's eyes were troubled. "I was scared, Keely," she said abruptly. "I couldn't face the fact that I'd helped kill a man, even if nobody knew. I started drinking and I couldn't stop. It helped me forget." She bit her lip again. "I should never have said that I didn't want you, Keely. Or that your father was disappointed you weren't a boy. I wanted you so much. I would have given up anything rather than lose you. Carly was right. I should never have said such a thing."

It didn't mean that Ella loved her. But it was something. "Thanks," Keely replied.

Ella cocked her head. "Are you getting involved with the Sinclair boy?" she asked worriedly. "Brent would find a way to use you to his advantage if he could, you know. He's an addict. He can't stop. He's more dangerous now than he ever was when I lived with him, especially in his situation and with Jock egging him on."

Keely was trying to come to grips with the idea that her own parents had a hand in the death of Sheriff Hayes's young brother, and that her father was a drug dealer. She'd known about deals he'd made to acquire animals that weren't quite what she thought of as legal. But he'd hidden his worst side from her during those two years they were together. From her vantage point now, she'd been naive and stupid. Perhaps, she thought, it wasn't so much ignorance as denial. She hadn't wanted a larcenous parent. Even an alcoholic, which is what she thought her father was, didn't have the stigma of a thief. Then again, it was a matter of degree.

"You're remembering things, aren't you?" Ella asked. "Listen, Keely, I may not be a good parent. I may be the worst alcoholic in town. But I've never laid a hand on you in anger or put your life at risk, and you know it."

That was the truth. Keely might feel used by her mother, but she'd never been afraid of her. She nodded.

"I'd like to tell you that I'm going to start over. That I'll stop drinking and carping and seducing married men." She shrugged and made a self-mocking smile. "But it would be a lie. I've been like this too long. I can't change. I don't want to change. I like getting drunk. I like men."

"I know that," Keely said in a resigned tone. "If you could just stop trying to make me feel inferior, that would be something. It hurts when you make fun of the way I am. Dad certainly isn't perfect, but he made me go to church every Sunday. He even said once that he was going to make sure I didn't end up like both of you."

Ella thought about that. She was still holding her drink. She took another sip. "Well, he was right to do that. Yes. He was. The best way to give up being an alcoholic is never to start drinking in the first place."

"I don't like the smell of it," Keely murmured.

Ella laughed. "Neither do I," she confessed. And she smiled, really smiled, at her daughter.

"Did either of your parents drink?" she asked out of the blue.

Ella's eyes darkened with pain. She took a big gulp of the drink. "My father did."

She waited, but no other confessions were forthcoming. She wondered at the hatred in Ella's eyes when she talked about her father. Keely remembered that she never had talked about him, or about her mother, either.

"More secrets," Keely murmured absently.

Ella only nodded. "Some are best kept forever." She got up. "Well, I'm going to bed. If the phone rings, do us both a favor and don't answer it."

"I wish I could," Keely confided, "but I still have a job that requires me to go out at all hours."

Ella frowned. "Do you have a cell phone?"

She flushed. "No." She couldn't afford even a cheap disposable one.

Ella went to her purse and dug out hers. "When you go out at night from now on, you take mine. I'll be with Carly if I go out." She waved away the instant objection. "We can use hers. You have to have a way to call for help. Your father and Jock might even try to kidnap you. Brent sounded desperate."

"Why don't they just rob a bank?" Keely asked, exasperated.

"Don't even joke about that," her mother said at once, and went pale.

"Sorry. I shouldn't have said it."

Ella turned toward the hall. "I'm going to bed. Be careful if you have to go out. Call the sheriff's office and have the deputies watch out for you."

"I will." She was thinking, though, of Sheriff Hayes's brother and how he'd grieved for him after he'd died of that so-called drug overdose. She couldn't bear the thought of being in any way involved, even if she'd had nothing to do with it. Her parents were responsible. Inevitably, one day it was going to come out. You never really knew people, she told herself. Not even your parents.

But despite everything, it made her feel warm inside, the unexpected concern from the one parent she'd thought hated her. She didn't go to bed at once. She savored the feeling of having a real mother for the first time in her life. Even if that mother was the next best thing to a killer.

Clark phoned her two days later and asked her to the big charity dance at the local community center on Saturday. She wasn't on call for that one night, so she couldn't refuse.

"Is this desperate or what?" he asked miserably. "It's the only thing going on in Jacobsville for the foreseeable future, unless you want me to sign us up for the summer square-dancing workshop," he added grumpily. "I'll never get to see Nellie."

"I like dancing," she replied. "It's okay. You can sneak out and nobody will even miss you. Then you can say you had a stomach upset."

"You're a genius," he exclaimed.

No, she was just getting good at lying, she thought. She still was concerned about Boone's perception and Clark's headlong fling into disaster. And in the back of her mind was the thought of her father and Jock and their schemes.

Things were routine at work. She and her mother were getting along for the first time. Even Carly was kinder to Keely. And it seemed that the work she did around the house was slowly appreciated, right down to her cooking. She felt as if she had a new lease on life.

But on Saturday morning, while she was worrying over the one good dress she had that she was wearing to the dance, there was a phone call.

She answered the phone herself. Her mother was sleeping late—she and Carly had gone out on the town the night before—and she was expecting to hear from Clark. But it wasn't Clark.

"Has your mother put the house on the market yet?"

She knew that voice. It wasn't her father's. It was Jock's.

She hesitated, sick with fear.

"Answer me, damn you!"

"N-no," she stammered. "She hasn't…yet…"

"You tell her she'd better get moving. I know what she and your father did. He may not want to tell, but I will. You hear me, Keely?" And he slammed the phone down.

Keely wouldn't have understood the threat even a week ago. She understood it now. She couldn't very well go to Hayes Carson and tell him that her mother had been accessory to a homicide. There could be no protection from that quarter, especially if Hayes found out who the homicide had been. Clark couldn't help her, either. She didn't dare involve Boone. She sat down, sick and frightened, and wondered what in the world they were going to do.

Later, when Ella woke up, Keely had to tell her about the phone call.

Ella was hungover, but she sobered quickly. "Jock knows, then? I was afraid Brent would get high enough to tell him."

"What can we do?" Keely asked miserably.

Ella drew in a long breath. "I don't know. I'll have to think about this."

"You don't have the time!" Keely said. "What if he goes to the sheriff?"

Ella looked at her daughter and actually smiled. "Thanks," she said huskily. "It means a lot, after the way I've treated you, that you'd mind if I went to jail." She shrugged. "Maybe it would be just as well to get it out in the open, Keely. It's been so many years…if I had a good lawyer…"

"Yes," Keely was agreeing.

She glanced at the younger woman, so hopeful, so enthusiastic. Ella knew that no judge in Jacobs County would let her walk away from a homicide; not when the sheriff's brother was the victim, regardless of how much time had transpired between the death and the present. Keely was young and full of dreams. Ella was long past them. But she might be able to do something to save her daughter. She might be able to spare Keely, if she had the guts to do what was necessary.

"We'll work something out," she assured the younger woman. "You're going to that dance with Clark, aren't you? He's very nice. Maybe he'll marry you." Her eyes looked dreamy for a moment. "He's a good man. He'd take care of you, and you'd have everything you wanted."

"Clark and I are just friends," she said.

Ella glanced at her curiously. "It's his brother, isn't it? I didn't do you any favors with the lies I told him. I could call him up and tell him the truth."

"No," Keely said at once.

Ella stared at her. "You loved him, and I screwed it up for you. I'm sorry."

"He thinks I'm much too young for him," Keely said with a sad smile. She was remembering the way Boone had talked to her at the library and hating circumstances that had robbed her of even a chance with him. Now that she knew the truth about her parents, any sort of a relationship with him would be impossible. Boone Sinclair, with his sterling reputation and impeccable bloodlines, wouldn't stoop so low as to marry the daughter of drug users and murderers.

"You look so sad," Ella said. "I really am sorry."

"I know. It's all right," she replied.

Ella got up. "You'd better finish pressing your dress. I'd offer you one of mine," she added, "but you're much too slender."

"Thanks for offering," Keely said gently.

Ella smiled back, and something twisted deep inside her as she recalled how cruel she'd been to her child. She was sorry about it now. Maybe she could make amends. Maybe, just maybe, she could spare Keely any more heartbreak if she went about it right.

Clark was right on time to pick up Keely. She was wearing a pretty green velvet dress that clung lovingly to her pretty figure all the way to her shapely ankles, with a fox stole that belonged to her mother. Ella had insisted that she take it. She also had high heels that were expensive and pretty, another loan from Ella, who wore the same shoe size. Keely had no evening shoes at all, never having had occasion to wear them. Her blond hair was clean and shiny, neatly combed, and her eyes were full of dreams.

"You look gorgeous," Clark said suddenly as he helped her into the car. "I mean it. You really do."

She smiled. "Thanks, Clark."

He got into the car, thoughtful. When he frowned like that, he reminded her of Boone.

"Is something wrong?" she asked.

He shrugged. "I was thinking that I've been using you and it's wrong."

"I don't mind."

"That's what makes it so bad," he replied. "I'm doing things I don't like just to keep Boone from asking questions about my girlfriend." He glanced at her. "If I really cared about her, I'd be doing things differently, wouldn't I, Keely?"

She was surprised by his attitude, and the question. "You're in love. It makes people do odd things."

"Am I? In love, I mean?" He accelerated around a curve. "I've invested in a king's ransom of jewelry and designer clothes for Nellie. She hasn't refused a thing. In fact, she's made suggestions about what I could buy her that she'd like best." He glanced at her. "I can't get you to accept a pair of inexpensive earrings."

She flushed. It sounded very much as if Boone had made some idle comment that had started his brother thinking about things.

"I don't like jewelry."

"Of course you like it, Keely. All women like jewelry," Clark replied. "But you won't accept it from me. You won't even tell me why."

She bit her lip. "It would be like accepting payment for helping you out."

"And that's wrong?"

"In my world, yes, it is. A small present at Christmas is one thing. But expensive jewelry, that's something else."

"That's what Boone says. His girlfriend was hinting that she'd like a diamond collar. He said she could whistle for it. He didn't have to pay women to go out with him. She was really mad. She stormed out without another word."

"I'll bet she came back," Keely said sadly.

"Of course she did. Boone's loaded, and he's a dish, and he's relentlessly chased by every spinster south of Dallas."

Keely's heart sank. Of course he was. Boone was every woman's dream. He was certainly Keely's.

"It started me thinking," Clark continued. "And not in a good way. If Nellie loved me, she'd be wanting to buy things for me."

"She couldn't afford your taste, Clark," she murmured dryly.

He thought for a minute and then laughed. "Well, no, she couldn't. But it's the point of the thing, Keely. She hasn't bought me anything since we started dating. Not even a handkerchief or a music CD. Nothing."

"Some people aren't givers."

"Some people are gold diggers, though," he replied.

She leaned back against the seat with a little sigh. "I guess so. I've never understood why. I love working for what I get. My paychecks may be small compared to a lot of others, but every one thrills me. I worked with my own hands for what I have."

"Boone admires that."

"Does he?" She tried not to sound impressed.

"Not that he wants to. He does his best to ignore you."

"I noticed."

"Maybe he's right, Keely," he said solemnly. "You're very young, even to be going out with me."

She threw up her hands. "What is it about my age? For heaven's sake, I'll be twenty on Christmas Eve!"

He smiled. She made him feel good. She always had. She and Winnie were closer to him than any other two women on earth.

"You're the nicest friend I have," he said out of the blue. "I'm going to start treating you better."

"Are you, really? Then if you want to get me something..."

"Anything!" he interrupted. "I mean that."

"I'd love to have mats for my car."

He blinked. "What?"

"Mats. You know, those black ribbed things that go on the floorboard. Just for the driver's side," she added quickly. "It was used, so it didn't come with the original equipment, and Dr. Rydel's parking lot isn't paved. I have to walk through mud to get to my car when it rains."

Clark was still absorbing the shock. Nellie had asked, petulantly, for a diamond pendant she'd seen advertised in a slick magazine and here was Keely asking for a single mat for her damned car.

"Not anything expensive," she said quickly, fearing she'd overstepped. "I mean, for Christmas. I'm going to get you something, too, but it will be inexpensive."

He pulled up at the community center, feeling two inches high. He turned to her in the car. "You make me ashamed," he said quietly.

"Of what?" she asked.

He shook his head. "Never mind. We'd better go in. I think we're a little late."

"My fault," she said, smiling. "You had to wait while I found my purse." She held it up. "It was an old one of mama's. She let me have it, and her cell phone, and she loaned me her fox fur—" she waved it at him "—and her shoes—" she held up one foot to show him.

He could have wept. She never asked for a thing. She wouldn't let Winnie loan her anything at all. He'd never felt so bad in all his life. He'd used her as a blind for his great love affair, put her in a position where Boone could savage her if he ever found out what she'd been doing and never even gave a thought to the consequences.

"Tonight is the last time I'm hiding Nellie behind you," he said suddenly. "I'll go off with her, this once. But from now on, I'm taking her right into the front door of my house."

"Have some catsup handy, won't you?" she teased. "Boone will have her for supper."

"I know that. Maybe it wouldn't be a bad thing to let him have a bite of her. For once, maybe she'd show her true colors."

She stopped smiling. "It might not be as bad as you think," she said softly. "I mean, she might care about you and still like jewelry."

"She might rather have just the jewelry," he returned cynically.

A big SUV pulled up into the parking lot. He grimaced. "She's early." He looked at Keely. "Want me to walk you in?"

She shook her head. "I can do it all by myself."

He handed her a ticket. "You're taking that, even if it's all you'll let me give you. I'll be back before you miss me."

She knew better than that. He might talk good, but he was still under Nellie's spell. She'd have him convinced by the end of the evening that he couldn't live without her. Poor man.

"Have fun," she said.

He harrumphed. "You have fun."

She got out of the car, closed the door and waved. She didn't look toward Nellie. She would have happily thrown rocks at her if it would have spared Clark.

Music poured out into the cold night air. They were playing a Latin number. She imagined all the town's excellent dancers, including Matt Caldwell and Cash Grier, were out on the dance floor dazzling the spectators. She was looking forward to watching them.

She gave her ticket at the door, tugged the fox fur closer and moved into the huge room where a live band was playing.

"I thought you'd be along when I heard Clark mention that he bought tickets," a deep, amused voice said behind her.

She turned and looked up into Boone Sinclair's dark, soft eyes.

CHAPTER EIGHT

Keely couldn't manage a single word. Boone caught her hand and tugged her into the community center with him.

"Should I ask where Clark is?"

She felt as if her feet weren't quite on the floor. "No need. I didn't see your car."

"That's because I didn't drive it here. I brought one of the trucks and parked it out back. I doubt Clark even noticed."

"He didn't." She looked around. "Is Winnie here?"

He hesitated. "No."

She stopped walking so that he had to stop, too.

He looked down at her appreciatively, his dark eyes lingering on the way the emerald-green dress fit her slender, pretty body. "Green suits you," he mused.

"Winnie didn't come…?" she prompted.

"Kilraven said he wasn't coming," he replied. "She said it was useless to let men she didn't even like parade her around the dance floor."

She cocked her head and looked up at him. "Maybe she has a point."

He lifted an eyebrow and looked wicked. "Maybe she does."

She felt suddenly uneasy. She looked around again, for Misty this time.

"She's not here."

Flushed, she looked back up into his amused eyes.

"I came alone," he told her. "I mentioned that I wasn't buying diamonds for a casual date and she took offense."

"I heard."

"Oh? Was Clark impressed?"

"Yes. But don't count on it lasting any length of time," she added. "Once he's alone with her, he'll forget everything he said."

"No doubt." He pursed his lips. "Do you dance, Miss Welsh?"

Her heart skipped at the way he said it. He had no date, and he'd come anyway. And he was looking at her as if he could eat her. That was thrilling, even if she couldn't hope for anything more.

"I do," she replied. She sounded breathless.

He took the fox stole and her purse and laid them on a table next to where Cag Hart and his wife, Tess, were sitting. "Do you mind watching them?" he asked.

Tess grinned. "Not if I get to try on that stole."

"Help yourself," Keely invited with a big grin.

Tess wound it around her neck and struck a pose. She batted her eyelids at her husband. Her blue eyes twinkled in their frame of red hair.

"I'm not buying you a dead fox," Cag informed her haughtily.

Keely recalled that Cag had watched the "pig" movie and gave up eating pork. She wondered if he'd recently seen any other animated animal films.

Tess looked up and grinned. "There was this foxhound movie..."

"Will you stop?" Cag muttered, looking oddly flushed. "I like animals."

Tess bent over and kissed him. "So do I. But this animal has probably been deceased for a number of years...."

He burst out laughing and kissed her back.

Boone tugged Keely toward the dance floor.

He slid one arm around her waist and pulled her closer, easing his fingers in between hers. She stumbled with nerves as he propelled her expertly into the slow rhythm, and he laughed, deep in his throat.

She felt like a fox, running for cover. Her heart was racing, her breath was stuck somewhere south of her windpipe. She barely noticed the music. She was too aware of Boone's powerful body against hers, the scent of his breath, the smell of his cologne. He made her feel weak and shaky all over.

His hand spread against her back over the soft velvet. "I like this dress," he murmured at her forehead.

"It's very pretty," she began.

"I like the way it feels," he corrected.

She laughed nervously. "Oh."

He nuzzled her cheek, so that she lifted her eyes to his. "Nineteen years old," he said quietly, studying her. He looked guilty.

She frowned. "You know, age isn't everything."

"If you trot out that tired old line about it being the mileage," he threatened softly.

"It's true, though," she replied.

He smoothed his fingers in between hers as they moved lazily to the music. "You've heard from your father, haven't you?" he asked suddenly.

She jerked in his arms.

He nodded. "I thought so. You've been jumpy since you walked in the door."

She felt miserable, when she remembered what her mother had said about Hayes Carson's brother. She would carry the guilt for her parents' actions until she died. And Hayes was trying to look out for her, not knowing the truth.

"Come here."

He stopped dancing, caught her hand and led her out the side door onto the dark patio, where only a strip of light from the room inside showed on the stones of the flooring.

"Tell me what's worrying you," he coaxed.

She leaned her forehead against his chest. If only she could. But Hayes was his friend. "It was Jock who called. He made threats. My father wants Mama to sell the house and give him the money," she said heavily. "He's got something on her, something he can use, if she doesn't do it. She's afraid of him."

"What does he have on her?"

She groaned softly. "I don't know."

He tilted her chin up. "Yes, you do, Keely," he argued, searching her eyes in the dim light from the patio windows inside.

Her eyes were tormented. "I can't tell you," she said sadly. "It isn't my secret."

His fingers caressed her chin. "You can tell me anything," he said, his voice deep and soft and seductive. "Anything."

He made her want to tell him. He was powerful and attractive. He made her blood run hot through her veins. She wanted to kiss him until the aching stopped. She couldn't tell him that, of course.

She didn't have to. Boone read the subtle signs of her body and her breathing and drew a conclusion. Slowly, so that he didn't frighten her, he bent toward her mouth. "I should be shot," he whispered.

His breath tasted of coffee. The exquisite feel of flesh against flesh in such an intimate way made Keely's head spin. She'd rarely been kissed at all, and never like this. His skill was apparent.

But he seemed to lose control, just a little, as the kiss lengthened. His mouth grew quickly hungry. His arms contracted and riveted her to the length of his body, bending her into its hard contours. She stiffened helplessly at the intimacy, to which she was completely unaccustomed.

Boone lifted his head, surprised by her posture, by her reaction. She responded as if she'd never been held and kissed in her life; as if the demanding ardor of an adult man was unknown to her. And perhaps it was. He considered what he knew of her life from Winnie's vague comments.

He let her move back, just a step, but he didn't let her go. "It's all right," he said softly, smiling. He framed her face in his big hands and held it where he wanted it. His thumb gently pulled down her lower lip as he bent again. "All we have to fear," he quoted amusedly, "is fear itself..."

It was different this time. He didn't demand. He teased her lips, brushing them in brief little caresses that made her want more. His hands smoothed back her hair. They moved down her back, to the curve of her hips, and coaxed her closer. She shivered at the contact and for an instant his mouth became demanding. But when she stiffened, he relented at once.

It was like a silent duel, she thought, fascinated. He advanced, and when she hesitated, he withdrew. It was as if he knew the difficulty she felt, as if he was aware of how new and frightening these sensations were to her. He calmed her, coaxed her, until she began to relax and stop fighting the slow, steady crush of his mouth.

"That's it," he whispered when she sank gently against him. "Just don't fight it. Don't fight me. I won't hurt you."

She knew that. But it was still difficult to give herself over to someone who didn't know about her past. She was terrified not of his exploring hands, but of what he might find if he persisted.

So when she felt his fingertips teasing just around the edge of her breast, she jumped and pulled back.

She expected an explosion. Once, just once, she'd given in to temptation in her adult years and agreed to go out with a salesman who came through town. He'd grabbed her in the car and she'd jerked away from him. He'd been furious, snapping at her about girls who teased. And then he'd forcibly run his hand over her shoulder and her breast. She could never forget the look of utter horror in his face. He'd pushed her away from him. He took her home without a single word. He hadn't even looked at her when she got out of the car. It wasn't as bad as the date she'd had at the tender age of sixteen that had ended in such trauma. But it was bad enough. That was the last time she'd ever gone out with a man on a date.

But Boone wasn't angry. In fact, he looked pleased rather than offended at her lack of response.

He withdrew his hand and traced her swollen lips with it. "Well!" he exclaimed softly, and he smiled.

She was worried. "You aren't…mad?"

He shook his head. "Virgins need gentle handling," he whispered, and bent to kiss her, tenderly, when she blushed.

When he drew back, his expression was solemn and gentle. He smoothed over her hair, touched her cheek, her mouth, her chin. "When are you going to be twenty?" he asked after a minute.

"Chr-Christmas Eve," she stammered.

"Christmas Eve. In four months." He kissed her eyelids closed, smiling against them. "We'll have to do something very special for your birthday."

"We? Oh, you mean Winnie and Clark and you?"

He lifted his head and searched her eyes. "Why wouldn't you think I meant just you and me?" he queried.

"There's Misty," she reminded him.

He frowned, as if he didn't know who she was talking about. The magic seemed to seep away. He withdrew his hand and became aloof. "Misty," he repeated.

The magic drained out of the night. He became the distant stranger, the aloof man of the past. At that moment, he looked as if he'd never considered touching Keely.

She wrapped her arms around herself against a chill that didn't come from the night air. "It's getting cool," she said, trying to sound nonchalant.

"Yes, it is." He moved away from her, deep in thought. He paused to open the door for her.

She went through it without looking up. She said nothing. He said nothing. She went to the refreshment table and got a small cup of soda and sat down with it over against the wall.

She watched Boone stop at a group of cattlemen and stand talking to them. Her eyes darted around to see if Clark had returned. When she glanced toward the group of cattlemen again, Boone was gone. She didn't see him again.

Clark picked her up. He looked disheveled and out of sorts.

"The pearls were the wrong color," he said dejectedly. "She wanted pink ones. I got gray ones."

"I'm sorry."

He glanced at her and grimaced. "I hated leaving you there alone," he confessed. "I'm really sorry. I won't do it again."

"It was all right," she said. "I liked the music."

"You're the nicest friend I've ever had," he said after a minute. "But you shouldn't let me take advantage of you like this."

She laughed. "Okay."

He gave her a rakish grin. "Good girl."

"What's our next project?"

He sighed. "I really don't know. I'll let you know when she decides if she wants to see me again."

"She will," she said with conviction.

"We'll see."

Dr. Rydel was raising more hell than usual when Keely went in to work the next Monday.

"I told you to reorder that low-fat dog food last week," he was raging at their newest clerk, Antonia.

"But I did, Dr. Rydel," she said, near tears. "They had it on back order."

He made a rude sound. "And I suppose the urn containing Mrs. Randolph's old cat is also on back order?" he added sarcastically.

Antonia was red by this time. "No, sir, I forgot to check on it is all. I'm sorry," she added quickly.

It didn't make any difference. He stood in front of her and glared. She burst into tears and ran into the back.

"Oh, nice job, Doctor," his colleague, Dr. Patsy King, muttered. "She'll quit and we'll have to break in yet another clerk. How many is that so far this year? Let me think…six, isn't it?" she added with as much sarcasm as she could muster.

Bentley glared at her. "Four!"

"Oh. Only four." She rolled her eyes. "That makes me feel better."

"Don't you have a patient waiting, Dr. King?" he drawled, eyes flashing.

She sighed. "Yes, I do, thank God, but I came out here to get our clerk to schedule her next appointment. I suppose I'll be doing that myself!" She looked pointedly toward the back where Antonia was audibly sobbing.

He cursed.

She made a face. "Oh, like that's going to help!" she grumbled. She sat down in Antonia's chair and used the computer to schedule the next visit for her patient. While she was at it, she added up the charges and printed out a sheet listing them.

"I could help you do that," Keely offered.

"No, you could not," Dr. Rydel muttered. "I need you to help with examinations, not making appointments."

"Speaking of which, Keely, could you carry this dog out to Mrs. Reynolds's car for her?" Dr. King asked, and smiled gently.

"Of course," Keely answered at once, and walked off with Dr. King, leaving a fuming Dr. Rydel behind.

After that morning, it was open war between the two senior veterinarians in the practice. Dr. King was three years younger than Dr. Rydel, married with two children, and she needed her job. But she threatened to leave if he didn't stop using the clerks for target practice. Keely and the senior vet tech and the other veterinarian, Dr. Dave Mercer, tried to keep out of Dr. Rydel's way until his temper improved. Nobody knew what had set him off, but he was like a prizefighter walking down the street wearing boxing gloves. He was spoiling for a fight.

It was a relief for Keely when the workweek was over and she could get away from the tension. She was still mooning over Boone and reliving the tender kisses he'd shared with her on the patio of the community center. She didn't understand his behavior at all. Everything had been fine until she'd mentioned Misty. Then he'd withdrawn as if he'd felt guilty about touching Keely. He'd left the dance rather than risk having to talk to her again.

Worse, people were gossiping about the two of them. Tess Hart had teased her about going out onto the patio with Boone and coming back inside flushed. She'd mentioned it to Cag. Probably he'd told his brothers and they'd told other people. So

Keely got teased when she went to the grocery store, because one of the checkout girls had a boyfriend on the Hart Ranch properties. Then she got teased at the bank, because one of the tellers was married to Cag Hart's livestock foreman. That teller's married daughter worked at the 911 center with Winnie.

"You and Boone are the talk of the town, did you know?" Winnie teased her friend when they had lunch together at Barbara's Café that Saturday.

"Boone's going to kill me," Keely said miserably. "Clark's probably going to want to kill me, too, when he realizes that Boone knows what he's up to."

"Oh, Boone always knows," Winnie said easily. "Clark can never hide anything from him—or from me. But just between us two, I don't think this Nellie thing is going very much further. She got mad because Clark gave her the wrong color pearls. That, after he's given her most of a jewelry store!" She leaned forward. "And it turns out that she's married."

"What?" Keely exclaimed. "Does Clark know?"

"That, and more," Winnie said. "When I left home, Boone was presenting our brother with a thick file on Miss Nellie Summers. He said Clark wasn't leaving the house until he'd read every sordid detail."

"Poor Clark."

Winnie chuckled. "He was cussing mad after he read the first page," she said. "He wouldn't have believed it even two weeks ago, but apparently Boone picked just the right time to tell him the truth."

"I'm glad," she confessed. "It was putting me right in the middle, being used as Clark's cover."

"Clark shouldn't have done that. Boone was angry. He said Clark had no right to use you that way."

"Clark's my friend. I could have said no," Keely said softly.

"You never say no to anyone," Winnie replied, concerned.

"You're too good to people, Keely. You won't stand up for yourself."

"I'm trying."

"Clark walks all over you. So does Boone. I'll bet Dr. Rydel does, too."

"Dr. Rydel walks all over everybody," Keely pointed out.

"Well, you do have a point there." She sipped coffee and then her eyes began to twinkle. "So what was going on with you and my brother at the dance?"

"Not you, too!" Keely wailed.

"I'm your best friend. You have to tell me."

Keely put on her best bland expression. "He wanted to talk to me about Clark without everybody eavesdropping."

Winnie's face fell. "Was that all?"

"What else would there be?" Keely replied. "You know Boone can't stand me. Usually he ignores me. But he knew Clark was up to something and that I was helping him. He got it out of me."

"He's good at that," Winnie had to admit. "They used to let him interrogate people when he was in the military." She toyed with her coffee cup. "He's changed so much since he came back from overseas. He used to be a happy sort of person. He's not happy now." She looked up. "He goes out with Misty, but he never touches her."

Keely's heart jumped. "How do you know?"

"He never picks up anything," she said with affection. "He just leaves his clothes lying around in his room. I gather them up and put them in the hamper for Mrs. Johnson. There are never any lipstick stains on his shirts." She paused, her lips pursed. "Well, that's not quite the truth. Last Saturday night, there were quite a few lipstick stains on his collar."

Keely's face flamed and Winnie laughed triumphantly. Keely knew that Winnie would go straight to Boone and tease him if she guessed what had happened. She couldn't let her friend know for sure. If Boone were teased about Keely at home, it would all be over before it had time to begin.

"No wonder he's been like a scalded snake all week," Winnie mused, watching Keely closely. "And he hasn't even called Misty. Odd, isn't it?"

"Just slow down, if you please. I danced with him," Keely muttered. "Of course I got lipstick on his collar."

Winnie's happy mood slowly drained away. She frowned. "Are you sure that's all?"

Keely gave her friend a speaking look. "Boone can't stand me. He was just trying to find out why Clark and I had gone to a dance and Clark was missing."

"Oh, Fish and Chips!" Winnie muttered.

"Excuse me?"

Winnie shifted. "Good Lord, I'm catching Hayes Carsonitis!" she exclaimed.

"What?"

"Hayes Carson doesn't cuss like a normal man. He says things like 'Crackers and Milk!' and 'Fish and Chips!' It rubs off when you're around him."

"What are you doing hobnobbing with Hayes Carson?" Keely asked.

"On the radio!"

"Oh. Right."

"He's not bad-looking," Winnie mused. "And he's much friendlier than Kilraven. I should really set my cap at him."

"You'd break Kilraven's heart," Keely teased.

Winnie wrinkled her nose. "Like he'd notice if I flirted with another man," she said shortly. "He's trying Boone's tactics. He's ignoring me."

"He's probably just busy."

Winnie toyed with her napkin. "Men are not worth the trouble they cause," she said irritably.

Keely laughed. "No," she agreed. "They aren't."

"And don't we both lie well?" Winnie retorted.

Keely nodded.

The little café was crowded for a Saturday, mostly with tourists trying to enjoy the last fleeting days of August. Jacobsville had an annual rodeo that drew crowds, because it attracted some of the stars of the circuit. The prize money wasn't bad, either.

"There are a lot of cars with out-of-state tags," Winnie murmured. "I guess it's the rodeo that draws them."

"I was just thinking about the rodeo." Keely chuckled. "Great minds running in the same direction."

"Exactly. I think—" Winnie's voice broke off. She was staring at the front door helplessly.

Keely glanced toward the entrance. Kilraven, still in uniform, was standing just inside the door. He really was hunky, Keely thought; tall, handsome and elegant with silver eyes and thick black hair. He was muscular without it being blatant.

"Excuse me," he called in his deep voice. "Is anyone here driving a red SUV with Oklahoma plates?"

A young man in jeans and chambray shirt raised his hand. "Yes. I am," he called. "Anything wrong, Officer?"

Kilraven walked to his table, spotted Winnie and Keely and nodded politely before he stood over the man. "Did you pick up a deer from the side of the road, sir?" he asked.

The young man laughed. "Yes, I did. It was just killed by a car, I think, because it was still warm and limp when I picked it up." The smile faded. "I was only going to take it home and cut it up for my freezer. Did I do something wrong?"

Kilraven cleared his throat. "You might want to call your insurance agent."

The young man looked blank. "Why?"

"The deer wasn't dead."

"Wasn't...dead?" He nodded.

"And it left the vehicle rather suddenly, through your windshield."

The young man was still nodding. "Through the windshield?" He stiffened. "Through my windshield? In my brand-new truck? Aaahhh!"

He jumped up, overbalancing his chair so that it fell. He almost trampled a couple getting out the door. His scream of dismay could be heard even with the door closed.

Kilraven shook his head as he paused beside Winnie. "The deer was just stunned," he said with faint amusement in his silver eyes. "We had a man make that same mistake about six months ago during hunting season. But fortunately for him, the deer came to before he could lift it into his truck."

Outside the café, the screams were getting louder.

Kilraven glanced outside and chuckled. "He'll want a report for his insurance agency. I'd better go write him up."

"Have they found Macreedy yet?" Winnie asked with a drawl and a grin.

Kilraven groaned. "He surfaced over in Bexar County about five yesterday afternoon trailing forty cars in a funeral procession. They were supposed to be headed for a cemetery in Comanche Wells, where they were due at three o'clock," he added, because Keely was looking puzzled. "He did finally get them to the right church...after several cars stopped to get gas."

"That's twice this month. They should never let Macreedy lead a funeral procession," Winnie pointed out.

Kilraven chuckled. "I told Hayes Carson the same thing, but he says Macreedy will never learn self-confidence if he pulls him off public service details now."

"Doesn't he have a map?" Keely wanted to know.

"If he does, he can't ever find it," Kilraven said with a sigh.

"He led the last funeral procession down into a bog near the river and the hearse got stuck." He laughed. "It's funny now, but nobody was laughing at the time. They had to get tow trucks to haul everybody out."

"Hayes should cut his losses and put Macreedy on administrative duties," Winnie said.

"Big mistake. Hayes put him in charge of the jail month before last and he let a prisoner out to use the bathroom and forgot to lock him up again. The prisoner robbed a bank while he was temporarily liberated." He shook his head. "I don't think Macreedy's cut out for a career in law enforcement."

"Yes, but his father does," Winnie reminded him.

"His father was a career state trooper," Kilraven told Keely. "He insisted that his son was to follow in his footsteps."

"Hayes Carson is our sheriff," Keely said, confused. "Macreedy's a sheriff's deputy."

"Yes, well, Macreedy started out working as a state trooper," Winnie began.

Kilraven was chuckling again. "And then he pulled over an undercover drug unit in their van just as they were speeding up to stop a huge shipment of cocaine. They'd been working the case for weeks. The drug dealers got away while Macreedy was citing the drug agents for a burned-out taillight. Macreedy's dad did manage to save him from the guys in the drug unit, but he was invited to practice his craft somewhere else."

"So Hayes Carson got him," Winnie continued. "Hayes is his second cousin."

"Sheriff Carson could have said no," Keely replied.

"You don't say no to Macreedy's father," Kilraven retorted.

"At least he's learning all the back roads," Winnie said philosophically.

Kilraven grinned at her. The look lasted just a second too

long to be conventional, and Winnie's delicate skin took on a pretty flush.

"*Where's my rifle?*" came a bellow from the parking lot. "Somebody stole my rifle!"

Kilraven glanced out the window. The young fellow who owned the red SUV was running down the street with a rifle, in the general direction that the escaped deer had gone. The gun's owner was jumping up and down in his rage and yelling threats after the deer hunter.

"I'd better go save the deer hunter," Kilraven remarked.

"I hope he has an understanding insurance agent," Keely mused.

"And a good lawyer. Stealing rifles is a felony." Kilraven nodded at them and went striding out the door.

"Well!" Keely teased softly. "And you don't think he likes you?"

Winnie's expression was so joyful that Keely envied her.

CHAPTER NINE

Keely had laughed at the predicament Hayes Carson was in with his cousin Macreedy, but it was impossible for her to talk about him or think about him without remembering her mother's pained confession about Hayes's brother, Robert.

She was feeling guilty about that when Clark phoned her.

"I'm sorry," she said as soon as she recognized his voice.

"You are?" He hesitated. "Oh. I guess you mean about Nellie. Boone knew all along, Keely," he added heavily. "I thought I was pulling the wool over his eyes. I always underestimate him. He'd hired his girlfriend's father's detective agency to investigate Nellie. I can't say I'm really surprised at what he found out. Well, I'm surprised that she was married and…fooling around with me, I mean."

"Boone is very intelligent," she said noncommittally.

"Yes, and he knows how to make people talk."

She grimaced. "I didn't mean to…"

"No! Not you. Me! He asked me what the hell I thought I was doing, leaving you at a dance alone all evening. He was furious."

"But I was all right."

"He knows that your father and his partner in crime might

make a grab for you, Keely. I knew it, or should have known it, and I put you at risk. Boone said anything could have happened. I'm really sorry, Keely. I was so crazy about Nellie that she was all I thought about. You're my friend. I should have been looking out for you."

It made her warm inside that Boone was worried for her safety. "It's okay, Clark," she said. "Honest, it is."

"He gets hot about you," he continued. "I'd almost say he's possessive of you, but that's ridiculous. He is fond of you, in his way, I think." He paused. "There was some talk about the two of you at the dance. You went outside together..."

"To talk about you," she countered. "He wanted to know where you were and what you were doing. He's very insistent."

There was a relieved sigh. "Yes, he is." He paused again. "Keely, you don't want to ever get mixed up with him," he said, in a stumbling sort of way that made her heart fill with disappointment. "Something happened to him overseas. He hated women for years after that she-cat dropped him when he was wounded. God knows why he's letting her lead him down the same path again. Maybe he wants revenge. He doesn't like women at all. He just uses them. Sort of like me," he added miserably.

Keely didn't know what to say, how to answer him. "He's not a bad person."

"I didn't say he was, just that he's hateful toward women. He's keeping Misty on a tight rein, and he doesn't watch his words when he talks to her. It's almost like he's keeping her around for some mysterious reason, but he doesn't really want to have anything to do with her. He couldn't care less if he's late for a date, or if he doesn't even show up. She spends most of their time together complaining about the way he treats her, and about you."

"Me?" she exclaimed. "But why? Boone doesn't give a hill of beans about me!"

"I don't really know. She's jealous of you."

"That's one for the books," she mumbled. "She's beautiful and rich. I'm plain and poor. I'm no competition at all."

"I could dispute that," Clark replied gently. "You have some wonderful qualities."

"I'm no beauty."

"Neither is she."

Keely laughed softly. "Of course she is."

"She's not a beauty inside," he said doggedly. "You are."

"Thanks, Clark. You're nice."

"Nice." He laughed. "Well, at least we're still friends. Aren't we?"

"Yes."

"Then you can go riding with me from time to time. At the ranch. When Boone isn't around," he added with a wicked chuckle.

"We both know you're not afraid of Boone," she chided.

"Not much, anyway."

"What did you tell Nellie, about not seeing her anymore?"

There was a long pause.

Her heart sank. "Clark, you're not still seeing her?"

There was a longer pause.

"Her husband might hurt you. Really hurt you," she warned.

He sighed. "You don't understand. It's complicated."

"I guess I don't," she replied. "Be careful. Okay?"

"I'll be careful. I know I have to break it off. But we had something special—on my side, at least. It takes a little time to adjust."

"You watch your back," she replied.

"I'll do that. See you."

"See you."

She hung up, but she was worried. Clark was playing with fire. If she and Boone were really friends, she'd tell him. But Boone hadn't called or come near her since the dance, when he'd kissed her so sweetly. She'd dreamed about him, ached to see him, but she hadn't had so much as a glimpse of him. Perhaps he'd just been leading her on, she thought sadly, to get information about Clark and Nellie. There was a miserable thought, and it kept her unhappy the rest of the day.

She and her mother were getting along better than they ever had, although Keely lived in terror that her father, or worse, Jock, might just show up at the door. Ella had talked to a Realtor about the house and land. She had to take Jock's threat seriously, she said, and she didn't want to go to jail. Keely was worried that the secret might come out anyway. She felt guilty just knowing about it.

Things got worse when Hayes showed up at the vet's office where she worked in the middle of the next week. He was somber and worried. He asked Keely out into the parking lot, away from the crowd in the waiting room, where they could talk undisturbed.

"What's wrong?" Keely asked him apprehensively.

"It's about your father," he began hesitantly. His face became hard. "I've heard something. A little gossip. It involves my brother..."

"Oh, heavens!" Keely ground out. "I'm so sorry!"

The expression on her face spoke volumes. She never could keep secrets, and this one had cost her many a night's sleep. If Hayes pushed, she'd have to tell him. She went pale.

"You know, don't you?" he asked quietly. "Tell me, Keely."

She wrapped her arms tight around herself. "If I do, my mother will go to jail," she said miserably.

"If you don't, your mother may die," he countered. "Your

father was seen at a roadhouse over in Bexar County two days ago."

She actually gasped. "With Jock?"

"The person who saw him didn't know about the other man. Probably wouldn't recognize him. What does Brent have on your mother, Keely, and what has it got to do with my family?"

She leaned back against his patrol car, looking at him with dead eyes. "My father was apparently dealing cocaine before he left here with me, and he had some pure stuff. He made a deal with..." She stopped and bit her lip. She hadn't thought how it would sound.

Hayes seemed to know. He shifted his tall frame. "I know what my brother was," he said quietly. "You don't have to pull any punches on his account. He's long dead and buried."

She drew in a long breath. "Yes, but he was still your brother and you loved him," she said gently. "I loved my father. I never dreamed..." She stopped. "Your brother saw my father make a drug buy. My father offered him a small fortune in cocaine not to tell you."

"So that was it."

"My father gave it to your brother. He didn't tell him that it was a hundred-percent pure. Your brother had his supplier inject him with it. That's why he overdosed." She lowered her eyes. "I'm so ashamed!"

"No!" He moved forward and framed her face in his big, warm hands. "No, Keely, it's not your shame or your guilt! You're as much a victim as Bobby was. Don't take that burden on your own shoulders. It's their crime, not yours!"

Tears were rolling down her cheeks. Hayes felt for a handkerchief, but he didn't have one. Keely laughed as she tugged a paper towel out of her jeans pocket. "I always carry them around," she explained, dragging at her eyes. "We're constantly cleaning up messes. Some dogs get sick when they're brought here."

"I can sympathize with them," Hayes said with a forced smile. "I don't like going to doctors myself."

She blew her nose. "I wanted to tell you. I couldn't. I haven't been close to my mother, until the last few days, and I knew if I told, she could go to prison."

"What for?" he asked heavily. "There's no evidence. Everybody directly connected with the case is dead. The woman who gave Bobby the drugs was Ivy Conley's sister, Rachel. She died of a drug overdose herself not long ago. She left a diary and confessed that she'd given Bobby the overdose," he said surprisingly. Actually Keely knew Ivy, who had just married Stuart York, her best friend's brother.

Hayes looked thoughtful. "Your father and Rachel handed Bobby the gun, but he pulled the trigger himself, figuratively speaking. Bobby was an addict from the time he was twelve. I knew and tried to stop him. I never could."

"You mean, Mama won't go to jail?" she worried.

"No." He hesitated. "But your father will, if I can find one damned thing to pin on him," he added in the coldest tone she'd ever heard him use.

She felt sad, because her father had been kind to her. She hadn't known about his dark past, and she'd loved him. It was hard to know that he was one jump ahead of the law. She wondered why, what he'd done to get in so much trouble that he was running scared. "If he's running, and he needs money," she reasoned out loud, "he must be desperate to get away."

He pursed his lips. "You think like a detective," he mused.

"He's done something bad," she continued. "Or Jock has, and he helped." Her eyes were sad as they met Hayes's. "He was good to me, those two years I lived with him. If he'd never got mixed up with Jock again, he might have stayed changed."

"Bad men don't change, Keely," Hayes said in a resigned tone. "A lot of them are easily led. Others are just lazy, and they don't want to have to work for a living. Some have been so badly abused that they hate the world and want to get even. In between, there are good kids who use drugs or get drunk and do things that they regret for the rest of their lives." He shrugged. "I guess that's why God made lawmen." He smiled.

She smiled back.

"If you hear anything from him," he said, "you have to tell me right away."

"Mama's talking to Realtors," she volunteered. "She's really afraid of what he might do."

"So am I," he said. "I've got a friend up in San Antonio talking to the man who recognized your father. He's got a lead, and he's following it up. Maybe we'll get lucky."

"What should I tell Mama to do?"

He thought for a minute. "Tell her to go ahead and put the property on the market."

She opened her mouth to protest.

He held up a hand. "She doesn't have to sell it. She just has to appear as if she's selling it. It might buy us a little time. I'd bet money that your father or his partner is keeping an eye out around here."

"I'll tell her," she promised.

"And keep your doors and windows locked, just in case," he added grimly.

"We always do that."

"Keep a phone handy, too," he advised.

She nodded.

"I'm sorry you ever got involved in this," he said.

"We don't get to choose our families," Keely said philosophically.

"Isn't that the truth?"

* * *

She went home after work and told her mother what she'd learned from Sheriff Carson. Ella was obviously relieved.

"I was scared to death," she confessed to her daughter. "Sheriff Carson isn't going to arrest me? He told you that?"

"He told me," Keely replied. "But he does want you to put the house up for sale."

"I can do that." Ella smoothed her hands over her silk slacks. "Yes. I can do that." She looked her age. She hadn't even put on makeup. "I've only had one drink today," she said after a minute, and smiled at her daughter. "I'm shaky. But maybe I can give it up, if I try."

Keely felt the beginnings of a real relationship with her mother. "Really?" she asked, and smiled.

"Well, just don't expect too much," Ella laughed. "I've been a heavy drinker most of my life. It isn't easy to quit."

"I understand. I'll help. Anyway I can."

Ella studied the younger woman quietly. "You're a good kid, Keely," she said. "I haven't been a good mother. I wish…" She shrugged. "Well, we don't get many second chances. But I'll try."

"That's all anyone can do," Keely replied. Impulsively she hugged her mother. Ella hesitated for a minute, but then she hugged her back. It was a moment out of time, when anything seemed possible. But it only seemed that way.

Keely had hoped that Boone might call her, or bring Bailey by the office for a checkup or even be at home when she went riding with Winnie on the occasional Saturday. But he stayed away.

She accepted an invitation to go riding at the Sinclairs', hoping for a glimpse of Boone. She knew it was pathetic, but she was hungry to see him, under any circumstances. Winnie led the way down a wooded path to the river that ran through the property. Keely started to get down off her horse.

"Don't," Winnie said quickly, indicating the tall grass. "Rattlers are crawling. One of the boys killed two of them near the river this week."

"It's really hot," Keely said, unnerved by the mention of snakes. She was terrified of them.

"Yes, and they like cool places," Winnie said. "We'd better get back," she added, checking her watch. "I have to go in this afternoon. One of our dispatchers had a death in the family and I promised to fill in for her."

"You're a nice person," Keely said. "I really mean that."

Winnie smiled. "Thanks, Keely. So are you. I mean it, too."

"How's Clark?" she asked on the way back.

"Heading for tragedy," Winnie said coolly. "He's still seeing that woman."

"How do you know?"

"He stuffed a jewelry box into his pocket when he thought I wasn't looking last night," she said.

"But she's married," Keely argued. "What if her husband finds out?"

"Clark will be very sorry," she replied. "That detective's report said that he was a truck driver who did long hauls, and he's got a prior for assault."

"Oh, boy," Keely muttered.

"One day we'll get a call for Clark at work, you wait and see," Winnie said grimly. "He won't listen. He thinks he can win her away from her husband. He's in love."

"That woman hasn't left her husband for a reason," Keely agreed. "She's probably afraid of him."

"That would be my guess."

They rode in silence until they were within sight of the barn.

"Boone's doing a stupid thing, too," Winnie said after a minute.

Keely's heart jumped. "What?"

"He's bringing that Misty person home for the weekend," she said tautly. "God knows why. He treats her badly, but she hangs on. I don't understand what's going on."

"Revenge," Keely guessed.

"That's what I thought, too. But Clark wasn't the only one hiding jewelry from me. Boone had a jewelry box in his pocket, too, just like Clark," she said, glancing worriedly at Keely. "I saw it. A little square one, like a ring comes in. He was hiding it."

Keely's world was ending. She tried to smile. "I guess he discovered he really does care about her, huh?"

Winnie looked worried. "My brothers are both idiots," she muttered.

"Love doesn't make people rational," she said, glancing around at the parched pasture. "If we don't get some rain, even the animals are going to go loco," she added, trying to change the subject. "This drought is terrible."

"Worse for small ranchers than for us," Winnie replied. "We can afford to buy hay to feed our cattle. Now, this corn thing for fuel is pushing those prices even higher." She shook her head. "You try to fix one thing, and it damages another thing."

"That's life, I suppose."

"Don't look so glum," Winnie said gently. "Maybe it was a lapel pin or something that Boone bought for a friend. It might not even be a ring."

"Of course."

Winnie knew the other woman was hiding a big hurt. She changed the subject as they rode back toward the ranch.

They met a furious Clark at the barn. He was pacing, steaming. He saw the women ride up and went to meet them, along with a wrangler who took the horses to unsaddle and stable.

"What in the world is the matter with you?" Winnie asked her brother when the horses had been led away.

"That damned private detective who works for Boone's girlfriend's father, that's what's the matter!" he raged. "Boone set me up!"

"Set you up? How?" Keely wanted to know.

"Nellie is *not* married," he ground out. "I was suspicious, because she lives in an apartment in town. None of her neighbors have ever mentioned that she had other men coming and going, much less that her so-called husband was parking his semi in an apartment parking lot. So I asked a friend of mine on the San Antonio police force to check her out for me, on the quiet. He found out that she's never even been married!"

Winnie was shocked. "Clark, I'm sure Boone didn't tell them to make up that report," she began.

"Boone hates Nellie," he shot back. "He'd do anything to break us up. And before you both say it, I know she has a mercenary streak. She likes pretty things, because she can't afford them. It's my business if I want to buy them for her...nobody's making me do it."

Winnie and Keely exchanged woeful glances.

"Anyway, she's furious because Boone checked her out and tried to break us up with lies," he added grimly. "She won't see me anymore."

Keely felt guilty. Although why she should was anybody's guess.

"I'm really sorry," Winnie said gently, kissing him on the cheek. "I wish I could stay and talk more about it, but I'll be late for work. We can talk later, can't we?" She frowned. "Oh, I forgot! I've got to drive Keely home...."

"I'll drive her," Clark volunteered. "She can console me."

Winnie hugged her brother, and then Keely. "I'll call you," she told her friend.

Keely nodded. She was disappointed that she didn't get to see Boone at all, and sad for Clark that he'd been lied to. It didn't seem at all like Boone to have people make up stories about Nellie.

Clark put her into his sports car and peeled out down the driveway. He was still furious, and it showed.

"What are you going to do?" she asked.

"I'm going to do what Boone wants me to do," he muttered. "I'm giving Nellie up before he finds a way to destroy her reputation."

She felt sad for him. "Boone is formidable," she said.

"He's too used to getting his own way. He's run things for so long that he thinks he can run people's lives, as well." He glanced at her. "Are you game for a little payback? After all, he's done his bit to hurt you, as well."

She felt a sense of dark foreboding. "What bit?"

"He told Misty that you were running after him at the charity dance," he said tautly. "I told you there was some gossip. She heard it and raised hell. Boone usually doesn't pay attention to her when she rants, but he did that time. He said you'd lured him onto the patio and flirted with him shamelessly."

She was so embarrassed and humiliated that she wanted to sink through the floor. That was an absolute lie, and Boone knew it. She bit her lip almost through.

Clark glanced at her stony expression and grimaced. "Sorry. I didn't mean to lay it on that thick."

"The truth is always best, Clark, even if it hurts."

"I couldn't believe it when I heard him," he said. "I know you don't chase men. And you never flirt. When she left, I gave him hell. He just walked away without a word. You can't argue with him. He ignores you!"

She felt very small. She'd gone running out to the Sinclair house to go riding with Winnie on the flimsiest excuse, hoping to see Boone. And he'd been telling lies about her to his girlfriend. It was the last straw. She felt sick to her stomach.

"Let's start going out together, for real," Clark said curtly.

"What good would that do?" she wanted to know.

"It would teach Boone a lesson about trying to run people's lives, that's what it would do," he gritted. "I'm sick of him leading me around like a kid. He can't stand Nellie because he says she's mercenary. But what is that gilt-edged gold digger he takes around with him, if she's not mercenary?"

"She isn't one of my favorite people."

"Or mine. And now he's talking about getting engaged," he muttered. "I heard him mention it to Hayes Carson on the phone. I couldn't hear everything he was saying, but he sounded furious. Then he mentioned that he was trying to get engaged. I couldn't believe it. But when I saw the rings sitting on his desk..."

Her heart fell the rest of the way into her shoes.

He sighed. "Well, I won't live in the house with that ratty woman, and Winnie says she won't, either. If she moves in, we're moving out. Boone can entertain her all by himself."

"I can't say I blame you," she said in a subdued tone. "She was willing to sacrifice poor old Bailey just to go to a concert."

"Something you'd never do in a lifetime," he replied and smiled across at her.

"I love animals."

"So do I."

"So what do you mean, that we'd pretend to go around together, like we were doing before? Boone saw right through it, Clark."

"He won't this time," he assured her.

She puzzled those words the rest of the way home while

she endured the pain of Boone's cruel taunts. The man who'd kissed her so tenderly on the patio of the community center hadn't seemed like someone who would humiliate a woman who responded to him. But she knew very little about men, and Boone had certainly pegged her for a novice. Perhaps he was just amusing himself. He'd moved away from her when she mentioned Misty, and he'd been remote. Maybe he felt guilty playing up to one woman when he was involved with another one. He had to explain the gossip to Misty, so he'd made Keely the fall guy. Gal. Whatever. She could almost hate him for that. For certain, it brought home the reality of her situation.

Boone was wealthy. Keely was poor. His girlfriend was socially acceptable and pretty. Keely's father was a criminal. That said it all.

Clark pulled up at her front door and cut off the engine. "We're going to San Antonio, to the ballet." He held up a hand when she started to protest. "I'm going to hire a bodyguard so Boone won't have the excuse that I'm putting you in danger."

That was a new twist. She felt new respect for her friend.

"And we're going shopping, whether you like it or not," he added firmly. "You need some pretty evening wear, something silky and off the shoulder," he added with a smile.

Keely felt sick. "I don't wear those sorts of things," she said primly.

"I'm not asking you to wear your underwear," he said gently. "Just something a little more feminine than what you usually go around in."

He couldn't know how he was hurting her pride. But it did show, and he noticed. He frowned.

"What's wrong?" he asked.

She clasped her hands together in her lap. "Clark, I can't wear clothes that don't button up to the neck, much less something off the shoulder," she said with grim pride. She raised her face.

"I had an…an accident, just before Dad brought me back to Jacobsville. There are, well, scars…"

"God, I'm sorry!" he said at once. "I didn't know!"

"Nobody knows, not even my mother," she said, tight-lipped. "And you can't tell anyone, either." She lowered her eyes to her jeans. "It's something I've learned to live with, in my own way. But I have to dress within the limitations of my injury."

"That weakness in your arm," he recalled out loud. "That's part of it, isn't it?"

She nodded. Her face was flushed. "I'm sorry."

"No. I'm sorry," he replied quietly. He reached over and clasped her hand in his. "I won't tell anyone," he promised. "And we'll buy very conservative clothes. But pretty ones."

"I won't let you do that," she said proudly.

He pursed his lips. "Suppose I made you a loan?"

"I could never pay it back. You'll just have to make do with what I can afford to wear. My mother can loan me some of her more conservative things, and her fox fur. I'll look presentable. I promise."

He smiled gently. "Okay. If that's what you want."

"This bodyguard, you should probably ask Sheriff Carson about it," she said.

"I will. Go on in. I'll be in touch."

"Are you sure you want to do this?" she asked as she opened her door. "Nellie might come back to you."

"I don't know that I want her to," he replied. "We'll take it one day at a time. If you need anything, though, you let me know, okay?"

She wouldn't, and he knew it, but she smiled.

His dark eyes narrowed. "And I'm sorry that I told you what Boone said," he added solemnly. "It hurt you."

"Life hurts, Clark," she said quietly. "There's no getting around that."

"So they say." He leaned over to close the door, and powered the window open. "Next Friday night. The ballet."

She smiled. "I'll ask Dr. Rydel if I can leave work early."

"I'll ask him, too," he volunteered.

"You brave soul!"

"Yes, I've heard that he's making meals of the staff lately, but we get along," he chuckled. "I'll call you. So long."

"So long."

CHAPTER TEN

The bodyguard was actually a Jacobsville police officer who worked odd jobs when he was off duty. He was powerfully built and never seemed to smile.

Instead of riding in the car with them, he drove his own private vehicle and followed behind them to San Antonio. Clark had paid for his gas and would have bought him a ballet ticket, as well, until he'd mentioned that he'd prefer being burned at the stake. So Clark had made other arrangements for when they were inside.

Keely was wearing the same green velvet dress she'd worn to the dance, and her mother's fox stole and high heels. She was nervous about mingling with the upper classes of San Antonio, but Clark held her hand and reassured her that they were just regular people like himself.

He recognized a friend of his and introduced Keely to him. The man was Jason Pendleton, who owned a truck farm in Jacobsville. He was usually with his stepsister, Gracie, but tonight he was with a redhead whom he introduced as his fiancée. The woman was brassy and not very polite. She dragged Jason away scant minutes later and led him to a local newspaper owner instead.

"I guess we aren't quite good enough company," Clark mused. "Old Peppernell over there does own a newspaper, but our family could buy most everything he owns out of petty cash. Jason will tell her that, at some point, and then she'll drag him back over here and gush and pretend that Peppernell is a cousin or something whom she had a duty to talk to. His sister, Gracie, isn't impressed by dollar signs. She has friends who don't have a penny. But Jason's fiancée apparently only associates with the ultrarich."

He was amused. Keely was mortified. "Is that the sort of people you know?" she asked uneasily. "They judge you by dollar signs?"

"Jason doesn't. His fiancée apparently does." He frowned. "I wonder where Gracie is? It's unusual not to see them together."

"Is it?" she countered, curious. "Brothers and sisters don't usually partner each other at social events, do they?"

"They're not related," he said carelessly. "Gracie's mother married Jason's father, and promptly died, leaving Jason to look after her. Gracie's mother is dead, but Gracie still lives with Jason. Until now, he hasn't been much for commitment. His fiancée is nice-looking, I guess, but she's grasping, too."

Keely had noticed that. She was watching the woman as Jason Pendleton bent his tall form to speak to her. The woman gaped at Clark and Keely and winced.

"She just got the bad news." Clark chuckled under his breath.

Keely laughed, too, but as she turned her head, her eyes collided with Boone Sinclair's. She shivered at the unexpected encounter. She averted her eyes at once and turned back to Clark, clinging to his hand. Her heart was racing again. Boone had accused her of chasing him shamelessly. She didn't want to have to speak to him at all.

Boone was with Misty. He tugged her over to where Keely and Clark were standing.

"Before you start," Clark told his brother belligerently, "I've got Jarrett from the Jacobsville Police Department acting as our bodyguard on the road, and Detective Rick Marquez has the seat on the other side of us at the ballet." He gave his brother a cold look. He was still smoldering about that private detective's report on Nellie. "I've covered all our bases."

Boone's dark eyes narrowed irritably. He looked at Keely until she was forced to meet that riveting stare, but she immediately turned her attention away from him. She couldn't forget what he'd said about her to his girlfriend.

"I still don't think it's a good idea," Boone said shortly.

"Boone, why don't we just enjoy our evening and let your brother and his…friend…enjoy theirs?" Misty asked haughtily. "He's over the age of consent, you know."

Boone gave Misty a look. He turned back to Clark. "Don't put her at risk," he said solemnly.

"I would never do that," Clark replied shortly. "And you know it."

Boone gave Keely a long look that she ignored. He was scowling when he escorted Misty to their seats.

"You invited Marquez?" Keely asked, for something to say.

"Yes. He loves the ballet, and he's our lookout inside, just in case your father and his friend decide to mount an attack in the audience," he added with pure sarcasm.

Keely laughed. "I don't think that's likely to happen."

"Neither do I. Boone's getting strange lately. He was giving Hayes Carson hell on his cell phone last night, God knows for what. Hayes is his best friend, but they're falling out."

"Are they?" she asked absently, still reeling from Boone's intense interest and not really hearing what Clark said. "Shouldn't we go in?"

"We probably…"

"Oh, *there* you are." Jason Pendleton's fiancée rushed up.

"I'm so sorry we rushed away, but we had to speak to that friend of Jason's!"

Clark glanced at Keely and had to bite his tongue to keep from laughing.

Jason was giving his fiancée an odd sort of look, as if he hadn't noticed this social climbing penchant of hers. He wasn't conventionally handsome, but Keely could see why he drew women; and it wasn't because of his money.

She gave the couple a shy smile as Clark led her into the auditorium.

Detective Marquez grinned at them as they sat down.

"You're alone?" Clark asked, surprised.

"I can't get girls." Marquez shrugged. "Once they see the gun—" he indicated his shoulder holster "—and they realize that I carry it all the time, they usually leave skid marks getting out of my life. But it's okay," he said pleasantly. "I always wanted to spend my whole life alone with no kids or grandkids."

Clark and Keely burst out laughing.

He just grinned.

All through the ballet, which was beautiful and riveting, Keely was aware of Boone's dark eyes watching her. She hated the feelings she couldn't help, because she knew what he really thought of her. It was humiliating that she couldn't wish them away.

When the performance was over, Boone stopped Clark, Keely and the bodyguard at the front door.

"We're stopping by Chaco's Bar and Grill for a nightcap. Why don't you join us? Your bodyguard is welcome to come in, too."

"I don't drink on the job," Jarrett said unapologetically. "But thanks."

"We should probably start toward home," Clark began, knowing Keely's reluctance to be around Boone.

"Just a nightcap," Boone said, and he had that expression that meant he was going to get his own way come hell or high water.

"Well, all right," Clark gave in, as he always did. He grimaced, because he'd had a glimpse of Keely's face when he agreed.

"We won't stay long," Boone promised.

He and Misty started toward his sports car. It was parked next to Clark's. Misty was complaining loudly about the intrusion on their privacy. Keely felt like doing the same. She didn't want a nightcap, especially with Boone.

But they ended up at the bar anyway. Keely ordered a soft drink. Misty glared at her while she ordered a whiskey sour with a smirk, as if she thought Keely was putting on some sort of Puritan act.

"Marquez would approve," Clark said gently when Keely was served. "You're not legal, yet."

"What?" Misty asked.

"You have to be twenty-one to have a drink in a bar," Clark said carelessly.

She frowned. "You're not even twenty-one?" she asked Keely.

"I'll be twenty on Christmas Eve, in four months," Keely said without looking at her.

Misty was irritable, and it showed. She sipped her drink and ignored Keely.

Boone didn't. He seemed restless. When Misty excused herself to go to the ladies' room—with obvious reluctance—and Clark decided to go, too, Keely was left alone with Boone.

She couldn't force herself to look at him. She sipped her soda with both hands wrapped around the glass and stared toward the bar.

"You haven't said a word to me all night," he said unexpectedly. "And you haven't looked at me once."

Keely did, then, and her eyes were blazing. "I didn't want it to seem as if I were chasing you," she told him coldly. "I understand that I threw myself at you at the charity dance and it offended you."

His jaw tautened. He looked away, as if the comment embarrassed him. "There are things going on that you don't know about. You shouldn't be wandering around the state with Clark."

"I'm as safe with him as I would be at home," she said. "Clark is a wonderful man. I'm very lucky that your private detective turned him off Nellie. Apparently," she added with a meaningful smile, "I'm more to his taste than she is."

His scowl was intimidating. But before he could speak, Misty was back. She swept into her chair and leaned against Boone's shoulder to distract him. Clark and Keely were stiff and uncomfortable, and they barely managed to remain civil for the time it took them to finish their drinks.

Misty made a point of getting Keely momentarily alone on their way out to the cars.

"He's talked about nothing except you all night, God knows why! Well, you won't get him," she said icily. "I'm going to fix you!"

Keely didn't get a chance to ask her what she meant. Misty ran to Boone and almost tripped getting to their car. Misty was apparently jealous that Boone had mentioned Keely. She couldn't imagine why, but it thrilled her to think he might be regretting his bad behavior.

"What the hell is wrong with Boone?" Clark asked on the way home. "I've never seen him so grim."

"I haven't the slightest idea," Keely said.

"I gave him the devil about that detective's report. He swore he hadn't put the man up to lying." He glanced at Keely. "It's hard for me to stay mad at him. But I'm sorry I couldn't get us out of that drink."

"It's okay, Clark," she replied. "He's a bulldozer. It's hard for anyone to say no to him."

"Especially me." He smiled. "When we were kids, Boone was always protecting me from the mean, older boys. He was never afraid of anything. I guess maybe he protected me too much. After our mom left, Dad was hell to live with. Boone took a lot of hits that were meant for me."

"He loves you."

"Yeah. I love him, too." He glanced at her. "Boone said that Sheriff Carson was out your way."

"Yes," she replied. "I had to tell him what Dad did."

"Excuse me?"

She bit her lower lip. Her father was a criminal. That was going to put Boone right out of her orbit forever. She was certain that Hayes Carson had already told him about Keely's parents. The two men had been best friends forever.

"My father was a drug dealer, Clark," she said quietly. "He supplied the cocaine that killed Sheriff Carson's brother, Bobby."

"Oh, boy," Clark said heavily. "You poor kid."

"Now my dad's back and he and his partner want money, lots of it..."

"I could give them whatever they want," he said at once.

"No!" Her eyes were eloquent. "Don't you see, the only way to stop them is to keep them hanging around while Mama puts the house on the market. The police might have a chance to catch them before they can hurt anyone."

"Do you think your father would hurt you?" he asked.

Keely had never liked looking back. Her accident had hurt more than her body. When the little boy dropped into the lion pit, Keely's father had been standing on the other side. He hadn't made a move to help.

"Yes, he would, wouldn't he?" Clark asked perceptively.

Keely drew in a long breath. It had been just after the court case that Keely's father had brought her back to Jacobsville. He hadn't said much to her, and he hadn't met her eyes. She'd tried to tell herself that he'd only hesitated because he was shocked. But Keely hadn't hesitated.

"I've spent all these years trying to pretend that he brought me back for my own good," she said. "But I think it was because I made him ashamed." She held up her hand when he started to ask a question. "I can't talk about it, not even now. It's so painful to think that my father was willing to stand by when a child's life was in danger. I loved him. But he was ready to sacrifice me to save himself." She looked up. "In the same situation, Boone wouldn't have hesitated a split second. Neither would you or Winnie."

Clark was solemn. "It's hard to lose faith in a parent. I know. When our mother ran off with our uncle, we were devastated. Three little kids, and she just left."

Keely was thinking that she would never have deserted her own flesh and blood. But she didn't say it.

Clark smiled. "You'll make a wonderful mother," he chuckled. "Your kids will be spoiled rotten."

She smoothed her right hand over her left arm. "No," she said absently. "I won't have children. I won't marry."

"A few little scars aren't going to matter," he told her.

She didn't reply. He had no idea. She couldn't tell him, either. She glanced at him. "I had a good time," she said. She smiled. "Mr. Pendleton's fiancée was a hoot." She chuckled. "Do you think he's really going to marry a woman who's that blatant about social climbing?"

"I think, like me, he got into a physical relationship that

blinded him to a woman's true nature," he said after a minute. "I hope he's lucky enough to see the light in time."

She frowned. "That doesn't sound like you."

"I was watching Misty tonight," he replied. "She was all over Boone, her eyes like dollar signs. She likes going first-class. She pretends to have money, but I don't think she does. I think she's putting on an act, to try to get Boone back. I hope he's got better sense." He gestured with his hand. "I saw myself when I looked at him. I was just as enchanted by Nellie. But what I saw was an illusion." He glanced at her. "You won't even let me give you emerald earrings, and you love them," he said softly. "I've never known a woman like you."

"Actually there are lots of them, and they all live in Jacobsville and Comanche Wells," she teased. "Just plain unsophisticated little country girls who love animals and like to plant things and don't think marrying a rich man is the greatest of life ambitions."

He grimaced. "I'd never get one of those kind of girls past Boone," he said with resignation. "He always expects the worst when I date anybody outside our own circles."

That stung, but she didn't say so. Clark had been kind to her. "I have to go," she said. "I had a wonderful time tonight, Clark," she added. "Thanks."

"We'll do it again." He frowned. "I didn't mean that like it sounded—about dating girls outside my own circle," he added. "I always think of you as family."

She smiled. "That's the nicest thing you've said to me."

He looked sheepish. "I guess you'd rather I thought of you as an eligible young woman?"

She shook her head. "I like being your friend."

"I like being yours." He bent and kissed her cheek. "If you ever needed help, you know you could ask me."

She chuckled. "Of course I do. But I can take care of myself. Good night, Clark."

"Good night."

He watched her go into the house before he drove away.

Her mother was unusually quiet. When Keely asked about the house, she only got evasive replies. Carly was nowhere in sight, and hadn't been for some time. She was out of town for a while, Ella said finally, and didn't refer to Carly again. There was also a disturbing phone call that Ella had answered with single syllable replies. She wouldn't tell her daughter what had been said or even who had called.

When a car pulled up at the front door on a rainy Saturday morning, Ella actually gasped. Keely ran to look out.

"It's Boone Sinclair," she stammered, shocked.

"Thank God," Ella said heavily. "Thank God." She walked back down the hall, went into her room and closed the door.

Surprised, Keely went out onto the porch as Boone exited the car and took the porch steps two at a time.

He was in working clothes, jeans and boots and white Stetson with a checked Western-cut long-sleeved shirt buttoned right up to the neck. He looked down at Keely, his eyes dark and stormy.

"Come for a drive," he said curtly.

She could have found a dozen reasons not to go. She wanted to come up with an excuse. Her mind agreed. But her body walked back into the house, grabbed her purse and a lightweight jacket and told her mother goodbye.

Boone opened the door of his car, helped her inside and went around to get in and start the engine. A minute later, they were speeding down the highway toward his ranch.

She was nervous, and it showed. Her hands played with her

small purse while she listened to the rhythmic sound of the windshield wipers as they brushed away the pouring rain.

Despite all their recent turmoil, she felt safe with Boone. Safe, excited, hopeful, breathlessly in love. Her whole body ached to be held again as he'd held her at the charity dance. She hoped that didn't show.

It did. Boone was far too experienced to mistake her body language. He smiled softly to himself. If she'd been involved with his brother, as Clark claimed, she wouldn't be this nervous in Boone's company. That meant there was still time. If he could convince her that he hadn't meant to humiliate her.

He pulled out onto a pasture track that led to a closed gate, stopped the car and cut off the engine.

The rain flooded onto the windshield, making the outside world a gray blur. He unfastened his seat belt, settled himself crossways in his seat and stared at Keely.

The silence was a little unnerving. She glanced at him and found her eyes captured and held.

"Clark says the two of you are going steady," he said.

Now what did she say, she wondered frantically. It wasn't true, but Clark was using her as a tool of vengeance, apparently, for Nellie's loss. She bit her lower lip and tried to find a graceful way out of the dilemma.

"Did he say that?" she asked, playing for time to think.

His dark eyes narrowed. "Don't play games with me," he said curtly. "Are you or are you not getting mixed up with my brother?"

Sorry, Clark, she said silently, but no mere woman could have resisted that look in Boone's eyes.

"I'm not," she said, sounding breathless, as though she'd run a long way.

The tautness seemed to go out of him. "Well, thank God for

one thing going right," he murmured. "I could have slugged Hayes Carson!"

While she was trying to work out that puzzle, he'd unfastened her seat belt and pulled her over the console into his arms.

"I thought this week would never end." His mouth ground down into hers as if he'd gone hungry for years and sought to satisfy the hunger in seconds. He crushed her up against him, mindless of her soft cry of protest. "I'm starving to death for you," he whispered into her mouth. "Dying for you—"

Had she really heard him say that? She gave up protesting. It didn't do any good, anyway. She curled up against him and ignored the pain in her shoulder and arm, going boneless as his ardor only increased at her response. Her head began to spin. It was the sweetest interlude of her life. Rain pounded on the roof, the hood, the trunk, the wind blew, but she heard nothing over the pounding of her own heart. She had no reserve left. Whatever he wanted, he could have.

Except when his hand searched under her blouse and up over her breast, inching toward the strap. She couldn't, didn't dare, let him feel her shoulder.

With a sharp little cry, she jerked away from him, her face flushed from his ardor, her eyes wild with passion and dread.

He misunderstood. His eyes grew cold. He pushed her away, dragging in harsh breaths, until he could control himself again. He'd taken her protests the first time he'd kissed her as virginal fears. But this wasn't. She'd rejected him. She'd lied about her feelings for Clark. She couldn't hide the fact that she didn't want intimacy with Boone. His ego hurt, almost as badly as it had when Misty shied away from him in the military hospital.

"Boone," she began slowly, dreading what she had to tell him now.

"Forget it," he said, interrupting her. He put his seat belt back on and started the car. "Obviously you can't get past your feelings for Clark. No sweat."

He didn't say another word, or even look at her, until they were sitting in front of her house with the engine running.

"It isn't what you think," she bit off.

"The hell it isn't," he returned icily. "Goodbye, Keely."

The way he said it, she knew it wasn't simply a temporary farewell. He meant that he wouldn't see her alone again, ever. Her heart broke. He thought she'd rejected him and it wasn't true. She couldn't bear to see the look on his face if he got her shirt off. That would end any chance she had with him. Of course, she'd just done that, without the added trauma of what he didn't know.

She drew in a quiet breath. "Thanks for the ride," she managed in a polite tone. She opened the door and got out.

He still hadn't said a word. He was down the driveway before her foot was on the first step up to the house. She didn't look back. It wouldn't help.

Her mother was still acting oddly. Almost a week had passed since Boone had taken Keely riding and kissed her. The rain had stopped and now the heat blazed. There were wildfires. Everyone was afraid to throw down a match or burn trash or even smoke a cigarette outdoors. It was almost time to harvest corn and hay and peanuts. The corn and hay would have to last the livestock through the winter; it was very important. Combines and tractors were sitting on ready, while the last days counted down to harvest.

On Saturday morning, the sounds of machinery could be heard everywhere. Winnie stopped by to pick up Keely for an impromptu lunch, assuring her first that Boone was out with the combines and wouldn't be in all day. He'd taken a cooler with him, bearing lunch and beer.

"I hope I have enough eggs to do the egg salad," Winnie murmured as they pulled up into her driveway past the huge posts that held the now-open gates that led to the house. "If I don't, I may have to run back to the store. Why didn't I think of it while I was in town?" she moaned. She glanced at Keely, who looked apprehensive. "Boone's really out with the combine," she promised. "I wouldn't lie."

Keely relaxed with a smile. "Okay. Sorry."

"Not your fault," Winnie replied, leading the way into the house. "Boone raged about you all week, in fact, not to mention Hayes Carson—God knows why. But this morning something came by express. He took it into the office, and got all quiet. He went out without a word, walking really slow." She grimaced. "God help the cowboys. Somebody will quit by sunset, you mark my words. He's seething!"

"You don't know why?" Keely had to ask. "It couldn't have been something about my father…?"

Winnie looked surprised. "What would Boone have to do with your father?"

Keely felt trapped. "You said he'd talked to Sheriff Hayes…"

Winnie scowled. "Keely, what's going on?"

She hesitated. "Did Clark say anything to you at all?"

"He said you had to take a bodyguard with you when you went to San Antonio," Winnie replied gently. "I'm not stupid. There's gossip about your father being in trouble and threatening you and your mother. But I don't think Boone would be mixed up with that."

"No. No, of course not," Keely said at once. She forced a smile. Winnie had no idea what was really going on with Boone and her best friend. It was probably better that she never did. Boone would never look twice at Keely again, anyway. She wondered how she was going to manage to draw back from her friendship with Winnie without making the other woman suspicious. She had to find a way. Just the thought of running into Boone again, after the way they'd parted Saturday, made her nervous.

They started lunch, but as Winnie had predicted, she should have bought eggs. She only had two.

"I can't make enough egg salad for us now and for the men later out of just two eggs," she laughed. She grabbed her car keys and her purse. "You finish the pasta salad and I'll run to the store. I'll only be fifteen minutes." She glanced at Keely's worried face. "He's over in the north pasture," she added ruefully. "Boone couldn't even *get* here in fifteen minutes. Feel better?"

"Yes," Keely said blatantly.

Winnie pursed her lips. "I do wonder what's going on between you and my big brother. But I won't ask. Yet."

She rushed out the back door and closed it behind her. Keely felt less secure.

She finished the pasta salad and put it into the refrigerator. She heard the front door open and close and felt a pang of relief. Winnie was back.

But the footsteps coming down the hall weren't soft and muffled. They were heavy and hard. Apprehensive, she turned.

And there was Boone, wearing stained jeans and boots, a shirt wet with sweat, his Stetson dangling from one hand. His eyes, as they met hers, were blazing with anger.

"Come into the office, Keely," he said tautly. "I've got something to show you." He turned and walked away, leaving her to follow.

She paused at the open door of the office, tugging at the buttons on her long-sleeved white shirt she was wearing over tan twill slacks. He was holding the envelope that Winnie said had come by express service this morning. He took out a photograph and held it out to her.

"Have a look," he said in a tone so threatening that it made the hair on the back of her neck stand up. "And then tell me you don't have anything going with Clark!"

CHAPTER ELEVEN

Keely moved slowly into the room and took the photograph Boone held out to her. She almost choked when she saw it. The picture showed two people in bed, in an intimate embrace. The man was Clark. The woman had Keely's face. But it certainly wasn't Keely's body. She almost laughed with relief at the very obvious attempt to frame her by putting her face on another woman's body.

She looked up with the amusement in her eyes, but Boone wasn't laughing. He was positively enraged, and he obviously believed the photograph was proof of her lies.

"This isn't me," she began.

"Like hell it isn't!" he raged. He tore the photograph from her fingers and ripped it to shreds, tossing it onto the carpet. "If you'd just told me the truth, I could have accepted it, Keely. You didn't have to lie!"

"But I didn't," she protested. "And I can prove it!"

Her hands went, reluctantly, to the buttons of her shirt. She didn't want to have to go to this extreme, but he wasn't going to be convinced easily.

He misunderstood the intent at once. "Spare yourself the embarrassment," he said curtly. "I don't care what you look like under that shirt. It was just a game on my part, Keely," he added with a cold smile. "A little flirting, a little teasing, a few kisses. I'm sure you didn't take it seriously. I only wanted to see how far you'd go. If you hadn't made it clear before, you certainly made it clear just now. Either of the Sinclair brothers will do, as long as you get enough to make it worth your while, is that right? And I thought you were so honest and upright and hardworking! It was just a sham. Like all the others, you're only after money!"

"That is not true!" she said defensively.

His eyes glittered again. "I don't want you here anymore. Ever. You get out of my house, Keely, and go home. And don't you come back again. I don't give a damn if Clark or Winnie invites you, don't come! Make an excuse, do whatever it takes. But don't come here again."

"You don't understand!" she began helplessly.

"I said, get out! Now! If you don't, so help me God I'll call one of Hayes's deputies and have you taken out in handcuffs!"

He was too angry to listen to reason, and he meant what he said. Keely couldn't bear the thought of being hauled off to jail for trespassing. It would be all over Comanche Wells and Jacobsville in no time, and she'd never live it down.

She sighed, feeling as if she'd been crushed. She loved him, and he could treat her so badly.

"I'm going," she said. "You don't have to make threats to get me to leave. Please tell Winnie something came up."

He didn't answer her. He swept back down the hall, out the door and into what sounded like a pickup truck. It roared away as Keely started down the long driveway. Boone didn't know that Winnie had driven her here. She didn't have a way home. But she was too wary of Boone to go down to the bunkhouse and ask for a ride. It would do no good, anyway—all the men were out in the pastures, bringing in the crops.

She was wearing a long-sleeved blouse, she had no water, she wasn't even wearing a hat. The sun was brutal. By the time she got out the gates and a quarter of a mile down the road, she was too sick and thirsty to go on. She'd sit in the shade by the highway, she thought. It was flat here. Winnie would come driving by sooner or later and spot her. Her white blouse would stand out in that grove of mesquite trees. She'd just have to be careful of the trees trailing limbs and long thorns, which were so dangerous that they could pierce a boot.

The big tree near the road afforded a little shade. There was a fallen limb next to it which seemed to have been there for a long time. She slumped down, exhausted by the heat, without looking first. That was a mistake. She heard the sound of frying bacon, which even her addled brain immediately connected with the source that would be making it this far away from a stove; a diamondback rattlesnake.

Before she could even turn her head to look for it, the snake struck. It bit her on the forearm and withdrew, still rattling.

Terrified, she jumped to her feet and ran backward before it could get her again. The bite mark was vivid, stained with blood. Tourniquet, she thought. Stop the blood running to the heart. Get the bite lower than the heart…

She dragged the handkerchief she always carried from her pocket and wrapped half of it around her forearm between the bite and her elbow. She grabbed up a stick and used it to tighten the handkerchief. Only use it to keep the poison below the skin, she recalled from the first-aid book she'd read, don't tighten it enough to stop the circulation. Once tightened, don't loosen it, get help.

Help? She looked both ways. The road was deserted. She'd been bitten by a poisonous snake. Her arm was already swelling as the poison tried to make its way to her heart. She kept her left arm down—it would be the one that was already damaged!—

and tried to breathe slowly and shallowly. She'd need antivenin. Did they have any at the Jacobsville hospital? She didn't have her mother's cell phone. It was still on the counter in Winnie's kitchen. The heat had already exhausted her and her head was swimming. She was nauseated. The bite hurt. It really hurt!

She closed her eyes, standing in the middle of the highway. If somebody didn't come down that road soon, it would be too late. She thought of Boone, the way he'd been at the charity dance, holding her, kissing her so tenderly, almost as if he… loved her.

"Boone," she whispered. And she fainted.

Winnie was cursing her own bad luck as she drove rapidly back to the ranch. Boone had called her, almost incoherent with fury, daring her to ever let Keely back in the front door. He had photos, he said harshly, of her with Clark that turned his stomach. He'd told her to get out and he never wanted to see her on the place again. He hung up before Winnie could tell him that Keely had no way home. Now she was hoping she could get back in time to save the poor girl a long and uncomfortable walk.

As she approached the ranch road, she noticed a bundle of rags in the road. But as she came closer, she realized it wasn't rags—it was Keely!

She wheeled her car around and left it running, the door open, as she rushed to Keely's side.

"Keely! Keely!" she called, as she whipped out her cell phone and dialed the emergency services number without hesitation.

Keely's eyes opened groggily. "Winnie…snake…rattler…" She tried to lift her left arm. It was swollen and almost black already.

"Dear God," Winnie whispered reverently. A voice spoke in her ear. "This is Winnie Sinclair," she said. "Shirley, is that you? I thought it was. Listen, I've got Keely Welsh here in the middle of the highway with snakebite. It was a rattler, she said. I'm taking her to Jacobsville General myself, no time to dispatch an ambulance. Have them waiting at the door with antivenin. Got that? Thanks, Shirley. No, I can't stay on the line, I have to get her in the car."

She hung up and managed to get Keely into the front seat and belted in, in a matter of seconds, with strength she didn't know she had. Her heart was pounding as she put the car in gear and left tire marks as she shifted into low gear.

A mile down the road she was met by flashing blue lights. She slowed. The car, Jacobsville Police, spun around in front of her. The door opened and Kilraven's head poked out. "Follow me!" he shouted.

She nodded, relieved to have help. He took off and she followed close on his bumper. Cars got out of the way. They went right through two red lights and turned into the emergency entrance to the hospital.

As soon as she stopped the car, Kilraven came running back to get Keely and carry her to her door where a gurney and Dr. Coltrain waited.

"Snakebite," Winnie panted. "Diamondback. She put on a tourniquet herself…"

"It's all right," Kilraven told her. "Shirley called them for you. Everything's ready, except the antivenin," he added quietly. "They don't have enough, so they're having a state trooper run it down here to the county line. Hayes Carson's going himself to meet him and relay it back here." He put a big hand on Winnie's shoulder. "She'll be all right. You did good."

She bit her lower lip. Tears rained down her face. She turned it away from him and started up the steps.

He pulled her around and into his arms. "Don't ever be

ashamed of tears," he said into her ear. "I've shed my share of them."

That was surprising and sort of nice. It meant he was human. "Thanks," she said huskily after a minute. She drew back and wiped at her eyes with the back of her hand. "I was scared stiff and I couldn't show it. She's my friend."

"I know. Come on. I'll walk you in. I had a call here anyway. Remember old Ben Barkley? His son put a bullet through his leg when he started beating the boy's mother."

"Riley shot him?" she asked, surprised. The boy was sweet and helpful when he called emergency services to get help saving his mother from his habitually drunk father.

"Riley did," he asserted. He grinned, and bent low. "We're going to take him out to our firing range and help him improve his aim, in case he ever does it again."

She burst out laughing. It was such an outrageous thing to say.

"That's better," he said when he saw her face. "Stiff upper lip, now."

"I'm not British."

"You aren't?" he exclaimed. "Why, what a coincidence… neither am I!"

She punched his broad chest, laughing. They walked together to the emergency waiting room.

Furious, helpless to do anything for her friend, Winnie took refuge in the only thing she could think of that might help—revenge. She phoned Boone and gave him hell.

"Slow down, slow down!" he complained. "I can't understand a word you're saying. Wait…" He cut off the engine on the tractor he was using to help with the harvest. "All right, what was that about Keely?"

"She was walking home, thanks to you, and she got bitten

by a rattlesnake! She's at Jacobsville General… Boone? Hello? Hello? Damn!"

She hung up, even more furious now, because he wouldn't listen to her. She called Clark. "Where are you?" she asked when he didn't answer for almost a minute.

He sounded out of breath. "I'm, uh, I had to run to catch the phone," he said lamely. In the background, music was playing and there was a faint protest, which sounded as if it came from a feminine throat.

"Oh, hell, never mind," she muttered and hung up. She didn't need to ask where he was. He was almost certainly with that damned Nellie again. So much for restraint.

But he phoned her back ten minutes later, while she was waiting, hoping, for some sort of report about Keely. She stopped nurses, who promised to go and check but never came back. She was getting frustrated.

"What did you want?" Clark asked.

"Never mind. Go back to Nellie," she muttered.

"Don't hang up!" he grumbled. "I'm not with Nellie. I'm over at Dave Harston's place helping him move a piano. His wife's making us lunch."

She felt her face go red. "Sorry."

He laughed. "I guess the sounds must be similar, but I swear I'm not doing anything I'd mind being seen doing. What's up?"

"Keely got bitten by a rattler," she said miserably. "I can't find out what's going on and I'm worried sick. Her arm was almost black, Clark. I'm scared—" Her voice broke.

"I'll be there in fifteen minutes. She'll be all right, sis. I know she will."

"Thanks," she said huskily, and hung up. She prayed that he was right.

A commotion at the desk caught her attention. Boone was bulldozing right past a nurse and a police officer—Kilraven—on his way back to the emergency room. Winnie almost cheered. If anybody could cut through red tape, it was her big brother. They could threaten, but they wouldn't stop him.

"Coltrain!" he bellowed.

"Over here," came a deep, resigned voice.

Boone hid it well, but he was terrified. Winnie's phone call made him feel guilty as hell, and he'd hardly managed to breathe as he rushed to the hospital. One of his cowboys had died from a rattler bite the year before. He was scared to death that Keely might not have reached help in time. If she died, he'd never forgive himself, never!

"Where is she?" Boone demanded, dark eyes flashing, face flushed. He'd come straight from work to the hospital in his work clothes, and never noticed how disheveled he was.

Coltrain nodded toward a cubicle where they were working on her. He knew better than to try to stop Boone. It would mean a brawl, where he could least afford one.

Boone walked into the cubicle and stopped dead. Everything seemed to go out of focus except for Keely's left arm. They'd bared her to the waist, pulling the sheet only over one breast, leaving the left one and her shoulder bare while they pumped antivenin into her in an attempt to save her life. She was unconscious. Her arm was almost black, swollen out of recognition. But it wasn't the swelling that Boone was fixated on. It was her shoulder. There were huge scars, which looked as if something with enormous teeth had taken a bite right out of her. The damage was staggering to look at. The pain she must have suffered—

He knew at once that his photographs had been faked, and later he was going to give somebody hell over that botched, so-called investigation. But right now, his whole focus was on this slip of a girl whom he'd misjudged, whom he'd almost killed with his outrage.

"What in hell happened to her?" Boone bit off.

"She was bitten..."

"Not the snakebite. That!" He pointed at her shoulder.

Coltrain wanted to tell him that he should ask Keely, but he knew it would do no good. "She jumped into a mountain lion pit at her father's game park to save a seven-year-old boy who sneaked under the rail when nobody was looking."

"Good God! And where was her father while all that was going down?" Boone demanded.

"Standing at the rail, watching," Coltrain said with utter disdain.

"Damn him," Boone said huskily.

"I couldn't agree more."

He held his breath as he looked at her. "Will she live?" he asked finally, having postponed the question as long as he could.

Coltrain looked at him. "I don't know, Boone," he said honestly. "The poison had a good bit of time to work before she was found..." He hesitated because of the torture in the other man's eyes.

Boone moved past the technicians to the head of the bed where Keely was lying, so white and still. He brushed back her sweaty hair with a hand that wasn't quite steady. He bent down to her ear.

"You have to live," he whispered, his voice forcibly steady. "You have to live. This is my fault, but I can't...live...if you don't, Keely..." He had to stop because his voice was breaking. She was blurring in his eyes. He never cried. His composure was absolute. But he was losing it. His thumb brushed her pale lips as he drew in an audible breath. "I'll kill that damned private detective," he whispered.

Keely stirred, just a heartbeat's movement, but he felt it. His forehead bent down to hers and his lips brushed against the pale, cold skin. "Don't die. Please..."

"You have to let us work," Coltrain said, catching the other man's arm. It was as rigid as metal. "Come on, Boone. Do what's best for her."

Boone hesitated just long enough to take one last look at her.

"Pity about those scars," one of the techs was saying.

"What scars?" Boone asked huskily.

Coltrain only smiled as he herded the rancher out of the cubicle and back out to the waiting room.

Winnie looked up as Boone was deposited in the waiting room. He paused, almost trembling with rage. He looked at his sister. "You call me if there's any change, any at all," he said heavily. "You hear?"

"Yes, of course," she replied. "Where are you going?"

"To kill a private detective," he said through his teeth. He'd added a few pithy adjectives to the sentence, which had Winnie's eyebrows arching toward her hairline.

He was gone in a flash. She connected the photos he'd mentioned to Keely's sudden departure and then to the private detective that Boone was going after. Clark walked in while she was mulling it over in her mind.

She turned to him. "Do we know any bail bondsmen?" she asked in an almost conversational tone.

Keely had been failing, but she rallied when they added the relayed antivenin to her drip catheter. She wasn't conscious, but she was groaning. Coltrain kept her under while they worked to stabilize her vital signs.

It was very late when he came out into the waiting room, smiling.

"She'll make it," he told them wearily. "But she'll be here for a few days."

"Thank God," they said almost in unison.

"We should send the boys out hunting rattlers," Clark suggested.

"Boone's already out after one of them, I'm afraid," Winnie said. She smiled at Coltrain. "Thanks."

"I like her, too," he replied. He smiled. "You'd both better get some rest. I'll have one of the nurses phone you if there's any change."

"Thanks," Winnie said again.

"It's why I'm a doctor," Coltrain said, grinning as he left them.

Winnie tried to phone Boone, but he didn't answer. She was about to try again when Sheriff Hayes Carson came into the room, his brown-streaked blond hair shining in the ceiling light. His dark eyes were turbulent.

"Have you been trying to reach your brother?" he asked Winnie. "Sorry, but they don't allow cell phones in detention."

Winnie groaned. "Oh, no."

"Oh, yes," Hayes replied. "Don't worry about calling anybody. I went and bailed him out myself while I was off duty." He put a hand to his ear. "I swear to God, the guards were writing down the words as he ripped them out. I've never heard such language in my life. At least the detective isn't pressing assault charges, however..."

"He isn't? Thank goodness," Winnie exclaimed. "But why?"

"He ran for his life. His employers weren't so fortunate." He actually smiled. "Detective Rick Marquez and I have been doing a little sleuthing of our own, after office hours, and with a little help from some friends. It turns out," he said in a low tone, wary of eavesdroppers, "that Boone's girlfriend, Misty, and her father are up to their necks in the regional drug traffic network. They ran for it when Marquez sent a DEA agent to their detective agency with a search warrant to have a look around. Last I heard," he added with a chuckle, "there was a statewide BOLO for them. I don't think we'll be seeing them again anytime soon."

Winnie was almost breathless. "Poor Boone. He and Misty were dating...."

"I asked him to do it," Hayes said quietly. "He was mad as hell, too. He said it was interfering with something very personal. I hated to strong-arm him into it, but he was the only person who had any sort of access to her."

Winnie's eyes lit up. "He didn't really care about her, then?"

"No. He couldn't stand her. He did it to help me cut off one of Jacobsville's top drug suppliers."

And Boone didn't want to because of something personal. Could it be Keely? She thought about the photos Misty's father's detective had dug up for him...

"They faked the photos," she burst out.

Hayes frowned. "What photos?"

"Never mind."

"How's Keely?" Hayes asked gently. "I heard about the snakebite from Boone."

"She's going to be fine. I still can't get him on the phone," she added worriedly.

"By now, he's made it to the nurses' station," he said. "He didn't stop cursing until we got to town. He's in the hospital somewhere. He'll turn up directly."

Even as they spoke, Boone walked in the door. He was disheveled, red-eyed and bruised.

"I know," Winnie said when he held up a bruised hand. "The other guy looks worse. Are you okay?"

He shrugged. "A little ragged, that's all. I called Coltrain. He says she'll be fine. The minute she can be moved, she's coming home with us," he added.

Winnie hesitated. "She's not going to want to do that."

"She's doing it anyway. Has anybody called her mother?" he asked.

Clark came in from the soda machine with two Cokes. "Do you want something to drink?" he asked the two men. He frowned at Boone. "What in hell happened to you?"

"A slight altercation," Boone said nonchalantly. "I'd like a black coffee, if you're taking orders."

Clark grinned. "Anything for my big brother," he murmured, and left again.

"I'll drive by Keely's house and speak with her mother," Hayes said. "I'm going back in tonight because we've got a case pending, but I'm off tomorrow." He wagged his finger at Boone. "You go home and wash your mouth out with soap."

Boone put an affectionate arm around his shoulders. "You're the only man I know who thinks 'Crackers and Milk' is a curse."

"I give talks to little kids about drugs," he pointed out. "What if I slipped in front of a classroom of kids?"

"They probably know more bad words than you do," Winnie chipped in, grinning. "You should hear some of their parents talk on the phone when they call for the police to come."

Hayes winced. "I know. I have to hear them." He grinned at Winnie. "You know, you're pretty good on that radio. Kilraven likes having you on duty. He says you brighten up dark nights."

"He does?" Winnie's face became radiant.

"Cut that out," Boone said severely. "She's going to go back to college and get a degree and marry an educated man."

"I am not going back to college," Winnie said pleasantly. "I don't want a degree, and I'm not marrying any man, educated or otherwise, until it pleases me."

"So there." Hayes chuckled.

Boone glowered at her. She glowered back.

"I, uh, wouldn't get too hopeful about Kilraven," Hayes

said gently, a little embarrassed. "He's had some tragedy in his life. He may act normal, but he hasn't gotten over the trauma."

Winnie moved closer to him. "Talk to me, Carson," she said quietly, using his last name, as she always did when she was really serious.

"A few years ago," he said quietly, "there was a violent murder up in San Antonio. Kilraven was working undercover there at the time, with the local police. It was a rainy Saturday night—when we always have dozens of wrecks—and he and his partner were closer than the patrol units, most of whom were tied up, so they volunteered to secure the crime scene. Kilraven recognized the address and ran in, before his partner could stop him." Hayes closed his eyes. "It was bad. Really bad." He paused. "What I'm telling you is that the man is an emotional train-wreck looking for a place to happen, regardless of his seeming composure. He's not going to put down roots in Jacobsville, Texas. He's put off dealing with his trauma too long. One day, he'll crash and burn."

"Did he know the murder victims?" Winnie asked hesitantly.

"He was related to them," Hayes said. "And that's all I'm saying about it."

Winnie wondered which relatives were involved. Poor man! "Did you speak to Dr. Coltrain about how soon we can take Keely home?" she asked her brother.

Boone shook his head. "No. But I will. I can guarantee it won't be tonight."

She managed a smile. Hayes had dashed her dreams to bits. She didn't want it to show. "I'm going home to get some sleep. You coming?" she asked Boone.

He hesitated. "I guess so." He looked at himself and grimaced. "I should have gone home and changed."

"Nobody will notice," she sighed. "A lot of people have been here all day and half the night, waiting for hope to make results." She indicated two families with white faces and red eyes. She smiled at them. They smiled back. Friends were made easily in emergency rooms. She said she was going home and asked if they needed anything that she could bring them. But they shook their heads. There were things they needed, but they didn't dare leave until they knew something. She understood.

Winnie and Boone slept for a while and then drove back to the hospital. They ate breakfast in the cafeteria without tasting what they ate, and drank black coffee.

"What did you say to Keely?" she asked.

His eyes were tortured. "Too much," he bit off. He looked down into his empty coffee cup. "Those damned photos were so convincing!" He realized, too, that Keely hadn't been trying to seduce him when she started to unbutton her blouse. She was going to show him the scars. It was an act of bravery that he hadn't appreciated at the time. Now, it hurt him.

"She'll be all right," Winnie assured him. "You can make peace."

He laughed hollowly. "Think so?"

The cafeteria door opened and Hayes Carson came in. He wasn't smiling. He made a beeline for the Sinclairs.

"I need to talk to you," he said tersely, looking around to make sure he wasn't being overheard. "I just found Ella Welsh, dead in her living room!"

CHAPTER TWELVE

"Dead?" Boone exclaimed, careful to keep his voice low. "Of what?"

"A gunshot wound," Hayes replied. He pulled out a chair and sat down. "I had the coroner out, along with a forensic team from the state crime lab and my own investigator. We found latent prints and a shell casing, but I don't need ESP to know who did it."

"Keely's father," Winnie guessed. "Or that partner of his, Jock."

"They were desperate for money, Keely said," Hayes replied. "I told Keely to tell Ella to put the house on the market, but not really sell it, to make Brent Welsh think she was complying. But the men must have gone to her and demanded immediate results. She either refused or infuriated them, I don't know." He sighed. "We don't dare let Keely see her body. It will have to be a closed casket."

"What?" Boone exclaimed.

Hayes's expression was eloquent. "They tortured her, probably to find out about any assets she hadn't produced."

"Good God!" Boone said heavily. "They'll come after Keely,

won't they?" he asked coldly. "She'll be next, because she'll inherit what little Ella had to leave her."

"We haven't heard anything about sightings of them since Misty and her father and the detective ran for the border," Hayes told him. "They may be spooked enough to keep running, if they were in the same network with the remnants of the Fuentes brothers' drug smuggling operation. Too, the murder may prompt them to keep running, since they know we'll be after them for it. On the other hand, if Ella left life insurance, Keely will get that. And Ella's savings accounts would mean ready cash. I talked to her banker already. He told me there is some money there."

"We'll need more men to protect the ranch," Winnie thought aloud.

"Several more, all ex-military, and I know where to find them," Boone said grimly. "I'll make the ranch into a fortress. Welsh will never get his hands on Keely!"

"I could make a comment here about vigilante justice," Hayes said with grim humor, "but I won't. Just don't step over the line. I can't afford any more bail money."

Boone chuckled. "You'll be paid back for that." The smile faded. "Poor Keely," he said heavily. "First the snake, now her mother."

"Someone will have to tell her." Hayes looked around him at the grim faces. "We could draw straws. Or we could ask Coltrain to do the dirty work."

"I'll tell her when the time comes," Boone said softly. "It's my responsibility now."

Winnie didn't say anything, but she looked thoughtful, and happy.

Which was a far cry from how Keely looked when she came out from under the effects of the medicines she'd been given.

Boone never left her bedside. She'd glared at him the first time she saw him there, when she was still too sick and weak to speak. By the third day, she was regaining some strength and she was furious.

"I know, I know," he said before she got started. "I got everything backward. I accused you of things you didn't do and threw you out of the house." He looked briefly tortured. "I know I caused this." He drew in a long breath, staring down at his boots. "God Almighty, I never meant for you to walk home with temperatures at the century mark! I must have been out of my head not to realize that you didn't even have a way to get home."

Keely wanted to rage at him, but she was still very sick and her arm hurt. She winced every time she moved. "It wasn't me…with Clark, in that picture you shoved in my face!"

He lifted his head and nodded. "I know," he said grimly.

That look, and the words, told her things she wouldn't have asked about. He knew. He knew about her shoulder. She closed her eyes and tears flowed out of them. She felt even worse now. She'd never wanted Boone, of all people, to know her secret. Her mind went back to the boy who'd thrown up when he saw her shoulder…

He moved close to the bed and bent over her, with one big hand beside her head on the pillow. "They'll kill me if I sit down here. I know you're still weak and you hurt like hell. But I want you to feel something." He drew her right hand up to his chest over the shirt and smoothed it down. He watched her eyes while she did it, saw the realization in her green eyes, and nodded.

She frowned as she met his eyes.

"There are more of them," he said stiffly, rising away from her. "A lot more—one that even took bone out of my thigh. When Misty saw me, in Germany, just after the bandages were removed, she ran out of the room. It's a little less messy now, after some plastic surgery, but the scars are too deep to be permanently erased, and it's noticeable. I don't go shirtless anymore," he added bitterly. "I haven't for years."

She felt the pain. She understood it. "I haven't worn anything short-sleeved since I was thirteen years old," she replied quietly. "When I was sixteen, a boy I liked asked me out on a date. He was just fumbling, you know, like boys will, but when he got my blouse half-off and saw the scars—they were fresh, then—he..." She closed her eyes. "He jerked the car door open and threw up. He was sorry, very sorry, but I was devastated. I knew, then, that I'd never have a normal life. I knew I'd never get married and have...have children..." Her voice broke and tears fell hotly onto her cheeks. She was weak and sick and in pain, or she'd never have let him see her devastation.

It affected him. He bent down again and drew his mouth over her eyes, her nose, her cheeks. "Don't," he whispered huskily. "You've been so brave, Keely. I can't bear to see you cry. Don't, honey. Don't."

Now she knew she was dreaming. Boone had never called her a pet name, and he didn't care if he hurt her. She closed her eyes, though, enjoying the dream. It was so sweet to have his breath on her lips, his mouth caressing her wet face, his deep voice murmuring sweet and impossible things.

The sound of the door opening stopped the dream, of course. Boone moved away and she was sure it had been her imagination. She'd been heavily sedated, after all, to compensate for the terrible pain. Boone's expression was taciturn, as usual, and he didn't look anything like a man who'd been whispering sweet endearments to her. Winnie and Clark came into the room, somber and worried, especially when they saw Keely's face.

"You didn't tell her?" Winnie asked angrily. "Coltrain said not to—"

"Tell me what?" Keely asked at once, dabbing her eyes with the sheet.

Winnie's face contorted. Boone glared at her. So did Clark.

"Tell me what?" Keely demanded, belligerent now, as she looked from one guilty face to the other.

"I said I'd tell her when it was time," Boone said shortly. "It's not time."

"Yes, but…" Winnie stopped, horrified, as the television, overhead, began with the lead story of the day's news. The first bit was a photo of Ella Welsh and news about her murder. That was what she and Clark had rushed back into Keely's room to tell him, because they knew the television had been on although turned down, so they could catch the evening news. They'd seen the beginning of this broadcast on the wall televisions as they passed through the waiting room. They hadn't thought about the murder story being broadcast so soon.

Keely burst into fresh tears, almost hysterical.

"Damn that thing! Shut it off!" Boone shot at Clark as he started toward the call button next to Keely's pillow. While Clark shut off the television, Boone pressed the button and asked the nurse to come in, before he bent to curl Keely's face into his shoulder. "It's all right, honey. It's all right. I'm so sorry. I never meant you to hear it like that!"

The nurse came in. Boone explained quietly what had just happened. The nurse grimaced and went to call Coltrain, who was, she explained, still making rounds.

The redheaded doctor was in the room scant minutes later. He ordered a sedative for Keely and waited until it took effect before he called the siblings out into the hall.

"It was the damned television," Boone said angrily. "Why do you have those things in every room in the first place?"

"It wasn't my idea, believe me," Coltrain replied at once.

"Keely's going to have a hard recuperation if she has to go back to that house alone."

"She won't," Boone said at once. "She's coming home with us. I've already discussed it with Hayes Carson."

"Good thinking," Coltrain replied. He drew in a heavy breath. "I never expected that story to come out so soon. Hell, we don't even have a local television broadcasting station in the county."

"San Antonio is plenty close enough to pick the story up, especially on a slow news day," Winnie murmured. "There's nothing but political news, and everybody's sick of that."

"You'd better hire some bodyguards to protect you at home," Coltrain advised. "These guys are desperate enough to go after money any way they can get it."

"Everybody knows they killed Keely's mother—at least locally we know it," Winnie said. "They'd be stupid to stick around."

"These guys will never get work building spaceships," Coltrain said, tongue-in-cheek. "Otherwise, they wouldn't have risked coming here in the first place. Hayes Carson would love to get Brent Welsh in his sights on any pretext."

"So would I," Boone replied grimly. "He stood by and watched while Keely got mauled saving a kid from a mountain lion. Those scars are going to be permanent, aren't they?" he asked Coltrain.

Coltrain grimaced. "We might be able to get a plastic surgeon to clean them up, but they're very deep. She'd have half a dozen surgeries to anticipate, at least. And there's something else—the sutures weren't done well, either. She may face some real problems down the road. I'd recommend plastic surgery for that reason alone. But she has no insurance, you know."

"What the hell does that matter?" Boone asked blithely. "I'll take care of it. You talk her into it, and I'll pay the surgeon."

Coltrain grinned. "That's a deal."

Winnie didn't say anything, but she felt terrible that she and Keely had been friends for so many years, and Keely had never told her about the encounter with the mountain lion. She wondered if she'd said or done something that would make her best friend uncomfortable telling her about it.

"Is Keely asleep?" Boone asked Coltrain.

He nodded. "She'll be out for a while. It's just as well. That snakebite is still giving her hell. If Winnie hadn't found her when she did… Well, it doesn't bear thinking about," he added, cutting short the remark when he saw Boone's tortured eyes. "I'd better get back to work. If you need me, just tell the nurse on duty. They can always find me."

"Thanks," Boone said.

Coltrain shrugged and smiled. "I like Keely."

The siblings gathered around to discuss their plans. Boone decided that he'd better go and see Eb Scott in person. He was going to need specialized talent. Clark and Winnie would take turns staying with Keely. Nobody was going to get past them. They weren't armed, but they could certainly call for help.

It was morning before Keely woke up again. The combination of all the drugs and the emotional upheaval of her mother's death had knocked her out for the night. She blinked sleepily, her mind clear and untroubled until she remembered quite suddenly what she'd seen on television the night before. It was like a rock on her heart. Tears stung her eyes, all over again.

"I'm so sorry, Keely," Winnie said gently, from her vigil in the chair beside the bed. "About your mother."

Keely glanced at her. She sighed. "I knew I'd lose her someday," she said, "and we were almost enemies for so long. But we were just getting to know each other again, and we were becoming friends..." She bit her lip, hard. "It's been a rotten week," she said after a minute.

"Yes, it has." She hesitated. "I wish you could have told me about your shoulder," she said. "I feel that I've failed you, because you couldn't trust me enough to tell me."

Keely grimaced. "I was afraid you'd tell Boone," she said softly. "Not that it would have mattered. He hated me..."

"No, he didn't," came the immediate reply. "You have no idea what's been going on, while you were out of it."

"He showed me a photograph of some woman with my head on another body, in a compromising situation with Clark," Keely said heavily. "I knew it was a fake, but Boone didn't. He was furious. I was going to sink my pride and show him...and he thought I was trying to seduce him!" Her eyes smoldered. "I should have hit him with something! Then he tells me to get out of the house, and stalks off before I can say I haven't got a way home. When I get out of this bed," she added, building up steam as she spoke, "I'm going to turn him every which way but loose! That man has some lumps coming!"

Winnie had to fight a smile. Keely was such a gentle person, but she was really angry. "I'll help you thump him," she promised. "But he didn't know, Keely. And you don't know how he reacted when he found out, either."

"What do you mean?"

"When he saw you in the emergency room, he came out raving that he'd been conned by Misty's father's detective. He left and the next thing we knew, Hayes Carson was here, telling us he'd just had to bail Boone out of jail in San Antonio."

"What?" Keely exclaimed.

"He beat up the detective who faked that photograph." Winnie chuckled. "He was arrested and Hayes had to bail him out and bring him home."

"Will they prosecute him?" Keely asked, her anger forgotten in concern for Boone's future. "He isn't going to have to go to jail, is he?" she asked fearfully.

"Not likely. The detective, Misty, and her father all ran for the border, and nobody's around to press charges," Winnie said smugly. "It so happens that they're involved with the Fuenteses' outfit, can you believe it? Boone was only seeing Misty to feed Hayes Carson information on her contacts. He was furious at Hayes for making him do it." She grinned. "I told you he wouldn't forgive her that easily after what she did to him."

"Boone got arrested." Keely said it, disbelievingly. "He never puts a foot wrong."

"He did this time. But there were extenuating circumstances. He was rather tipsy at the time."

"He was drinking?"

"From what we hear," Winnie agreed. She laughed. "My spotless big brother, drunk and beating up detectives." She shook her head. "What is the world coming to?" She grinned at Keely. "Apparently he thinks a little more of you than he let on, I'd say."

Keely was afraid to hope for much, especially after Boone had seen her wrecked shoulder. But his actions indicated more feeling for Keely than he'd expressed verbally. There was hope, she thought. He had scars, too. Perhaps he'd had worse experiences than she had, with people of the opposite sex who didn't understand or care about his scars.

By the time Boone came back to the hospital, Winnie and Clark had gone home for supper and to get a room ready for Keely when she was discharged. Coltrain had said she'd be ready to go the next day if she continued improving.

Keely didn't want to go home with them if Boone only offered out of guilt. But she didn't want to go to her home, either, with Ella's death so fresh on her mind. Nobody had told her where Ella died, but Keely suspected that it was at the house.

She had an unexpected visitor while she was worrying her choices to death in her mind. Ella's best friend, Carly, came in, dressed in black, red-eyed from crying.

"Did they tell you?" she asked gently, because she didn't want to upset Keely.

"Yes," Keely said huskily. "We were doing so well together..." Her voice broke.

Carly bent over the bed, and hugged her gently. "I've been out of town. There was a missed call on my cell phone, but when I tried to call Ella back, there was no answer. I got worried when I couldn't get you, either, so I cut my trip short and came home." She grimaced. "What a homecoming! Ella dead, and you in the hospital in serious condition. Are you going to be all right?"

"Yes," Keely said. "But I understand that the snake died."

It took a minute for Carly to get the dry humor. She smiled. "Poor snake."

"I expect his relatives are all sad." She dabbed at her eyes with the sheet. "I haven't had time to make any arrangements about the funeral."

"Do you want me to do that?" Carly asked solemnly. "Ella gave me a copy of her will and instructions for her funeral two years ago. I never really thought they'd be needed, but I humored her."

"Could you call Lunsford's and make the arrangements?" Keely asked gently. "She has a burial policy with them, which should cover everything. She paid it off a few years ago."

"I'll be glad to do that," Carly replied. Fresh tears rolled down her cheeks. "She was the only friend I had—the only real one."

Keely reached out her good hand and squeezed Carly's. "You were her only real friend," she replied. "I'm glad she had you."

Carly cried even harder. "I wish I could take back every mean thing I ever said to you, Keely," she sobbed. "I didn't really mean any of it. In the old days, I took care of you a lot when Ella couldn't. I lost sight of that. But I'll do anything to make it up to you now, if I can."

"Look after Mama's funeral arrangements," Keely said, "and we'll call it even."

Carly dried her eyes. "When do you want to have it?" she asked worriedly. "You don't look up to a funeral."

She wasn't. She hesitated. Boone came in the door, gave Carly a cold appraisal and moved to Keely's bed.

"I've arranged for some additional manpower at the ranch," he said without preamble. "What do you want to do about your mother?"

"Carly's going to take care of that," Keely said. "She knows where everything is, and she has copies of Mama's will and last wishes."

Boone glanced at the older woman. "If there are any outstanding accounts, I'll take care of them," he said.

Carly nodded. Her eyes were as red as Keely's. "Thanks." She hesitated. "You know," she said, staring meaningfully at Boone, "it might not be a bad idea to have her cremated, and the ashes buried in the family plot."

Boone knew then that Carly had seen Ella and wanted to spare Keely the trauma of it. His eyes narrowed. "I think that's a good idea. Keely?"

Keely wasn't sure. She hesitated.

"A Viking funeral," Boone said quietly. "Appropriate for a brave woman."

Keely burst out crying again. "Yes," she agreed, choking. "She was brave. Okay. That's okay."

Boone leaned over and gathered her as close as he could, kissing the tears away. "It passes," he said softly. "Everything passes. You'll be able to remember her with happiness one day."

"Yes, you will," Carly seconded. She went on the other side of the bed, and bent and kissed Keely's disheveled hair. "I'll go and get things started. The hospital and the funeral home may need your approval before they can proceed. I'll have them call you here."

"Do that," Boone said quietly. "But I don't think there will be a problem. You stuck by Ella when nobody else would go near her."

Carly took that for a compliment and smiled. "Thanks."

"If you can find that snake," Keely told Boone, trying to lighten the somber mood, "we can arrange the same sort of funeral for him. Of course, if he didn't die from biting me, we'll have to kill him first."

Boone managed a chuckle. "I'm glad to see that you're better."

She smiled weakly, grimacing as she moved her arm.

"Coltrain says she can go home tomorrow, so we'll have her with us," Boone told Carly. He pulled out his wallet, got out a business card and handed it to her. "If you need help with the arrangements, let me know."

"Okay. If we cremate her, we can schedule a memorial service when this is all over," Carly told him. She glanced at Keely worriedly. "You're not going to be able to manage a funeral in the condition you're in right now."

"I have to agree," Keely said. She caught her breath. "Oh, my gosh! My job! I didn't even call Dr. Rydel! He's going to fire me!"

"I phoned him," Boone said at once. "He's got a temp filling in for you. He and the staff send their best wishes. They sent you a big fruit basket. It just came, so the nurses gave it to me, but I took it out to the car. I'm taking it home. You can have it tomorrow."

"Thanks," she told him. "I was afraid of losing my job. I was too sick to call and tell them what was going on."

"Oh, everybody in Comanche Wells and Jacobsville knows everything that's going on already," Carly said. She glanced amusedly at Boone. "And I mean everything."

Boone's eyes actually twinkled, but Keely didn't see it.

Carly said her goodbyes and left Boone alone with Keely. He stuck his hands in his slacks' pockets and stood over her, his eyes soft and quiet.

"You look a little better," he commented.

"I wish I felt it. I'm still sick at my stomach and my arm throbs," she said huskily. She looked up at him. "I hate snakes."

"They don't like people sitting on them," he pointed out.

"I didn't. He was just all of a sudden there. I didn't even look at him sideways. He just rattled his head off and struck at me."

"Nervous."

She blinked. "Excuse me?"

"Rattlesnakes are nervous. They rattle to try to scare people into going away."

It had never occurred to her that a snake could be nervous. She said so.

He sighed. "Anyway, we got him."

"You got him? You did?" She was excited.

"The boys found him about twenty feet from where you were sitting when he bit you."

"What did they do with him?"

He pursed his lips. "Do you like cowboy hats?"

"I guess so. I don't wear them much, except when I go riding."

"You'll wear this one. It's just your size and it's got a nice new rattlesnake hatband. Or it will have, when the skin's tanned out."

"You didn't!"

"I did." He grinned down at her. "We'll go riding, when you're better."

"We will?"

One eye narrowed. "You go riding with Clark and Winnie all the time. You can go riding with me now," he said with faint belligerence.

"Okay," she said, fascinated. It almost sounded as if he were jealous of her. That was ridiculous, of course.

"I had a television put in your room. You can watch movies on pay-per-view. We've got satellite, too, so you can watch programs from all over the world." His eyes twinkled. "Then, there's the national news, with the presidential race on every channel, every hour, every day."

She sighed. "I haven't watched the national news for weeks. I can't stand the monotony. The only news they report is on the presidential election and every detail of the private lives of celebrities."

"The Spanish channel has the real news," he pointed out. "If you want to know what's going on in the world, that's where to find out."

She smiled. "I can't speak Spanish."

"I'll teach you," he said quietly, and his eyes were insinuating that he had in mind teaching her other things, as well.

She flushed a little. Her life had been a closed, painful book, her future a dream that she never thought would be realized. Now, here was this dishy man with whom she'd been in love for years, looking at her with acquisitive eyes and smiling at her. It felt as if her heart might burst from joy.

He smiled. "Mrs. Johnston has an assistant cook, Melinda.

She's from Guatemala. She's teaching us Mayan. You can learn, too."

"Mayan?" She caught her breath. "Their culture had astronomy and the concept of zero and raised beds for planting and irrigation while Europeans were knocking each other over the head with rocks."

"I know." He chuckled. "You spend your time off at the library reading books about them. Or so I hear from the head librarian."

She flushed. It flattered her that he'd learned things about her. "I'd love to go and see some of the Mayan ruins," she said. "I'd love to go to Peru and see the Inca ruins, too."

"So would I," he told her. "Maybe we can both go, one day."

For her, that was a pipe dream. She'd never save enough to pay for a plane ticket even to south Texas for a vacation. Her smile was wistful.

He saw that. "What else do you like?"

She smiled. "Ancient history."

"The Caesars, the philosophers, the politicians…?"

"Don't mention politicians!"

"What sort of history?" He chuckled. "And which historians do you read?"

"Tacitus. Thucydides. Strabo. Arrian. Plutarch. Those ones."

"Deep authors for a young mind," he commented.

"You listen here, I may be young, but I have an old mind," she told him. "I was pretty much on my own when my father took me out to west Texas to live in an animal park, and I was really on my own when I came back here, because Mama was drunk so much." Mama. The thought sobered her, made her aware of her recent tragedy. "I can't believe my own father would kill her," she said. "He was a little out of the bounds of law sometimes, but he never hurt anybody."

"He sold drugs," Boone reminded her. "That does hurt people."

"Yes, but you know what I mean," she replied. "He isn't a killer."

"Baby, all people are killers, given the right incentive," he said. "Anybody can kill."

She sighed. "I suppose so," she said sadly.

He bent and kissed her, gently, on her mouth. "I'm going to get a cup of decent coffee. What can I bring you?"

"A nice juicy steak with hash browns?" she asked hopefully.

"No chance I could get that past the nurses' station, unless they were all wearing nose plugs. Try again," he invited.

"I guess I'll wait for supper here," she said with resignation.

"When you're well again, I'll fly you up to Fort Worth and take you to this little steak place I know," he said.

Her heart jumped up into her throat. "You mean it?"

He drew in a long breath. "I had to date Misty to feed information to Hayes, and I gave him hell twice a day about it. I was over her years ago. But I had to put on an act, to keep her from getting suspicious." His eyes darkened. "Hayes has a lot to answer for. She's vindictive. She set you up, and I was too angry to think straight when I saw those photographs."

Keely recalled that Misty had promised to get even with her. She'd done a good job of it. "She'll get her just deserts one day," Keely replied.

"We all do," he said philosophically. He glanced at his watch. "I have to make a few phone calls and get something to eat, then I'll be back."

Her eyes lit up. "Okay."

He smiled slowly. Disheveled, her hair uncombed, her face devoid of any makeup, she was beautiful to him. So easily, she could have been dead. He'd never have been able to live with that, knowing he caused her death.

He bent and kissed her again with breathless tenderness. "I'll be back soon," he whispered.

She smiled. "Okay. I'll wait."

He chuckled as he walked out.

Ten minutes later the phone rang. She answered it, thinking it must be Carly or Winnie or Clark.

"Keely, is that you?"

It was her father's voice.

CHAPTER THIRTEEN

"You killed my mother!" Keely choked, overwhelmed with rage at just the sound of his voice. "How could you!"

"It wasn't me, I swear it wasn't!" he replied, and he sounded frightened. "Keely, I've never killed a person in my life. You have to believe me."

"You threatened her for money—"

"I had to! Listen, if I don't pay them, they'll…well, they'd already threatened to kill your mother, now they say they'll get you, too," he said nervously. "It's the Fuentes gang! I got mixed up with them because of Jock," he said bitterly. "He's been working for Fuentes for years. He even went to prison for him, just after you came to live with me. He said they paid better than any of the other distributors, and that he'd get me in because he had a cousin in the organization. But there was trouble right up-front because Jock double-crossed one of the bosses and pocketed some drug money. Then he hid out and left me holding the bag. They're after me, now." There was a sigh. "Your mother was right about Jock. She said he'd destroy me if I stuck with him, and he has. He keeps calling me, making threats toward you if you don't come up with enough money to help him to get out of town before the drug lords kill him. I don't know what to do!"

She had to clamp down hard on her feelings. He was rationalizing his behavior, but she remembered that he'd stood by while the mountain lion dragged her away to what would have been her death.

"You go to Sheriff Carson," she told him. "Tell him what you've told me, and help him find Jock. That's what you have to do."

"Hell, Carson will lock me up and throw away the key!" he muttered. "I gave his brother the coke that killed him. No, I'm not going to the law."

"What else can you do?" she asked.

"Get enough money to pay Jock, so he'll get off my back. The Fuentes organization want Jock. They want to kill him, but they don't know where he is. They thought Ella did and they..." He was going to say they tortured her, but he couldn't make himself say that to his daughter, whom he'd failed in so many ways already. "Well, they killed her. Now, the only hope I have is to raise enough money to help Jock get out of the country before they catch up with him. He swore if I didn't, he'd tell them I was the one who double-crossed them. He'd give them back what he took and blame it on me!"

"If you give him money," she said in a weary tone, "he'll only want more."

"There's a chance he won't. He just wants to get out of the country before they do to him what they did to those drug agents they killed. He won't say so, but I think he's afraid of Fuentes's new partner. The partner is called Machado and he hates Jock. He'll kill him before Fuentes does if he gets the chance, and Jock knows it."

"Let him," Keely said coldly.

"Jock was the only friend I had, Keely," he said heavily. "He stood by me when everybody else jumped ship."

Just as Carly had stood by Ella. But that had been because Carly genuinely loved Keely's mother. Jock had stood by Brent Welsh because he knew Ella had money, Keely thought, and he could use Brent to get some of it. But she didn't say that. He wouldn't have listened anyway.

"I don't have any money," Keely told him. "I work as a veterinarian technician and I make minimum wage. Mama—" Her voice broke. She composed herself. "Mama had some money in a savings account, but it's in her name and it's tied up in probate. I won't be able to get it for weeks." She didn't know if that was true, but it sounded convincing.

He cursed sharply. "There must be something you can sell!"

"She already sold it all," she said bitterly.

He muttered again, incoherent. "Then those friends of yours, the Sinclairs—they've got money. Ask them for it!"

"I won't."

"Your life is on the line, Keely!" he raged. "It's not a game! Jock's already said that he's got nothing to lose. He'll kill you if you don't help us."

She felt very old. Her mother was dead, she'd almost died herself. Boone knew her darkest secret and would surely not want her anymore, even if he was compassionate and understanding about her injury. He was scarred himself. But Keely saw no future for herself.

"I don't care," she said passively. "Let Jock do his worst. He might be doing me a favor," she said with black humor. "God knows, I'm never going to have a husband or a family, the way I look."

"I'm…sorry," he said slowly. "I'm very sorry, for what happened. I was so shocked that I couldn't even do anything. I feel bad about that. And I didn't think about how the scars might affect your life."

"Pity," she said, and felt hatred seethe through her. "Until that moment, I thought you cared about me."

"I do care, in my way," he said. "My parents were ice-cold with each other and with me. They never went out of their way to do one charitable thing for anyone else. I learned that you take care of number one."

"So did Mama," she replied. "Neither of you was fit to raise a child."

"Tell me about it," he laughed hollowly. "Once you came, our lives changed forever. She was too unstable emotionally to cope with a baby." He sounded bitter. "You spent a lot of time with Carly."

A light flashed in her mind as she recalled Carly's face. It was far more familiar to her than Ella's. No wonder the other woman had been so protective of her.

"But that's all in the past, and I've got bigger problems now. You have to try to get me some money. Jock says he won't wait much longer."

"Tell him to come see me. I can borrow a shotgun," she mused.

"It's not funny!"

"If you were in my position, it might be."

"Ask your friends if they'll help out. Even two thousand might be enough," her father persisted. "Take this number down, Keely. You can reach me here."

She grabbed a pencil and pad from inside the drawer by her bed. "Okay."

He gave her the number. "Do your best, honey," he pleaded. "You lived against all the odds. I don't want you to die over a handful of money."

"I'll see what I can do," she said heavily, and hung up. It wasn't until then she realized that she was shaking.

When Boone came back, he found Keely quiet and preoccupied, staring into space.

"What's wrong?" he asked, because he knew at once that something was. He could feel it.

She frowned. "How do you know something is?"

He moved to the bed and dropped down lazily into the armchair by her bed. "I read minds. Come on. Tell me."

She sank back into the pillows wearily. "My father called. Jock's running from the drug lords and he wants money to get out of the country. He told my father that if I don't get it for him somehow, he'll kill me. The drug dealers will probably send him back to wherever he came from in a shoebox."

He took off his hat and dropped it on the floor by his chair. He ran a big, lean hand through his black hair. "I'll turn Bailey loose on him, and when he gets through, Jock will fit in the shoebox. Or parts of him will."

"Is Bailey all right?" she asked.

He smiled. "Doing great, thanks to you." His smile faded. "I still can't believe I listened to that self-centered little cheater when you told me what was wrong with Bailey. I wish I could go back and live those few minutes over."

"It turned out all right."

He nodded. "Only because you had the guts to do what you knew was right. You've got grit, Keely."

"I'm just stubborn," she replied. "What am I going to do? I don't have anything I could sell that would bring enough money to buy Jock a plane ticket."

"We'll talk to Hayes," he told her. "He'll know what to do."

And Hayes did. They arranged for a sum of money that Boone would give her father to lure him into a trap. Keely had already given Hayes the number where her father could be reached when she got the money.

"You're not going," she told Boone when he and Hayes were discussing who was going to take the money to Jock.

"Excuse me?" Boone asked haughtily.

She flushed, but she wouldn't backtrack. "You're not going. Everybody around me is either dead or in danger, and you're not going to join my mother at the local funeral home. Let him do it." She pointed at Hayes. "He knows how to deal with criminals. He's good at it."

"Thanks," Hayes mused.

"I was with a Special Forces unit in the Middle East," Boone reminded Keely. "I came home."

She looked to Hayes for assistance.

He grimaced. "Okay, I'll work out the details once you get the money together. With any luck, we can nab both men."

"I'll call you," Boone promised.

When Hayes left, Boone watched Keely with faint amusement. "You're afraid I'll get hurt."

She shifted on her pillows. "My mother is dead because my father wanted money. I don't want to lose you… I mean, I don't want Clark and Winnie to have to lose you."

He pursed his lips. "I could have wrung your neck when I saw those photos," he said conversationally. "I could have wrung Clark's, too."

"I know you don't want him around me because I'm in another social class…"

"Stop that," he muttered. "I didn't want him around you because you're mine, Keely," he said curtly.

Warmth shot through her body like fire. Surely she was hearing things. Her expression said so.

"We'll have to do something about that self-image." He chuckled. "I don't know why you ever thought I didn't want you. Even Clark realized I was jealous as hell."

"You hated me," she exclaimed. "You ignored me when you came to bring Bailey to Dr. Rydel!"

"Camouflage," he replied. "I didn't know about your shoulder, then," he added, in a subdued tone. "All I could think about was my own defects. I'd already had evidence of how a woman would react to them. You're so young, Keely. I thought you were too young to cope."

"I'm older than I look," she replied.

"We both are." His dark eyes grew intent on her face. "I don't care about the obstacles anymore. We'll improvise."

She was tingling at the way he looked at her, but she was a little apprehensive. It was a modern world, in the circles Boone frequented. But Keely was living in the past. "I've never been… I've never had… I don't know how…" She gave up, exasperated.

"I know all that," he said gently. "We'll go slow. I won't rush you."

"Yes, but it won't matter," she said earnestly. "Don't you see? I was raised religiously, despite the bad role models my parents were. I don't believe people should sleep together if they aren't married."

"Funny," he returned with a smile, "that's exactly the way I feel, too."

She seemed to stop breathing. Her eyes were held by his. She felt funny. "It is?" she parroted.

"It is. So we'll get to know each other a lot better, then we'll make long-term decisions. Okay?"

She smiled. Her heart was soaring in her chest. "Okay."

He chuckled deep in his throat. It was the first time he'd felt happy since the ordeal began.

He got the money out of his bank, in cash, and phoned Hayes, who had Keely call her father and set up a time and place for the money to change hands.

"You got it!" her father exclaimed. "Keely, you're a wonder! This will save my life!"

"I thought it was going to save mine," she replied suspiciously.

"Of course, yours!" he said quickly. "I meant it will save us both! Where do you want me to meet you?"

"Dad, I'm still in the hospital," she pointed out.

"Oh! That's right. I guess I could meet you in the hospital, then," he said.

She repeated what he said, so that Boone and Hayes could hear him. Hayes nodded enthusiastically.

"Yes, that would be fine," Keely said. "When do you want to come?"

"Ten minutes," he said, and hung up.

She put the receiver back down. "He's on his way here," she said. Her tone was bitter. "He said it would save his life. He wasn't ever concerned about mine."

"I'm sorry, Keely," Hayes told her. "But he never was concerned about the welfare of other people. If he had been, he'd never have sent Bobby that totally pure cocaine, knowing it would kill him."

Keely sighed. "I had hoped that—" She broke off, flushed. "Well, it would have been nice if he'd cared a little about me. But if he had, he'd have dived into that mountain lion pit without thinking about the consequences when that little boy's life was at stake."

"Which you did," Boone replied.

She nodded. "I didn't think at all, I just reacted. Dad got sued by the parents because of it, but they called me to the stand and described the wounds I sustained trying to save the little boy. The family was shamefaced and asked their lawyer to withdraw the case. The little boy wasn't even frightened, and he didn't have a mark on him. But the judge wasn't so forgiving.

He said that Dad should have had better fencing in place, and he named a figure for Dad to pay the family. But by then, Dad spent all his money on his pretty gold digger and had to borrow on the game park to pay off the little boy's family, and to take care of his legal fees. He lost everything. I guess he thinks I owe him for that."

"It seems to me that he owes you," Boone said coldly.

"Same here," Hayes agreed. He got to his feet. "I'd better get some backup over here. I'll talk to the security guard, too." He glanced at Boone. "You staying?"

"You bet I am," Boone replied doggedly. "I'm not leaving her in here alone in case her father gets past you."

Hayes smiled. "I don't think he will, but better safe than sorry. Want a gun?"

Boone chuckled. "I never needed one. I still don't."

"Okay. Sing out if you need help. Thanks, Keely," he told her.

She nodded.

Hayes left and she stared curiously at Boone. "Why don't you need a gun?" she asked him.

"I had the highest score in my unit in hand-to-hand combat," he said simply. "I could even disarm my men when they came at me with weapons."

Her eyes sparkled. "Wow."

He shrugged. "It's a skill. We all have them." He smiled at her. "Yours is handling animals. I never told you that Bailey bites, did I?"

"He's never bitten me," she said, confused.

"You're the only person who knows him who can say that," he told her with a twinkle in his eyes. "Like I said. You have skills."

She smiled back.

He got to his feet and moved to the door, opened it and looked both ways. He came back into the room. He'd just turned toward the closet when the door opened suddenly and Brent Welsh came into the room.

"Quick, Keely, give me the money!" he told Keely abruptly. "Hayes Carson was downstairs—he got Jock the minute we walked in the door! Somebody tipped them off!"

"Then you should be safe," Keely told him. "If Sheriff Carson has Jock."

"I'll never have enough money to be safe," he said. "But at least I can get away from the Fuentes bunch. Where's the—"

In a movement so fluid that Keely almost missed it, Boone caught Welsh's arm, swung him around and pinned him to the wall. He held him there with one big hand while he flipped open his cell phone and pushed a button.

"Let me go!" Brent pleaded with his captor. "I can't go to jail here, they'll kill me!"

"What a tragedy that would be," Boone drawled.

The door burst open and Hayes walked in, closing his cell phone. He put away the .40 caliber Glock he'd been holding even with his right temple, and grinned at Boone. "You don't forget that military training, do you?" He chuckled.

Boone grinned. "I get in some practice on stubborn bulls at roundup. Here." He propelled Welsh around so that Hayes could handcuff him.

"Keely, tell them to let me go!" Brent called to his daughter. "I'm innocent. It was Jock! He did it!"

Keely felt sick. She'd almost believed her father's false apology. "I can't help you," she said sadly. "Nobody can, now."

Brent's face darkened and he began to curse. Hayes grimaced as he pushed the man out of the room ahead of him and turned him over to a deputy.

"Sorry about that," he told Keely. "We had him, but he slipped away. We've got him now, thanks to you," he told Boone, "and his partner, as well. I'll talk to you later. Don't worry, Keely," he added. "These two are wanted for murder in Arizona. I imagine there'll be an extradition hearing very soon. Good job, Boone. If you ever want to work for me…?"

"I'd never fit in," Boone told him. "I use real curse words."

Hayes made a face at him. "'Crackers and Milk' is a perfectly good curse," he informed his friend.

"Ha!"

Hayes left with his dignity intact.

Boone moved to the bed and tugged Keely up into his arms, careful not to jar her sore arm. "And now we can concentrate on happier times," he said gently, smiling as he kissed her with breathless tenderness.

She had a room next to Winnie's upstairs, the most beautiful bedroom she'd ever seen in her life. She was afraid to walk on the carpet, which was pure white, dramatic against the blue curtains and bedspread and the blue tile in the bathroom.

"Gosh, the bathroom is bigger than my whole bedroom at home," she exclaimed when Boone carried her in and laid her on the bed.

"We like a lot of space," he told her, smiling. "Comfortable?"

She sank into fathoms of feathery softness. "Oh, yes!"

Winnie and Clark came in behind them, bearing flowers and fruit.

"The flowers came from the girls at your office," Winnie told her, "and the fruit's from Dr. Rydel."

"Does he often send you presents?" Boone asked darkly.

"Only when I get bitten by rattlesnakes and end up in the hospital," she told him solemnly.

Winnie and Clark burst out laughing.

Boone flushed a little. "Cut it out," he muttered. He pulled his hat low over his eyes. "I've got to get the boys working out on the west pasture. I'll be back in time for supper." He grinned at Keely. "When you're better, you can make us some more yeast rolls."

She laughed, flattered that he'd liked them. "Okay."

"But not yet," he cautioned.

She saluted him. He laughed out loud, winked at his siblings, and left them with Keely.

"Imagine that," Winnie sighed, smiling. "You and Boone."

Keely flushed. "He's just being kind."

"Do you think so?" Clark mused. "I don't."

"Shoo," Winnie told her brother. "I'm going to settle Keely, then I have to go in and work for a few hours. I'm on a split shift this week."

"You're worth a fortune, and you're working for wages," Clark sighed.

Winnie made a face at him. "I like working for wages."

Clark's eyes twinkled. "You like working with Kilraven."

Winnie blushed. "He's just one of the guys I work with, now that I'm working dispatch full-time."

Clark wiggled both eyebrows and laughed as he walked out.

"Besides," Winnie told her best friend, "Kilraven doesn't like me."

Keely had doubts about that, but she didn't say a word. She just smiled.

Winnie helped her get into a flowered-print ankle-length cotton gown with short puffy sleeves and a high neckline. She winced at the scars. "You poor thing," she said with genuine sympathy. "It must have been so painful!"

Keely lost her self-consciousness at that expression. "Most people would have said how horrible it looks. Yes, it was terrible. The first few days were the worst of my life. And then, even when it started healing, there were the scars." She shivered and leaned back into the pillows with a sigh. "But I guess it was really a blessing in disguise, because Jock had just gotten out of prison after two years, and he came on to me the day he got back. The scars were all that saved me from him. He thought I was repulsive." She looked at Winnie meaningfully. "I was thirteen years old," she said bitterly.

Winnie sat down on the bed beside her and squeezed her hand. "Some men are animals," she said gently. "Men used to come on to me when I went to parties because they knew who I was, who my family was. They didn't really want me, they wanted the wealth and power I had access to. Boone spent a lot of time making threats." She laughed. "That's why I like working for the emergency management center," she added. "Some of the newer people don't even know I come from a wealthy background. They treat me like everybody else. It's flattering."

Keely was curious. "Kilraven knows who you are."

Winnie nodded. She frowned. "It's odd, isn't it, that he doesn't seem to mind." She hesitated, looking down at her lap. "But most of the time he treats me just like he does the other dispatchers."

"I've always dreamed about Boone," Keely said. "I never thought he might feel the same way about me."

Winnie laughed. "I had a hunch about that when he went off and beat up the private detective," she mused. "That's not like Boone. It wasn't just guilt, either. He may think you're too young, Keely, but he seems to have come to grips with your age."

Keely smiled. "I'm old for my age," she said dryly.

"And I'll say amen to that!"

CHAPTER FOURTEEN

Boone came home dusty and worn-out, having helped move steers from summer pasture into the holding pens nearby, where they'd be held until they could be shipped to a feedlot for finishing as yearlings.

It was a long, arduous process, and somebody always got hurt. Fortunately, Keely noted, it wasn't Boone.

"You pay your foreman a fortune to do that job, and then you go out and work like you're him," Winnie fussed as he came into Keely's bedroom after he'd showered.

"I'm not cut out for the life of a gentleman of leisure," he pointed out, smiling. "How're you doing, sprout?" he asked Keely.

"Much better," she assured him. "Have you heard anything from Hayes Carson?"

He shook his head. "He'll get back in touch with us when he's got something to say. Meanwhile, stop worrying. You're safe here."

She smiled. "I know. It wasn't that. I just wondered."

"I'm starved," he told Winnie. "When are we eating?"

"Mrs. Johnston's outdone herself," Winnie replied with a grin. "Beef stew and Mexican corn bread."

"Worth working all day for," he said. "I'll bring yours up," he told Keely.

"I could come downstairs," she began.

"Not until Coltrain says you can," he replied firmly. "We don't want a relapse, now, do we?"

"I guess not. My arm's better, though," she said, moving it gingerly. "The swelling's gone down a lot."

"Damned snake," he muttered.

"That's exactly what I said when it happened," Keely assured him.

He grinned. "You do look better." His eyes slid over the flowered gown. They were bold and possessive.

The memory of that look kept her occupied all through supper. He'd brought it himself, on a tray, to the amusement of Winnie, Clark and Mrs. Johnston, who added a flower in a vase to the tray.

After supper, Winnie went straight to her bedroom to change clothes. Clark went out. Boone changed into pajamas and a robe and came walking into Keely's bedroom with a file folder in his hand, reading glasses on and a pencil over one ear. He piled into bed with Keely, propping himself up on two of the mound of pillows Mrs. Johnston had brought her. He proceeded to open the folder and read.

Keely was fascinated. "What are you doing?"

"Working on printouts of the breeding program that our cow and calf foreman brought me," he told her. "We breed for certain traits, like low birth weight and lean conformation, and we use computers to make projections for us." He showed her the information on the pages.

"No. I mean… I mean, what are you doing in here, like that?" She indicated his pajamas and robe.

He gave her a conspiratorial grin. "I'm sleeping with you."

"You are not!" she gasped. "In the first place, I can't—"

"Sleeping," he emphasized. "You close your eyes and the next thing you know, it's morning."

She relaxed a little, but she was still wary.

"All the doors are open," he pointed out, nodding toward the hall. "They'll stay open. Nobody will notice that I'm in here."

Winnie walked past the doorway and smiled. She stopped suddenly, turned and stared.

Boone glowered at her. "What's the matter with you?" he asked his sister. "Haven't you ever seen a man in pajamas and a robe before?"

"You're in bed with Keely," she stated. "She's still fragile," she added worriedly.

"That's true, but her father's friend is something of an escape artist," he agreed. He reached into his pocket and pulled out a worn-looking Smith & Wesson .38 caliber police special. He put it up again. "Nobody's getting past me."

Winnie stopped looking shocked and began to grin. "I get it."

"Good. While you're getting things, how about getting Bailey and his bed out of my room and bringing them both in here?" he added. "He'll start howling if the light goes off and he's alone in there."

"He really does," Winnie told Keely. "He thinks Boone will die if he isn't there to protect him."

Keely smiled. "He's a sweet old boy."

"Who, me?" Boone drawled, peering at her wickedly over his reading glasses.

"The dog!" she emphasized.

"Oh." He went back to his spreadsheets, oblivious to the world.

Winnie chuckled. "I'll get Bailey."

She did. She also got Clark and Mrs. Johnston. They all peered in from the hall, fascinated. Boone had never even brought a woman upstairs in living memory, and here he was in bed, in his pajamas, with Keely.

Clark started to speak. Boone lifted the gun, displayed it, put it back in his pocket without looking up from the spreadsheet.

"I haven't said anything!" Clark protested. "You shouldn't threaten people with guns just because they're curious!"

"It's for Keely's father's evil friend," Winnie told him.

"Oh. Oh!" Clark finally got it. "Okay."

Mrs. Johnston was grinning from ear to ear. Her white hair seemed to vibrate. She and Clark and Winnie just stood, staring and grinning. Boone reached in his other pocket and brought out a jeweler's box, just the size to contain a ring. He displayed it, still without looking up from the spreadsheet, and put it away again. Now Keely was looking breathless, too.

"Here's Bailey and his bed," Winnie said as she put the dog pallet on Boone's side of the bed. "We'll close the door on our way out."

"You'll do no such thing," Boone told her curtly. "This is a respectable household. No hanky-panky above stairs." He glared at Clark. "From anybody."

Clark threw up his hands. "I once, only once, sneaked a girl into my room for immoral purposes. He never forgets!"

"It was an act of charity," Winnie chided Boone. "He found her wandering all alone on a street corner and brought her home to get a blanket to put around her."

Everybody burst out laughing, even Clark.

"All right, that's enough. Everybody out. I've got work to do, then we're going to have a decent night's sleep." He glanced down at Keely, who was watching him with openly worshipful eyes. He smiled tenderly. "Some of us could use it more than others."

"I won't argue with that," Keely replied.

While they were looking at each other, their audience vanished.

Boone glanced at the doorway and chuckled deep in his throat as he looked down at his bedmate. "I do have evil purposes in mind," he confided in a low tone, "but they're probably all hiding ten feet from the door, waiting for developments. So we have to behave."

She sighed deeply. "Okay," she replied. Her hand, under the sheet, reached over to touch his muscular arm. She closed her eyes, comforted by the contact. "I've been afraid to sleep for days," she whispered. "Now I'm not."

He smoothed a hand over her blond hair. "Go to sleep," he said. "I'll keep you safe."

"I know that."

He went back to the spreadsheet. Seconds later, in the long silence that followed, three sets of eyes peered cautiously in the door.

"What?" Boone asked belligerently.

They scattered to the four winds. Bailey climbed into his bed, circled a few times, lay down and yawned and went back to sleep.

The next morning, Keely heard a car drive up. She opened her eyes slowly, disoriented. She was lying next to a warm, hard body that had her wrapped up gently against it. They were both under the covers.

Boone looked down at her warmly. "Ready for breakfast?" he asked softly. "I hear movement from the general direction of the kitchen."

She curled closer. "I could eat."

They were both on her side of the bed, and had apparently been close like that all night. Keely felt so safe and cozy that she was reluctant to move.

Voices murmured downstairs, and heavy, quick footsteps came up the staircase. Hayes Carson walked in, his uniform a little rumpled, like his blond, brown-streaked hair under his Stetson.

He stopped, lifting both eyebrows.

Boone yawned. "I've got a gun," he murmured.

"I haven't said anything yet," Hayes protested.

Boone glared at him. "To protect Keely with," he added.

"Oh."

Hayes marched over to the bed, threw his hat on the carpeted floor, climbed in next to Boone and lay back on the pillows. "God, I'm tired! I've been up all night helping interrogate Keely's father and his friend."

"Make yourself comfortable," Boone drawled sarcastically.

"Thanks, I will," Hayes replied. "This is the most comfortable bed I've ever been in," he added. He reached down, scooped up his hat and set it over his eyes. "I could sleep for a week!"

"Tell me what you're doing here first," Boone said.

"In order to save his skin, Keely's father made a plea deal. He gave us his friend Jock on a murder charge. It seems that Jock killed a woman in Arizona. He was the chief suspect, but they couldn't get the evidence to convict him. Keely's father has a watch that belonged to the dead woman, and he can put Jock there at the time of the murder." He smiled under the hat.

"What about my father?" Keely wanted to know.

"Three to five, on accessory charges. We talked to the assistant D.A. last night, too."

"Maybe it will teach him something," Keely said, but she didn't sound convinced.

"Don't look for miracles," Boone advised. "With lawbreakers, they rarely happen."

"Like you know," Hayes drawled from under the hat. He crossed his long legs.

There was the sound of another car arriving. A car door slammed. Voices murmured. Another sound of footsteps, but these were soft and quick and almost undetectable.

Kilraven poised in the doorway, staring. "Well, if that isn't just like county law enforcement," he muttered. "Walk out in the middle of an interrogation and leave the hard work to the local law!"

"Shut up, Kilraven," Hayes said pleasantly. "I haven't slept since night before last."

"Like I have!" Kilraven shot back. He scowled. He shrugged. "Hell, maybe you're right. A little rest might perk us all up. Hi, Keely," he greeted as he sank down onto the foot of the bed and sprawled across it at Hayes's booted feet. "Say, this is a really soft bed," he mused, closing his own eyes.

There were other footsteps. "Isn't anybody coming down for breakfast…?"

Winnie stood in the doorway, absolutely dumbstruck. There were four people in the bed. Two of them were in uniform.

"I'm not bringing trays up here," she announced. "Anybody who wants breakfast has to come downstairs and get it." She grinned. "There's enough for company, too."

"Are we company?" Hayes asked drowsily.

"Apparently," Kilraven replied.

"I suppose we all have to get up," Hayes sighed.

"It is my bed," Boone pointed out. "And Keely and I were here first."

Hayes sat up. He frowned. "What are you doing in bed with Keely?"

He produced the revolver from his pocket.

"Gun!" Kilraven exclaimed.

Boone just shook his head and laughed.

* * *

The guests stayed for breakfast and then went on their way. Kilraven was giving Winnie an odd look. She was subdued with him now. It was as if all the joy and bubbly fun had gone out of her forever. She knew there was no chance that he'd ever care for her in any permanent way, and she wasn't the sort for temporary liaisons. It broke her heart.

Kilraven tried to catch her eye as he and Hayes headed out the front door, but she wouldn't look at him. She said goodbye in a perfectly natural, pleasant tone and went back to the table. Kilraven was frowning when he left.

"Don't you have a meeting with some visiting cattlemen today?" Winnie asked Boone.

"Yes, for a couple of hours. They want to see our artificial insemination labs."

"I have to get to work," Winnie said reluctantly. She glanced at Keely. "Clark's already gone up to Dallas for a meeting with some investors, and Mrs. Johnston's gone shopping."

"Bailey will protect me," she told them, reaching down to pet the old dog.

"You won't need protecting now," Boone said gently. "Your father and Jock are safely behind bars at the detention center in San Antonio. They don't lose prisoners."

"So we hear," Winnie had to agree. "Make sure you keep the doors locked," she cautioned Keely.

"Of course I will," she said, smiling. "Don't worry. I survived a rattlesnake bite."

"You're tough all right," Winnie had to admit. "I'll be back as soon as I get off work. Take care."

"You, too," Keely said gently.

Winnie bent to kiss her and Boone before she left for her job. She managed to hide her heartbreak from them. She didn't want to spoil their joy in each other.

***

The house was very quiet, with only the two of them in it, both still in their pajamas. Boone looked at Keely with an expression she'd never seen on his face before. He got up slowly, pulled out her chair, swung her up into his arms and started for the staircase.

"Time for dessert," he whispered, bending to her mouth.

"It was breakfast. You don't have dessert with breakfast."

"Yes, we do."

He kissed her hungrily. After a few seconds, Keely forgot her protests, wrapped her good arm around his neck and kissed him back with enthusiasm. He laughed softly at her innocent eagerness, and proceeded to teach her the proper technique. By the time they got back to his room, she was ready for promotion to the next level.

He put her down long enough to close and lock the door. His high cheekbones were faintly flushed with the force of his desire. "It's been years," he bit off, his dark eyes blazing down into hers. "I want you."

She was breathless, frightened, exhilarated, all at once. But those old scruples were grinding away at her.

"I know," he said softly. "You want to wait for a ceremony. That's weeks away." He pulled her to him, pushed her hips against the hard thrust of his body. "Don't make me wait," he whispered huskily.

"Boone..." She was torn, tortured.

He reached into his pocket and pulled out the jewelry box. He opened it. Inside were an emerald solitaire and an emerald and diamond studded yellow gold set of rings. "Everybody in this house knows that I intend to marry you. I've had this set of rings for weeks, waiting for Hayes to get enough evidence to put damned Misty and her father out of business! A piece of paper with a seal isn't going to make that much difference.

With this ring," he said tenderly, sliding the emerald solitaire onto her ring finger, "I thee wed. The rest will come later. I love you, Keely," he added with reverence. "I'll love you until I die. Will you marry me?"

She could barely see the ring or him for the blur of tears. "Yes," she whispered.

He bent and drew his lips over hers, teasing them apart, coaxing them to admit the long, slow thrust of his tongue into her mouth.

She gasped as a charge of passion as powerful as a lightning strike shook her slender body. The shock was in her eyes when she met his.

"We begin here, now, Keely," he said solemnly. "The first day of the rest of our lives. Let me love you."

She was already too far gone to think of refusing him. His hands were under the gown, making nonsense of her fears about her scars. She closed her eyes, moaning softly, as his fingers smoothed expertly over the thrust of her breasts, followed in short order by his hungry mouth.

"Yes," she whispered unsteadily. And for long, passionate minutes, she said nothing more.

He paused just long enough to protect her. "It's too soon for babies," he whispered against her damp breasts. "We have a lot of living to do first. Then, when we're comfortable with each other, they'll come naturally."

"I love children," she said softly.

He smiled. "So do I."

Her arm protested when she reached up to him, but she ignored the pain. He pleasured her for a long time, until she was shivering all over with desire, pleading for an end to the anguish. At that moment, she felt him lose control. She arched up eagerly to meet the hard downward thrust of his body and tensed, crying out softly, as the barrier protested its invasion.

He hesitated, his whole body pulsing. "I hurt you," he ground out.

"Only a little," she whispered, because he looked as if it hurt him, too. "Don't stop."

"As if I could," he managed to say. He laughed as he moved again, and then he groaned and drove for fulfillment, helpless to stop himself.

She moved with him, blind with need, pulsating with delight that grew sharper and more pleasurable with every single second. She felt him in an intimacy that she'd never dreamed possible. Her last thought was that the culmination was going to kill her. The pleasure was so intense that, at the end, she cried out in a high-pitched, keening little tone that she'd never heard torn from her throat in her lifetime.

They clung together in the aftermath. He was spent. He could hardly breathe. Under him, Keely was holding tight, biting into his muscles with her short nails, still moving helplessly against him as the pleasure ebbed and flowed in her untried body. She was only just learning that the peak wasn't really the peak. She could feel the echoes of that intense, shattering climax happen over and over, just by moving in the right way.

He indulged her for a time, but then his lean hand caught her hip and stilled her. "No more," he whispered. "You're very new to this. It will be uncomfortable if we don't stop."

"Oh," she protested.

He kissed her tenderly. "Besides," he whispered, "we're tempting fate. These things are only good for one use. They can break."

Her eyes opened and looked up into his. They widened. "They can?"

She'd sounded almost hopeful. He chuckled. "It's rare, when that happens. We don't need a baby right now, at the beginning of our marriage."

"Are you sure we don't?" she asked.

He kissed her again. "I'm sure. And it isn't because I don't want one," he clarified. "I want time for us to travel and learn about each other."

"Travel."

He chuckled. "Anywhere you want to go."

"You mean, we could go to Wyoming and see Old Faithful?" she asked excitedly.

He propped up on one elbow. "I was thinking of someplace more exotic."

"Oh. Like Florida." She nodded.

He scowled. "The pyramids. Chichén Itzá. Sacsayhuamán. Zimbabwe. Those sorts of places."

"You mean, go overseas?" she exclaimed. "We could do that?"

He studied her rapt, pretty little face, and he smiled again. "Yes. We could do that."

"Wow."

He kissed her once more and withdrew, wincing when she winced. "I told you," he mused. "It takes time and practice to avoid these little pitfalls."

"I suppose so." She looked at his broad chest, where deep scars cut across it. There were more on his belly, and one, much worse, on his broad thigh. She reached out and touched them, testing the hard ridges with her fingertips, exploring. "Badges of honor," she murmured aloud.

He was watching her watching him, his dark eyes keen and alert. He smiled. "I've been self-conscious about these for years."

"They aren't that bad," she replied.

His own eyes were on her shoulder, her scars equally as deep as his and less cared for. "If you want to have plastic surgery, you can," he told her. "But I'd love you if you were missing an arm or a leg. Nothing will ever change the way I feel. And I don't mind your scars."

"I don't mind yours." She reached over and kissed his chest, where the thickest, hardest ridge ran right across it, diagonally. "I'm so glad that stupid woman ran from you," she murmured.

He laughed. "So am I, now."

She cuddled close to him, more secure and less embarrassed. It seemed to be a natural thing, this combining of bodies. It was certainly fulfilling.

He wrapped her up in his arms, careful not to jar the sore one any more than he already had. He closed his eyes. He'd never been so happy in all his life.

He'd planned to have a big wedding, but his conscience got the better of him, so the next day he drove Keely over to the probate judge's office in Jacobsville and married her.

"You really are a prude, you know," Keely teased him when they were back on the street wearing wedding bands, with the license in Keely's handbag.

He shrugged. "Pot calling the kettle black," he replied, smiling tenderly.

She pressed close against him, still a little weak and shaky from the snakebite, but so happy that she felt like bursting. "There's one thing left that we have to do," she said reluctantly.

"Yes. Do you want to call Carly, or shall I?"

She linked her fingers into his. "I'll call her."

They had the funeral a week later, a small memorial service at the cemetery, where Ella Welsh was buried next to her parents. It was a sad interlude in a happy whirl, because Winnie had insisted on a society wedding. Boone and Keely reluctantly gave in. Winnie's enthusiasm was contagious.

So they were married in the autumn, with the maples wearing glorious red and gold coats, and chrysanthemums for Keely's bouquet. She tossed it outside the church and watched with amusement as her bridesmaids scrambled for it. But it was the best man, Hayes Carson, who caught the bouquet. He grinned widely and gave a courtly bow when everyone stared at him. A glowering Dr. Bentley Rydel had also attended the wedding, along with Keely's coworkers, and Carly, who cried buckets and said that Keely was the most beautiful bride she'd ever seen.

Boone and Keely went away for a month, touring Spain and Africa and much of Europe. They came home weary of travel, but with beautiful memories.

"You're not going to be happy giving morning teas for brides and hostessing dinner parties, are you?" Boone asked when they'd finished supper and were sitting in front of the fireplace in the living room.

"I'm not cut out for it," she replied worriedly.

He grinned and pulled her close. "Then do what you please."

"I'd like to go back to work for Dr. Rydel," she said slowly. "I guess you wouldn't like that?"

He looked down into her wide, soft green eyes. "We've already agreed that you have skills, and they apply to animals. I think it would be a good idea. I'll have days when I have to be out of town on business, and I'll have workshops and conferences to go to. You can come to some of them, but you won't like being on the road so much. Work for Rydel." He kissed her. "Just don't forget where you live and who loves you."

She grinned and kissed him back. "I could never forget that."

He stretched and yawned. "Clark's got a new girl, Winnie says," he murmured after a peaceful silence. "A nice one, this time. She works in a library."

Keely smiled. "Good for Clark. How about Winnie?"

He hesitated. "I don't know. She's changed. She's gone all silent lately. Probably mooning over Kilraven." He shook his head. "That bird isn't going to settle down in some small town. He's got big city written all over him."

Keely promised herself that she'd make time to talk to her best friend and let her cry it all out.

"Sleepy?" he asked.

She nuzzled against his shoulder. "Not really. Why? Did you have something in mind?" she teased.

"In fact, I did." He leaned closer, brushed his mouth over hers in a whisper of contact. "Yeast rolls."

Unprepared, she burst out laughing. "Yeast rolls?"

"I haven't had a decent roll since before we married," he pointed out, "and you're all healed now. Besides, nobody makes bread like you do."

"Well, if that's how you feel, I'd love to bake you some yeast rolls!" she replied. Her eyes shimmered with amusement. "But I'd need a little encouragement, first."

He pursed his lips. "What sort of encouragement?"

"Be inventive," she coaxed.

He got to his feet, swung her up into his arms, and started for the staircase. "Inventive," he assured her with a chuckle, "is my middle name."

She tucked her face under his chin and listened to the heavy, hard beat of his heart and smiled with anticipation. She felt as if she were being reimbursed for all the long years of loneliness and sorrow that she'd endured. Her scars, she decided, didn't matter so much after all. And the happiness she'd found with Boone was worth every one.

★★★★★